BEASTLY

DELUXE EDITION
FEATURING LINDY'S DIARY

Also by
ALEX FLINN

BEASTLY

DELUXE EDITION
FEATURING LINDY'S DIARY

ALEX FLINN

HARPER TEEN

An Imprint of HarperCollins Publishers

HarperTeen is an imprint of HarperCollins Publishers.

ISBN 978-0-06-211391-7 (pbk.)

Typography by Sasha Illingworth
12 13 14 15   CG/BV   10 9 8 7 6 5 4 3 2
❖
First Deluxe Edition
Beastly was previously published in 2007.

To my daughter Katherine,
who is finally old enough to read one of my books!

Trying something new is hard. I'd like to thank
the following people for their help, and also for
reassuring me that it wasn't just a crazy idea:
Joyce Sweeney (and various members of her
Friday group), Marjetta Geerling, George
Nicholson, Phoebe Yeh, Catherine Onder,
Savina Kim, and Antonia Markiet.

Special thanks to my daughter Meredith
for listening to numerous versions of
Beauty and the Beast, often without pictures.

Mr. Anderson: Welcome to the first meeting of the Unexpected Changes chat group.

Mr. Anderson: Anyone here? Or should I say, anyone going to admit being here?

BeastNYC joined the chat.

Mr. Anderson: Hello, BeastNYC.

Mr. Anderson: Hello? I see you there, BeastNYC. Want to introduce yourself?

BeastNYC: Don't want to talk 1st . . . anyone else here?

Mr. Anderson: Yes, we seem to have a lot of lurkers who joined the chat before you.

BeastNYC: Let them talk 1st then.

Mr. Anderson: Anyone else want to give a shout-out to BeastNYC?

SILENTMAID: Hello, BeastNYC. Should we call you Beast?

BeastNYC: Whatever. Doesn't matter.

Mr. Anderson: Thanks for speaking up, Silent—pardon the pun. What sort of creature are you?

SILENTMAID: A mermaid. Just a little one.

Mr. Anderson: You were transformed into a mermaid?

SILENTMAID: Actually, I'm currently a mermaid, but I'm *considering* a transformation. I thought this group might help me make my decision.

Mr. Anderson: That's what we're going to talk about tonight—the experience of transformation, how you became what you are.

Froggie: wer u trnsfrmd, Andy?

Mr. Anderson: Well, no. But I've set this up to help you all.

BeastNYC: You're a girl, SilentMaid? I mean, a female, er, fish. A mer*maid*

Froggie: Hw cn u hlp us wen u dnt know wat is like

SilentMaid: Beast, yes, I am. I'm thinking of becoming a human girl.

Mr. Anderson: Froggie, I've studied your type of case. Extensively. I've written a thesis on The Effects of Transformation on True Love, based upon the works of Grimm, LePrince de Beaumont, Aksakov, Quiller-Couch, and Walt Disney . . .

BeastNYC: Location, Silent?

SilentMaid: I'm sure you're very qualified, Andy. It was nice of you to set this up :)

Mr. Anderson: Thanks, Silent.

SilentMaid: Beast, I'm in Denmark. Actually, the Atlantic Ocean, near Denmark.

BeastNYC: Denmark?

Froggie: Frgve me asking bt is hard typin w webbed fet.

SilentMaid: Denmark. It's in Europe.

Froggie: I mean FEET.

Mr. Anderson: Understood, Froggie. I think it will be good for you guys—and girl too—to get together and chat.

Grizzlyguy joined the chat.

Grizzlyguy: I want to talk about these 2 girls I saw.

BeastNYC: I know where Denmark is. Since the curse, I've had lots of time to study, cuz I have no life.

Mr. Anderson: Good observation, BeastNYC. We'll also discuss the lifestyle changes brought about by transformation.

BeastNYC: Cold there, Silent!

SILENTMAID: Yes, it is. <grin> But it's warm under the water.

Grizzlyguy: I want to talk about these 2 girls!

BeastNYC: U single, Silent?

Grizzlyguy: These 2 girls—1 is RoseRed & she's really hotttt!!!

SILENTMAID: Sort of single, Beast. I think I know where this is going . . .

Froggie: hardest prt 4 me is eatin flys

Grizzlyguy: The other one is Snow White

SILENTMAID: I'm single, but there's this one particular guy . . . a sailor

Grizzlyguy: Not *that* Snow White. A different one—

RoseRed's sis. Quiet. She's nice 2.

Froggie: dont lk flys

BeastNYC: Thing is, Silent, I'm looking to meet a girl, a girl who could love me.

SILENTMAID: Flattering, Beast, but I'm in love w/ another. There was a boy on a sailboat. I saved him from drowning.

Mr. Anderson: Can we not *all* talk at once?

BeastNYC: But we don't have anyone 2 talk 2 usually.

Froggie: Lnly being a frg when ur not rlly 1.

Mr. Anderson: Understood. Still, we need to take turns so the threads aren't too confusing. This is the first session, so I thought we'd discuss how we got the way we are—how we were transformed.

Froggie: Thts ez—pissed off a witch.

BeastNYC: Ditto.

SILENTMAID: Considering a deal with a witch, here. Sea Witch, actually. My voice for human legs. That's why I'm Silent.

BeastNYC: U type great, Silent.

SILENTMAID: Thanks, Beast. I have fingers, not claws.

Grizzlyguy: La-ti-da.

Mr. Anderson: Beast, why don't you tell us about your transformation?

BeastNYC: I don't feel like it.

Mr. Anderson: You're among friends, Beast.

Grizzlyguy: Yeah, go ahead so I can talk about the 2 girls.

BeastNYC: You know *2* girls, Prince??? Where are *you* located???

Mr. Anderson: This isn't a dating service, Beast.

BeastNYC: Yeah, well I could use one. It's hard meeting girls when you look like Chewbacca! And I need to meet 1 to end my curse.

Mr. Anderson: You need a support network too. That's why I set this up.

SILENTMAID: Please, talk to us, Beast. You're among friends.

BeastNYC: All right, all right. The first thing you need to know about me is, I'm a beast.

Froggie: henc the SN.

Mr. Anderson: No flames, Froggie.

BeastNYC: Yeah, right. But there was a time when I would have said about a fat girl, "She's a beast." I'm not a beast like that. I'm an animal. Fur, claws, you name it. Everything about me is an animal, except the inside. On the inside, I'm human still.

Grizzlyguy: Ditto here.

BeastNYC: It's really hard for me because before I was a beast, I was . . . well, beautiful. Cool, popular, rich. Like, my friends at school, they'd elected me their prince.

Grizzlyguy: Elected? Prince?

Froggie: princ not elcted Bst . . . i ws a princ once

BeastNYC: It's a long story.

Froggie: i ws a princ

Mr. Anderson: We have nothing but time, Beast. Talk to us.

BeastNYC: <sigh> OK. It all started because of a witch.

Froggie: thts hw they all strt

PART 1

A Prince and a Witch

1

I could feel everyone looking at me, but I was used to it. One thing my dad taught me early and often was to act like nothing moved me. When you're special, like we were, people were bound to notice.

It was the last month before the end of ninth grade. The substitute teacher was giving out ballots for spring dance court, something I'd normally have thought was lame.

"Hey, Kyle, your name's on this." My friend Trey Parker flicked my arm.

"No duh." When I turned Trey's way, the girl next to

him—Anna, or maybe Hannah—looked down. Huh. She'd been staring at me.

I examined the ballot. Not only was my name, Kyle Kingsbury, there for ninth-grade prince, but I was the sure winner. No one could compete with my looks and my dad's cash.

The sub was a new one who might still have been under the mistaken impression that because Tuttle was the type of school that had a salad bar in the cafeteria and offered courses in Mandarin Chinese—i.e., a school where the serious money people in New York sent their kids—we weren't going to bust on him like public school dregs. *Big* mistake. It wasn't like anything the sub said was going to be on an exam, so we were trying to figure out how to make reading the ballot and scratching in our choices take the entire fifty-minute period. At least most of us were. The rest were texting each other. I watched the ones who were filling out their ballots glancing over at me. I smiled. Someone else might have looked down, trying to act all shy and modest, like they were ashamed of having their name there—but it doesn't make sense to deny the obvious.

"My name's there too." Trey flicked my arm again.

"Hey, watch it!" I rubbed my arm.

"Watch it yourself. You've got this stupid grin on your face like you already won, and now you're giving the paparazzi a chance to snap your picture."

"And that's wrong?" I grinned wider, to bug him, and

gave a little wave like people in parades. Someone's camera phone snapped at just that moment, like an exclamation point.

"You shouldn't be allowed to live," Trey said.

"Why, thank you." I thought about voting for Trey, just to be nice. Trey was good for comic relief, but not too gifted in the looks department. His family was nobody special either—his dad was a doctor or something. They might post the vote totals in the school newspaper, and it'd be pretty embarrassing for Trey if he came in last or even didn't get any votes at all.

On the other hand, it would be cool if I got two or three times the votes of the next-closest person. And besides, Trey worshipped me. A real friend would want me to win big. That's another thing my dad always said: "Don't be a sucker, Kyle, and do things out of friendship or love. Because what you always end up finding out is the only one who really loves you is you."

I was seven or eight when he first said that, and I asked, "What about you, Dad?"

"What?"

"You love . . ." *Me.* "Us. Your family."

He gave me a long look before saying, "That's different, Kyle."

I never asked him again if he loved me. I knew he'd told the truth the first time.

I folded my ballot over, to keep Trey from seeing I'd

voted for myself. Of course, I knew he voted for himself too, but that was different.

That's when a voice came from the back of the room.

"This is disgusting!"

We all turned.

"Maybe someone left a booger under her desk," Trey whispered.

"Was it you?" I said.

"I don't do that anymore."

"Disgusting," the voice repeated. I stopped talking to Trey and looked at where the voice was coming from, this Goth freak sitting in back. She was a fat chick, dressed in the kind of flowing black clothes you usually only see on witches or terrorists (we don't have uniforms at Tuttle; it would piss off the parents not to be able to buy Dolce & Gabbana), and her hair was green. Obviously a cry for help. Weird thing was, I'd never noticed her before. Most people here I'd known my whole life.

The sub was too stupid to ignore her. "What's disgusting, Miss . . . Miss . . ."

"Hilferty," she said. "Kendra Hilferty."

"Kendra, is there something wrong with your desk?"

"There is something wrong with this world." She stood like she was making a speech. "Something very wrong when it's the twenty-first century and this type of elitist travesty is still being perpetuated." She held up her ballot. People giggled.

"It's a ninth-grade dance ballot," Trey volunteered. "To choose the royalty."

"Exactly," the girl said. "Who are these people? Why should they be treated as royalty? Based upon . . . what? The people on this ballot were chosen on one basis and one basis only—physical beauty."

"Sounds like a good basis to me," I said to Trey, not too softly. I stood. "That's BS. Everyone voted, and this is who they chose. It's a democratic process."

Around me there were some thumbs-ups, some *Yeah, man*s, particularly from Anna or Hannah. But I noticed that a lot of people, mostly the ugly people, were silent.

The girl took a few steps toward me. "They're sheep, following the herd. They vote for the so-called popular people because it's simple. Surface beauty: blond hair, blue eyes"—she was looking at me—"is always easy to recognize. But if someone is braver, stronger, smarter, that's harder to see."

She pissed me off, so I jumped on her. "If someone's so smart, they'd figure out how to *get* better-looking. You could lose weight, get plastic surgery, even get your face scraped and your teeth bleached." I emphasized the *you* in the sentence, so she'd know I meant her and not just some general sort of *you*. "My dad's a network news guy. He says people shouldn't have to look at ugly people."

"Is that what you think?" She raised a dark eyebrow. "That we should all transform ourselves to be as you want us to be, Kyle Kingsbury?"

I started at my name. I was sure I'd never seen her before. But of course she knew me. Everyone did. Probably had some pathetic crush on me.

"Yeah," I said. "Yeah. That's what I think. That's what I *know*."

She walked toward me. Her eyes were light green and her nose was long and hooked down. "Then you'd better hope you never get ugly, Kyle. You are ugly now, on the inside, where it matters most, and if you ever lost your good looks, I bet you wouldn't be smart or strong enough to get them back. Kyle Kingsbury, you are beastly."

Beastly. The word was from another time and place. It made me think of fairy tales, and I felt this weird tingling, like the hairs on my arms had caught fire from her eyes. I brushed it off.

2

Beastly.

"That Goth chick in English was weird," I said to Trey when we were dressing out for PE.

"Yeah, she really freaked you out," he agreed.

"After ten years looking at your ugly face, nothing freaks me out."

"Oh, okay, so that's *not* why you've been beastin about it ever since we left English?"

"Have not." But it was true. When the girl said that thing about how I'd better not ever get ugly, when she looked at me that last time, it was like she knew stuff about me, things like how I used to cry when my mom ditched 'cause I didn't think I'd ever see her again (which wasn't far from what happened). But that was stupid. She knew nothing.

"Whatever you say," Trey said.

"It was scary, all right," I agreed. "Scary that people like that even exist."

"And go to this supposedly exclusive school and ruin it for the rest of us."

"Yeah. Someone ought to do something about her."

I really did believe that. I'd been trying to act like it wasn't a big deal, being elected prince and all, but it kind of was. It should have been a good day for me, but that witch had to ruin it.

That was how I was thinking of her: a witch. Ordinarily, I'd have used a different word, a word that rhymed with *witch*. But something about the girl, the way she'd looked at me with those freaky eyes, a color green I'd never seen before, made me think *witch*. *Witch* totally described her.

Later, in the gym, I saw the witch again. We were running the indoor track, but she wasn't. She hadn't dressed out but was still wearing the black flowing clothes from before. She sat on a bench below the skylight. Above her, the sky was dark. It was going to rain.

"Someone ought to teach her a lesson." I thought of her words: *You are ugly now, on the inside, where it matters most . . . you are beastly.* What utter crap. "She's no different than anyone else. If she could hang with our crowd, she would. Anyone would."

And in a second, I knew what I was going to do.

I sped up my pace. We had to do five laps around the track, and usually I did it at a leisurely pace, because once you finished, Coach made you start something else. It was BS that I even had to take PE when I was on two school teams. But I knew Coach thought so too, so I could usually get out of it. If you gave Coach the right respectful look—the type of look that made him remember the kind of checks your dad wrote for athletic association fundraisers to make up for not showing up—you got away with stuff.

Even going slow, I finished half a lap ahead of the next-closest person and started across the track to the bench where the witch was sitting, looking at something in her lap.

"Kingsbury!" Coach yelled. "If you're through, you can get out the basketballs."

I said, "All right, Coach." I started to walk away, like I was going to do it, then winced. "Oh, I've got a cramp I need to work out. Can I go stretch? Wouldn't want to get an injury."

Insert respectful look here.

"Aw, go ahead." Coach laughed. "You're miles ahead of the others anyway."

Worked. "You rock, Coach!"

He laughed.

I limped until his back was turned, then strolled over to the bench where the witch girl was sitting. I started to stretch.

"You're really good at playing the adults, aren't you?" she said.

"I'm excellent at it." I smiled at her. "Hey." I saw the object in her lap. It was a mirror, one of those old-fashioned ones with a handle, like in *Snow White*. When she saw me looking at it, she quick slipped it into her backpack.

"What's the mirror for?" I asked, thinking it was weird for an ugly chick to be carrying around a big mirror. Weird for anyone, really.

She ignored the question. "How's your leg?"

"What?" I stopped in mid-stretch. "Oh, it's fine, actually. Fine. I really just came over to talk to you."

She raised an eyebrow. "To what do I owe this honor?"

"I wouldn't say it was an honor. I was just . . . thinking."

"That must have been quite an experience for you."

"I was thinking about what you said in class. And I decided you're right."

"Really?" She blinked a few times, like a rat coming out of its dark hole.

"Yeah, really. We do judge people by looks around here. Someone like me . . . face it, I'm a lot better than average-looking, and I have an easier time than . . ."

"Me?"

I shrug. "I wasn't going to get that specific. My dad, he's on the news, so I know how it is. In his business, you lose your looks, you lose your job."

"Does that seem right to you?"

"I never had to think about that, you know? I mean, you

can't help what you're born with."

"Interesting," she said.

I smiled at her, the way I did at girls I liked, and moved closer, even though I almost hurled doing it. "You're pretty interesting yourself."

"By *interesting*, you mean *weird*?"

"You can be weird in a good way, can't you?"

"Fair enough." She looked at her watch, like there was somewhere she had to be, like we weren't all trapped like rats in PE. "So was that what you came over to tell me?"

Witch.

"No, actually. I was thinking about what you said, and I thought maybe I ought to . . . expand my horizons a little." That was a Dad phrase. He was always saying I should expand my horizons, which usually meant doing more work. "You know, meet other kinds of people."

"Ugly people?"

"Interesting people. People I haven't met before."

"Like me?"

"Exactly. So I was wondering if, um, if you'd go with me to the dance next week. I think we'd have a good time."

She stared at me, and the green parts of her eyes seemed to flash and looked like they might boil over the sides of her skinny nose. Impossible. Then she smiled. It was a weird kind of smile, a secretive one.

"Yes. Yes, I want to go with you."

Of course she did.

3

I wasn't home two minutes when Sloane Hagen, a typical toned, BlackBerry-wired, Evian-swigging, fake blonde,
belly-pierced daughter of a CEO and my *real* date for the
dance, called my cell. I hit *Ignore*. She rang again. And again.
Finally, I caved.

"Some Goth chick is telling everyone she's your date for
the dance!" she shrieked.

Play it cool. You expected this.

"Does it sound likely that I'd ask some misfit to the
dance?"

"Then why's she telling everyone you did?"

"I can't control what every unbalanced freak says about me."

"So you didn't ask her?"

"Are you trippin'? Why would I ask some skank when I'm already going with the hottest girl in school?" I put on my special "just for Sloane" voice. "We're the perfect couple, babe."

She giggled. "That's what I thought. I'll just tell everyone she's messed up."

"No, don't."

"Why not?" She was suspicious again.

"Well, it's kind of funny, isn't it? Some loser telling everyone she's going to the biggest dance of the year with *your* date?"

"I guess so."

"So picture it. She tells everyone I'm her date. Maybe she even believes it and gets a fancy dress. Then I show up at the dance with you. It's classic."

"I love you, Kyle." Sloane giggled. "You're so evil."

"Evil genius, you mean." I laughed a wild laugh like a villain in a cartoon. "So what do you think?"

"When you're right, you're right. It's classic."

"Exactly. So you just have to do one thing to make it happen—keep your mouth shut."

"Sure. But Kyle?"

"Yeah?"

"You'd better not try anything like that on me. I wouldn't be dumb enough to fall for it."

I wasn't so sure about that, but said, "Never, Sloane," obedient as a Labrador.

"And Kyle?"

"Yeah, what?"

"My dress is black and it has very little material."

"Hmm. Sounds nice."

"It is. So I'd like an orchid to go with it. A purple one."

"Sure," I said, thinking that was the great thing about Sloane. With most people I knew, actually. If they could get what they wanted from you, they'd give you what you wanted back.

After I got off the phone, I looked in the school directory for that Kendra girl. I didn't really trust Sloane when she said she wouldn't tell Kendra anything, so I figured I should call Kendra for some damage control.

But when I looked in the directory under *H*, there was no Kendra Hilferty. So I went through every single name in the book, *A* to *Z*, and then back again, and still didn't find any Kendra. I tried to remember if she'd been there at the beginning of the year but gave up. A girl like her wouldn't be on my radar.

Around nine, I was watching the Yankees kick butt when I heard Dad's key in the lock. That was weird. Most nights, Dad was out until I went to bed. I could have watched in my room, but the plasma screen was in the living room. Plus I sort of wanted to tell Dad about the dance court thing. Not that it was a big deal, but it was the kind of thing he might at least notice.

"Hey, guess what?" I said.

"What? I'm sorry, Aaron. I didn't hear you. Someone was trying to talk to me." He waved his hand to me to keep quiet and gave me a "Shut up!" look. He was using the Bluetooth. I always thought people looked totally stupid doing that, like they were talking to themselves. He went into the kitchen and kept talking. I thought about turning up the sound, but I knew he'd freak. He said it sounded low class, having the TV on when he was on a call. Problem was, he was *always* on a call.

Finally, he got off. I heard him rifling through the Sub-Zero (which was what he always called the refrigerator), looking for the dinner stuff the maid left. Then I heard the microwave open and shut. I knew he'd come out then, because he now had exactly three minutes to kill by talking to me.

Sure enough. "How was school today?"

It was fun. Trey and I ran all the wires we'll need to detonate the bombs tomorrow. We just have to figure out how to get hold of some submachine guns without you finding out. Shouldn't be hard considering you're never around. I stole your credit card yesterday. Didn't think you'd mind. Or notice.

"Great. They put up the finalists for spring dance court, and I'm one of them. People say I'll probably win."

"That's great, Kyle." He looked down at his cell phone.

I wondered, if I'd said the other thing, would he still have said, "That's great, Kyle."

I tried the one thing that usually got a response from him. "Heard from Mom lately?" Mom left when I was eleven because "there has to be something else out there." She ended up marrying a plastic surgeon and moving to Miami, so she could soak up the rays all she wants and never worry about getting old. Or calling me.

"What? Oh, she's probably drying out somewhere." He looked toward the kitchen, like he was urging the microwave to hurry up. "They canned Jessica Silver today." Jessica was his coanchor, so the conversation was squarely back to his favorite subject: himself.

"Why?" I said.

"The official word is that it was a slipup in reporting the Kramer incident."

I had no clue what the Kramer incident was.

Dad was still going. ". . . but between you and me, if she'd lost the last twenty pounds after she had the baby—or, better yet, not had the baby in the first place—she'd still have a job."

Which made me think of what Kendra said. But so what? People wanted to look at someone hot instead of someone fugly. It was human nature. Was that wrong?

"She's totally stupid," I agreed. Dad was looking toward the kitchen again, so I said, "Yankees are kicking butt."

That was when the microwave beeped.

"What?" Dad said. He focused on the TV for maybe a tenth of a second. "Oh, I've got a lot of work to do, Kyle."

Then he took his plate into the bedroom and closed the door.

4

Okay, maybe Sloane didn't tell Kendra she was my date for the dance. But she definitely told everyone else. When I got to school, two girls who apparently dreamed I was going to ask them blew me off, and Trey was at my side as soon as I walked in the door.

"Sloane Hagen." He held up his hand to high-five. "Nice job."

"Nice enough."

"Nice enough," he imitates. "She's, like, the hottest girl in school."

"Why would I settle for less than the best?"

I figured for sure Kendra knew too, so I was surprised when she came up to me in the hall between classes. "Hey." She linked her arm through mine.

"Hey." I tried not to pull my arm away or see who might be looking at me with this defective attached to me. "Tried to call you last night."

For the first time, she looked flustered. "I'm not in the directory. I'm . . . um, new this year. Transfer student."

"Figured it was something like that." She was still hanging on me. Some friends of mine walked by, and it was just automatic that I tried to squirm from her grip.

"Ouch!" One of her nails scraped me.

"Sorry."

"So, we still on for the dance?"

"Sure. Why wouldn't we be?" She gazed at me.

I was just about to lay it on her, the part about how we needed to meet at the dance because my dad couldn't drive on account of the six o'clock news, when she said, "I think we should just meet there."

"Really? Most girls want, like, a royal escort."

"Nah. It's weird, but my mom might not be totally thrilled about me going to a dance with a boy."

As opposed to what? A werewolf?

This was too good to be true. "Okay. I'll buy your ticket and see you there."

"See you there." She started to walk away.

I did too, then remembered what Sloane had said, about the corsage. I figured I should ask her, to make it seem real. "Kendra, what color dress are you wearing? My dad says I'm supposed to get a corsage."

"Oh, I haven't decided what I'm wearing yet. Something black—it's my signature color. But a single white rose goes with everything, doesn't it, and it symbolizes purity."

She was so incredibly ugly that I imagined for a second what it would be like if I actually *was* planning on taking her to the dance, leaning toward her, looking at her mossy teeth and hooked nose, and those weird green eyes, and pinning on the corsage while all my friends stood and laughed at me. For a second I wondered if she really was a witch. Impossible. There was no such thing as witches.

"You got it," I said. "So I'll see you at the dance?"

"It will be a night to remember."

5

The day of the dance, I got into the tuxedo Magda, the new maid, rented for me with Dad's credit card. One great thing about having a dad who's never around is they buy you stuff because it's easier than arguing. Trey's parents, for example, were total cheapskates—like they told him he had to choose between an Xbox and a Wii. Worried about "spoiling" him or something. My dad bought me both. Then I talked to Trey on my cell phone (from Dad) while waiting for the limo (sponsored by . . . Dad) to arrive. I checked the Sub-Zero for the corsage Magda was supposed to pick up from the florist. Sloane had told me about fifteen or sixteen more times that her dress was "black, very hot" and that I wouldn't be sorry if I got her an orchid corsage. So, of course, that's what I told Magda to buy.

"You ever think that school dances are a form of legalized prostitution?" I said to Trey on the phone.

He laughed. "What do you mean?"

"I mean I—by which I really mean my dad—drop five hundred or so on a tuxedo, a limo, tickets, and a corsage, and in return I get some. What does that sound like to you?"

Trey laughed. "Classic."

I looked in the refrigerator for the corsage. "Where the—"

"What's the matter?"

"Nothing. I gotta go."

I plumbed the depths of the Sub-Zero, but there was no orchid corsage. The only flower in there was a single white rose.

"Magda!" I yelled. "Where the hell's the orchid corsage you were supposed to get? What's up with the rose?" I was pretty sure roses were way cheaper than orchids. "Magda!"

No answer.

I finally found her in the laundry room, slopping detergent on the collar of one of Dad's shirts. Pretty cushy job if you asked me. Dad worked 24/7 and didn't mess the place up. I was mostly at school or, if not, I stayed as far away from home as possible. So basically, she got a salary and free use of our apartment, and all she had to do was laundry and vacuuming and watch soap operas and fan her butt all day.

That and run a few simple errands, which she obviously couldn't even do right.

"What's this?" I said, shoving the plastic corsage box under her nose. Actually, that wasn't exactly what I said. I added a few swear words that she probably didn't even understand.

She stepped back from my hand. All the necklaces around her neck made a jingling sound. "Beautiful, isn't it?"

"Beautiful? It's a rose. I said an orchid. Or-chid. Are you so stupid you don't know what an orchid is?"

She didn't even react to *stupid*, which just showed how stupid she was. She'd only been there a few weeks, but she was even dumber than the last housekeeper, who got canned for putting her cheap red Wal-Mart T-shirt in with our laundry. Magda didn't stop folding laundry, but stared at the rose, like she was high on something.

"I know what an orchid is, Mr. Kyle. A proud, vain flower. But can you not see the beauty of this rose?"

I looked at it. It was pure white and almost seemed to be growing before my eyes. I glanced away. When I looked back, all I could see was Sloane's face when I showed up with the wrong kind of corsage. I'd get no love from her tonight, and it was all because of Magda. Stupid rose, stupid Magda.

"Roses are cheap," I said.

"A beautiful thing is precious, no matter the price. Those

who do not know how to see the precious things in life will never be happy. I wish you to be happy, Mr. Kyle."

Yeah, and the best things in life are free, right? But what would you expect from someone who makes a living washing other people's Jockey shorts?

"I think it's ugly," I said.

She put down the laundry she was holding and, quick as can be, snatched the rose away. "Give it to me, then."

"Are you on crack?" I knocked the box from her hand. It bounced to the floor. "That's probably how you planned it, huh? Get the wrong thing so I don't want it, and I'll give it to you. I don't think so."

She looked at the rose lying on the floor. "I pity you, Mr. Kyle."

"You pity me?" I laughed. "How can you pity me? You're the maid."

She didn't answer, just reached for another of Dad's shirts, like she got off doing laundry.

I laughed again. "You should be scared of me. You should be pissing in your pants. If I tell my dad you wasted his money like that, he'll fire you. He'll probably have you deported. You should be *so* frightened of me."

She kept folding laundry. She probably didn't even understand English enough to get what I was saying. I gave up. I didn't want to take the rose corsage because that would be admitting I was going to give it to Sloane. But what choice did I have? I picked it up from where it had bounced in the corner. The plastic box was broken, and the corsage was on the floor, a petal knocked off. Cheap junk. I stuck the loose petal into my pants pocket and put the rest of the corsage back in the box best I could. I started to walk away.

That's when Magda said—in perfect English, by the way—"I am not frightened *of* you, Kyle. I am frightened *for* you."

"Whatever."

6

I had planned on picking Sloane up in the limo, giving her the corsage, and then reaping the benefits of all that advance planning by at least making out with her in the limo. After all, my dad had spent big, and it was supposed to be the most important night of my life. Being a prince had to be good for something.

That's not how it went down.

First off, Sloane practically burst a vein when she saw the corsage. Or she would've, if there was any room for any bursting in that tight dress she had on.

"What are you, blind?" she demanded, her already toned arm muscles sticking out more from clenching her fists. "I said my dress was black. This totally clashes."

"It's white."

"It's *off*-white. Duh."

I didn't see how off-white could clash. But hotness had its privileges.

"Look," I said. "The stupid maid screwed up. It's not my fault."

"The *maid*? You didn't even care enough to go buy it yourself?"

"Who buys things themselves? I'll get you flowers another time." I held out the corsage box. "It's pretty."

"Pretty cheap." She knocked it from my hand. "It's not what I asked for."

I stared at the corsage box on the floor. I wanted to just leave. But at that moment, Sloane's mom showed up with all the latest technology necessary to take both still and action photos of Sloane on my left side, Sloane on my right side, Sloane slightly in front of me. The camera was recording and Ms. Hagen, who was single and who probably wouldn't have minded an intro to my dad, was cooing, "Here's the future prince and princess." So I did what the son of Rob Kingsbury would do. I kicked the cheapo corsage aside and smiled nice for the camera, saying all the right things about how beautiful Sloane looked, how great the dance would be, blah, blah, blah.

And then, for some reason, I picked the corsage off the floor. Another petal had fallen, and I put it in my pocket with the first one. I took the box with me.

The dance was at the Plaza. When we got there, I handed my tickets to the girl who was checking them. She looked at the corsage.

"Pretty flower," she said.

I looked at her to see if she was kidding. She wasn't. She was probably in my classes, a sort of mousy-looking girl with a red braid and freckles. She didn't look like she belonged at the Plaza. She must have been a scholarship student because they made them do all the grunt work like taking tickets. Obviously, no one had asked her to the dance, or ever bought her flowers, not even a cheap, broken rose. I glanced at Sloane, who was having a joyous reunion with fifty close friends she hadn't seen since yesterday, since all the girls blew off school the day of the dance to get pedicures and spa treatments. Sloane had spent most of the ride griping about the corsage—not exactly what I'd planned—and she'd still refused to wear it.

"Hey, you want it?" I said to the girl.

"That's not nice," she said.

"What?" I tried to remember if I'd ever picked on her. Nah. She wasn't ugly enough to tease, just a total zero, not worth my time.

"Goofing on me, pretending you're going to give it to

me, then taking it back."

"I wasn't pretending. You can have it." It was so weird that she even cared about a stupid rose. "It's not the right color for my girlfriend's dress or something, so she won't wear it. It's just going to die, so you might as well take it." I held it out to her.

"Well, since you put it that way . . ." She smiled, taking it from me. I tried not to notice her crooked teeth. Why didn't she just get braces? "Thanks. It's beautiful."

"Hey, enjoy it."

I walked away sort of smiling. Why had I done that? I for sure wasn't in the habit of doing favors for uglies. I wondered if all poor people got that excited over stupid little things like that. I couldn't remember the last time I was excited about anything. Anyway, it was fun, knowing Sloane would eventually stop whining and want the rose, and I'd be able to say I didn't have it.

I looked around for Kendra. I'd almost forgotten about Kendra, but my timing was, as usual, perfect because there she was, slinking into the front entrance. She wore a black and purple dress that looked like a costume for *Harry Potter Goes to the Prom* and she was looking for me.

"Hey, where's your ticket?" one of the ticket-taking drones said to her.

"Oh . . . I don't have . . . I was looking for someone."

I saw a flash of pity on the ticket taker's face, like she knew exactly what was going down, loser to loser. But she said, "Sorry. I can't let you in without a ticket."

"I'm waiting for my date."

Another pitying look. "Okay," the volunteer said. "Just stand back a little."

"Fine."

I went to Sloane. I pointed at where Kendra was loserishly standing. "Showtime." That was when Kendra spotted me.

Sloane knew just what to do. Even though she was pissed at me, she was the type who'd never miss the opportunity to cause another girl permanent emotional damage. She grabbed me and planted a big kiss on my lips. "I love you, Kyle."

Sweet. I kissed her again, not repeating what she'd said.

When we finished, Kendra was staring at us. I walked over to her.

"What are you looking at, Ugly?"

I expected her to cry then. It was fun to kick the nerds, make them cry, then kick them some more. I'd been looking forward to this night for a while. It almost made up for the corsage crap.

But instead she said, "You really did it."

"Did what?" I said.

"Look at her." Sloane giggled. "She's all dressed up in that ugly dress. It makes her look even fatter."

"Yeah, where'd you find that?" I said. "A trash heap?"

"It was my grandmother's," Kendra said.

"Around here people buy *new* dresses for a dance." I laughed.

"So you're actually doing this, then?" she said. "You really did invite me to a dance even though you had another date, just to make me look stupid?"

I laughed again. "You actually thought someone like me would take someone like you to a dance?"

"No, I didn't. But I hoped you wouldn't make my decision so easy, Kyle."

"What decision?" Behind me, Sloane was cackling, chanting, "Loser," and soon other people started in until finally the whole room was buzzing with the word so I could barely think straight.

I looked at the girl, Kendra. She wasn't crying. She didn't look embarrassed either. She had this intense look in her eyes, like this chick in this old Stephen King movie I once saw, *Carrie*, where this girl developed telekinetic powers and took her enemies out. And I almost expected Kendra to start doing that—killing people just by looking at them.

But instead she said in a voice only I could hear, "You'll see."

And she walked out.

7

Fast-forward through the evening. Picture a typical dance, lame music, chaperones trying to keep us from actually mating on the dance floor. All sort of a preparty for the real party to follow. But I kept hearing Kendra's words, ringing in my ears: *You'll see.* Sloane got friendly, and once we got crowned prince and princess, she got even friendlier. With some girls, popularity and the power that goes with it are some kind of aphrodisiac. Sloane was like that. We stood onstage, getting crowned. Sloane leaned toward me.

"My mom's out tonight." She took my hand and put it on her butt.

I removed it. "Great."

You'll see.

She continued, pressing closer, her breath hot in my ear. "She went to an opera—three and a half hours. I called the Met to find out. And she usually gets dinner after. She won't be home until almost one . . . I mean if you wanted to come over awhile." Her hand slipped down my stomach, edging closer to the Danger Zone. Unbelievable. She was groping me in front of the whole school?

I moved away. "I only have the limo until midnight." Brett Davis, who'd been prince last year, came toward me with my crown. I bowed my head to humbly accept it.

"Use it wisely," Brett said.

"Cheap," Sloane said. "I'm not worth taking a cab? That's what you're saying?"

What did "You'll see" mean? And Sloane and Brett were too close, cutting off my air. Things and people were coming at me from all sides. I couldn't think straight.

"Kyle Kingsbury, answer me."

"Will you just get away from me?" I exploded.

It seemed like everyone and everything in the room stopped when I said that.

"You bastard," Sloane said.

"I have to go home," I said. "Do you want to stay or take the limo?"

You'll see.

"You think you're leaving? Leaving me?" Sloane whispered, loud enough for anyone in a ten-mile radius to hear. "If you leave here, it will be the last thing you'll ever do. So smile, and dance with me. I'm not going to let you ruin my night, Kyle."

So that's what I did. I smiled and danced with her. And afterward, I took her back to her house and drank Absolut vodka, stolen from her parents' bar ("Absolut Royalty!" Sloane toasted), and did everything else she expected and I'd been expecting too, and tried to forget the voice in my head, the voice saying, "You'll see," over and over. And finally, at eleven forty-five, I made my escape.

When I got home, the light was on in my bedroom. Weird. Probably Magda had been cleaning in there and forgot it.

But when I opened the door, the witch was sitting on my bed.

8

"What are you doing here?" I said it loud enough to hide the fact that my voice was shaking, and sweat was dripping out of every pore, and my blood was pounding like I'd been running the track. And yet I couldn't say I was surprised to see her. I'd been expecting her since the dance. I just didn't know when or how.

She stared at me. I noticed her eyes again, the same bottle color as her hair, and I had this weird thought: What if it was natural, the hair as well as the eyes? What if they'd grown that way?

Crazy.

"Why are you in my house?" I repeated.

She smiled. I noticed for the first time that she held a mirror, the same one she'd had the first day on the benches. She peered into it as she chanted, "Retribution. Poetic justice. Just deserts. Comeuppance."

I stared. In the moment she spoke, she didn't look as ugly as I remembered her. It was those eyes, those glowing green eyes. Her skin glowed too.

"What do you mean, 'Comeuppance'?"

"It's an SAT word, Kyle. You should learn it. You will learn it. It means well-deserved punishment."

Punishment. Over the years, lots of people—housekeepers, my teachers—had threatened me with punishments. They never stuck. Usually, I could charm my way out of them. Or my dad could pay someone off. But what if she was some kind of crazy psycho?

"Look," I said. "About tonight. I'm sorry. I didn't think you were really going to show up. I knew you didn't really like me, so I didn't think you'd get your feelings hurt." I needed to be nice. She *was* obviously crazy. What if she had a gun under those big clothes?

"I didn't."

"Didn't what?"

"Like you. Or get my feelings hurt."

"Oh." I gave her the look I usually used on teachers, the "I'm a good kid" look. When I did, I noticed something weird. Her nose, which I'd thought was long and witchlike before, wasn't. Must have been the shadows. "Good. So we're all squared?"

"I didn't get my feelings hurt because I *knew* you'd blow me off, Kyle, knew you were cruel and ruthless and that, given the opportunity, you would hurt someone . . . just to show you could."

I met her eyes. Her eyelashes looked different. Longer. I shook my head. "That's not why."

"Then why?" Her lips were bloodred.

"What's going on here?"

"I told you. Comeuppance. You will know what it is like not to be beautiful, to be as ugly on the outside as on the inside. If you learn your lesson well, you may be able to undo my spell. If not, you will live with your punishment forever."

As she spoke, her cheeks reddened. She shed her cloak to reveal that she was a hot—though green-haired—babe. But something was weird—how could she transform like that? I was getting freaked out. But I couldn't back off. I couldn't be afraid of her. So I tried again. Where charm didn't work, bringing my dad in usually did.

I said, "You know my dad's got a lot of money—connections too."

Everyone wants something, Kyle.

"So?"

"So I know it must be hard being a scholarship student at a school like Tuttle, but my dad can sort of grease the wheels, get you what you want. Money. College recs, even a shot on the evening news if I asked him. What, did you have on a disguise before? You're actually pretty hot, you know. You'd be good on TV."

"Do you really think so?"

"Sure . . . I . . ." I stopped. She was laughing.

"I don't go to Tuttle," she said. "I don't go to school at all or live here or anywhere. I am old as the ages and young as the dawn. Otherworldly beings cannot be bribed."

Oh. "So you're saying you're a . . . a . . . witch."

Her hair flowing around her face seemed now green, now purple, now black, like a strobe light. I realized I was holding my breath, waiting for her answer.

"Yes."

"Right." I said, understanding. She was truly crazy.

"Kyle Kingsbury, what you did was ugly. And it wasn't the first time. All your life you've gotten special treatment because of your beauty, and all your life you've used that beauty to be cruel to those less fortunate."

"That's not true."

"Second grade, you told Terry Fisher that the reason her head was lopsided was because her mother had slammed it in the car door. She cried for an hour."

"That was kid stuff."

"Maybe. But in sixth grade you had a party at Gameworks and invited the whole class—except two kids, Lara Ritter and David Sweeney. You told them they were too ugly to be allowed in." She looked at me. "Do you think that's funny?"

Yeah. Kind of. But I said, "That's still a long time ago. I had problems then. That was the year my mom left." Kendra seemed inches taller now.

"Last year, Wimberly Sawyer had a crush on you. You asked for her number, then had all your friends torment her with obscene phone calls until her parents got the number changed. Do you know how embarrassing that was for her? Think about it."

For one second I imagined it, what it would be like being Wimberly, telling my dad that everyone at school hated me. And for one second I couldn't bear to think of it. Wimberly hadn't just changed her number. At the end of the year, she'd left Tuttle too.

"You're right," I said. "I was an asshole. I won't do it again."

I almost believed it. She was right. I *should* be nicer. I didn't know why I was mean and cruel sometimes. Sometimes I'd told myself I'd be nicer to people. But always, in an hour or so, I forgot it, because it felt good to be on top of them all. Maybe a psychologist, one of those guys on TV, would say I did it to feel important, because my parents didn't pay attention to me or something. But that wasn't it, not really. It was just, like, sometimes I couldn't help it.

In the living room, the grandfather clock started to strike midnight.

"You're right," the witch said, spreading her now ripped

arms. "You won't do it again. In some countries, when a man steals, they cut off his hand. If a man rapes, he is castrated. In this way the tools of crime are removed from those who commit them." The clock was still striking. Nine. Ten. The room was glowing and almost spinning.

"Are you crazy?" I looked at her hands, to see if she had a knife, if she was going to try and cut something off me. I thought I must be really drunk because this couldn't be happening. She couldn't be doing magic. That's it. It had to be a drunken hallucination.

The clock finished striking. Kendra touched my shoulder, turning me away from her so I faced the mirror over my bureau. "Kyle Kingsbury, behold."

I turned and gaped at the sight that met my eyes.

"What have you done to me?" When I said it, my voice was different. It came out a roar.

She waved her hand with a shower of sparks.

"I have transformed you to your truer self."

I was a beast.

Mr. Anderson: I'm glad so many of you have come back this week. Today, we'll be talking about your family's and friends' reactions to your transformation.

BeastNYC: <— Not talking this time bc spilled guts last time

Mr. Anderson: Why are you so angry, Beast?

BeastNYC: Wouldn't you be angry if you were me?

Mr. Anderson: I'd be trying to think of a way out of my situation.

BeastNYC: no way out.

Mr. Anderson: There's always a way out. No spell is cast without a reason.

BeastNYC: You're taking the WITCH'S side???

Mr. Anderson: I didn't say that.

BeastNYC: Besides, how can you be so sure there's a way out?

Mr. Anderson: I just am.

BeastNYC: How do you know there aren't lots of fish and birds and spiders out there who got transformed and *never* came back?

SILENTMAID: I'm sure there are no fish. I'd know about it.

BeastNYC: Do you have some kind of magic powers that let you know that? Because if so, use your powers to put me back the way I was.

Mr. Anderson: Beast . . .

SILENTMAID: Can I say something?

BeastNYC: Please, Silent. Maybe he'll leave me alone.

SILENTMAID: It's just, I'd like to talk about the planned topic instead of listening to Beast's rants. I'm considering a transformation, and I'm most concerned about my family's reactions.

Mr. Anderson: Interesting. Why is that, Silent?

SILENTMAID: Should be obvious. I'd be doing this voluntarily, unlike the others, and even in the best-case scenario, I'd be rejecting not only my family, but my species.

Mr. Anderson: Tell us more, Silent.

SILENTMAID: Well, I love this guy, the one I saved, and I could become human and meet him if I sacrifice my voice. If he falls in love with me = happily ever after. But if he doesn't . . . well, there's some risk involved.

BeastNYC: How do you know it's true love?

Grizzlyguy: There's always some risk involved when dealing with persons of the witch persuasion.

SILENTMAID: It's love on my side, Beast.

Grizzlyguy: <– doesn't think Silent should risk it.

BeastNYC: <– doesn't believe in love.

Froggie: Cn I say smthing & cn you wat 4 me bc i typ slo

SILENTMAID: Sure, Froggie. We'll wait.

Froggie: It ws hrd 4 me bc my famy nvr saw me as a frg. I couldnt talk 2 thm. Thy think i disapprd but i didnt. my sis saw me the 1st day and said eek, a warty frog! She thru me outsid in the muk. Thru me!! it hrts 2 not be able 2 tell them wat hapend.

SᴵLENTMᴬID: That's terrible, Frog. I'm so sorry. {{{{{Froggie}}}}}

BeastNYC: UR better off not talking 2 thm, Froggie.

Grizzlyguy: U don't know what its like, Beast. You can speak.

SᴵLENTMᴬID: You be nice, Beast. Be a little human.

BeastNYC: I CAN'T BE HUMAN!

Mr. Anderson: No yelling, Beast.

Froggie: u thnk so bc u dont no wot its lik not 2 be abl to talk 2 yr fam NE more

BeastNYC: No, Frog. I think so bc I know what it's like to be able to talk to your family and have them not want you around, be ashamed of you.

SᴵLENTMᴬID: Wow, Beast, sounds awful.

Grizzlyguy: Yeah, sorry. Tell us about it.

BeastNYC: I don't want to talk about it!

SᴵLENTMᴬID: Talk to us, Beast.

Mr. Anderson: You brought it up. I think you do want to talk about it.

BeastNYC: NO I DON'T!

Mr. Anderson: Shouting, Beast. If you do it again,

I'll have to ask you to leave.

BeastNYC: Sorry. Caps lock got stuck. Hard typing w/ claws.

BeastNYC: Hey, Grizz, how does a bear have Internet access anyway? Or a frog?

Mr. Anderson: Please don't change the subject, Beast.

Froggie: i sneak in2 the castl 2 use the computr

Grizzlyguy: I took my laptop w me. There's Wi-Fi all over the place now, even in the woods.

Mr. Anderson: I want to hear about your family, Beast.

BeastNYC: Just my father. I only have a father. Had a father.

Mr. Anderson: Sorry. Go on.

BeastNYC: I don't want to talk about my father. Let's change the subject.

SILENTMAID: I bet it hurts too much to talk. {{{{{Beast}}}}}

BeastNYC: I didn't say that.

SILENTMAID: No, you didn't. You didn't have to.

BeastNYC: Fine. OK fine. It hurts 2 much so i don't want 2 talk about it. Boohoohoo. Everyone happy? Can we talk about someone else now?

SILENTMAID: Sorrrreee!

PART 2

The Beast

1

I was a beast.

I stared into the mirror. I was an animal—not quite wolf or bear or gorilla or dog, but some horrible species that walked upright, that was almost human, yet not. Fangs grew from my mouth, my fingers were clawed, and hair grew from every pore. I, who'd looked down on people with zits or halitosis, was a monster.

"I am allowing the world to see you as you truly are," Kendra said. "A beast."

And then I was pouncing on her, my claws dragging into

the flesh of her neck. I was an animal, and my animal voice formed not words, but sounds I couldn't have made before. My animal claws raked her clothes, then her flesh. I smelled blood, and I knew without even having words for it that I could kill her like the animal I was.

But some human part of me made me say, "What have you done? Change me back! Change me back, or I'll kill you." My voice was beyond recognition as I howled, "I'll kill you."

Then, suddenly, I felt myself being lifted off her. I started to see her ripped flesh, then her clothes repair themselves as if they'd never been torn.

"You can't kill me," she said. "I will simply move on to a new form, perhaps a bird or a fish or a lizard. And changing you back isn't up to me. It's up to you."

Hallucination. Hallucination, hallucination. This type of thing didn't happen to real people. It was a dream helped along by seeing the school production of *Into the Woods* and a few too many Disney movies. I was tired, and all that Absolut I'd had with Sloane didn't help. When I woke up, I'd be fine. I had to wake up!

"You're not real," I said.

But the hallucination ignored me. "You've lived your life being cruel. But in the hours before your transformation, you performed one small kindness. It is because of this one bit of goodness that I see fit to offer you a second chance, because of the rose."

I got what she meant. The rose. The rose corsage I'd

given to that nerdy girl at the dance. I'd only given it to her because I didn't know what else to do with it. Did that count? Was that the only nice thing I'd ever done for anyone? If so, it was pretty lame.

She read my mind. "No, not much of a kindness. And I haven't given you *much* of a second chance, only a little one. In your pocket you'll find two petals."

I reached down to my pocket. There were the two petals I'd shoved in when they'd fallen off the rose. She couldn't have known about them, which maybe proved it was all in my mind. But I said, "So?"

"Two petals, two years to find someone willing to look beyond your hideousness and see some good in you, something to love. If you will love her in return and if she will kiss you to prove it, the spell will be lifted, and you will be your handsome self again. If not, you'll stay a beast forever."

"Not much of a chance is right." A hallucination, a dream. Maybe she'd slipped me something like acid? But like all dreamers, I went along. What else could I do since I wasn't waking up? "No one could ever fall in love with me now."

"You don't believe anyone could love you if you're not beautiful?"

"I don't believe anyone could love a monster."

The witch smiled. "Would you rather be a three-headed winged snake? A creature with the beak of an eagle, the legs of a horse, and the humps of a camel? A lion, perhaps, or a buffalo? Hey, at least you can walk upright."

"I want to be like I was."

"Then you'll have to hope to find someone better than yourself and that you are able to win her love with your goodness."

I laughed. "Yeah, goodness. Girls really think *goodness* is hot."

Kendra ignored me. "She has to love you *despite* your looks. Different for you, isn't it? And remember, you have to love her back—that will be the hardest part for you—and prove it all with a kiss."

A kiss, right. "Look, this has been real fun. Now change me back or whatever you did. This isn't a fairy tale—it's New York City."

She shook her head. "You have two years."

And then she was gone.

That was two days ago. Now I knew it was real, not a dream, not a hallucination. Real.

"Kyle, open the door!"

My father. I'd avoided him all weekend, Magda too, camping out in my room, living on snacks I'd stored. Now I looked around the room. Almost every object that could be broken was. I'd started with the mirror, for obvious reasons. Then I'd moved on to the alarm clock, my hockey trophies, and every piece of clothing in my closet—nothing fit me anyway. I picked up a shard of glass and stared into it. Horrible. I lowered the glass, considering one quick slice to the jugular that would end it all. I'd never have to face my friends, my father, never have to live as what I'd become.

"Kyle!"

His voice startled me, and I let the glass fall to the floor. The shock was what I needed to come to my senses. Dad could fix this. He was a rich man. He knew plastic surgeons, dermatologists—the best in New York. He'd fix this.

And if he couldn't, there was still plenty of time for the other.

I headed for the door.

Once, when I was a little kid, I was walking in Times Square with my nanny, and I looked up and saw Dad on the JumboTron, up there above everyone. The nanny tried to hurry me along, but I couldn't stop staring, and I noticed other people looking up at the television too, watching my dad.

The next morning, Dad was in his bathrobe, talking to my mother about whatever big story he'd been broadcasting the night before that had made all those people look up. I was scared even to look at him. I could still see him, bigger than everything and high above me, a part of the skyline like a god. I was afraid of him. At school that day, I told everyone my dad was the most important man in the world.

That was a long time ago. Now I knew Dad wasn't perfect, wasn't God. I'd walked into the bathroom after he'd been there, and I knew it stunk too.

But I was afraid again when I walked to the door. I stood, hand on the doorknob, my hairy face close to the wood.

"I'm here," I said very soft. "I'm going to open the door."

"Then open it."

I pulled the door open. It seemed like all the sounds of Manhattan stopped, and I could hear that moment like I was out in the woods: my bedroom door scraping against the carpet, my breathing, my heartbeat. I couldn't begin to imagine what my father would do, how he'd react to his son being turned into a monster.

He looked . . . annoyed.

"What the . . . why are you dressed that way? Why aren't you in school?"

Of course. He thought it was a costume. Anyone would. I kept my voice soft. "This is my face. Dad, I'm not wearing a mask. This is my face."

He stared at me, then laughed. "Ha-ha, Kyle. I don't have time for this."

You think I'd waste your precious time? But I tried my best to stay calm. I knew if I got upset, I'd begin to growl and snarl, to paw the floor like a caged beast.

Dad grabbed a chunk of my face fur and pulled it hard. I yelped, and before I could even think, my claws were out, close to his face. I stopped myself as my paw met his cheek. He stared at me, panic in his eyes. He let go of my face and backed away. I could see he was trembling. My God, my father was trembling.

"Please," he said, and I saw his knees begin to buckle.

He stumbled against the door. "Where's Kyle? What have you done with my son?" He looked behind me, like he wanted to push past, to come inside, but he didn't dare. "What have you done? Why are you in my home?"

He was practically crying, and I was too, looking at him. But I kept my voice steady when I said, "Dad, I *am* Kyle. I'm Kyle, your son. Don't you know my voice? Close your eyes. Maybe you'll recognize it." Though even as I said it, the horrible thought grew. Maybe he wouldn't. We'd spoken so little the past few years. Maybe he wouldn't recognize my voice. He'd throw me into the street looking like this, and tell the police his son had been kidnapped. I'd be forced to run away, to live underground. I'd become an urban legend—the monster who lived in the New York sewer system.

"Dad, please." I held out my hands, checking to see if I still had fingerprints, if they were even the same anymore. I looked at him. He was closing his eyes. "Dad, please say you know me. Please."

He opened them again. "Kyle, is it really you?" When I nodded, he said, "You're not playing a joke on me? Because if you are, I don't think it's the least bit funny."

"No joke, Dad."

"But what? How? Are you sick?" He passed his hand across his eyes.

"It was a witch, Daddy."

Daddy? I'd reverted to the word I'd used for two minutes

between the time I'd learned to talk and the time I'd realized that Rob Kingsbury wasn't anyone's "Daddy."

But I said, "There are witches, Daddy. Right here in New York City." I stopped. He was staring at me as if he'd been turned to stone, as if I'd *turned* him to stone. Then, slowly, he sank to the ground.

When he came to, he said, "This . . . this thing . . . this disease . . . condition . . . whatever's happened to you, Kyle . . . we'll fix it. We'll find a doctor, and we'll fix it. Don't you worry. No son of mine is going to look like this."

Then I felt relieved, yet nervous. Relieved because I was sure that if anyone could fix it, my father could. My father was a household name. He was powerful. But nervous because of what he'd said: *"No son of mine is going to look like this."*

Because what would happen to me if he couldn't fix it? I didn't believe for one second in Kendra's second chance. If my father couldn't fix it, I was finished.

2

Dad left, promising to be back for lunch after he did some research. But the clock dragged past one o'clock. Two o'clock. Magda went out shopping. I learned that it's almost impossible to eat breakfast cereal if you have claws. Hard to eat anything, actually. I fed my beast face with an entire package of Boar's Head ham. Would I start eating raw meat soon?

By two thirty, I knew Dad wasn't coming home. Was he trying to do anything to help me? But who'd believe him? What would he say: "Hey, my son's been transformed into some kind of fairy tale beast"?

By three, I'd come up with a backup plan. Unfortunately, it involved Sloane. I called her cell.

"Why haven't you called me?" Do I need to add, *she whined*?

"I'm calling you now."

"But you were supposed to call me before now, over the weekend."

I pushed back my annoyance. I had to be nice to her. She was my best chance. She was always saying she loved me. So if she'd just kiss me, this could be over before Dad consulted with the first plastic surgeon. I realized it was crazy to believe that a kiss would change me, like believing in magic. But how could I not believe in magic now?

"Baby, I'm sorry. I wasn't feeling well. Actually, I think I was coming down with something Friday. That's why I was in such a bad mood." I coughed a few times.

"You sure were."

Which pissed me off, but I said, "I know. I was a jerk, and I ruined everything, didn't I?" I took a deep breath and said what I knew she wanted to hear. "And you looked so beautiful Friday. God, you were the most beautiful girl I've ever seen."

She giggled. "Thanks, Kyle."

"Everyone was eating their hearts out, seeing me with you. I was so lucky."

"Yeah, me too. Listen, I'm in SoHo, shopping with

Amber and Heywood. But I could come over after, maybe. Your dad's not home, right?"

I smiled. "Right. Put your ear real close to the phone. I want to tell you something, but I don't want Amber and Heywood to hear."

She giggled again. "Okay. What?"

"I love you, Sloane," I whispered. "I love you so much . . ."

"I love you too," she said, giggling. "You never said it first before."

"You didn't let me finish. I love you so much, I'd love you even if you weren't so hot."

"Huh?"

"It's true. I'd love you even if you were ugly." I heard Magda puttering around outside my door. I lowered my voice so she couldn't hear me. "Wouldn't you love me even if I was ugly?"

Another giggle. "You could never be ugly, Kyle."

"But if I was. If I had, like, some huge zit on my nose, could you still love me?"

"On your nose? You have a zit on your nose?"

"It's just a rhetorical question. Would you still love me?"

"Sure. This is weird, Kyle. You're being weird. I've gotta go."

"But you'll come over, after you're done?"

"Sure. Yeah. But I have to leave now, Kyle."

"Okay. See you later."

As she hung up, I heard her, giggling higher, telling her friends, "He said he loved me."

It would all be right.

It was six. I'd told Magda, through the door, that if Sloane came over, she should send her into my room. I was sitting on my bed, shades drawn, lights off except the closet light. Waiting. In the darkness, with any luck, Sloane might not even realize how I looked. I wore a pair of Dad's old jeans, larger than my own, to cover me better, and a long-sleeved shirt. All I needed was one kiss. Love and a kiss, the witch had said. Then, it would be fine. I'd be my old beautiful self again, and this cosmic joke would be over.

Finally, a knock came at the door.

"Come in," I said.

She opened the door. I'd worked hard, cleaning up the shattered glass and paper. I had found the two petals and hidden them under the lamp on my dresser, so they wouldn't get lost.

"Why's it so dark in here?" she said. "What, you don't want me to see your zit?"

"I wanted it to be romantic." I patted a spot on the bed. I tried to keep my voice steady. "I wanted to make up for Friday. I love you so much, Sloane. I don't want to do anything to lose you."

"Apology accepted." She giggled.

"That's great." Again, I patted the bed for her to sit.

"Can we make out or . . . something? My dad's on TV, so he won't be home for a while." She finally sat, and I put my shirt-covered arms around her, pulling her close.

"Oh, Kyle. I love having your arms around me." Her own hands moved down the outside of my shirt and . . .

No. She was going for the crotch again. The fur would be a dead giveaway. All I needed was one fast kiss before she noticed it.

"Let's just kiss a while."

"Mmm, okay for a little while."

And I kissed her right on the mouth. I expected to feel something, like when I'd changed the other night. But nothing.

"Ick, Kyle. You feel so hairy. You need to shave."

I scrambled away from her, trying to stay between her and the window. "No, I didn't shave today. I told you I've been sick."

"Well, did you shower? Because you're getting nowhere with me if you didn't."

"Of course I showered."

"Let me turn on the light. I want to see." She reached for the lamp.

The light blazed on.

Then I heard a scream.

"Who are you? What are you?" She started hitting me. I cowered, afraid of killing her with my claws. "Get away from me!"

"Sloane! It's me, Kyle."

She kept hitting. She'd taken karate, and it wasn't for nothing. It hurt.

"Sloane, please! I know it's crazy, but you have to believe me! That Goth chick—she was really a for-real witch."

Sloane stopped hitting me and stared. "A witch? You think I'm stupid? You expect me to believe there was a witch?"

"Look at me! How else can you explain this?"

Sloane was reaching out, as if to touch my hairy face, then jerked her hand back. "I've got to get out of here." She started toward the door.

"Sloane—" I went after her and blocked her way.

"Get away! I don't know what's wrong with you, but get away, freak boy!"

"Please, Sloane. You can fix this. She said I'd be this way until someone loved me and kissed me to prove it. We have to try again."

"You want me to *kiss* you now?"

This wasn't going well. But maybe it was better that she knew. Maybe she had to know she was kissing a beast. "Kiss me, and then I'll be back to normal." I felt myself shaking, the way you do when you're about to cry. But that was pathetic. "You *said* you loved me."

"That was when you were hot!" She tried to get past me, but I blocked her again. "What really happened to you?"

"I told you, it was a—"

"Don't say it again! Like I believe in spells, you loser!"

"I'm the same, underneath, and if you kiss me, it will all be like it used to be. We'll rule the school. Please. Just one more kiss."

She looked like she might do it. She leaned toward me. But when I bent to kiss her, she ducked under my arm and ran out of the room.

"Sloane! Come back!" I chased her out into the apartment, not even thinking of Magda or anything. "Please! I love you, Sloane."

"Get away from me!" She opened the door. "Let me know if you get over whatever this is." She ran out into the hallway.

I ran to the door. "Sloane?"

"What?" She was jiggling the elevator button, trying to hurry it there.

"Don't tell anyone, huh?"

"Oh, believe me, Kyle, I won't tell a soul. They'd think I was nuts. I must be nuts." She looked at me again and shuddered.

The elevator came, and she was gone. I went back to my room and lay on the bed. I could still smell the scent of her, and it didn't smell good. I hadn't loved Sloane, so it was no surprise she didn't love me either. That must be why the kiss didn't work. The witch had meant it—I had to be in love.

I'd never loved anyone, even when I was normal, never had anyone want to be with me, other than because of who I was, how much stuff I had, and how good I was at partying. I hadn't cared much. I just wanted the same thing the girls wanted, a good time. There was time for the other stuff later.

But what were the chances I'd ever find someone to really love me now? And maybe loving her back would be the hardest part of all.

3

Good to know: Doctors can't cure you of being a beast.

Over the next weeks, my father and I traveled all over New York and talked to a dozen doctors, who told us in various languages and accents that I was screwed. We traveled outside New York and visited witches and voodoo people too. They all said the same thing: They didn't know how I'd become what I was, but they couldn't cure it.

"I'm sorry, Mr. Kingsbury," the last doctor told my father.

We were sitting in an office in the middle of nowhere in Iowa or Idaho or maybe Illinois. The drive had taken thirteen long, silent hours, and when we'd gotten off at a rest stop, I'd dressed like a Middle Eastern woman, with robes covering my body and face. The doctor worked at a hospital in a nearby city, but Dad had arranged to meet him privately at his weekend home in the country. Dad didn't want anyone to see me. I looked out the window. The grass was a green I'd never seen before, and there were rosebushes in every color. I stared at them. They were beautiful, just like Magda had said.

"Yes, I am too."

"We really enjoy you on the news, Mr. Kingsbury," Dr. Endecott said. "My wife, especially, seems to have a bit of a crush on you."

God! Was this guy going to ask for an autograph, or suggest a threesome?

"Could I go to a blind school?" I interrupted.

The doctor stopped in the middle of his proposal, or proposition. "What, Kyle?"

He'd been the only one to call me by my name. There was this voodoo guy in the East Village who'd called me devil's spawn (which, I thought, was every bit as insulting to Dad as to me). I'd wanted to leave at that point, but Dad kept talking to him until the bitter end when—surprise, surprise—he couldn't help me. Not that I really blamed anyone for not wanting to hang with me. I wouldn't have wanted to hang with me either, which is why I thought what I was suggesting was so brilliant.

"A school for the blind," I said. "Maybe I could go to one of those."

It would be perfect. A blind girl wouldn't be able to see how ugly I was, so I could turn on the Kingsbury charm and make her love me. Then, once I was transformed, I could just go back to my old school.

"But you aren't blind, Kyle," the doctor said.

"Couldn't we tell them I am, though? That I lost my sight in some freak hunting accident or something?"

He shook his head. "It's not that I don't understand what you're feeling, Kyle."

"Yeah, right."

"No, really. I do, a little. When I was a teenager, I had a very bad complexion. I tried every medication and preparation, and it would get better for a little bit, then worse again. I felt so ugly and shy, I was sure no one would ever care for me. But eventually, I grew up and married." He pointed to a picture of a pretty blonde woman.

"*Eventually* meaning after you finished med school and made a ton of money so women would look past your looks?" Dad snapped.

"Dad . . ." I said. But I'd been thinking the same thing.

"You're comparing this to *acne*?" Dad said, gesturing toward me. "He's a beast. He woke up one morning, and he's an animal. Surely, medical science—"

"Mr. Kingsbury, you have to stop saying these things. Kyle is not a beast."

"What would you call it? What terminology is there?"

The doctor shook his head. "I don't know. But what I do know is that only his physical appearance is affected, what he is on the outside." He put his hand on mine, which no one had *ever* done. "Kyle, I know it's difficult, but I'm sure that your friends will learn to accept you and be kind."

"What planet do you live on?" I shouted. "Because it's definitely not Earth. I don't know anyone *kind*, Dr. Endecott. And what's more, I don't want to know anyone like that. They sound like losers. I don't have some little problem. I'm not in a wheelchair. I'm a complete and total freak." I turned away, so they couldn't see me lose it.

"Dr. Endecott," my father said, "we've been to more than a dozen doctors and clinics. At some point . . ." He stopped. "You came highly recommended. If it's a matter of money, I'll pay anything to help my son. This won't be an insurance job."

"I understand that, Mr. Kingsbury," the doctor said. "I wish—"

"Don't worry about the risk. I'll sign a waiver. I think Kyle and I both agree that we'd rather risk . . . anything than have Kyle continue to live like this. Right, Kyle?"

I nodded, even though I realized my father was saying he'd rather see me dead than alive the way I looked. "Yeah."

"I'm sorry, Mr. Kingsbury, but it's really not a matter of money *or* risk. It's simply that there's nothing to be done. I thought perhaps with skin grafts, even a face transplant, but

I did some tests, and . . ."

"What?" my father said.

"It was the oddest thing, but the structure of the skin remained unchanged whatever I did, almost as if it *couldn't* be changed."

"That's insane. Anything can be changed."

"No. It's like nothing I've ever seen. I don't know what could have caused it."

Dad shot me another look. I knew he didn't want me telling anyone about the witch. He still didn't believe it himself. He still thought I had some weird disease that could be cured by medicine.

Dr. Endecott continued. "I'd really like to do some more tests, for research purposes."

"Will they help my son look normal?"

"No, but they might help us to learn more about his condition."

"My son won't be a guinea pig," Dad snapped.

The doctor nodded. "I'm sorry, Mr. Kingsbury. The only thing I can suggest is that you get Kyle into counseling, to learn to deal with this as best he can."

Dad gave a thin smile. "Yes, I'll be sure to do that. I already looked into it."

"Good." Dr. Endecott turned to me. "And Kyle, I'm very sorry I can't help you. But you need to understand that this isn't the end for you unless you let it be. Many people with disabilities go on to great achievement. Ray Charles, a blind man, had tremendous musical accomplishments, and Stephen Hawking, the physicist, is a genius despite motor neuron disease."

"But that's the problem, Doc. I'm no genius. I'm just a guy."

"I'm sorry, Kyle." Dr. Endecott stood and patted my shoulder again, in a way that said both *There, there* and *Please leave now.* I understood and got up.

Dad and I barely spoke on the drive home. When we got there, Dad walked with me from the limo to the back service entrance door of our building. I pulled the dark veil away from my face. It was July and hot, and even though I tried to keep my face hair trimmed, it grew back almost instantly. Dad gestured for me to go in.

"Aren't you coming?" I said.

"No, I'm late. I've missed enough work for this crap." He must have seen my face because he added, "It's a waste of time if it's not accomplishing anything."

"Sure." I walked in. Dad started to close the door, but I let it hit my back. "Will you still keep trying to help me?"

I watched Dad's face. My father was a news guy, so he was really good at keeping a straight face even when he was BS-ing. But even Dad couldn't help the twitch his lips gave when he said, "Of course, Kyle. I'll never stop trying."

4

That night I couldn't stop thinking about what Dr. Endecott had said, about how he couldn't help me because I *couldn't* change. It made sense now—how it seemed like as soon as I cut my hair, it grew right back. Same with my nails—claws now.

Dad wasn't home, and Magda was gone for the night. Dad had raised her salary and sworn her to secrecy. So I took out a pair of kitchen scissors and a razor. I hacked the hair on my left arm as short as I could, then shaved the rest off until it was smoother than before my transformation.

I waited, staring at my arm. Nothing happened. Maybe

the secret was to get it as smooth as possible, not to trim it, but to obliterate it. Even if Dad had to pay off someone to pour hot wax on me every day, it would be worth it if I could just look a little more normal. I walked back to my room, feeling a surge of something—hope—that I hadn't felt since that first day I'd called Sloane to get her to come kiss me.

But when I returned to the bright light of my bedroom, the hair had grown back. I looked at my arms. If anything, the hair on my left arm seemed thicker than before.

Something—maybe a cry—was stuck in my throat. I rushed to the window. I wanted to howl at the ever-loving moon like a beast in a horror movie. But the moon was hidden between two buildings. Still, I opened the window and roared into the hot July air.

"Shut up!" A voice came from the apartment below. On the ground, a woman scurried, clutching her purse. A couple made out in the shadows away from the lamppost. They didn't even notice me.

I ran to the kitchen and chose the biggest knife from the chopping block. Then I barricaded myself in the bathroom and, gritting my teeth against the pain, I sliced away a section of my arm. I stood watching the blood ooze from the gash. I liked the raging red hurt of it. On purpose, I looked away.

When I looked back, the hole had healed. I was indestructible, unchangeable. Did this mean I was superhuman, that I couldn't die? What if someone shot me? And, if so, which was worse—to die, or to live forever as a monster?

When I returned to the window, there was no one on the street. Two o'clock. I wanted to go online, IM with my friends like I used to. I'd gone along with Dad's pneumonia story until school ended, then told them all that I was going to Europe over the summer, then boarding school in the fall. I told them I'd see them before I left in August, but that was a lie. It wouldn't matter. They'd barely e-mailed. I didn't want to go back to Tuttle, of course, not as a freak. At Tuttle, we'd treated people bad if they had cheap shoes. They'd come after me with pitchforks, the way I looked. They'd think I had some disease like Dad thought, and stay away from me. And even if they didn't, I couldn't deal with being a freak in a school where I used to be one of the Beautiful People.

In the street below, a homeless guy trudged by with an enormous backpack on his shoulders. What was it like to be him, to have no one expect, no one want anything from you? I watched him until he disappeared, like the moon, between the two buildings.

Finally, I stumbled to bed.

When my head hit the pillow, there was something hard there. I slid my hand under the pillow and pulled out an object, then turned the light on to see.

It was a mirror.

I hadn't looked in a mirror since my transformation, not since the day I'd broken the one in my room. I picked up this one, a square hand mirror with a silver frame, the same one Kendra had been holding that day at school. I thought

I'd smash it into as many pieces as possible. You have to find your bliss where you can.

But I caught sight of my face in it. It was my own face—my *old* face, that blue-eyed, perfect face that was still mine in my dreams. I held the mirror close, using both hands, like it was a girl I was kissing.

The reflection melted away, and there was my beast face once again. Was I insane? I raised the mirror.

"Wait!"

The voice came from the mirror. Slowly, I brought the mirror down.

The face inside it had changed again. Kendra, the witch.

"What are you doing here?"

"Don't smash this mirror," she said. "It has magical powers."

"Yeah?" I said. "So?"

"I'm totally serious. I've been watching you for over a month now. I see you've realized that you can't get out of this with Daddy's money—dermatologists, plastic surgeons. Your dad even called that clinic in Costa Rica where he had his last top-secret procedure. They all told you the same thing—'Sorry, kid. Learn to live with it. Get counseling.'"

"How did you—"

"I saw you strike out with Sloane too."

"I didn't strike out. I kissed her before she saw me."

"She didn't change you back, did she?"

I shook my head.

"I told you, you have to love the person. She has to love you. Do you love Sloane?"

I didn't answer.

"Didn't think so. The mirror has magic powers. Look inside, and you can see anyone you want, anywhere in the world. Think of someone's name, one of your former friends maybe . . ." In the glass, I could see her sneer when she said *former*. "Ask, and the mirror will show you that person, wherever they may be."

I didn't want to. I didn't want to do anything she said. But I couldn't help myself. I thought of Sloane, and just as quick, the picture in the mirror changed to Sloane's apartment, just the way it had been the day of the dance. Sloane was on the sofa, making out with some guy.

"Okay, so what?" I yelled, before wondering if Sloane could hear me.

The face in the mirror changed back to Kendra's.

"Can she hear me?" I whispered.

"No, only me. With everyone else, it's a one-way thing like a baby monitor. Anyone else you want to see?"

I started to say no, but again, my subconscious betrayed me. I thought of Trey.

The mirror returned to Sloane's apartment. Trey was the one with Sloane.

After a minute, Kendra said, "What's next for you? Are you going back to school?"

"Of course not. I can't go to school as a freak. I've been

bonding with Dad." I looked at the clock. After ten, and Dad still wasn't home. He was avoiding me. The few weeks with the doctors was the most time we'd spent together in . . . well, ever. But I'd known it wouldn't last. I was back to my former life of only seeing Dad on television. I hadn't cared before, when I had a life. But now I had nothing and no one.

"Have you given any thought to how you're going to break the spell?"

I laughed. "You could change me back."

She looked away again. "I can't."

"You won't."

"No, I can't. The spell, it's yours to break. The only way to undo it is by its terms—finding true love."

"I can't do that. I'm a freak."

She smiled a little. "Yeah, you sort of are, aren't you?"

I shook the mirror. "You made me this way."

"You were a hateful jerk." She grimaced. "And stop shaking that mirror!"

"Does it bother you?" I gave it another shake. "Too bad."

"Maybe I wasn't wrong to transform you. Maybe I was wrong to consider helping you now."

"Help? What kind of help can you give that I'd want? I mean, if you can't change me back."

"I can give you advice, and my first is, don't break the mirror. It might help you out sometime."

And then she disappeared.

I put the mirror—gently—down on the nightstand.

5

Sometimes, when you're walking in New York—probably anywhere, but especially in New York because it's so crowded—you see these people, like guys in wheelchairs with stumps of legs just reaching the edge, or people with burns on their faces. Maybe their legs got blown off in a war, or someone threw acid at them. I never really thought about them. If I thought about them at all, what I thought was how to get past without them touching me. They grossed me out. But now I thought about them all the time, how one minute you can be normal—beautiful, even—and then something can happen the next minute that changes it. You can be damaged beyond repair. A freak. I was a freak, and if I had fifty, sixty, seventy years left, I'd spend them as a freak because of that one minute when Kendra put the spell on me after what I did.

Funny thing about that mirror. Once I looked in it, I got obsessed. First, I looked at each of my friends (former friends, as Kendra said), catching them in weird moments—getting ragged on by parents, picking their noses, naked, or just generally not thinking about me. I watched Sloane and Trey too. They were together, yeah, but Sloane had another boyfriend, a guy who didn't go to Tuttle. I wondered if she'd cheated on me too.

Then I started watching other people. The apartment was empty those long August weeks. Magda made my meals and left them for me, but I only came out if I heard her vacuuming in a different part of the house, or if she went out. I remembered her saying she was frightened for me. Probably, she thought I'd gotten what I deserved. I hated her for thinking that.

I started this thing where I'd take out my yearbook and choose a page, then point to some random person—usually some loser I wouldn't have bothered with when I was at the school. I'd read their name, then look in the index to see what activities they did. I thought I'd known everyone at that school. But now I saw that I hadn't known many of them. Now I knew all their names.

The game I played was I chose a person then tried to decide where they'd be in the mirror. Sometimes it was easy. Technogeeks were *always* by the computer. Jocks were mostly outside, running around.

Sunday morning, the picture I chose was Linda Owens. She looked familiar. Then I realized it was the girl from the dance, the one I'd given the rose to who'd gotten so jacked up about it, the one who'd gotten me my second chance. I'd never noticed her at school before that day. Now I looked at her yearbook pages, which were like a résumé: National Honor Society, French Honor Society, English Honor Society . . . well, *all* the honor societies.

She *had* to be at the library.

"I want to see Linda," I told the mirror.

I watched for the library. The mirror usually panned its location, like a movie. So I expected a shot of the cement lions, then Linda, studying even though it was August.

Instead, the mirror panned a neighborhood I'd never seen before—and wouldn't want to see. On the street, two worn-out women in tube tops argued. A junkie slumped on a doorstep, shooting up. The mirror panned up a stoop, through a door, up a staircase with a broken step and a bare lightbulb with wires hanging from it, and landed in an apartment.

The apartment had peeling paint and coming-up lino-leum. There were boxes for bookshelves. But everything looked clean, and Linda sat in the middle of it, reading. At least I was right about that.

She turned a page, then another, and another. I must have watched her read for ten minutes. Yes, I was that bored. But it was more than that. It was sort of cool that she could read like that, and not pay attention to anything around her.

"Hey, girl!" a voice called, and I jumped. It had been so quiet up until then that I didn't realize there was anyone else in the apartment with her.

Linda looked up from her book. "Yes?"

"I'm . . . cold. Bring me a blanket, huh?"

Linda sighed and put her book facedown. I glanced at the title. *Jane Eyre*, it was called. I was bored enough at that point that I thought maybe I'd read it someday.

"Okay," she said. "Want some tea too?" She was already standing, walking toward the kitchen.

"Yeah." The answer was barely more than a grunt. "Just hurry."

Linda turned on the faucet and let it run while she took out a battered red teakettle. She filled the kettle and placed it on the stove.

"Where's that blanket?" The voice was angry.

"Coming. Sorry." With a backward glance at her book, she walked toward the closet and unfolded a skimpy blue blanket. She took it to a man huddled on an old sofa. He was covered in another blanket, so I couldn't see his face, but he shivered even though it was August. Linda tucked the blanket around his shoulders. "Better?"

"Not much."

"Tea will help."

Linda made the tea, and searched through the mostly empty refrigerator for something, gave up, and brought the tea to the man. But he'd fallen asleep. She knelt by him a second, listening. Then she reached her hand under the sofa cushion like she was looking for something. Nothing. She went back to her reading, drinking the tea. I kept watching, but nothing else happened.

Usually, I only watched a person once. But in the next week, I kept going back to Linda. It wasn't like she was hot-looking or even did anything interesting. Most people at Tuttle were away at camp, or even in Europe. So I could have looked in on someone at the Louvre if I'd wanted. Or, more like it, I could have seen a camp shower room full of naked girls— okay, I did do that. But usually, I watched Linda read. I couldn't believe she'd read so much in summer! Sometimes she laughed, reading her book, and once she even cried. I didn't know how anyone could make such a big deal about books.

One day, while she was reading, there was a noise— banging on the door. I watched her open it.

A hand grabbed her. I started.

"Where is it?" a voice demanded. A hulking shape came into view. I couldn't see his face, only that he was big. I wondered should I call 911.

"Where's what?" Linda said.

"You know what. What'd you do with it?"

"I don't know what you're talking about." Her voice was calm, and she wiggled away from his grip and started back toward her book.

He grabbed her again and pulled her to him. "Give it to me."

"Don't have it anymore."

"Bitch!" He slapped her hard across the face. She stumbled and fell. "I need that. Think you're better than me, that you can steal from me? Give it to me!"

He started toward her like he was going to grab her again, but she recovered herself, stood, and ran behind the table. She grabbed her book and held it in front of her, like it would shield her. "Stay away from me. I'll call the cops."

"You wouldn't call the cops on your own dad."

I started at the word *dad*. That sleaze was her father? The same one she'd tucked the blanket around the week before?

"I don't have it," she said. Her face had the busted-up look of someone trying hard not to cry. "I threw it out, flushed it down the toilet."

"Flushed it? Hundred bucks' worth of horse? You—"

"You shouldn't have it! You promised . . ."

He threw himself at her, but he was unsteady on his feet, and she got away and ran to the door. Still holding her book, she ran from the scummy apartment, down the cracked, cobwebby stairs toward the street.

"Run away!" he yelled after her. "Just leave like your slut sisters did!"

She ran into the street and to the subway station. I watched her down the stairs, until she got onto the car. Only then did she burst into tears.

I wished I could go to her.

Mr. Anderson: Thanks for coming. Today, we'll be talking about living arrangements after transformation.

Froggie: i nvr lkd ponds & I sur dont lk em now

SILENTMAID: Froggie, why not?

Froggie: why not??? theyr wet!!!!!

SILENTMAID: But you're an amphibian.

Froggie: So???

SILENTMAID: So you consider living on dry land to be preferable to water, even though you can breathe underwater. Why? I really want to know!

Froggie: for 1 thing my stuf keeps floting awy!

BeastNYC joined the chat.

BeastNYC: You all can start now. im here.

SILENTMAID: We started.

BeastNYC: I wz kidding.

Mr. Anderson: We can't always be sure with you, Beast. But welcome.

BeastNYC: I'm moving this wk. Not sure where.

SILENTMAID: I had a bit of an announcement today.

Mr. Anderson: What is it, Silent?

SILENTMAID: I've decided to go through with it.

Froggie: go thru w the trnsformtin?

SILENTMAID: Yes.

BeastNYC: Why would u do a stupid thing like that?

Mr. Anderson: Beast, that isn't polite.

BeastNYC: But it's stupid! why would she risk a spell when she doesn't have 2?

SILENTMAID: I've thought long and hard about this, Beast.

Grizzlyguy joined the chat.

SILENTMAID: I know there'll be a risk involved, a huge risk. If I don't get the guy, I'll be reduced to sea foam. But I think it's a risk I have to take for true love.

Grizzlyguy: Sea foam?

Froggie: tru luv is worth it

BeastNYC: Can i say something?

Froggie: Cn NE1 evr stop u?

BeastNYC: All guys r jerks. U could be giving up your chance for some guy who doesn't deserve it. No one's worth being turned to sea foam.

SILENTMAID: You don't even know him!

BeastNYC: Neither do u. U r undersea & he's on land!

SILENTMAID: I know all I need to know. He's perfect.

Froggie: im sur he is.

BeastNYC: I'm just being realistic . . . . he might not notice you. didn't you say you have to give up your voice?

SILENTMAID: I saved him from drowning! Oh, forget it.
Froggie: beest is a beest, slnt. Dont let him get u down.

SilentMaid has left the chat.

BeastNYC: sorry but it's really hard being a beast in nyc.

PART 3

The Castle

PART 3

1

The next month, I moved. My father bought a brownstone in Brooklyn and informed me we were moving there. Magda packed my stuff with no help from me.

The first thing I noticed was the windows. The house had old-fashioned stick-out windows with fancy frames around them. Most houses on the block had windows with sheer curtains or shades that looked out on the tree-lined street. Dad obviously didn't want me looking at trees—or, more to the point, anyone looking at me. Our house had thick, dark, wooden blinds that, even when opened, blocked most of the light and view from the front of the house. I could smell the fresh wood and the stain, so I knew that they were new. There were alarms on every window and surveillance cameras on every door.

The house was five stories, each story almost as big as our whole apartment in Manhattan. The first floor was a complete private apartment with its own living room and a kitchen. That was where I'd live. A huge plasma screen took up most of a wall in the living room. It had a DVD player and the entire stock of Blockbuster. Everything an invalid needs.

In back of the bedroom was a garden area so bare and brown I almost expected tumbleweeds. A new-looking wooden fence stretched across the back. Even though there was no gate, there was a surveillance camera trained on the fence, in case anyone broke in. Dad didn't want to take any chances someone would see me. I didn't plan to go outside.

In keeping with the invalid theme, there was a study off the bedroom with another plasma screen, just for the PlayStation. The bookshelves were lined with games, but no actual books.

The bathroom on my floor had no mirror. The walls had been freshly painted, but I could see an outline where a mirror had been unscrewed and spackled over.

Magda had already unpacked my stuff—except for two things I hadn't let her see. I took out two rose petals and Kendra's mirror. I put them under some sweaters in my bottom dresser drawer. I walked up the stairs to the second floor, which had another living room, a dining room, and a second kitchen. This place was too big for just us. And why would Dad want to move to Brooklyn?

The bathroom there had a mirror. I didn't look at it.

The third floor had another big bedroom, which was decorated like a living room, but empty, and a study with no books. And another plasma screen.

The fourth had three more bedrooms. The smallest one had some suitcases in it I didn't recognize. The fifth floor just had a bunch of junk in it—old furniture and boxes of books and records, all covered in a thick blanket of dust. I sneezed—dust stuck in my beast fur more than it did on regular people—and went back down to my own apartment and stared out the French doors at the garden fence. While I was looking around, Magda walked in.

"Knock much?" I said.

"Ah, I am sorry." And then she started chirping, like a Spanish squirrel. "You like you room, Mr. Kyle? I do for you—a good, cheerful room."

"Where's my dad?"

She looked at her watch. "He at work. News on soon."

"No," I said. "I mean, where's he staying? Where's his room? Is he upstairs?"

"No." Magda stopped chirping. "No, Mr. Kyle. He no upstairs. I stay."

"I mean when he comes back."

Magda looked down. "I stay with you, Mr. Kyle. I am sorry."

"No, I mean . . ."

Then I got it. *I stay.* Dad had no room because he wasn't living here. He wasn't moving to Brooklyn, only me. And Magda, my new guardian. My warden. Just the two of us, forever, while Dad lived a happy Kyle-free existence. I looked around at the mirrorless, windowless, endless walls (all painted in cheerful colors—the ones in the living room were red; mine were emerald green). Could they swallow me up so there was nothing left but the memory of a good-looking guy who'd disappeared? Could I be like that one guy at school who died in an accident in seventh grade? Everyone cried, but now I'd forgotten his name. I bet everyone had, just like they'd forget mine.

"It's nice." I walked over to the night table. "So where's the phone?"

A pause. "No."

"No phone?" She was a bad liar. "Are you sure?"

"Mr. Kyle . . ."

"I need to talk to my dad. Is he planning on just . . . dumping me here forever without saying good-bye . . . buying me DVDs"—I swept out my hand, catching a shelf and sending most of its contents crashing to the floor—"so he won't feel guilty about ditching me?" I felt the bright green walls closing in on me. I sank to the sofa. "Where's the phone?"

"Mr. Kyle . . ."

"Stop calling me that!" I knocked down more DVDs.

"You sound like a moron. What's he paying you to stay with me? Did he triple your salary to get you to stay here with his freak son, to be my jailer and keep your mouth shut? Well, your job goes bye-bye if I run away. You know that, don't you?"

She kept staring at me. I wanted to hide my face. I remembered what she'd said that day about being frightened for me.

"I'm evil, you know," I told her. "That's why I look this way. Maybe some night I'll come and get you in your sleep. Don't people in your country believe in that stuff—voodoo and Satan's spawn?"

"No. We believe—"

"Know what?"

"Yes?"

"I don't care about your country. I don't care about anything about you."

"I know you are sad . . ."

I felt a wave rising in my head, welling up in my nose. My father hated me. He didn't even want me in the same house with him.

"Please, Magda, please let me talk to him. I need to. He's not going to fire you over letting me talk to him. He couldn't find anyone else to stay with me."

She stared a moment longer. Finally, she nodded. "I will get the phone. I hope it will help you. I try myself."

She walked away. I wanted to ask her what she meant

by "I try myself." That she'd tried to talk my dad into staying with me, to being human, but failed? I heard her trudging upstairs to her room, which must have been the one with the suitcases. God, she was all I had. She could poison my food if I got too obnoxious. Who'd care? I knelt on the floor to pick up the DVDs I'd knocked down. It was hard with claws, but at least my hands were still shaped the same, with a thumb like a gorilla's, not like a bear's paw. In a few minutes, Magda came back carrying a cell phone. So the place really did have no phone service. What a piece of work my dad was.

"I . . . I picked up most of the stuff I threw." I gestured with my arms full of stuff. "I'm sorry, Magda."

She raised an eyebrow, but said, "Is all right."

"I know it's not your fault my father's . . ." I shrugged.

She took the games I was still holding. "You want I call him?"

I shook my head and took the phone. "I need to speak to him alone."

She nodded, then put the games back on the shelf and left the room.

"What is it, Magda?" My father's voice oozed irritation when he answered. It wouldn't get better when he heard it was me.

"It's not Magda. It's me, Kyle. We need to talk about some things."

"Kyle, I'm in the middle of—"

"You always are. I won't take long. It'll be quicker to listen to what I have to say than to argue with me."

"Kyle, I know you don't want to be there, but really it's for the best. I've tried to make you comf—"

"You dumped me here."

"I'm doing what's best for you, I'm protecting you from people staring, from people who'd try to use this to their advantage and—"

"That's a load of crap." I looked around at the green walls closing in on me. "You're just protecting yourself. You don't want anyone to know about me."

"Kyle, this conversation is over."

"No, it's not. Don't you hang up on me! If you do, I'll go to NBC and give them an interview. I swear to God I'll go right now."

That stopped him. "What is it you want, Kyle?"

I wanted to go to school, to have friends, to have everything back the way it used to be. That wasn't going to happen. So I said, "Look, there are a few things I need. Get them for me, and I'll go along with what you want. Otherwise, I'll leave." Through the almost opaque blinds, I could see the sky was dark.

"What things, Kyle?"

"I need a computer with Internet. I know you're worried I'll do something crazy like tell the press to come over here and take my picture." *Tell them I'm your son.* "But I won't—not if you do what I ask. I just want to be able to see the world still, and maybe . . . I don't know, maybe join an e-group or something." This sounded so lame I almost had to cover my ears against its patheticness.

"Okay, okay, I'll work on it."

"Second, I want a tutor."

"A tutor? You were hardly a star student before."

"Now's different. Now I have nothing else to do."

Dad didn't answer, so I kept going.

"Besides, what if I snap out of this? I mean, I got this way in a day. Maybe in another day, I'll be better. Maybe the witch will change her mind and switch me back." I said this even though I knew it couldn't happen, and he didn't believe me. In the back of my mind, I still thought maybe I could meet someone, a girl, maybe online. That's why I wanted the computer. I didn't really understand why I wanted a tutor. Dad was right—I'd hated school. But now that it was being taken away from me, I wanted it. Besides, a tutor would be someone to talk to. "It just seems like I should keep up."

"All right. I'll look for someone. What else?"

I took a deep breath. "The third thing is I don't want you to visit me."

I said it because I already knew he wouldn't. Dad didn't want to see me anyway. He'd made that completely clear. If he did come, it would be because he felt like he had to. I didn't want that, didn't want to sit there, waiting to see if he'd show and getting bummed every day that he didn't.

I waited to see if he'd argue, pretend to be a good dad.

"All right," he said. "If that's what you want, Kyle."

Typical. "It's what I want."

I hung up before I could change my mind and beg him to come back.

2

Dad was quick. The tutor showed up a week later.

"Kyle." I noticed Magda had stopped calling me Mr. Kyle after I had screamed at her. This made her very slightly less annoying. "This is Will Fratalli. He is teacher."

The guy with her was tall, late twenties, and major geeky. He had a dog with him, a yellow Lab, and he had on worn jeans, too baggy to be fitted but not big enough to be cool, and a blue button-down shirt. Obviously public school, and not even cool public school. He stepped forward. "Hello, Kyle."

He didn't run screaming at the sight of me. That was a point in his favor. On the down side, he didn't look at me. He sort of looked to the side of me.

"Over here!" I waved. "This isn't going to work if you can't even look at me."

The dog let out a low growl.

The guy—Will—laughed. "That might be a bit difficult."

"Why's that?" I demanded.

"Because I'm blind."

Oh.

"Sit, Pilot!" Will said. But Pilot was pacing, refusing to sit.

This was so totally alternative universe. My dad had gone out and found—or, most likely, got his secretary to find—a blind tutor, so he wouldn't be able to see how ugly I was.

"Oh, wow, I'm sorry. Is this . . . this is your dog? Will it be living here? Will you?" I'd never met a blind person before, though I'd seen them on the subways.

"Yes." Will gestured to the dog. "This is Pilot. We shall both be living here. Your father drives a hard bargain."

"I'll bet. What'd he tell you about me? I'm sorry. Do you want to sit down?" I took his arm.

He jerked it away. "Please don't do that."

"Sorry. I was just trying to help."

"Don't grab people. Would you like it if I grabbed you? If you'd like to offer assistance, ask if the person needs it."

"Okay, okay, sorry." This was getting off to a great start. But I needed to get along with this guy. "Do you?"

"Thank you, no. I can manage."

Using a cane I also hadn't noticed, he made his way around the sofa and sat. The dog kept glaring at me, like he thought I was some animal that might attack his master. He let out another low growl.

"Does he tell you where to go?" I asked. I wasn't scared. I knew if the dog bit me, I'd just heal. I leaned down and stared right into the dog's eyes. *It's okay*, I thought. The dog sat, then lay down. He stared at me, but he stopped growling.

"Not really. I find my own way, but if I'm about to walk down a flight of stairs, he stops walking."

"I never had a dog," I said, thinking how dumb it sounded after I said it. Poor little deprived New York kid.

"You won't have this one either. He's mine."

"I understand." *Strike two.* "Chill." I sat on the chair opposite Will. The dog kept looking at me, but the look was different, like he was trying to work out whether I was an animal or a man. "What did my father tell you about me?"

"He said you were an invalid who needed home teaching to keep up with your studies. You're a very serious student, I gather."

I laughed. "Invalid, huh?" Invalid was right. As in in*val*id. Not valid. "Did he mention what disease I have?"

Will shifted in his seat. "Actually, no. Was it something you wanted to discuss?"

I shook my head before realizing he couldn't see me. "Something you might want to know. See, the thing is, I'm perfectly healthy. I'm just a freak."

Will's eyebrows went up at the word *freak*, but he didn't say anything.

"No, really. First off, I have hair all over my body. Thick hair like a dog's. I also have fangs, and claws. Those are my bad points. The good point is I seem to be made of Teflon. Cut me, and I heal. I could be a superhero except that if I ever tried to save someone from a burning building, they'd take one look at my face and run screaming into the flames."

I stopped. Will still didn't answer, just stared at me almost like he could see me better than other people, like he could see what I used to look like.

Finally, he said, "Are you quite finished?"

Quite finished? Who talked like that? "What do you mean?"

"I'm blind, not stupid. You won't be able to put stuff over on me. I was under the impression . . . your father said you *wanted* a tutor. If that isn't the case . . ." He stood.

"No! You don't get it. I'm not trying to yank your chain. What I'm saying is true." I looked at the dog. "Pilot knows it. Can't you tell how freaked out he's been acting?" I reached out my arm to Will. The dog let out another growl, but I looked into his eyes, and he stopped. "Here. Touch my arm."

I rolled up my shirtsleeve, and Will touched my arm.

He recoiled. "That's your . . . it's not a coat you're wearing or something?"

"Feel it. No seams." I turned my arm, so he could feel underneath. "I can't believe he didn't tell you."

"He did have some rather odd . . . conditions for my employment."

"Like what?"

"He offered an enormous salary and use of a credit card for all expenses—I can't say I argued with that. He required me to live here. The salary was paid through a corporation, and I was never to ask who he was or why he'd hired me. I was required to sign a three-year contract, terminable at his will. If I stayed three years, he'd pay off my student loans and send me to a doctoral program. Finally, I had to agree not to tell my story to the media or write a book. I rather assumed you were a movie star."

I laughed at that one. "Did he tell you who he was?"

"A businessman, he said."

And he didn't think I'd tell you?

"We'll talk," I said. "That is, assuming . . . do you still want to work here, now that you know I'm not a movie star, that I'm just a freak?"

"Do you wish me to work here?"

"Yes. You're the first person I've spoken to in three months besides doctors and the housekeeper."

Will nodded. "Then I want to work here. I was actually kind of put off when I thought you were a movie star, but I needed the money." He put his hand out. I took his. "I'm happy to work with you, Kyle."

"Kyle Kingsbury, son of Rob Kingsbury." I shook his hand, enjoying his shocked expression. "Did you say my dad gave you a credit card?"

3

You'd have to say Will and I bonded in the next week, over Dad's credit card. We ordered books first, because I was such a serious student now. Schoolbooks, but novels too, and Braille versions for Will. It was pretty cool watching him read with his hands. We bought furniture and a satellite radio for Will's room. He tried to say we shouldn't spend so much, but he didn't argue too hard.

I'd told Will all about Kendra and the curse.

"Preposterous," he said. "There's no such thing as witches. It must be a medical condition."

"That's because you can't see me. If you could, you'd believe in witches."

I told him about how I needed to find true love to break the curse. Even though he said he didn't, I think he finally sort of believed me.

"I chose a book I think you'll like." Will pointed to the table. I picked up the book, *The Hunchback of Notre-Dame*.

"Are you crazy? It's, like, five hundred pages long."

Will shrugged. "Give it a whirl. It has lots of action. If it turns out you're not smart enough to read it, we'll choose something else."

But I read it. The hours and days just went on and on, so I read. I liked to read in the fifth-floor rooms. There was an old sofa that I'd pulled up to a window. I'd sit for hours, sometimes reading, sometimes watching the streams of people below on the way to the subway station or out shopping, the people my age going to school or skipping. I felt like I knew all of them.

But I also read about Quasimodo, the hunchback, who lived in Notre Dame Cathedral. I knew why Will had suggested the book of course, because Quasimodo was like me, locked away somewhere. And in my fifth-floor room, watching over the city, I felt like him. Quasimodo watched the Parisians and a beautiful gypsy girl, Esmeralda, who danced far below. I watched Brooklyn.

"That author, Victor Hugo, must've been a real fun guy," I told Will in one of our tutoring sessions. "I think I'd have liked to have him at a party."

I was being sarcastic. The book was totally depressing, like the author hated people.

"He was subversive, though," Will said.

"Why? Because he made the priest the bad guy and the ugly guy good?"

"That was part of it. See, you are smart enough to read that long book."

"It isn't a hard book." I knew what Will was trying to do—build me up so I'd try harder. Even so, I felt myself smile. I'd never thought of myself as smart. Some of my teachers had said I was, that I didn't get good grades because I didn't "apply myself," which is this thing teachers say to get you in trouble with your parents. But maybe it was true. I wondered if maybe being ugly made me smarter. Will said that when a person is blind, the other senses—like hearing and smell—grow stronger to compensate. Could I be getting smarter to compensate for my hideousness?

Usually, I read in the morning, and we talked in the afternoon. Will would call up to me around eleven.

One Saturday, Will didn't call up. I didn't notice at first because I was reading an important part of the book, where Quasimodo rescues Esmeralda from execution, then carries her into the cathedral, yelling, "Sanctuary! Sanctuary!" But even though Quasimodo rescued Esmeralda, she couldn't even look at him. He was too ugly.

Talk about depressing! I heard the clock striking noon. I

decided to go downstairs.

"Will! Rise and shine! Time to instill knowledge!"

But Magda met me at the third-floor landing. "He is not here, Kyle. He had an appointment, very important. He said tell you take the day off."

"My whole life's a day off."

"He will be back soon."

I didn't want to read anymore, so after lunch, I logged on to the Internet. The week before, I'd found this great Web site where you could see a satellite view of the world. So far, I'd found the Empire State Building, Central Park, and the Statue of Liberty. I'd even found my house. How cool would it be to find the Notre Dame Cathedral in Paris? I tried New York again, zooming from the Empire State Building to St. Patrick's. Was Notre Dame as big as St. Patrick's? I really needed an atlas, and a travel guide. I ordered them online.

Then, since I was online and didn't have anything to do, I checked out MySpace.com. I'd heard about people in school who hooked up online. Maybe I could meet someone that way, get her to fall in love with me through IM, then sort of gently explain about the whole beast thing later.

I logged on to MySpace and searched for girls. I still had a profile from back when I was Normal Kyle. I'd never tried to meet anyone on MySpace before, never had to. So I added a few more photos, a few more descriptions, and answered all the questions about my interests (hockey), favorite movie

(*Pride and Prejudice*—Sloane had made me watch it, and I hated every minute, but I knew girls went for that stuff), and heroes (my dad, of course—it sounded sensitive). For *I'd like to meet*, I wrote "my true love" because it was true.

I started searching. There was no category for my age, so I tried ages 18 to 20, since I knew everyone lied about that anyway. I got seventy-five profiles.

I clicked on some. A bunch of them turned out to be pay sex sites. I tried to avoid anything that had the word *kinky* in it, but finally, I found one that sounded normal. The member name was Shygrrl23, but the profile was anything but.

> I'm considered to be a rare type chick. I don't think there is really anyone out there like me. I'm 5'2" blond and blue-eyed. Well, you see the pics. I love to dance and spend time with my friends. I love people who can keep it real. I love to go to parties too. I go to UCLA, where I'm studying to be an actress. I like having fun and living life to the fullest. . . .

I looked at the mirror. "Show me Shygrrl23," I told it.

The mirror panned a classroom and settled on a girl—a girl who was clearly not a second over twelve years old. I hit the Back button on the keyboard.

I clicked on another profile, and another. I tried to

choose profiles that were in other states, because then I wouldn't have to meet them too soon. After all, what was I going to say, "I'm the beast with the yellow flower in my lapel"? I had two years to fall in love and make her love me.

"Show me Stardancer112," I commanded the mirror.

She was in her forties.

For the next three hours, I trawled MySpace and Xanga. Actually *trolled* would be a more accurate term. The next profiles I looked at turned out to be:

A 40-something housewife who asked for a naked picture

An old guy

A 10-year-old girl

A police officer

All said they were my age and female. I hoped the cop was there trying to catch the other pervs. I typed a warning to the ten-year-old, and she messaged back, yelling that I wasn't her mother.

Magda came in with the vacuum cleaner.

"Ah, I did not know you were in here, Kyle. Is okay I vacuum in the room?"

"Sure. I'm just on the Internet." I smiled. "Trying to meet a girl."

"A girl?" She came closer and looked at the screen. "Ah." She sort of frowned, and I thought that I wasn't even sure if she knew what a chat room was, or what the Internet was, for that matter. "Okay, I be very quiet. Thank you."

I looked around a little longer. There were a few people

who seemed normal, but none of them were online. I'd come back later.

Then I spent another half hour Googling words like *beast, transformation, spell, curse*—you know, just to see if this type of thing had happened to anyone else outside of Grimms' fairy tales or *Shrek*. I found the weirdest Web site, run by some guy named Chris Anderson, with all kinds of chats listed, including one about people who'd transformed into other things. It was probably just some teen group, full of the type of people who liked writing Harry Potter fan fiction. Still, I planned to go back there another day.

Finally, I logged off. I'd heard Will come in hours earlier, but he hadn't come up to talk to me. "Will, vacation day's over!" I yelled.

No answer. I checked out the other floors. No Will. Finally, I went back to my own apartment.

"Kyle, is that you?" His voice came from the garden. I hadn't been there since the first day. It was too depressing to look at the eight-foot wooden fence Dad had put in to keep people from seeing me, so I kept the curtains closed.

But Will was out there. "Little help here, Kyle?"

I stepped outside. Will was surrounded by pots and plants and dirt and shovels. In fact, he was trapped against a wall by a huge bag of dirt.

"Will, you look like hell!" I yelled through the glass door.

"I can't say how you look," he said. "But if you look like you sound, you look like a jerk. Please help me."

I went and helped him lift the bag of soil. It spilled everywhere, mostly on Will. "Sorry."

That's when I saw he'd been planting rosebushes, dozens of them. Roses in the once empty flowerbeds, roses in pots, and rose vines climbing on trellises. Red, yellow, pink, and, worst of all, white roses that reminded me of what had ended up being the worst night of my life. I didn't want to look at them, and yet I stepped out farther. I reached out to touch one. I jumped. A thorn. My claws went out. Like the lion and the mouse, I thought. I plucked the thorn and it came out. The hole sealed up.

"What's with the roses?" I said.

"I like gardening and the way roses smell. I got tired of you moping around with the curtains drawn. I thought maybe a garden might cheer things up. I decided to take your advice about spending your dad's money."

"How do you know the curtains are closed?"

"A room is cold when it's all shut up and empty. You haven't seen sun since I've been here."

"You think planting some flowers will change that?" I took a punch at one of the rosebushes. It got its revenge by stabbing me in the hand. "Sure, I'll be like one of those Lifetime channel movies—'Kyle's life was empty and desperate. Then a gift of roses changed everything.' Is that what you think?"

Will shook his head. "Everyone can use a little beauty . . ."

"What do you know about beauty? You don't know me from anyone."

"I wasn't always blind. When I was little, my grand-mother had a rose garden. She showed me how to tend them. 'A rose can change your life,' she used to say. She passed away when I was twelve. That was the same year I began losing my vision."

"Began?" But I was thinking, Yeah, a rose can change your life.

"At first, I just couldn't see at night. Then tunnel vision, which drove me crazy because I couldn't play baseball any-more, which stunk because I was pretty good. Finally, I could hardly see at all."

"Wow, that must have really freaked you out."

"Thanks for the sympathy, but don't go all Lifetime channel on me." Will sniffed a red rose. "The smell reminds me of those times. I can see them in my mind."

"I don't smell anything."

"Try closing your eyes."

I did. He touched my shoulder, guiding me toward the flowers.

"Okay, now smell."

I inhaled. He was right. The air was filled with the scent of roses. But it brought back the odor of that night. I could see myself onstage with Sloane, then back in my room with Kendra. I felt a stirring in my stomach. I backed away.

"How'd you know which ones to buy?" My eyes were still closed.

"I ordered what I wanted and hoped for the best. When the delivery man came, I color-coded them. I can see colors a bit."

"Oh, yeah?" I still had my eyes closed. "What color are these, then?"

Will let go of me. "These are the ones in the pot with the cupid's face on it."

"But what color are they?"

"The ones in the cupid pot were white."

I opened my eyes. White. The roses that had brought back such a strong memory were white. I remembered Magda saying, "Those who do not know how to see the precious things in life will never be happy."

"Do you want to help plant the rest?" Will asked.

I shrugged. "It's something to do."

Will had to show me how much dirt to put in the pot, and peat moss and plant food. "City kid never did this before?" he teased.

"The florist delivered an arrangement each week."

Will laughed, then said, "You're serious."

I squeezed the plastic container to loosen the dirt, the way Will had shown me, then lifted the plant out and put it in the bed. "Magda likes white roses."

"You should bring her some."

"I don't know."

"Actually, it was she who suggested the garden. She told me you spend your mornings on the top floor, staring out the window. 'Like a flower, searching for sun' is what she said. She's concerned for you."

"Why would she be?"

"I have no idea. Perhaps she has a kind heart."

"No way. It's because she gets paid to."

"She gets paid whether you're happy or not, doesn't she?"

He was right. It made no sense. I'd never been anything but rude to Magda, but here she was, doing extra stuff for me. Will was too.

I started another hole. "Thanks for this, Will."

"No problem." He kicked the bag of plant food in my direction, to remind me that was what I was supposed to put in next.

Later, I picked three white roses and brought them up to Magda. I meant to give them to her, but when I got upstairs, I felt all stupid. So I just left them by the stove where she was cooking dinner. I hoped she'd know they were from me, not Will. But when she came down to bring my dinner tray, I pretended to be in the bathroom and yelled at her to leave it by the door.

4

That night, for the first time since moving to Brooklyn, I went out onto the street. I waited until night, and even though it was early October, I wore a big coat with a hood, which I pulled up over my face. I wrapped a scarf around my chin and cheeks. I walked close to the buildings, turning so people wouldn't see me, ducking into alleys to avoid coming too close to anyone. I shouldn't have to do this, I thought. I am Kyle Kingsbury. I'm someone special. I shouldn't have been reduced to skulking in alleyways, hiding behind garbage Dumpsters, waiting for some stranger to yell, "Monster." I should have been with people. Yet, I hid and ducked and skulked and luckily went unnoticed. That was the weird thing. No one noticed me, even those who seemed to look right at me. Unreal.

I knew where I wanted to go. Gin Elliott, from my class at Tuttle, had the hottest parties at his parents' place in SoHo when they were away. I'd been watching the mirror, so I knew they'd be away this weekend. I couldn't go to the party—not as a stranger, and certainly not as myself, as Kyle Kingsbury reduced to nothing.

But I thought that maybe—just maybe—I could stand outside the party and watch people going in and out. I could watch them from Brooklyn, sure. But I wanted to be there. No one would recognize me. My only risk was that maybe someone would see me, that I would be captured, held as a monster, maybe made a zoo creature. Not a small risk. But my loneliness made me brave. I could do it.

And still, people passed me, seeming to look, but not seeing me.

Did I dare take the subway? I did dare. It was the only way. I found the station I'd seen so many times from my window, and pushing back once again the thought of being placed in a zoo and having my friends come there on field trips to see me, I bought a MetroCard and waited for the next train.

When it arrived, it wasn't crowded. Rush hour was over. Still, I sat away from the other passengers, taking the worst seat in back. I faced the window. Even so, a woman in a nearby seat moved away when I sat. I watched her, reflected in the windowpane, as she passed me, holding her breath. She would have been able to see my animal reflection if she'd looked. But she didn't, just walked, lurching against the movement of the train, wrinkling her nose as if she smelled something bad. She went to the farthest part of the car to sit, but she didn't say anything.

Then I figured it out. Of course! It was warm. In my heavy coat and scarf, I looked like a homeless person. That's what they thought I was, the people on the street and the train. That's why they hadn't looked at me. No one looked at the homeless. I was invisible. I could walk the streets, and as long as I kept my face sort of hidden, no one would notice me. It was freedom, in a way.

Braver, I looked around. Sure enough, not one eye met mine. Everyone looked at their books, or their friends, or just . . . away.

I got to Spring Street and got out, not so carefully this time. I made my way along the brighter streets, pulling my scarf closer around my neck, ignoring the suffocating feeling of it, and staying to the side. My big fear was Sloane seeing me. If she'd made the mistake of telling anyone about me, they'd have made fun of her for sure. And then she'd be eager to point me out to them, so they'd know she wasn't lying.

I got to Gin's apartment. It had a doorman, so I couldn't

go in the lobby. I didn't want to anyway, didn't want to deal with the light, the faces, the fact that the party was going on without me, like I didn't matter. There was a large planter by the door. I waited until no one was near, then slid down, making myself comfortable beside it. A familiar scent filled the air, and I glanced up at the planter. Red roses. Will would have been proud of me for noticing.

The party had probably started around eight, but even at nine, the late arrivals poured in. I watched like the party was a hidden-camera TV show, seeing the things I wasn't meant to see, the girls pulling the underwear from their butts, or slipping a last dose of something before entering the building, the guys talking about what they had in their pockets and who they'd use them on. I could have sworn a few of my friends looked right at me, but no one saw me. No one screamed, "Monster!" No one even seemed to notice. It felt good, yet bad at the same time.

And then she was there. Sloane. She was liplocked with Sullivan Clinton, one of last year's juniors, in a major Public Display of Affection unfolding before my eyes like an R-rated movie. They could do it in front of me because I was, once again, invisible. I started to wonder if maybe I really was. Finally, they went inside.

That was how the night went. People came. People left. Around midnight, tired and way too hot, I thought about leaving. But that was when I heard a familiar voice from the steps above my head.

"Wild party, huh?" It was Trey.

He was with another former friend of mine, Graydon Hart. "The best," Graydon said. "Even better than the one last year."

"Which one was last year?" Trey said. "I was probably too trashed to remember."

I hunkered farther down, wishing they'd leave. Then I heard my name.

"You know," Graydon said. "Last year—the one where Kyle Kingsbury brought that skanky girl who spent half the night with her hand in his pants."

Trey laughed. "Kyle Kingsbury—a name from the past. Good old Kyle."

I felt myself smile and get even warmer in my long coat.

"Yeah, what ever happened to him?" Graydon said.

"Went to boarding school."

"Guess he thought he was too good for us, huh?"

I stared at them, especially Trey, waiting to see him defend me.

"Wouldn't surprise me," Trey said. "He always thought he was so big when he was here—Mr. My-Father-Reads-the-News."

"What a putz."

"Yeah. I'm glad that guy's gone," Trey said.

I turned my face away from them. Finally, they walked away.

My face, my ears stung. It had all been a lie—my friends

at Tuttle. My whole life. What would people say if they saw me now—they'd hated me even when I was hot-looking. I don't even know how I got home. No one noticed me. No one cared. Kendra had been right, about everything.

5

I was on MySpace again. "Show me Angelbaby1023," I told the mirror.

Instead, it showed me Kendra's face.

"It won't work, you know."

"What are you doing here?"

"Relieving you of your delusions. It won't work, trying to meet someone online, find true love that way. It won't work."

"Why the hell not? I mean, sure some of them are full of it, but they can't all—"

"You can't fall in love with a computer. Not true love."

"People meet online all the time. They even get married."

"It's one thing to meet online, then meet in person and fall in love. It's another thing entirely to conduct a whole relationship online, convince yourself you've fallen in love from thirty states away . . ."

"What's the difference? You think looks shouldn't matter. With the Internet, they really don't. It's all about personality." Then I figured out her problem. "You're just mad because I figured out a way around your curse, a way I can meet someone without them getting freaked about what you've done to my looks."

"That's not it. I cast the spell to teach you a lesson. If you learn it, great. I'm not rooting for you to screw up; I'm trying to help you. But this just won't work."

"But why?"

"Because you can't fall in love with someone you don't know. That profile of yours is full of lies."

"You read my mail. Isn't that against the—"

"'I love to go out and party with my friends . . .'"

"Stop it!"

"'My dad and I are really close . . .'"

"Shut up! Shut up! Shut up!" I covered my ears, but her words still taunted me. I wanted to break the mirror, the computer monitor, anything, but it was all because I knew it was true. I'd just wanted someone to love me, someone to break the curse. But it was all hopeless. If I couldn't meet someone online, how could I meet anyone?

"Do you understand, Kyle?" Kendra's muffled voice penetrated my thoughts.

I looked away, refused to answer. I felt my throat getting tight, and I didn't want her to hear it.

"Kyle?"

"I get it," I roared. "Now can you please leave me alone?"

6

I've changed my name.

There was no Kyle anymore. There was nothing left of Kyle. Kyle Kingsbury was dead. I didn't want his name anymore.

I looked up the meaning of *Kyle* online, and that clinched it. *Kyle* means "handsome." I wasn't. I found a name that means "ugly," *Feo* (who would name their kid that?), but finally settled on Adrian, which means "dark one." That was me, the dark one. Everyone—by which I mean Magda and Will—called me Adrian now. I was darkness.

I lived in darkness too. I started sleeping during the day, walking the streets and riding the subways at night when no one could really see me. I finished the hunchback book (everyone died), so I read *The Phantom of the Opera*. In the book—unlike the dorky Andrew Lloyd Webber musical version—the Phantom wasn't some misunderstood romantic loser. He was a murderer who terrorized the opera house for years before kidnapping a young singer and trying to force her to be the love he was denied.

I got it. I knew now what it was to be desperate. I knew what it was to skulk in darkness, looking for some little bit of hope and finding nothing. I knew what it was to be so lonely you could kill from it.

I wished I had an opera house. I wished I had a cathedral. I wished I could climb to the top of the Empire State Building like King Kong. Instead, I had only books, books and the anonymous streets of New York with their millions of stupid, clueless people. I took to lurking in alleys behind bars where couples went to make out. I heard their grunts and sighs. When I saw a couple like that, I imagined I was the man, that the girl's hands were on me, her hot breath in my ear, and more than once, I thought about how it would be to put my claws on the man's neck, to kill him, and to take the girl back to my private lair and make her my love whether she wanted me or not. I wouldn't have done it, but it scared me that I thought of it at all. I scared me.

"Adrian, we need to talk."

I was still in bed when Will came in. I'd been looking through the window at the garden he'd planted, my eyes half closed.

"Most of the roses are dead, Will."

"That's what happens to flowers. It's October. Soon they'll be gone until spring."

"I help them, you know. When I see one that's turned brown but it doesn't fall off, I help it. The thorns don't bother me too much. I heal up."

"So there are some advantages, then."

"Yes. I think it's good to help them die. When you see something struggling like that, it shouldn't have to suffer. Don't you think?"

"Adrian . . ."

"Sometimes, I wish someone would help me like that." I saw Will staring at me. "But there's a few like that red rose, still clinging to the branch. It doesn't fall. It's freaking me out."

"Adrian, please."

"You don't want to talk about the flowers? I thought you liked flowers, Will. You were the one who planted them."

"I like flowers, Adrian. But right now I wanted to talk about our tutoring relationship."

"What about it?"

"We don't have one. I was hired as a tutor, and lately all that means is that I receive an enormous amount of money to stay here and catch up on my reading."

"That doesn't work for you?" Outside, the last red rose drifted on a sudden wind.

"No, it doesn't. Taking money and doing nothing in return is stealing."

"Think of it as redistribution of wealth. My dad's a rich bastard who doesn't deserve what he has. You're poor and deserving. It's sort of like that guy who robbed from the rich and gave to the poor. I think there's a book about that."

I noticed Pilot, sitting by Will's feet. I wiggled my fingers at him to try and get him to come over. "I've been studying anyway. I read *The Hunchback, Phantom of the Opera, Frankenstein*. Now I'm reading *The Picture of Dorian Gray*."

Will smiled. "I think I detect a theme here."

"The theme is darkness—people who live in darkness." I kept wiggling my fingers at Pilot. The dumb dog didn't come.

"Perhaps if we discussed the books. Do you have any questions about—"

"That Oscar Wilde guy—was he gay?"

"See? I knew you'd have some keen insights, something clever to contribute to—"

"Don't screw with me, Will. So was he?"

"Rather famously so." Will jerked on Pilot's harness. "That dog is not going to come to you, Adrian. He is as disgusted with you as I am, lying in bed in your pajamas at one in the afternoon."

"What makes you think I'm in my pajamas?" I was.

"I can smell you. The dog certainly can. And we're both disgusted."

"Okay, I'll get dressed in a minute. Happy?"

"I might be—particularly if you took a shower."

"Okay, okay. So tell me about Oscar Wilde."

"He was put on trial after he had an affair with the son of a lord. The young man's father said that Wilde had enticed his son into the relationship. He died in prison."

"I'm in prison," I said.

"Adrian . . ."

"It's true. When you're a kid, they tell you that it's what's on the inside that counts. Looks don't matter. But that's not true. Guys like Phoebus in *The Hunchback*, or Dorian, or the old Kyle Kingsbury—they can be scumbags to women and still get away with it because they're good-looking. Being ugly is a kind of prison."

"I don't believe that, Adrian."

"The blind guy has insights. You can believe it or not. It's true."

Will sighed. "Adrian, can we return to the book?"

"The flowers are dying, Will."

"Adrian. If you don't stop sleeping all day and let me tutor you, I will quit."

I stared at him. I knew he was mad at me, but I never thought he'd leave.

"But where would you go?" I said. "It must be hard for

you to find jobs when you're . . . I mean, you're . . ."

"It is hard. People think you can't do things, and they don't want to take a chance. They think you're a liability issue. I once had a guy at an interview say, 'What if you tripped and injured a student? What if the dog bit someone?'"

"So you get stuck tutoring a loser like me."

He didn't nod or say yes. He said, "I studied hard so that I *can* work, so I wouldn't have to be supported by someone else. I can't give that up."

He was talking about my life. That's what I was doing, living off Dad, would always do if I couldn't figure out a way to break the spell.

"You gotta do what you gotta do," I said. "But I don't want you to leave."

"There's a solution. We can go back to our regular tutoring sessions."

I nodded. "Tomorrow. Not today, but tomorrow. I have something I need to do today."

"Are you sure?"

"Yes. Tomorrow. I promise."

7

I knew my days of being able to go out in the world were
dwindling. As it got colder, my wearing a coat seemed less
weird, less homeless-looking. More than once recently,
someone had started to make eye contact, and it had been
only my quick reflexes that allowed me to turn away fast
enough, so when the stranger looked again, they saw only
my back and thought my monster face was just a figment of
their imagination. I couldn't take chances like that. I began
to go out later, when the streets and subways were less
crowded, when I was less likely to be caught. But that didn't

satisfy me. I wanted to be part of the life of the streets. And now there was my promise to Will. I couldn't stay up all night and still study the next day. And I couldn't let Will leave.

It would be a long winter. But today, I knew I could go out without fear. It was the one day of the year that no one would look twice at me. Halloween.

I'd always loved Halloween. It had been my favorite holiday since I was eight years old, and Trey and I had egged Old Man Hinchey's apartment door because he hadn't signed up for building-wide trick or treat—and got away with it because we were two of the approximately two hundred thousand kids in the city dressed as Spider-Man. If there was any doubt that it was my favorite holiday, it ended when I went to my first middle school party and got surrounded by Tuttle girls dressed in French maid outfits with fishnets.

And now it would still be my favorite holiday, because tonight, for once, everything could be normal.

I wasn't really thinking of meeting a girl to break the spell. Not really. I just wanted to talk to a girl, maybe dance with her and have her hold me, even if it was for only one night.

Now I was standing in front of a school that was having a party. It was the fifth party I'd passed, but a few of them had signs that said, PLEASE, NO SCARY COSTUMES. I didn't want to take a chance that my face would be too gross. It must have been a private school because the kids looked pretty clean, but it wasn't a school like Tuttle, a school that mattered. Through the gym door, I could see people dancing in a dimly lit room. Some were in groups, but a lot were alone. Outside, a girl sold tickets, but she wasn't checking IDs. The perfect party to crash.

So why wasn't I going in?

I stood a few feet away from the ticket seller, who was dressed like Dorothy from *The Wizard of Oz* except with magenta hair and tattoos. I watched people—especially the girls—go in. No one much looked at me, so that was good. I recognized all the usual types—the cheerleaders and the trust fund babies, the future politicians and the current ones, the jocks, and the kids who went to school just to be picked on. And people who didn't belong to any group. I stood by the door, watching them, for a long time.

"Cool costume."

The DJ was playing "Monster Mash" and some people started dancing.

"Hey, I'm talking to you. That's a really cool costume."

It was the ticket seller girl. Dorothy. Things had cleared out around her since everyone had gone in. We were alone.

"Oh. Thanks." It was the first time I'd talked to someone my own age in months. "Yours is cool too."

"Thanks." She smiled and stood up so I could see her fishnet stockings. "I call it 'Definitely Not in Kansas Anymore.'"

I laughed. "Are the tattoos real?"

"No, but I Jell-O-dyed my hair. I haven't broken it to my

Mom yet that it will last a month. She thinks it's a spray. It should be fun at my nana's seventy-fifth birthday party next week."

I laughed. She wasn't bad-looking, and her legs looked hot in fishnets.

"So aren't you going in?"

I shook my head. "I'm supposed to be meeting some-one."

Why did I say that? Obviously, I'd passed the test. This girl thought I just had on a really elaborate costume. I should have bought my ticket and gone in.

"Oh," she said, looking at her watch. "Okay."

I stood there another fifteen minutes, watching. Now that I'd told her I was waiting for someone, I couldn't change my story, couldn't go in. What I should do was walk away, pretend I was just pacing, then pace farther and not come back, go somewhere else. But something—the lights, the music, and the dancing inside—made me want to stay, even if I couldn't go in. I liked being outside, actually. The air felt cool on my face.

"You know what I like best about your costume?" the girl said.

"What?"

"I like the way you're wearing regular clothes over it, like you're a half man, half monster."

"Thanks. We're doing a unit on literary monsters in English class—*Phantom of the Opera, Hunchback of Notre-Dame,*

Dracula. Next we're doing *The Invisible Man*. Anyway, I thought it would be cool to go as a man who's transformed into a monster."

"Cool. Very creative."

"Thanks. I took an old gorilla suit and modified it."

"What English class is that?"

"Um, Mr. . . . Ellison." I tried to decide how old she was. About my age, no older. "Twelfth-grade honors."

"I'll have to try and get him. I'm only a sophomore."

"I . . ." I stopped myself from saying I was too. "I really like his class."

We stood for another minute. Finally, she said, "Look, I don't usually do stuff like this, but it looks like your girlfriend maybe ditched out, and my shift selling tickets is over in five minutes. Would you go in with me?"

I smiled. "Sure."

"That is really freaky."

"What is?"

"I don't know. It's almost like your mask has facial expressions, like you just smiled." She held out her hand. "I'm Bronwen Kreps."

I took it. "Adrian . . . Adrian . . . King."

"That feels really real." She meant my hand. "It's freaky."

"Thanks. I've been working on it for weeks, putting together pieces of other costumes and stuff."

"Wow, you must really love Halloween."

132

"Yeah. I was really shy as a kid. I liked to pretend I was someone else."

"Yeah, me too. I'm still shy, actually."

"Really? I'd never have guessed from the way you started talking to me."

"Oh, that," she said. "Well, your girlfriend stood you up. You seemed kind of like a kindred spirit."

"Kindred spirit, huh?" I smiled. "Maybe so."

"Stop doing that."

She meant my smile. She was a freaky-looking girl with white skin and the magenta hair—not the type who'd ever wear a slutty French maid outfit. Probably had parents in theater or something. A few months ago, I'd have totally blown her off. Now, talking to anyone was a thrill.

Another girl came to take over Bronwen's shift, and we went into the dance. Now that she was standing and her hair was out of the way, I saw that she'd ripped the neckline of her Dorothy pinafore and had the shirt open so it looked sort of sexy. There was a tattoo of a spider over her left breast. "This is my favorite," I said, brushing it, taking a chance that she'd think I was just touching her with some fake rubber hand so she wouldn't mind.

"I've been sitting on my butt for hours," she said. "Let's dance."

"What time is it?"

"Almost midnight."

"The witching hour." I led her out onto the dance floor.

The fast song that had been playing before melted into a slow one, and I pulled her close.

"So what do you really look like under there?" she asked.

"Why does it matter?"

"I was just wondering if I'd seen you before."

I shrugged. "I don't think so. You don't look familiar."

"Maybe not. Are you into a lot of activities?"

"I used to be," I said, remembering what Kendra had said about lying. "But now I mostly read. I've been doing a lot of gardening too."

"Gardening's a weird hobby around here."

"There's a garden behind my house, a little one. I like to watch the roses grow. I was thinking about building a greenhouse so I can see them in winter."

As I said it, I realized I did plan to do that, for real.

"That's cool. I never met a guy who cared about flowers."

"Everyone needs beauty in their lives." I pulled her closer, feeling the warmth of her against my chest.

"But seriously, Adrian, what do you look like?"

"What if I looked like the Phantom of the Opera or something?"

"Hmm." She laughed. "He was pretty romantic—Music of the Night and everything. I almost wanted Christine to end up with him. I think a lot of women do."

"What if I looked like this for real?" I gestured toward my beast face.

She laughed. "Take off the mask, and let me look."

"What if I was really handsome? Would you hold that against me?"

"Maybe a little . . ." When I frowned, she said, "I'm kidding. Of course not."

"Then it doesn't matter. Please just dance with me."

She pouted but said, "Okay," and we danced closer.

"But how will I find you at school Monday?" she whispered in my ear. "I really like you, Adrian. I want to see you again."

"I'll find you. I'll look for you in the hallways and find—"

She had slipped her hand under the collar of my shirt and was fumbling, looking for the bottom of the mask.

"Hey, stop it!"

"I just want to see."

"Stop it!" I struggled away from her. She was still holding on to my neck.

"How does this . . . ?"

"Stop it!" It came out a roar. Now people were staring at us, at me. I pushed her away, but we were too entangled and she stumbled, making a final grab for my neck. I grabbed her arm, twisting it behind her, hearing a gruesome crack. Then her screams.

I ran, her screams still ringing in my ear, until I reached the subway.

Mr. Anderson: Thanks for coming back this week. I decided to have open chat since it's been so hard to stay on topic other times.

Grizzlyguy: I have an important announcement

Froggie: ne1 hear frm silent

Grizzlyguy: Im in! im sleepng in a condo!! They let me in.

BeastNYC: Who did???

Grizzlyguy: the 2 girls . . . . they took me in.

Froggie: thats awsum grizz!!!

BeastNYC: <— very jealous

Mr. Anderson: Tell us about it, Grizzlyguy?

Grizzlyguy: 1 night they let me in & i slept on the bathmat. When I didn't eat anyone, I guess they thought it was ok for me 2 come back every night.

BeastNYC: That's great!

SilentMaid joined the chat.

Froggie: Hello silent

SILENTMAID: Hi, Froggie. Hi everyone. You'll never guess where I'm writing from.

BeastNYC: where (r u speaking 2 me, or r u still mad?)

SILENTMAID: Yes, I'm speaking to everyone. I'm writing from his house!

Froggie: house? Evry1 gets 2 b in a house

BeastNYC: That's great!

Froggie: im stil in a pond

SILENTMAID: I met him out dancing in a club. He danced with me. I don't have my voice, but I danced and he liked it, even though it hurt my feet. He talked his parents into letting me sleep on the sofabed in their study. We're good friends, but of course, I want it to be more.

Grizzlyguy: of cours

SilentMaid: We go sailing together and for long walks.

Grizzlyguy: That's right. U can walk now.

BeastNYC: How is it?

SILENTMAID: It's hard for me. My feet bleed and bleed, but I always act like it's no big deal because I don't want him to feel bad. I love him so much even though he calls me dumb.

Mr. Anderson: Dumb?

BeastNYC: What a jerk! You're not dumb!

SILENTMAID: Dumb as in unable to speak. Mute. Not as in stupid.

BeastNYC: Still don't like it

SILENTMAID: Anyway, I think it's going well. I'm sorry to talk about myself so much. How's it going with everyone else?

Grizzlyguy: U get 2 sleep on a sofabed. i hav 2 sleep on a mat!

Froggie: stil no hop here. i meen ther is hop but not HOPE

BeastNYC: Ditto here. Waiting 4 something 2 happen.

PART 4

The Intruder in the Garden

7 Months Later

1

I picked up one petal from my dresser, dangled it out the window, then watched it fall. One year left. Since Halloween night, I'd only talked to Will and Magda. I hadn't been outside. I'd seen no light except in the rose garden.

On November 1, I told Will I wanted to build a greenhouse. I'd never built anything—not even a birdhouse or a napkin holder in camp. But now I had nothing but time and Dad's Amex card. So I bought books about greenhouses, plans for greenhouses, materials for greenhouses. I didn't want a cheapo plastic one, and I needed the wall to be solid enough to hide me from view. I built it myself on the ground floor behind my apartment, a big one that took up the whole yard. Magda and Will helped by doing everything that had to be done from outside. I worked by day, when neighbors were mostly at work.

By December, it was finished. A few weeks later, shocked by the sudden spring, yellowish leaves began to grow from the branches, then the green buds. By first snow, everything was in full bloom, the red roses showing in the winter sun.

The roses became my life. I added additional beds and pots until there were hundreds of flowers, a dozen colors and more shapes, hybrid teas and climbing roses, purple cabbage roses the size of my outstretched hand, and miniatures barely the size of my thumbnail. I loved them. I didn't even mind the thorns. All living things needed protection.

I stopped playing video games, stopped looking for lives in my mirror. I never opened the windows, never looked out. I endured my teaching sessions with Will (I didn't call them tutoring anymore; I knew I wasn't ever going back to school), then spent the rest of my day in the garden, reading or looking at my roses.

I read gardening books too. Reading had become my perfect solution, and I researched the best food, the perfect soil. I didn't spray for pests, but washed off those that came with the roses with soapy water, then guarded against reinvasion. But even with the hundreds of flowers, I was aware of the small deaths brought by each morning, as one by one, the roses withered. They were replaced by others, of course, but it wasn't the same. Each tiny life that bloomed into being would live only in the greenhouse, then die. In that way, we were alike.

One day, when I was plucking a few dead friends from the vine, Magda came in.

"I thought I would find you here," she said. She had a broom with her, and she began to sweep up some of the fallen leaves.

"No, don't," I said. "I like to do that. It's part of my work each day."

"There is no work for me. You never use your rooms, so nothing to clean."

"You make my meals. You shop. You buy plant food. You wash my clothes. I couldn't live the way I do without you."

"You have stopped living."

I plucked a white rose from a vine. "You said once that you were afraid for me. I didn't understand what you meant, but I do now. You were scared I'd never be able to appreciate beauty, like this rose." I handed it to her. It was hard for me to do, to pick my prizes, knowing they'd die sooner that way. But I was learning to let go. I'd let go of so much already. "That night, there was a girl at the dance. I gave her a rose. She was so happy. I didn't understand why she cared so much about a rose, a stupid rose that was missing petals. I understand now. Now that all the beauty of my old life is gone, I crave it like food. A beautiful thing like this rose— I almost want to eat it, to swallow it whole to replace the beauty I've lost. That's how that girl was too."

"But you do not . . . you will not try to break the spell?"

"I have everything I need here. I can never break the

spell." I gestured for her to give me the broom.

She nodded a little sadly, and handed it to me.

"Why are you here, Magda?" I said, sweeping. It was something I'd been wondering about. "What are you doing here in New York, cleaning up after a brat like me? Don't you have a family?"

I could ask that because she knew about my family, that I didn't have one anymore. She knew they'd abandoned me.

"I have family in my country. My husband and I, we came here to make money. I used to be a teacher, but there was no work. So we came here. But my husband, he couldn't get his green card, so he had to go back. I work hard to send money back to them."

I stooped to get the leaves with the dustpan. "Do you have children?"

"Yes."

"Where are they?"

"They grow. Without me. They are older than you now, with children of their own I have never seen."

I lifted the dead leaves. "So you know what it's like, then, to have no one?"

She nodded. "Yes." She took the broom and dustpan from me. "But I am old now; my life is older. When I made the choice I made, I did not think it was forever. It is another thing to give up so young."

"I haven't given up," I said. "I've just decided to live for my roses."

That night, I looked for the mirror. I had brought it upstairs, to the fifth-floor rooms, where I'd left it on top of an old armoire.

"I want to see Kendra," I said.

It took a few moments, but when she finally showed, she looked happy to see me. "It's been a while," she said.

"Why does the mirror take so long to show you to me, but others I see instantly?"

"Because sometimes I'm doing something you shouldn't see."

"Like what? In the bathroom?"

She scowled. "Witch things."

"Right. Got it." But under my breath, I sang, "Kendra's on the potty."

"I was not!"

"Then what do you do when I can't see you? Turn people into frogs?"

"No. Mostly I travel."

"American Airlines or astral projection?"

"Commercial airlines are tricky. I don't have a credit card. Apparently, paying in cash makes one a security risk."

"You are, aren't you? I'd think you could just wiggle your nose and blow up a plane or something."

"It's frowned upon. Besides, I can time-travel if I travel my way."

"Really?"

"Sure. You say you want to go to Paris to see Notre Dame. But how about if you could see it being built? Or Rome at the time of Julius Caesar?"

"You can do that, but you can't undo your spell? Hey, can you take me?"

"Negative. If I hung around with a beast, they'd know I was a witch. And witches got burned in those days. That's why I prefer this century. It's safer. People do all sorts of weird stuff, especially in New York City."

"Can you do other magical stuff? You said you felt sorry about the spell. Can you do me a favor to sort of make up for it?"

She frowned. "Like what?"

"My friends, Magda and Will."

"Your friends?" She looked surprised. "What about them?"

"Will's a great teacher, but he can't get a good teaching job—meaning a job other than sitting around tutoring me—because no one wants to hire a blind guy. And Magda works really hard to send money to her kids and grandkids, but she never gets to see them. It's not fair."

"The world just reeks of unfairness," Kendra said. "When did you get so philanthropic, Kyle?"

"It's Adrian, not Kyle. And they are my friends, my only friends. I know they get paid to be here, but they're nice to me. You can't undo what you did to me, but could you do something for them—help Will see again, and bring Magda's

146

family here, or send her there, at least, for a vacation?"

She stared at me a second, then shook her head. "That would be impossible."

"Why? You have incredible powers, don't you? Is there some kind of witch code that says you can turn people into beasts but not help people?"

I thought that would shut her up, but instead she said, "Well, yes. In a way. The thing is, I can't grant wishes just because someone asks for something. I'm not a genie. If I try to act like one, I could end up stuck in a lamp like one."

"Oh. I didn't know there were so many rules."

She shrugged. "Yeah. It sucks."

"So the first time I want something for someone else, I can't have it."

"I already agreed it sucks. Hold on one second." She reached over and took out a big book. She flipped through a few pages. "It says here that I can do you a favor if and only if it is tied to something you have to do."

"Like what?"

"Well, let's say that if you break the spell I placed on you, I'll also help Magda and Will. That's okay."

"That's the same as saying no. I can never break the spell."

"Do you want to?"

"No. I want to be a freak all my life."

"A freak with a beautiful rose garden . . ."

". . . is still a freak," I said. "I love gardening, yeah. But

147

if I was normal-looking, I could still garden."

Kendra didn't answer. She was looking at her book again. She raised an eyebrow.

"What now?"

"Maybe it isn't so hopeless," she said.

"It is."

"I don't think so," she said. "Sometimes, unexpected things can happen."

2

That night, as I lay in bed on the edge of sleeping, I heard a crash. I put my hands to my ears and willed it not to wake me. But then I heard glass falling, and I was awake.

The greenhouse. Someone was invading my greenhouse, my only sanctuary. Without even dressing, I ran to my living room and flung open the door that led out.

"Who dares disturb my roses?"

Why did I say that?

The greenhouse was bathed in moonlight and streetlights, brighter still for the hole in one of the glass panes. A shadowy figure was in the corner. He'd chosen a poor entry point, near a trellis. It had fallen over and lay on the floor, the rose branches broken, surrounded by dirt.

"My roses!" I lunged at him at the same time he lunged toward the hole in the wall. But my animal legs were too fast for him, too strong. I sank my claws into the soft flesh of his thigh. He let out a yelp.

"Let me go!" he screamed. "I have a gun! I'll shoot!"

"Go ahead." I didn't know if I was invincible to gunshots. But my anger, pulsing, pounding through my veins like fireblood, made me strong, made me not care. I'd lost everything there was to lose. If I lost my roses too, I might as well die. I threw him to the floor, then pounced on him, wrestling his arms to the ground and prying the objects from his hands.

"Was this what you were going to shoot me with?" I growled, brandishing the crowbar I'd stripped from him. I held it aloft. "Bang!"

"Please! Let me go!" he yelled. "Please don't eat me. I'll do anything!"

It was only then that I remembered what I looked like. He thought I was a monster. He thought I'd grind his bones to make my bread. And maybe I was, and would. I laughed and grabbed him in a headlock, him struggling against me. Holding his arms with my free paw, I dragged him up the stairs, one flight, then two, heading to the fifth floor, to the window. I held his head out of it. In the moonlight, I could see his face. It looked familiar. Probably I'd just seen him in the street.

"What are you going to do?" the guy gasped.

No clue. But I said, "I'm going to drop you, scumbag."

"Please. Please don't. I don't want to die."

"Like I care what you want." I wasn't going to drop him, not really. It would bring the police there, with all their questions, and I couldn't have that. I couldn't even call the police to arrest him. But I wanted him to fear, to fear for his life. He'd hurt my roses, the only thing I had left. I wanted him to pee in his pants in fear.

"I know you don't care!" The guy was shaking, not just in terror, I realized, but because he was coming down. A junkie. I put my hand in his pocket for the drugs I knew were there. I pulled them out along with his driver's license.

"Please!" he was still begging. "Let me live! I'll give you anything!"

"What do you have that I'd want?"

He squirmed and thought. "Drugs. You can keep those! I can get you more—all you want! I've got a lot of customers."

Ah. A small businessman. "I don't do drugs, you sleaze." It was true. I was too scared I'd do something crazy, like go outside, if I was high on something. I pulled him farther out the window.

He screamed. "Money, then."

I held his neck tight. "What would I do with money?"

He was choking, crying. "Please . . . there must be something."

Tighter. "You have nothing I want."

He tried to kick me, to get away. "You want a girlfriend?" He was choking harder, crying.

"What?" I almost lost my grip, but I dug my claws in harder. He screamed.

"A girlfriend? Do you want a girl?"

"Don't screw with me. I warn you . . ."

But he could see my interest. He pulled away, and I let him. "I have a daughter."

"What about her?" I loosened my grip a little, and he came inside.

"My daughter. You can have her. Just let me go."

"I can *what*?" I stared at him.

"You can have her. I'll bring her to you."

He was lying. He was lying so I'd let him go. What kind of father would give his daughter away? To a beast? But still . . . "I don't believe you."

"It's true. A daughter. She's beautiful . . ."

"Tell me about her. Tell me something to let me know you're telling the truth. How old is she? What's her name?"

He laughed like he knew he had me. "She's sixteen, I think. Her name's Lindy. She loves . . . books, reading, stupid things. Please, just take her, do what you want with her. Take my daughter, but let me go."

It began to be true. A girl! A sixteen-year-old girl! Would

he really bring her here? Could she be the girl for me, the one I needed? I thought of Kendra's voice. *Sometimes, unexpected things can happen.*

"She'd sure be better off without you," I said. Then I realized I believed it. Anyone would be better off without him for a father. I'd be helping her too. At least, that's what I told myself.

"You're right." He was crying, laughing. "She would be better. So take her."

I decided. "In a week, you'll bring your daughter here. She'll stay with me."

He was laughing now. "Sure. Absolutely. I'll go now, and I'll bring her back."

I knew his game. "But don't think you can get away with not doing it." I pulled his face through the window again, farther than before. He screamed like I was going to push him, but I pointed below, to the surveillance equipment by the greenhouse. "I have cameras all over the house to prove what you did. I have your driver's license, your drugs. And I have something else." His hair was long and greasy. I seized him by it and dragged him to the old armoire where I kept the mirror. "I want to see his daughter. Lindy."

The mirror image changed, from my grotesque image to that of a bed, a girl sleeping in it. The image took greater shape. I saw a long red braid. Then her face. Linda. Linda Owens from school, the one with the rose, the one I'd watched in the mirror. *Linda.* Could she be *the* girl?

I shoved the mirror in the scumbag's face. "This her?"

"How did you . . . ?"

Now I said to the mirror, "I want to see the address where she is."

The mirror panned out to the door of an apartment, then a street sign.

"You can't escape." I showed it to him. "Wherever you go, I will know exactly where you are." I looked at his driver's license. "Daniel Owens, if you don't return, I'll find you, and the consequences will be terrible."

The consequences will be terrible? Sheesh, who talked like that?

"I could go to the police," he said.

"But you won't."

I dragged him back downstairs to the greenhouse. "We understand each other?"

He nodded. "I'll bring her." He reached out, and I realized he was trying to get the bag of drugs and the driver's license I held. "Tomorrow."

"In a week," I said. "I need time to get ready. And I will keep these in the meantime, to make sure you come back."

I let him go then, and he scurried into the night like the thief he was.

After I watched him go, I went downstairs. I was almost skipping. Linda.

I saw Will on the third-floor landing. "I heard the

commotion," he said. "But I thought it was better to leave you to your own devices."

"You thought right." I was smiling. "We'll be having a visitor soon. I'll need you to go and buy some things to make her comfortable."

"Her?"

"Yes, Will. It's a girl. *The* girl who'll break the spell maybe, who could . . . love me." I almost choked on the words, they were so hopeless. "It's my only chance."

He nodded. "How do you know she's the one?"

"Because she has to be." I thought about her father, ready to trade his daughter for his drugs and his freedom. A real father would have said no, even if he got arrested. My father would have done what hers had. "And because no one cares about her either."

"I see," Will said. "And when will she be coming?"

"A week at most." I thought about the drugs still in my hand. "Probably sooner. We'll need to work fast. But everything has to be perfect."

"I know what that means," Will said.

"Yeah. Dad's credit card."

3

In the next days, I worked harder than I'd ever worked at anything, decorating the empty third-floor master suite. Linda's room. The furniture in it was living room stuff, and empty bookshelves—just to remind me that my father didn't plan to visit. Now I made it over into the perfect girl's bedroom and library, sending Will out for furniture catalogs, paint, paper, everything.

"And you think this is right?" Will said. "Forcing her to come here? I don't know that I can take part in—"

"Kidnapping?"

"Well, yes."

"You didn't see the guy, Will. He broke in, probably to steal my stuff for drug money. And then, to get out of trouble, he offered me his daughter. Maybe he's done it before—ever think of that? So I said yes. You know I don't plan to do anything bad to her. I want to love her." *God, I sounded like the Phantom of the Opera.*

"I still don't think it's right. Just because there's a benefit to you. What about her?"

"What about her? If her father would give her to me, who's to say he wouldn't give her to someone else? Sell her into slavery? Or something worse, to buy drugs? I know *I'm* not going to hurt her. Can you be so sure about the next guy he tries this with?"

Will was nodding, so I knew he was at least thinking about it. "And how do you know she'll be someone appropriate for you to fall in love with?" Will asked. "If the father's a sleaze?"

Because I have watched her. "This is my one chance. I have to love her," I told Will. "And she has to love me back or it's over for me." And if she could love that loser of a father, maybe she could see past my looks and love me too.

Three days passed. I chose blankets and pillows filled with down. I imagined her sinking onto the bed, the nicest she'd ever had. I picked the finest Oriental rugs, crystal lamps. I could barely sleep those days, so I worked from four in the morning into the night. I painted the study turned library a warm yellow with white trim. For her bedroom, I chose wallpaper with a trellis of roses. Will helped, and Magda, but only I worked through the night. Finally, the rooms looked perfect. Almost unable to believe she was coming, I did more. With the mirror, I visited her house and explored her closets, then went online and bought out the Macy's Juniors department in her size. I arranged it all in the walk-in closet in her new rooms. And I bought books— hundreds of books—and arranged them on ceiling-high shelves. I bought out all the online booksellers and included all my own favorites, the titles I'd been reading. We could talk about them. It would be so great to have someone my own age to talk to, even if it was just about books.

Each afternoon brought a new rush delivery from UPS, and each morning found me working long and hard, painting and sanding and decorating. I had to make everything perfect, had to so maybe she'd look past my ugliness and find some happiness here, find some way to love me. I didn't begin to think about how that would happen, that she'd probably hate me for taking her from her father. I had to make it work.

On the night of the sixth day, I stood in the suite of rooms that would be hers. I still had to fix my greenhouse, my beautiful greenhouse. But fortunately, it was warm out. I'd fix it next. For now, I studied the room. The floors, waxed to perfection, gleamed next to rugs in shades of green and gold. The air smelled of lemon cleaner and dozens of roses. I'd chosen yellow ones, which I read symbolized joy, gladness, friendship, and the promise of a new beginning, and placed them in Waterford crystal vases throughout the suite. In her honor, I'd planted a new rose, a yellow miniature called "Little Linda." I hadn't cut any of those, but would show them to her when she first visited the greenhouse. Soon. I hoped she'd like them. I knew she would.

I walked to the door of her suite and, using a stencil and a tiny brush dipped in gold, painted the finishing touch on the door. I had never been neat in my former life, but this was important. In perfect script, the door said:

Lindy's Room

When I went back to my room, I checked the mirror, which I was keeping by my bed again. "I want to see Lindy," I tried.

It showed her. She was asleep because it was after one o'clock. One small battered suitcase stood beside the door. She was really coming.

I lay down and fell into the perfect sleep for the first time in over a year—not the sleep of boredom, failure, or exhaustion, but the sleep of anticipation. Tomorrow, she'd be here. Everything would change.

4

Someone was knocking. Someone was knocking! I couldn't answer it. I didn't want to terrify her at first sight. I stayed in my rooms, but I watched in the mirror as Will let her in.

"Where is he?" It was the scumbag father. But where was the girl?

"Where is who?" Will asked, all polite.

The guy hesitated, and in that moment, I saw for the first time that she was with him, standing in the shadow behind him. Even though she was shadowed, I could see she was crying.

It was really her. I realized I hadn't believed it.

Lindy. Linda. She was really here!

She'd love the roses. Really, it was she who'd first taught me to appreciate them. Maybe I should go up to meet her after all, show her to her room, and the greenhouse.

Then I heard her voice. "My father has the crazy idea there's a monster here, and that I need to be locked in a dungeon."

A monster. That was how she'd see me if I went upstairs. No, I would let her see the place first, the beautiful rooms and the roses, before she had to see the horror of me.

"No monster, miss. At least, none I can see." Will chuckled. "My employer is a young man of—I am told—unfortunate appearance. He doesn't go outside because of it. That's all."

"Then I'm free to leave?" Lindy asked.

"Of course. But my employer struck a deal with your father, I believe—your presence here in exchange for his cooperation in not reporting certain criminal acts that were caught on tape. Which reminds me . . ." He reached into his pocket and took out the bag I'd taken from the intruder. "Your drugs, sir?"

Lindy grabbed the bag from him. "That's what this is about? You're making me come here so you can get your drugs back?"

"He caught me on tape, girl. Breaking and entering."

"I'm guessing this wasn't a first offense," Will said, and I could tell from his face that he'd checked the guy out with his special blind person sixth sense and found him exactly as I'd said. "And the drugs alone would result in a serious sentence, I believe."

He nodded. "Minimum mandatory—fifteen years to life."

"Life?" Lindy turned on Will. "And you agree to this . . . my imprisonment?"

I held my breath, waiting for Will's answer.

"My employer has his reasons." Will looked as if he wanted to put his hand on Lindy's shoulder or something, but he didn't. He probably sensed that she would deck him if he did. "And he'll treat you well—better, probably than . . . Look, if you want to leave, you may, but my employer has the break-in on tape and will bring it to the police."

The girl looked at her father. Her eyes were pleading.

"You're better off." He snatched the bag from her fingers. "I'll take that."

And without a good-bye, he was out, slamming the door behind him.

Lindy stood staring at the spot he'd occupied. She looked as if she'd crumple to the floor. Will said, "Please, miss. I can tell you've had a hard day, even though it's only ten o'clock. Come. I'll show you to your rooms?"

"Rooms? With an *s*?"

"Yes, miss. They're beautiful rooms. Master Adrian—the young man I work for—he's worked very hard to make

162

certain they're to your liking. He asked me to tell you that if there's anything you require—anything at all other than a telephone or an Internet connection—to be certain to ask for it. He wants you to be happy here."

"Happy?" Lindy's voice was flat. "My jailer thinks I'll be happy? Here? Is he crazy?" In my room, I cringed at *jailer*.

"No, miss." Will reached over and used a key to lock the door. Just a formality. I counted on her staying to protect her father. The sound of the doors locking was terrible to me. I was a kidnapper. I didn't want to kidnap her, but it was the only way to get her to stay. "I'm Will. I too am at your service. And Magda, the maid, whom you'll meet upstairs. Shall we go?"

He offered her his arm. She didn't take it, but casting one last reluctant glance at the door, followed him upstairs.

I watched as Will brought her up the stairs and opened the door. Her cheeks and eyes were stained red from crying. She gasped as she entered, taking in the furniture, the artwork, the walls, painted the exact shade of yellow as the roses in their crystal vases. She gazed at the king-sized bed with its designer sheets. She walked to the window.

"It would be very far to jump, wouldn't it?" She touched the thick glass.

Will, behind her, said, "Yes it would. And the windows don't open that far. Perhaps if you give it a chance, you won't find it so terrible, living here."

"Not so terrible? Have you ever been a prisoner? Are you now?"

"No."

I studied her. I remembered her, from the day of the dance. I'd thought she was homely then, with her red hair, freckles, and bad teeth. The teeth hadn't changed, but she wasn't, really, just plain-looking. I was glad she wasn't beautiful, as her father had said. Someone beautiful could never see past my ugliness. Maybe this girl could.

"I have," she said. "For sixteen years, I've been a prisoner. But I've been digging myself a tunnel. On my own, I applied and got a scholarship to one of the best private schools in the city. I took a train there every day. The rich kids there ignored me because I wasn't one of them. They thought I was scum. Maybe they were right. But I studied my hardest, got the highest grades. I knew it was the only way out of my life, to get a scholarship, go to college, get out of here. But instead, to keep my father out of jail, I have to be a prisoner here. It isn't fair."

"I understand," Will said. I knew he had to be impressed with her, with the way she spoke. She'd even used a metaphor, about the tunnel. She was really smart.

"What does he want from me?" the girl cried. "To make me work for him? To use me for sex?"

"No. I wouldn't go along if that were the case."

"Really?" She looked a little relieved, but said, "What, then?"

"I think . . ." Will stopped. "I *know* he is lonely."

She stared at him but didn't say anything.

Finally, he said, "I'll give you a chance to rest and look over your new home. Magda will bring your lunch at noon. You can meet her then. If you need anything, ask and it's yours."

He walked out and closed the door behind him.

I watched Linda as she walked around the room, touching various objects. Her eyes lingered longest on one of the vases of roses. She picked up a yellow bloom that I thought was the prettiest. She held it to her face a moment, smelling it, then pressing it to her cheek. Finally, she replaced it in its vase.

She walked through the suite, opening doors and drawers. The elaborate wardrobe had no effect, but at the library door, she gasped and stopped. She tilted her head upward, taking in the rows of books that stretched to the ceiling. I'd noticed her homework and tried to buy things she'd like, not only novels, but books about physics, religion, philosophy, and duplicate volumes for myself so I could read anything that caught her attention. I'd started work on a database with all the books listed by title, author, and subject, like the real library, but it wasn't finished yet.

She climbed the ladder and chose a book, then two. She held them close to her, like a security blanket, or a shield. This, at least, was a success. She took the books back to the bedroom, placed them on the night table, then collapsed onto the bed, sobbing.

I wanted to comfort her, but I knew I couldn't, not now. I hoped that someday she'd understand.

5

At noon, Magda brought Lindy her lunch. I watched in the mirror. Some days, Magda bought take-out for lunch, because I missed fast food. But today, I'd asked her to make something a girl would like—sandwiches with no crusts, fancy, girly soup. The china was edged in pink roses. Her water was in a crystal glass with a stem. The knife and fork were sterling silver. The meal looked delicious.

I watched. She didn't eat it and returned it to Magda when she came back. She sank into bed, reading a book from the shelf. I checked the title. Shakespeare's sonnets.

I was afraid to knock on the door. I had to make my move sometime, but I didn't know how to do it without terrifying her. Would it be too much to yell, "Please let me in, and I promise not to eat you"? Probably. Probably she'd be scared even at the sound of my voice. But I wanted her to know that if she'd just come out, I'd be nice to her.

Finally, I wrote her a note.

> Dear Lindy,
> Welcome! Do not be afraid. I hope you will be comfortable in your new home. Whatever you want, you only have to ask. I will see that you get it immediately.
>
> I am looking forward to meeting you at dinner tonight. I want you to like me.
>
> Sincerely,
> Adrian King

I deleted the last sentence, printed it out, then brought the letter up to her room and slipped it under the door. I waited, afraid to move in case I made a noise.

A minute later, the note came back.

The word *NO* was written in large letters across the page.

I sat there a long time, thinking. Could I write her letters like some romantic hero, get her to fall in love with me that way? No way. I was no writer. And how could I get to love her when I'd only seen her in the mirror? I had to get her to talk to me. I walked up to the door and knocked, tentative and soft. When she didn't answer, I tried again, louder.

"Please," came her answer. "There's nothing I want. Just go away!"

"I have to talk to you," I said.

"Who . . . who is that?"

"Adrian . . ." *Kyle . . . the master of this house . . . the beast who lives here.* "My name is Adrian. I'm the one . . ." *The one who is holding you prisoner.* "I wanted to meet you."

"I don't want to meet you! I hate you!"

"But . . . do you like the rooms? I've tried to make everything nice for you."

"Are you crazy? You've kidnapped me! You're a kidnapper."

"I didn't kidnap you. Your father gave you to me."

"He was forced to."

That got me mad. "Yeah, right. He broke into my house. Did he tell you that? He was robbing me. I have the whole thing on surveillance. And then, instead of taking his punishment like a man, he brought you here to take it for him. He was willing to sell you to save himself. I'm not going to hurt you, but he didn't know that. For all he knew, I could be keeping you in a cage."

She didn't say anything. I wondered what story he'd told her, if this was the first she knew of the truth.

"What a scum," I muttered, starting to walk away.

"Be quiet! You have no right!" She pounded the door hard, maybe with her fist, maybe with something else, like a shoe.

God, was I dumb. Of course that wasn't the smartest thing to say. Story of my life lately. Had I always said stark-raving stupid things before? Maybe so, but I'd gotten away with them. Until Kendra.

"Look, I'm sorry. I didn't mean that." *Stupid, stupid, stupid.*

She didn't answer.

"Did you hear me? I said I was sorry."

Still nothing. I knocked on the door, I called her name. Finally, I left.

An hour later, she was still in the room, and I was pacing the floor, thinking of what I should have said. So what if I'd kidnapped her? She didn't have anything to leave behind anyway. This house was nicer than anything she'd ever had, ever imagined, but was she grateful? No. I don't know what I expected, but not this.

I went to Will. "I want her to come out. Can you get her to?"

"How do you propose I do that?" Will said.

"Tell her I want her to, that she has to."

"That you order her to? The way you ordered her father to give her over? That worked . . . well."

It wasn't the way I'd thought of it, but yes. I guess it

was what I wanted. "Yes."

"And how do you think she'll feel about that?"

"How does she feel? What about how *I* feel? I worked all week to make her comfortable, to make it nice for her, and the ungrateful . . . girl . . . she doesn't even come out to see me?"

"See you? She doesn't want to see the person who took her from her home, from her father. Adrian, you're holding her prisoner!"

"Her father's a lowlife." I hadn't told Will about the mirror, about how I'd watched her in the mirror before, seen her father hit her. "She's better off without him. And I don't mean her to be a prisoner. I want—"

"I know what you want, but she doesn't. She doesn't see the roses in the vases, or the way you've painted the walls. She only sees a monster, and she hasn't even looked at you yet."

My hand flew to my face, but I knew Will was talking about my behavior.

"A monster," he continued, "who brought her here for God knows what purpose—to murder her in her sleep. Or to keep her as a slave. She's afraid, Adrian."

"Okay, I get it. But how can I let her know that's *not* why I have her here?"

"You're really asking my advice?"

"You see anyone else around?"

Will grimaced. "Nope. No one." Then he reached out

toward me. He found my shoulder, finally, and put his hand on it. "Don't tell her to do anything. If she wants to stay in her room, let her. Let her know that you respect her right to choose."

"If she stays in her room, I'll never get her to care about me."

Will patted my shoulder. "Just give it a chance."

"Thanks. That's helpful." I turned and started to walk away.

Will's voice stopped me. "Adrian."

I turned back.

"Sometimes it also helps to have a bit less pride."

"Another winner," I said. "I have no pride at all at this point."

But an hour later, I knocked on Lindy's door once again. I'd show no pride, only remorse. This was hard to do, because I wasn't going to let her go. I *couldn't.*

"Go away!" she yelled. "Just because you have me here doesn't mean I'll do—"

"I know," I answered. "But can I just . . . can you listen to me for a minute?"

"Do I have a choice?" she said.

"Yes. Yes, you have a choice. You have tons of choices. You can listen to me, or you can tell me to screw off. You can ignore me forever. You're right. You did your end by coming here. We don't have to be friends."

"Friends? Is that what you call it?"

"It's what I . . ." I stopped. It was too pathetic to say it was what I'd hoped, that I had no friends, and I wanted—so wanted—her to talk to me, to be with me, to say something that would make me laugh and bring me back to the real world, even if it was nothing more. What a loser I'd be if I said that.

I remembered what Will said about pride. "I hope we can be friends someday. I understand if you don't want to be, if you're . . ." I choked on the words *disgusted, revolted by me, terrified of me*. "Look, what you need to know is, I don't eat human flesh or anything. I *am* human, even if I don't look it. And I'm not going to make you do anything you don't want except stay here. I hope you'll decide to come out soon."

"I *hate* you!"

"Yeah, you mentioned that." Her words were like whips, but I continued. "Will and Magda, they work here. Will can tutor you if you like. Magda will make your meals. She'll clean your room, shop, do your laundry, whatever you want."

"I . . . I don't want anything. I want my life back."

"I know," I said, remembering what Will said about her feelings. I'd been thinking for an hour about her feelings, about how maybe she actually cared about her horrible father the same way, damn it—I hated admitting this—I'd cared about mine. "I hope . . ." I stopped, thinking about it, then decided Will was right. "I hope you'll come out sometime because . . ." I couldn't choke the next words out.

"Because what?"

I caught sight of my reflection in the glass of one of the framed pictures in the hallway, and I couldn't say it. I couldn't. "Nothing."

An hour later, dinner was ready. Magda had made a wonderful-smelling arroz con pollo. At my request, she knocked on Linda's door carrying a tray.

"I don't want any dinner," came Linda's answer. "Are you kidding?"

"I have brought you a tray," Magda asked. "You eat in there?"

A pause. Then: "Yes. Yes, please. That would be fine. Thank you."

I ate dinner, as always, with Magda and Will. After dinner, I said, "I'm going to bed." I gave Will a look that said, *I did everything you said, and it didn't work.*

Even though he couldn't see it, he said, "Patience."

But I couldn't sleep, knowing she was two floors above me, feeling her hatred coming through the vents of the air conditioner, the walls, the floors. This was not what I'd wanted. It would never work. I was a beast, and I would die a beast.

6

"I thought of something helpful," Will had said the day after she came.

"What's that?" I asked.

"Silence. If you leave her alone, perhaps she'll come around."

"This may be why you're not actually surrounded by girls."

"Talking to her didn't work, did it?"

I had to admit, he was right, so I decided to do what he said. What scared me was she hadn't seen me yet. What would she say when she did?

In the next days, I was silent. Lindy stayed in her room. I watched her in the mirror. The only things she liked were the books and the roses. I read every book she read. I stayed up late into the night reading, to keep up with her. I didn't even try to talk to her again. And every night, when I got so tired the book fell from my hand, I lay in bed, feeling her hatred like a phantom walking the night hallways. Maybe this was a bad idea. But what other hope did I have?

"I underestimated her," I told Will.

"Yes, you did."

I looked at him, surprised. "You think so too?"

"I always thought so. But tell me, Adrian, why do you think so?"

"I thought she'd be impressed with the stuff I bought her, the beautiful furniture, and the clothes. She's poor, and I thought that if I bought her jewelry and pretty things, she'd give me a chance. But she doesn't want any of it."

Will smiled. "No, she doesn't. She just wants her freedom. Don't you?"

"Yes." I thought of Tuttle, of the dance, of what I'd said to Trey about how the school dance was legalized prostitution. It seemed so long ago. "I've never met anyone who couldn't be bought. It makes me sort of like her."

"I wish that understanding that was enough to break the curse. I'm proud of you for it."

Proud of you. No one had ever said that to me, and for a

second, I wished I could hug Will, just to feel the touch of another human being. But that would be very strange.

That night, I lay awake later than usual, hearing the sounds of the old house. "Settling," some people would call it. But I thought I heard footsteps upstairs. Were they her footsteps? Impossible, through two floors. But still I couldn't sleep.

Finally, I got up and went to the second-floor living room, turned on ESPN real soft, so it wouldn't bug her. I put on jeans and a shirt to do this, which in the past I'd have done in my boxers. Even though she'd pledged to stay in her room forever, I didn't want to take a chance of her seeing more of me than my face. My face was bad enough.

I'd almost bored myself to sleep when I heard a door open. Could it be her? In the hall? Probably only Magda, or even Pilot, wandering. Yet it sounded like it was on the next floor, Lindy's floor. I willed myself not to look, to keep my eyes glued to the television so she wouldn't be frightened by my face in the darkness. I waited.

It was her. I heard her in the kitchen, rattling a plate and fork, rinsing them and putting them into the dishwasher. I wanted to tell her she didn't have to do it, that Magda did that, that we pay her to. But I stayed quiet. But when I heard her footsteps in the living room, so close she had to see me, I couldn't stop myself.

"I'm sitting here." I said it soft. "I want you to know so you won't freak."

She didn't answer, but her eyes darted toward me. The

light in the room was dim, coming only from the television. Still, I wanted to pull a pillow over my face, to cover myself. I didn't. She'd have to see me sometime. Kendra had made that clear.

"You've come downstairs," I said.

She faced me, and I saw her eyes go toward me, then away, then back. "You *are* a beast. My father . . . he said . . . I thought it was a trip he was on. He says crazy things a lot. I thought . . . But you really are. Oh, my God." She looked away. "Oh, my God."

"Please. I won't hurt you," I said. "I know I look this way, but I'm not . . . please. I won't hurt you, Lindy."

"I just didn't think. I thought you were some guy, some pervert who'd . . . and then when you didn't break down the door or anything . . . But how could you be—"

"I'm glad you've come down, Lindy." I tried to keep my voice even. "I'd worried so much about when we'd meet. Now it's over, and maybe you'll get used to me. I was worried you wouldn't come out, maybe ever."

"I had to." She took a deep breath, then exhaled. "I've been walking at night. I couldn't stay in those rooms. I felt like an animal." She stopped herself. "Oh, God."

I ignored her nervousness. Maybe by acting human, I could show her that I *was*. I said, "The picadillo Magda made for dinner. It was good, wasn't it?" I didn't look at her. Maybe she'd be less afraid if she couldn't see my face.

"Yes, it was fine. Wonderful." She didn't thank me. I

didn't expect her to. I knew better now.

"Magda's a great cook," I said, wanting to keep the conversation going, now that we'd started, even if I had to talk about nothing. "When I used to live with my father, he never wanted her to make Latin dishes. She just made regular stuff then, meat and potatoes. But when he left us here, I didn't really much care what I ate, so she started making this stuff. I guess it's easier for her, and it's better." I stopped babbling, trying to think of something else to babble about.

But she spoke. "What do you mean he left you here? Where's your father now?"

"I live with Magda and Will," I said, still looking away. "Will's my tutor. He can tutor you too, if you want."

"Tutor?"

"Teacher, really, I guess. Since I can't go to school because . . . Anyway, he homeschools me."

"School? But then, you're . . . how old are you?"

"Sixteen. Same as you."

I could see from her face that this surprised her, that she was thinking all along that I was some old perv. Finally, she said, "Sixteen. Then where are your parents?"

Where are yours? We were in the same boat, sort of, being abandoned by our dear old dads. But I didn't say it. "Silence," Will had said. Instead, I said, "My mother left a long time ago. And my father . . . well, he couldn't handle that I looked like this. He's into normalcy."

She nodded, and there was pity in her eyes. I didn't

want pity. If she pitied me, she might think that I was some pathetic creature who was going to try to drag her off and force her to be mine, like the Phantom of the Opera. Still, pity was better than hatred.

"Do you miss him?" she asked. "Your father?"

I told the truth. "I try not to. I mean, you shouldn't miss people who don't miss you, right?"

She nodded. "When things started getting really bad with my dad, my sisters moved out to live with their boyfriends. I was really mad because they didn't stay and, you know, help me with him. But I still missed them."

"I'm sorry." The subject of her father was getting too risky. "Would you like Will to teach you? He tutors me every day. You're probably smarter than me. I'm not a very good student, but I bet you're used to having some kids who aren't as smart in regular school, aren't you?"

She didn't answer, and I said, "He could just tutor you, separately from me, if you want. I know you're mad. You have every right to be."

"Yes, I do."

"It's just that I have something I'd love to show you."

"Show me?" I could hear the wariness in her voice, like a curtain going down.

Quickly, I said, "No! Not that. You don't understand. It's a greenhouse. I built it myself from plans I bought. And all the plants in it are roses. Do you like roses?" I knew she did. "Will turned me on to them. I guess he thought I could use a hobby. My favorites are the floribunda—climbing roses. They aren't as detailed as the hybrid tea roses. I mean, they have fewer layers of petals. But they can grow so high—sometimes ten feet if they're supported right. And I make sure they're supported right."

I stopped. I sounded like those nerdy kids at school, the ones who spouted baseball stats or knew *Lord of the Rings* like Frodo, the Hobbit, was a long-lost cousin.

"The roses in my room," she said. "They're from you? You grew them?"

"Yes." In the days she'd been there, I'd had Magda remove the yellow roses as they'd died and replace them with white ones, symbolizing purity. I hoped to replace them someday with red ones, which stood for romance. "I liked having you see my roses. I had no one to give them to before except Magda. But I have dozens more. If you want to come down to see them—or for tutoring—I can have Will or Magda there the whole time, so you wouldn't worry I'll hurt you."

I didn't point out the obvious, that she was alone with me now, that she'd been with me for days, guarded only by a blind man, an old woman, and a flimsy door, and I hadn't done anything to her. But I hoped she'd noticed.

"And this is really how you look?" she said finally. "It's not a mask you're using to hide your face? Like kidnappers do?" A nervous laugh.

"I wish it was. I'll come around the sofa, so you can see for yourself." I did, cringing to have her examine me. I was glad I was covered up as much as possible, but I squinted in the glare. I thought of Esmeralda, unable to look at Quasimodo. I was a monster. A monster.

"You can touch it—my face—if you'd like to make sure," I said.

She shook her head. "I believe you." Now that I was closer, her eyes traveled up and down my body, taking in my clawed hands. Finally, she nodded, and I knew from her eyes she felt sorry for me. "I think I would like for Will to tutor me. We could try him tutoring us together, to save his time. But if you're too stupid to keep up, we'd have to make a change. I'm used to honors classes."

I could see she was joking, but also a little serious. I wanted to ask about the greenhouse again, and if she'd come down early to have breakfast with Will, Magda, and me. But I didn't want to freak her out, so I said, "We study in my rooms, by the rose garden. It's on the first floor. We usually get started at nine. We're reading Shakespeare's sonnets."

"Sonnets?"

"Yes." I searched my mind for a stanza to recite. I'd memorized pages and pages of poetry during this solitary confinement. This was my chance to impress her. But the silence of my stupidity was deafening. Finally, I broke it. "Shakespeare's great."

Duh. Shakespeare's cool, man.

But she smiled. "Yes. I love his plays and his poetry." Another nervous smile, and I wondered if she was as relieved at our first meeting as I was. "I should get to bed, then, to be ready."

"Yeah."

She turned and went upstairs. I watched her as she walked to the stairs, then up, then listened as her footsteps reached the next floor landing.

Only when I heard her bedroom door open and close did I give in to my beast instincts and do a wild animal dance around the room.

7

I woke before sunrise, to remove the dead leaves from the roses, sweep the greenhouse floor, and water the plants. I wanted to do this well before our tutoring session, so everything would have a chance to dry. I didn't want mud. I even rinsed the wrought-iron furniture in the greenhouse, though it was already clean and it was also probably too warm to sit out there. I wanted all options open.

By six, everything was perfect. I'd even rearranged some of the vines to climb higher, like they were trying to escape. Then I woke Will by knocking loudly on his door.

"She's coming," I told him.

"Whoshe?" Will's voice was still groggy with sleep.

"Shh," I whispered. "She'll hear you. Lindy's coming to our tutoring session."

"Terrific," Will said. "That's in—what—five hours?"

"Three. I told her nine o'clock. I couldn't wait any longer. But I need your help before that."

"Help with what, Adrian?"

"You have to teach me everything ahead of time."

"What . . . and why would I do that instead of sleeping?"

I knocked on the door again. "Will you open up? I can't stand out here and have this conversation with you. She might hear."

"Then go back to bed. There's an idea."

"Please, Will," I stage-whispered. "It's important."

Finally, I heard him moving around the room. In a moment, he appeared at the door. "What's so important?"

Behind him, Pilot hid his head in his paws.

"I need you to teach me now."

"Why?"

"Didn't you hear me? She's coming to our tutoring session."

"Yes. At nine. She's probably still asleep now."

"But I don't want her to think I'm stupid—besides being ugly. You need to teach me everything ahead of time so I can be smart in front of her."

"Adrian, be yourself. It will be fine."

"Be myself? Maybe you've forgotten that *myself* is a beast?" The word *beast* came out a frantic roar, though I was trying to stay calm. "This is the first time she'll be seeing me in daylight. It's taken her over a week. I want to at least be smart."

"You are smart. But she's smart too. You want to be able to talk to her, not just repeat what I've told you."

"But she was an honors student at Tuttle. She was on scholarship. I was just a screwup with Daddy's money."

"You've changed since then, Adrian. I'll throw you some soft pitches if it seems like you need them, but I doubt you will. You're a smart kid."

"You just want to go back to bed."

"I do want to go back to bed. But I don't *just* want to go back to bed." He started to close the door.

"You know, the witch said she'd give you back your sight if I broke this curse."

He stopped. "You asked her for that?"

"Yeah. I wanted to do something for you, since you've been really nice to me."

"Thank you."

"So you can see how it's really important that I do well. So can you give me something, some hint? She says that if I turn out to be stupid, she'll want to study separately. That would be double the work for you."

He must have thought about that because he said, "Okay, check out Sonnet Fifty-four. I think you'll like it."

"Thanks."

"But, Adrian, sometimes it's nice to let her be smart too."

He closed the door.

I'd parked my chair in front of the French doors of the rose garden for her arrival. It took me a while to decide whether I looked better against the beauty of the roses, or if they just called attention to my ugliness. But finally, I decided something in the room should be beautiful, and it definitely wasn't me. Even though it was July, I wore a long-sleeved blue Ralph Lauren button-down, jeans, and sneakers with socks. Prep Beast. I held a book of Shakespeare's sonnets in my hand and read Sonnet 54 for about the twentieth time. Vivaldi's *The Four Seasons* played in the background.

The whole thing was shattered when she knocked. Will wasn't there yet, so I had to stand, ruining my picturesque (or—let's be honest here—slightly less repellant) arrangement. But I couldn't leave her standing out there, so I hurried to the door and opened it. Real slow. So as not to shock her.

In the morning light, more than the night before, I could feel her *not* looking at me. Was it because I was too hideous to take up space in her eyes, like a crime scene photo? Or was she just trying to be polite and not stare? I believed she'd gotten past her hatred of me, turning to pity instead. But how could I make that into love?

"Thank you for coming," I said, motioning her into the room, but not touching her. "I set up next to the greenhouse."

I'd moved a dark wood table next to the French door that led out. I pulled out a chair for her to sit in. In my former life, I'd never have done that for a girl.

But she was already at the door. "Oh! It's so beautiful. May I go out?"

"Yes." I was behind her already, reaching for the lock. "Please. I've never had a visitor before, never shared my garden with anyone but Will and Magda. I hoped . . ."

I stopped. She had already stepped outside. The sound of Vivaldi's strings swelled around her, playing the part called "Spring" just as she stepped out among all the flowers.

"It's glorious! Just smell it—to have such riches in your home!"

"It's your home too. Please come anytime."

"I love gardens. I used to go to Strawberry Fields in Central Park after school. I would sit there for hours, reading. I didn't like to go home."

"I understand. I wish I could go to that garden. I've seen pictures of it online." And passed it a thousand times in my past life. I'd barely looked. Now I yearned to go and I couldn't.

She was kneeling by a bed of miniature roses. "They're so precious."

"Girls always like little things, I guess. I prefer the climbers. They're always looking for the light."

"They're beautiful too."

"But this one . . ." I knelt to point out a light yellow

miniature I'd planted a little over a week ago. "This one's called a Little Linda rose."

She gave me a weird look. "Do all your flowers have names?"

I laughed. "I didn't name it. The horticulturalists, when they develop a new rose variety, they name it. And this one happens to be called 'Little Linda.'"

"It's so perfect, so delicate." She reached for the rose. When she did, her hand knocked against mine, and I felt a chill of electricity run through my body.

"But strong." I pulled my hand away before she could be disgusted by it. "Some of the miniatures are heartier than the tea roses. Would you like me to cut some for your room, since it's your namesake?"

"It would be a shame to cut it. Maybe . . ." She stopped, holding the small bloom on two fingers.

"What?"

"Maybe I'll come back to see them."

She said she'd come back. But maybe.

Just then, Will came in.

"Guess who's here, Will?" I said, like I *hadn't* talked to him about it. "Lindy."

"Wonderful," he said. "Welcome, Lindy. I hope you'll liven things up. It's pretty boring with just Adrian."

"It takes two to be boring," I said.

Then, as I knew he would, he said, "We'll be discussing Shakespeare's sonnets today. I thought we'd start with number fifty-four."

"Did you bring the book?" I asked her. When she shook her head, I said, "We could wait for you to go get it. Right, Will? Or you could share with me?"

Her eyes still drifted to the rose garden. "Oh, I guess we can share. I'll bring my own book tomorrow."

She'd said, "Tomorrow."

"All right." I pushed the book over, so it was closer to her than to me. I didn't want her thinking I was trying to make a move on her. But still, I was closer to her than I'd ever been. I could have touched her so easily, and made it seem like an accident.

"Adrian, do you want to read it aloud?" Will asked.

A softball, as he'd said. Teachers had always praised my reading. And I'd read this poem over and over.

"Sure," I said.

> *"O! how much more doth beauty beauteous seem*
> *By that sweet ornament which truth doth give!*
> *The rose looks fair, but fairer we it deem*
> *For that sweet odour, which doth in it live."*

Of course, with her sitting so close, I screwed up, stumbling over "beauty beauteous seem." But I kept going.

> *"The canker-blooms have full as deep a dye*
> *As the perfumed tincture of the roses,*

190

Hang on such thorns, and play as wantonly
When summer's breath their masked buds discloses:
But, for their virtue only is their show,
They live unwoo'd, and unrespected fade;
Die to themselves. Sweet roses do not so;
Of their sweet deaths are sweetest odours made:
And so of you, beauteous and lovely youth,
When that shall vade, my verse distills your truth."

I finished and glanced up. Lindy wasn't looking at me, though. I followed her eyes and saw that she was staring out the French doors, at the roses. *My* roses. Did the beauty of my roses make up for the ugliness of me?

"Adrian?" Will was saying something, maybe for the second or third time.

"I'm sorry, what?"

"I asked what the rose symbolizes in the poem."

Having read the poem twenty times, I thought I knew what it meant. But now I held back. I realized I wanted to let her be smart. "What do you think, Lindy?"

"I think it signifies truth," she said. "Shakespeare talks about how the rose has perfume that makes it beautiful on the inside. And the scent of the rose can last even after the bloom dies."

"What's a canker-bloom, Will?" I asked.

"A dog-rose. It looks like a rose, but it doesn't have the perfume."

"So it looks good, but it's not as true?" I said. "Like Lindy was saying. Just because something is beautiful doesn't mean it's good. That's his point."

Lindy looked at me like I was smart, not just ugly. "But something with inner beauty will live forever, like the scent of a rose."

"But does the scent of a rose live forever?" Will asked Lindy.

Lindy shrugged. "I once had a rose someone gave me. I pressed it in a book. The scent didn't last."

I stared at her, knowing the rose she meant.

The morning passed quickly, and even though I hadn't pre-studied the other subjects, I managed not to look like a total moron, but always I let her be a little bit smarter. It wasn't difficult.

At twelve thirty, Will said, "Will you be joining us for lunch, Lindy?"

I was glad he'd asked and not me. I held my breath. I think we both did.

"Sort of like the school cafeteria?" Lindy said. "Yes, that would be nice."

If anyone thinks I hadn't prepped Magda for this, they'd be wrong. I'd woken her up at six too—though she was nicer about it than Will—and we talked about possible menus that included no soups, no salads, no messy items that I might spill with my clawed hands. I hated that being a beast made me eat like a beast. But I'm happy to say I didn't make an ass of myself, and we studied that afternoon too.

That night, I lay in bed, remembering the moment when her hand touched mine. I wondered what it would be like to have her touch me not by accident, to maybe have her let me touch her.

Mr. Anderson: Thanks for coming. This week we're going to talk about transformation and food.
BeastNYC: But I wanted to talk about this girl. I have a girl. We're friends but i think we could be more.

Grizzlyguy joined the chat.

Froggie: hi, grizz.
Grizzlyguy: I have news! I'm human! I'm not a bear anymore!
BeastNYC: Human?
Froggie: congratz.
BeastNYC: <– Very jealous of Grizz.
Grizzlyguy: The girl, her name is Snow White (not *that* Snow White), she followed me out into the woods when they were leaving for their summer place. She saw the evil dwarf who put a spell on me, and she helped me kill it.
Froggie: U killd a dwarf
Grizzlyguy: an *evil* dwarf.
Froggie: stil . . . . . .
Grizzlyguy: It wasn't a crime for me to kill the dwarf because I did it as a bear.

SilentMaid joined the chat.

SILENTMAID: I'm afraid I have some very bad news.

Froggie: Grizzlyguy is a guy agin!

SILENTMAID: That's wonderful. But I'm afraid it hasn't been going as well with me.

BeastNYC: What happened, Silent?

SILENTMAID: Well, I thought it was going really well. He said I reminded him of the girl who saved his life (which was me, of course) and even though his parents wanted him to go meet this other girl, this girl with rich parents, he said he'd rather be with me.

Grizzlyguy: That's great, Silent. I'm sure it will work out.

BeastNYC: Yeah, he won't care about her!

SILENTMAID: But that's the problem. He does. His parents said, "Well, at least *she* can talk" and set him up on a blind date. And would you believe, now he thinks *she's* the one who saved his life. And since I can't talk, I can't tell him different.

Mr. Anderson: I'm so sorry, Silent.

SILENTMAID: I saw them kissing. He's with her. I failed.

BeastNYC: #@*!

BeastNYC: I'm sorry. Isn't there any way out of the spell, Silent?

SILENTMAID: My sisters tried to get the Sea Witch to let me out of the spell. They gave her their hair and everything. But she said the only way I could get out of the spell is for me to kill him.

Froggie: R U going 2 do it?

BeastNYC: Ask Grizzlyguy to help you. He & his gf killed a dwarf.

Grizzlyguy: It's not funny, Beast.

BeastNYC: I'm sorry, Grizz. Sarcasm is how i deal w/ being upset.

SILENTMAID: I understand, Beast. You all have been very good friends.

Froggie: hav been? Tht means u arnt going 2 do it?

SILENTMAID: I can't, Froggie. I can't kill him. I love him too much. It was my mistake to make, and I made it.

BeastNYC: Let me get this straight—UR going 2 be sea foam

SILENTMAID: I'm told that if I wait 300 years, the sea foam I am will float to heaven

Froggie: 300 yrs! Thts nothing.

Grizzlyguy: Frog's right. It'll seem like a day or two. You'll see.

SILENTMAID: I think I need to go now. Thanks for everything. Bye.

SilentMaid has left the chat.

BeastNYC: Wow. I can't believe it.

Froggie: mee eithr.

Grizzlyguy: I don't really feel in the mood for chatting today.

Mr. Anderson: Maybe we should just adjourn until next time.

PART 5

Time Lapses, Autumn and Winter

1

Outside the closed windows, leaves began to fall, but inside, everything stayed the same. Everything except Lindy and me. We changed. We studied together, and I saw that while she was smart, I wasn't glaringly *not* smart. I didn't think she hated me anymore. Maybe. Maybe she even liked me.

One night, there was a storm, a big one with lightning like sheets of metal across the sky and thunder that showed it was all way too close. It shook my bed, rattled the world, and woke me. I stumbled upstairs to the living room, only to find myself not alone.

"Adrian!" Lindy was sitting in the dark on the sofa, watching the sky light up from the farthest distance out the window. "I was frightened. It sounded like gunfire."

"Gunfire." I wondered if she'd heard gunfire at night where she was from. "It's just thunder, and this old house is sturdy. You're safe."

I realized how crazy it was, saying she was safe when I was holding her prisoner. But she said, "Not every place I've lived has been safe."

"I notice you've chosen the spot farthest from the window."

"You think I'm being silly."

"Nah. I'm here, aren't I? The noise woke me up. I was going to pop some popcorn and see if there's anything on TV. Want some?" I moved toward the kitchen. I was being careful. I decided it was best to move away, not to scare her by being too close. It was the first time we'd been alone since that day in the rose garden. Always, we had Will when we studied, Magda at meals. Now, alone with everyone else asleep, I wanted her to know she could trust me. I didn't want to screw it up.

"Yes, please. Can you make two bags, though? I really like popcorn."

"Yeah." I entered the kitchen and found the microwave popcorn. Lindy flipped through the television channels and landed on an old movie, *The Princess Bride*. "This is a good one," I said as the popcorn started popping.

"I've never seen it."

"You'll like it, I think. It has something for everyone—sword fights for me, princesses for you." The first bag finished popping, and I took it out. "Sorry. That was probably sexist."

"It's okay. I'm a girl. Every girl pretends she's a princess at one point, no matter how little her life is like that. And I like the idea of 'happily ever after.'" She left the television on that channel. I stood there watching the second bag swell up and considered what to do with them—put the popcorn in a bowl to share, like Magda would have with girls I used to know, or leave it in a bag.

Finally, I said, "Should I put them in a bowl?" I didn't even know where Magda kept the bowls. How sad was that?

"Oh, no, don't go to all that trouble."

"It's no trouble." But I took the bag out, opened it, then carried both bags over to the living room. Probably, she'd asked for her own bag so our hands wouldn't touch. I didn't blame her. I sat about a foot away from her watching the movie. It was the scene where Westley, a pirate, has challenged the killer, Vizzini, to a battle of wits.

"You fell victim to one of the classic blunders!" Vizzini said onscreen. ". . . Never go in against a Sicilian when death is on the line!"

By the time Vizzini fell over, dead, I'd finished my popcorn and put the bag down. I wanted some more. It seemed like the beast was always hungry. I wondered, if I was transformed back, would I be fat?

"Do you want some more?" she said.

"Nah. You said you really like popcorn."

"I do. But you can have a little bit." She held the bag out to me.

"Okay." I moved a few inches closer. She didn't scream or move away. I took a handful of popcorn, hoping I wouldn't drop it. There was a terrific clap of thunder, and she jumped, spilling half of what was left.

"Oh, sorry," she said.

"Don't be." I picked up the obvious pieces and threw them into my empty bag. "We can get the rest in the morning."

"It's just that I get really scared of thunder and lightning. When I was little, my father used to go out at night, after I went to sleep. And then, if some noise woke me, I'd find him not there. I'd get so scared."

"That must have been hard for you. My parents used to yell at me when I got up at night. They'd tell me to be brave, which meant leave them alone." I passed her the popcorn. "You have the rest."

"Thanks." She picked at it. "I like . . ."

"What?"

"Nothing. It's just . . . thanks for the popcorn."

She was so close I could hear her breathing. I wanted to move closer, but I wouldn't let myself. We sat in the blue-white light of the television, watching the movie in silence. Only when it was over did I see she'd fallen asleep. The storm had subsided, and I wanted just to sit there, watching her sleep, staring at her as I stared at my roses. But if she woke, she would think it was strange. And she already did think I was strange enough.

So I turned off the television. The room was pitch-black, and I picked her up to carry her to her room.

She woke halfway up the dark staircase. "What the . . . ?"

"You fell asleep. I was carrying you to your room. Don't worry. I won't hurt you. I promise. You can trust me. And I won't drop you." Her weight was barely anything in my arms. The beast was strong too.

"I can walk," she said.

"Okay, if you want to. But aren't you tired?"

"Yes. A little."

"Trust me, then."

"I know. I thought if you were going to hurt me, you'd have done it already."

"I'm not going to hurt you," I said, shuddering to know that was what she's been thinking about me. "I can't explain why I want you here, but it's not for that."

"I understand." She settled back into my arms, against my chest. I carried her to the top of the stairs and tried the doorknob. She grabbed it. Her voice came through the darkness. "No one's ever carried me, not that I can remember."

I tightened my grip on her. "I'm very strong," I said.

She didn't say anything else after that. She'd fallen back asleep. She trusted me. I trod on in the darkness and into her bedroom, thinking it must always be like this for Will, being careful, hoping for no obstacles. When I reached her bed, I lay her down and pulled the soft down comforter around her. I wanted to kiss her, there in the darkness. It had been so long since I'd even touched anyone, really touched them. But it would be wrong to take advantage of her sleeping, and if she woke, she might never forgive me.

Finally, I said, "Good night, Lindy," and started to move away.

"Adrian?" At the door, I heard her voice. "Good night."

"Good night, Lindy. Thanks for sitting up with me. It was nice."

"Nice." I heard her shifting on the bed, rolling over, maybe. "You know, in the darkness, your voice seems so familiar."

2

It got colder and wetter, and I got so I could talk to Lindy without worrying about every word. One day, after our tutoring session, Lindy said, "So, what's on the fifth floor?"

"Huh?" I'd heard what she said, but I wanted to stall and think up an answer. I hadn't been up to the fifth floor since she'd come. To me, the fifth floor meant hopelessness, meant sitting at the window reading *The Hunchback* and feeling as lonely as Quasimodo. I didn't want to go up there.

"The fifth floor," Lindy said. "You're on one, the kitchen and living room are on two, I'm on three, and Will and Magda are on four. But when I came here, I saw five sets of windows."

Now I was ready. "Oh, nothing. Old boxes and stuff."

"Wow, that sounds interesting. Can we go look?" Lindy started toward the stairs.

"It's just boxes. What's interesting about that? It will make you sneeze."

"Do you know what's in the boxes?" When I shook my head, she said, "That's what's interesting. There could be buried treasure up there."

"In Brooklyn?"

"Okay, maybe not real treasure, but other treasure—old letters and pictures."

"You mean junk."

"You don't have to come. I can look by myself, if it isn't your stuff."

But I went. Even though the idea of the fifth floor brought a sense of dread that sat in my stomach like rotten meat, I went because I wanted to spend time with her.

"Oh, look. There's a sofa by the window."

"Yeah, it's pretty cool to sit there and watch the people go by. I mean, it must have been for whoever lived here."

She climbed on the window seat, my window seat. I felt a twinge. She must have missed going outside. "Oh, you're right. You can see all the way to the subway station from here. Which station is that?"

But I was talking. "You can watch people go from the

train to their jobs, and come back in the afternoon." When she looked at me, I said, "Not that I've ever done that."

"I would. I bet people did that all the time. You can see whole lives here."

She leaned over, staring down into the street. I stared at her, the way her red braid hung thick down her back, turning golden in the afternoon sun, the freckles on her white skin. What was the deal with freckles? Did you get them one at a time or all at once? Last, I noticed her eyes, pale gray, surrounded by whitish lashes. They were kind eyes, I thought, but could any eyes be kind enough to forgive my beastliness?

"How about the boxes?" I gestured to the stacks in the corner.

"Oh, you're right." But she looked disappointed.

"The window gets more interesting around five. That's when people start coming from work." She looked at me. "Well, I might have sat in that seat . . . once or twice."

"Oh, I see."

The first box she opened was full of books, and even though Lindy had hundreds of books, she got all excited. "Look! *A Little Princess!* That was my favorite in fifth grade!" And I went to her side to look. How did girls get so excited over such dumb things?

The next Lindy squeal was louder. I hurried over to make sure she hadn't hurt herself, but she said, *"Jane Eyre!* It's my all-time favorite!"

I remembered she'd been reading it the first time I'd

watched her. "You have a lot of favorites. Don't you already have that?"

"Yeah. But look at this one."

I took the book from her. It smelled sort of like the subway. It was dated 1943 and had these mostly black illustrations that took up whole pages. I opened it to a picture of a couple making out under a tree. "I never saw a grown-up book with pictures before. They're cool."

She took the book from me. "I love this book. I love how it shows how if two people are meant to be together, they will be, even if something separates them. That there's a magic to it."

I thought of how Lindy and I had met at the dance, then I'd seen her in the mirror, and now she was here. Was that magic? Kendra's type of magic? Or just luck? I knew there was magic. I just didn't know if it could work for good.

"Do you believe that?" I said. "That magic stuff?"

Her face darkened, like she was thinking about something else. "I don't know."

I glanced at the book again. "I like the pictures."

"Don't they capture the book perfectly?"

"Don't know. I've never read it. Isn't it kind of a girly book?"

"You've never read it? Really?" I knew what was coming. "Well, you have to read it. It's the most wonderful book in the world—a love story. I read it every time we had a power outage. It's the perfect book for candlelight."

"Power outage?"

Lindy shrugged. "We had more than most people, I guess. Sometimes things got in the way of my dad paying the electric bill."

Things like feeding his nose and his bloodstream. Gotta have priorities. I thought, again, of how alike Lindy and I were. And how alike our dads were—with my dad, work was his drug.

I took the book from her. I knew I'd stay up all night to read it.

Finally, we moved to the other boxes. The second was full of scrapbooks and clippings, all about some actress named Ida Dunleavy. I took out posters: Ida Dunleavy as Portia in *The Merchant of Venice*. Ida Dunleavy in *The School for Scandal*.

There were reviews too. "Listen to this," Lindy said. "'Ida Dunleavy will be remembered as one of the great stage starlets of our time.'"

"Guess not. I've never heard of her." I looked at the date on the clipping. 1924.

"Look how pretty she was." Lindy showed me another clipping, this one a picture of a beautiful dark-haired woman in an old-fashioned dress.

The next clippings were about a wedding. "Actress Ida Dunleavy Weds Prominent Banker, Stanford Williams."

Then the clippings about plays and acting turned to news of babies. Eugene Dunleavy Williams, born in 1927, Wilbur Stanford Williams in 1929. The pages were covered with notes in fancy, old-fashioned writing and golden locks of hair.

A clipping from 1930 said, "Banker Stanford Williams Takes Own Life."

"He killed himself," Lindy said, reading. "Jumped out a window. Poor Ida."

"He must've been one of those guys who lost everything in the '29 market crash."

"Do you think they lived here?" Lindy fingered the yellow-gold paper.

"Or maybe their kids or grandkids."

"That's so sad." She flipped through the rest of the scrapbook. There were a few more articles about Stanford, a photo of two little boys of about three or four, then nothing else. Lindy put the scrapbook aside and reached underneath. She took out a box, opened it, and removed wads of tissue paper that crumbled to powder in her hands. Finally, she removed a green satin dress, halfway between the color of mint and the color of money. "Look! It's Ida's dress from the photo." She held it in front of her.

It seemed exactly her size. "You should try it on."

"Oh, it'd never fit me." But I noticed she kept holding it, fingering the yellowed lace on the front. A few beads were hanging by threads, but other than that, it looked pretty good.

"Try it," I said. "Go downstairs if you're worried about me looking."

"It's not that." But she lifted the dress high and spun around with it. Then she disappeared downstairs.

I went to the trunk. I was going to find something cool to show her when she got back. In a hatbox, I found a top hat. I tried it, but it kept slipping off my animal head. I hid it behind the sofa. But there was also a pair of gloves and an evening scarf. Those fit with a little pulling. Stanford must have had big hands. I opened another box and found an old Victrola and some records. I was about to take them out when Lindy returned.

I'd been right about the dress. It fit her like it had been sewn on her body—her body, which I'd assumed was nothing special because of the way she hid it under sweatshirts and baggy jeans, usually. But now, with satin and lace hugging every curve, I couldn't stop looking. And her eyes, which I'd previously thought were gray, now seemed exactly the same green as the dress. Maybe it was because I'd had minimal access to girls lately, but she looked hot. Had she transformed as much as I had? Or had she always been this way, and I'd never noticed?

"Take your braid out," I said before I thought. Was that a weird thing to say?

She made a face, but obeyed, taking down her hair so it spilled down her shoulders like a waterfall of flame.

I stared at her. "God! You're beautiful, Lindy," I whispered.

She laughed. "Oh, right. You only think I'm beautiful because . . ." She stopped.

"Because I'm ugly?" I finished for her.

"I wasn't going to say that." But she was blushing.

"Don't worry about hurting my feelings. I know I'm ugly. How could I not?"

"But I really wasn't. What I was going to say was you think I'm beautiful because you don't know any other girls, any beautiful ones."

"You're beautiful," I repeated, imagining how it would be to touch her, what it might be like to run my hands over the slippery cold satin, and feel her warmth beneath. I had to stop thinking like that. I had to keep in control. If she knew how much I wanted her, it might freak her out. I handed her a mirror—*the* mirror. And as she examined her reflection, I checked her out, secretly, the way her red hair crinkled down her back. She'd put on makeup too, cherry lipstick and a pink blush. She never had before. But, of course, I told myself it was because of the dress, not me.

"I saw an old Victrola in one of the boxes," I said. "We should see if it works."

"Oh really? Cool." She clapped her hands.

I showed her the old windup record player. The label on the small, fat disc said "The Blue Danube." "I think we put this like this." I positioned the needle over the record. "Then wind it up." But when I wound, no sound came out.

Lindy looked disappointed, then laughed. "I don't know how to waltz anyway."

"I do. My f—" I stopped. I'd been about to say that my friend Trey had dragged me to some fancy dance class his

214

mom made him take at their country club when we were eleven. But I caught myself. "There was a dance lesson on TV once. I could show you. It's easy."

"Easy for you."

"For you too." I pulled the gloves and scarf from the box. I wanted to touch her, but I didn't want to gross her out with my disgusting animal paws. I held a gloved hand out to her. "May I have this dance?"

She shrugged. "What do I do?"

"Take my hand."

She did. I stood there, dumbly, for a second. "What about the other hand?" she prompted.

"Um, on my shoulder. And mine . . ." I slid it up to her waist, looking out the window as I did. "And then just mirror what I do." I showed her the simple waltz step. "Forward, side, close."

She tried and didn't get it.

"Here." I pulled her closer than I should, so her leg was against mine. I felt every nerve, every muscle in my body tense, and I hoped she couldn't feel the quickening of my heartbeat. Still, I guided her along, and after a few tries, she got the steps.

"There's no music," she said.

"Yes there is." I started to hum "The Blue Danube" and glided with her away from the boxes and across the floor. We got a little tangled in each other, doing this, and I was forced even closer. Not that I minded. I noticed she was wearing perfume too, and between that and the humming, I felt a little dizzy. But I kept gliding, now taking her around in a little circle like the dance teacher had taught us, wishing I could remember more of the song, to make it last longer. But finally, I ran out of notes and had to stop.

"You dance divinely, my dear Ida," I said. What a dork I was!

She giggled and released my hand, but she stayed close. "I've never known anyone like you, Adrian."

"Huh. I guess not."

"No. I mean I've never had a friend like you, Adrian."

Friend. She'd said *friend*, which was better than the words she'd used before. *Kidnapper. Jailer.* But it wasn't good enough. I wanted more, and not just for the spell. I wanted everything about her. Did it bother me knowing that the only reason we weren't kissing, the only reason she didn't want me was because I looked like I looked? You bet. But maybe if I worked harder, she would look past it, see the real me. Except I didn't even know who "the real me" was anymore. I had been transformed—not just my body, but all of me.

"I hated you for forcing me to be here," Lindy continued.

"I know. But I had to, Lindy. I couldn't be alone anymore. That's the only—"

"You think I don't see that? You must have been so lonely. I understand."

"Do you?" She nodded, but I wished she hadn't, almost,

wished I could let her go and have her say, "No. I'll stay. Not because you're forcing me to, or I feel sorry for you, but because I want to be here with you." But I knew I couldn't, and she wouldn't. I wondered that she didn't ask me to let her leave. Could it be that she didn't want to anymore, that she was happy? I didn't dare to hope. Still, I smelled her perfume, the perfume she'd never worn before. Maybe.

"Adrian, why are you . . . like this?"

"Like what?"

"Nothing." She turned away. "I'm sorry."

But I remembered my cover story. "I've always been like this. Am I too horrible to look at?"

She didn't say anything for a moment, didn't look at me. For a minute, it seemed like we both forgot to breathe, and everything was ruined, ruined.

But finally, she said, "No."

We breathed again.

"Your looks mean nothing to me," she continued. "I've gotten used to them. You've been so kind to me, Adrian."

I nodded. "I'm your friend."

We stayed up there all afternoon and didn't do a bit of studying. "I'll ask Will to start late tomorrow," I told Lindy. "I have pull."

At the end of the day, Lindy removed the green dress and folded it back into its box. But that night, I snuck upstairs by moonlight and secretly carried the dress downstairs with me. I put it under my pillow. The faint smell of her perfume was clear to my animal senses, and I remembered reading that smell is the sense most connected with memory. I slept with that dress by my face and dreamed of holding her, of having her want me to. It was impossible. She'd said I was her friend.

But the next morning, when Lindy came down to breakfast, her hair was down, brushed and gleaming. I smelled her perfume.

I began to hope.

3

Lindy's room was two floors above mine. It made me restless knowing she was there, in the same house, asleep, alone. At night, I could almost feel her body, slipping between cool white sheets. I wanted to know each golden freckle on her skin. But now I was restless. My own sheets felt hot, sometimes sweaty, and itchy. I ached for her, lying in my bed, imagining her in hers. I went to sleep thinking of her, and woke soaking wet, sheets tangled around my legs. I imagined what it would be like to be tangled around her. I wanted to touch her. I'd seen her softness the day she'd tried on the dress. Somehow, I knew she would be soft enough to make up for me.

"I wish we could go to school together," Lindy said one day when we'd finished studying. "I mean that you could go to my school, my old school."

She was saying, I realized, that she still wanted to go, but she wanted to be with me too.

"Would I like it?" It was late afternoon. I'd opened the shutters—brazenly—and the light streamed across her hair, making it gold. I longed to touch it, but didn't.

She thought about it. "Probably not. The kids there, they're all rich and snotty. I didn't fit in."

I had. It amazed me now. "What would your friends say if they saw someone like me there?"

"I didn't have any friends." She smiled. "But I'm sure some of the parents in the PTA would have problems with you."

I laughed, imagining it. Of course, I knew exactly the parents she was talking about—certainly no one related to me, but there were parents who went to all the PTA meetings and volunteered at the school and just generally complained about stuff. They would care. I helped her gather her books. "'I don't want any beasts in school with my child!' That's what they'd say at the PTA meeting. 'I pay good money for this school. You can't let in riffraff.'"

She laughed. "Exactly." She left her books on the table

and started toward the greenhouse. It had become our daily routine. After our tutoring session was finished, we would have lunch, then read and discuss what we'd read—homework for people who never left home. Then we'd walk through the greenhouse, and she would help me with the watering and other work.

"We could start studying out here now that it's cool," I said.

"I'd like that."

"Do you need any flowers?" I asked her this every day. If the blooms in her room had wilted, we picked some. It was the only gift I could give her, the only thing she wanted from me. I'd offered other gifts. She always said no.

"Yes, please. If you won't miss them."

"I'll miss them. But it makes me happy to give them to you, Lindy, to have someone to give them to."

She smiled. "I understand, Adrian." We paused before a white tea rose. "I know what it is to be lonely. I've been lonely all my life, until . . ." She stopped.

"Until what?" I asked.

"Nothing. I forgot what I was going to say."

I smiled. "All right. What color do you want this time? I think you had red last time, but the red ones don't last, do they?"

She leaned forward, fingering a white rose. "You know, I had a huge crush on this guy at my school once."

"Really?" Her words were an ice pick, and I wondered if

it was anyone I knew. "What was he like?"

"Perfect." She laughed. "The typical guy you'd have a crush on, I guess. Beautiful, popular. I thought he was smart too, but maybe I just wanted him to be smart. It bothered me that I could like someone just for his looks. You know how that is."

I looked away so I couldn't see my animal hand on the roses. Between the roses and her memories of this hot guy, I felt particularly hideous.

"It's strange, though," she said. "People make such a big deal about looks, but after a while, when you know someone, you don't even notice anymore, do you? It's just the way they look."

"You think?" I edged closer, imagining what it would be like to trace the line of her ear with my clawed finger, smelling her hair. "So what was this guy's name?"

"Kyle. Kyle Kingsbury. Isn't that an incredible name? His father's this big network anchor. I watch him sometimes and remember Kyle. They look just alike."

I crossed my arms in front of me to hold in what I was feeling. "So you liked this Kyle guy because he was so great-looking and had a rich father and an incredible name?"

She laughed, like she realized how shallow it sounded. "Well, not just that. He was so confident, fearless like I'm not. He spoke his mind. He didn't know I existed, of course, except this one time . . . it was silly."

"No. Tell me." But I knew what she was going to say.

"I was helping out at a dance. I hated helping at dances. I felt stupid and poor, but it was . . . encouraged if you were on scholarship. Anyway, he was there with his girlfriend—this completely evil girl named Sloane Hagen. I remember he'd gotten her a corsage—a glorious white rose." She fingered the roses in front of her. "Sloane was having a hissy because it wasn't an orchid, wasn't expensive enough, I guess. But I remember thinking that if I could have a rose like that from a guy like Kyle Kingsbury, I'd be happy forever. And just as I was thinking that, he walked over and gave it to me."

"Yeah?" I was about to choke.

She nodded. "I could tell he thought it was no big deal, but in my entire life, no one had ever given me a flower. Ever. I spent the whole night looking at it, the way its calyx cradled it like a tiny hand. It even had a little vial of water to keep it alive longer. And the scent—I took it home on the subway, smelling it the whole time, and pressed it in the pages of a book so I could remember it forever."

"Do you still have it?"

She nodded. "In a book upstairs. I brought it with me. That Monday, I wanted to find Kyle, to thank him again for it, but he wasn't in school. He'd gotten sick over the weekend and missed the rest of the year. Then he went to boarding school. I never saw him again."

She looked so sad, and I thought about how I would have laughed at her if she'd come up to me Monday and thanked me for giving her that old, broken rose. I'd have laughed in her face. For the first time, I was glad I hadn't gone to school that Monday. Kendra had protected her from me.

"Should we pick some now?" I said.

"I love the roses you give me, Adrian."

"Do you?"

She nodded. "I've never had beautiful things. It makes me sad to see them die, though. The yellow roses last the longest, but it's still too short."

"That's why I built this greenhouse, so I could have them all year long. It's never winter, even though there will soon be snow on the ground."

"But I like winter. It's almost Christmas. I miss being able to go outside and touch the snow."

"I'm sorry, Lindy. I wish I could give you everything you want."

And I did. I'd tried so hard to make things perfect for her, bringing her roses and reading poetry. All handsome Kyle Kingsbury had to do to make her love him was walk on the planet being handsome. If she was trapped here with him, if she knew she was, she'd have been happy. But trapped here with me, she thought about him. Yet I would not have become my old self, with all that involved, even if I could. I could have lived like my father, who had nothing in his life but looks and money. I would have been unhappy but never known why.

If I hadn't been transformed, I would never have known what I was missing.

Now, at least, I knew. If I stayed a beast forever, it was

better than I had ever been before.

I took a clipper from my pocket, found the most perfect of the white roses, and handed it to her. I wanted to give her everything, even her freedom.

I love you, I thought.

But I didn't say it. It was not that I feared she would laugh in my face. She was far too kind for that. My fear was a greater one—that she wouldn't say it back.

"She'll never love me," I said to Will, later in his room.

"Why do you say that? It's been going so well. We have a wonderful time in class, and I can feel the chemistry between you."

"That's because it's chemistry class. But she doesn't want me. She wants a normal guy, someone who can take long walks in the snow with her, someone who can leave the house. I'm a monster. She wants someone human."

Will gave Pilot a pat and whispered something to him. The dog came to me. Will said, "Adrian, I can assure you, you are more human than most people. You've changed a great deal."

"But it's not enough. I don't look human. If I went outside, people would scream at the sight of me. Looks matter to most people. That's reality in the world."

"Not my world."

I petted Pilot. "I like your world, Will, but it doesn't have a very big population. I'm going to let her go."

225

"And you believe this is what she wants?"

"I believe she's never going to love me, and . . ."

"What?"

"Do you know what it's like, to want to touch someone so much and not be able to? If she's never going to love me, I shouldn't torment myself."

Will sighed. "When will you tell her?"

"I don't know." My throat hurt almost too much to say the words. It would be unfair of me to ask her to visit. She might do it out of pity, but I'd had my chance to make her fall in love with me, and I'd failed. "But soon."

"I'm letting her go," I told Kendra in the mirror.

"What? Are you psycho?"

"No. I'm letting her go."

"But why?"

"It's not fair to keep her as my prisoner. She hasn't done anything wrong. She should have freedom to do as she pleases, to have her own life, to walk around in the stupid, stinking snow." I thought of this poster a girl I'd known had in her room—a picture of a butterfly with the words IF YOU LOVE SOMETHING, SET IT FREE. Needless to say, I'd thought it was superdumb.

"Snow?" Kendra said. "You could take down the green-house and there'd be snow."

"Yeah. She misses going outside in the real world."

"This is your life, Kyle. It's more important than—"

"Not Kyle, Adrian. And nothing's more important to me than what she wants. I'm going to do it tonight at dinner."

Kendra looked thoughtful. "This means you may never break the curse."

"I know. I was never going to break it anyway."

That night, I took my time brushing my hair and washing up for dinner. I heard Magda calling my name, but I still dawdled. I didn't want to have dinner because it might be our last. I hoped Lindy would want to spend the night and leave in the morning, or better yet, take a few days to pack her things—the books and clothes and perfumes I'd bought her. What would I do if she left without them? They'd only remind me of her, like she'd died.

Of course, really, I really, really hoped she'd say, "Oh, no, Adrian, I couldn't dream of leaving you. I love you too much. But it was so sweet and unselfish of you to let me go that I think I'll kiss you." And then we'd kiss and the curse would be broken, and I'd have her forever. Which was what I really wanted, to be with her forever.

But I couldn't hope for that.

"Adrian!" Magda was knocking. I was five minutes late. "Come in."

She came in in a rush. "Adrian. I have an idea." I tried to smile. "You no have to let Miss Lindy go. I think of how you can let her be more free, give her more everything she wants."

"I can't go out." I thought of the girl at the Halloween

party. "It's impossible."

"Not here," she said. "But listen. I think of a way."

"Magda, no."

"You love her, no?"

"Yes, but it's hopeless."

"This girl needs love too. I see it." She gestured for me to sit in a chair near the door. "You listen this once."

4

Two days later, at four A.M., I waited downstairs while Magda woke Lindy and walked her to the door. It was dark, so I stared out the window since there was no one to see. Around us, the City that Never Sleeps slept. The streets were empty. It had snowed a little bit overnight, and the sidewalks were footprint free. Even the garbage trucks weren't out yet.

"Where are we going?" Lindy said when she came downstairs.

"Trust me?" I held my breath for her answer. She had every reason not to trust me. I'd been her kidnapper, her captor, yet I'd rather have died than hurt a single hair on her head. I hoped that after five months of living with me, she knew that.

"Yes," she said, seeming as surprised at the news as I was.

"We're going someplace great. I think you'll really like it."

"Do I have to pack any bags?"

"I have everything you'll need."

Will arrived, and I walked Lindy around to the security entrance of our building. I held her wrist, but I didn't use force. She was no longer my prisoner. If she ran, I would have let her go.

She didn't run. My heart hoped that she didn't run because she didn't want to leave, but perhaps she simply didn't know that I wouldn't hold her. She followed my lead to the waiting limo.

The limo had been my father's doing. After I spoke to Magda, I'd called him at work. It had taken some time to get through the studio phone system, but finally I heard that famous voice, full of fatherly concern.

"Kyle, I'm almost on the air." It was five fifteen.

"This won't take long. I need your help. You owe this to me."

"I *owe* this to you?"

"You heard me. You've had me locked up in Brooklyn for over a year, and I haven't complained. I also haven't gone to the Fox network with my story of Rob Kingsbury's beast son. Face it, you owe me."

"What is it you want, Kyle?"

I explained. When I finished, he said, "You mean to say you have a girl living there?"

"It's not like we're doing it."

"Think of the liability."

You know, Dad, when you ditched me with the maid, you forfeited the right to supervise my conduct.

But I didn't say that. After all, I wanted something from him.

"It's fine, Dad. I'm not hurting her. I know you're as concerned as I am about my getting out of this curse." I tried to think of what Will would say. Will was smart. "That's why it's really important that you help me with this. The sooner I get out of this, the less chance there is of anyone finding out."

I made it all about him because that's the way he'd think of it.

"Okay," he said. "Let me see what I can do. I have to go on the air now."

What he'd done was take care of everything—the place, the transportation, everything but a guy to feed the roses. That I'd done. Now I watched Lindy as she dozed, her head lolling close to my shoulder, and the car made its way across the Manhattan Bridge. I felt like someone who'd been thrown a rope at the cliff's edge. There was a chance that this would work, but if it didn't, I would fall, and fall hard.

Though Lindy slept, I couldn't. I watched the early

traffic rolling into the city's waning lights. It wasn't that cold. By noon, the light snow would be a slushy mess, but soon there would be cold and Christmas and so much to look forward to. Magda and Will slept on the other side of the seat. The driver had had a fit when he saw Pilot.

"He's a service dog," Will had explained.

"Does that mean he won't poop on the seats?"

I'd suppressed a laugh. I'd dressed as a Bedouin once again, but now, with the wall up between me and the driver, I removed my disguise. I stroked Lindy's hair.

"Are you going to tell me now where we're going?" she asked when we exited the Holland Tunnel.

I started. "I didn't know you were awake." I took my hand off her hair.

"It's okay. It felt nice."

Does she know I love her?

"Have you ever seen the sunrise?" I pointed back to the east, where a few streaks of red were making their way over the buildings.

"Beautiful," she said. "We're leaving the city?"

"Yes." *Yes, my love.*

"I never have before. Can you believe that?"

She didn't ask again where we were going, just curled up on the pillow I'd brought her and fell back asleep. I watched her in the dim light. We were going north slowly, but even so, she wasn't going to jump out. She didn't want to leave. When we reached the George Washington

232

Bridge, I fell asleep myself.

I next awoke at almost nine on the Northway. Snow-covered mountains loomed in the distance. Lindy gazed out the window.

"I'm sorry we can't stop for breakfast," I told her. "But it might start a panic. Magda brought some bread and stuff."

Lindy shook her head. "Look at those hills. It's like a movie—*The Sound of Music*."

"They're mountains, actually, and we're going to get a lot closer."

"Really? Are we still in the United States?"

I laughed. "We're in New York, if you can believe it. I'm taking you to see snow, Lindy—real snow, not gray slush pushed by the roadside. And where we're going, we can go outside and roll in it."

She didn't answer, just kept staring at the distant mountains. Every mile or so, we saw a farmhouse below, sometimes with a horse or some cows. A while later, she said, "People live in those houses?"

"Sure."

"Wow. They're so lucky to have all that space to roam around."

I felt a twinge for keeping her inside all these months. But I would make it up to her. "It'll be great, Lindy."

An hour later, we pulled off of Route 9 and in front of one house, the best house, I thought, surrounded by snow-whitened pines. "This is it."

"What?"

"Where we're staying."

She gaped at the snow-shingled roof and red shutters. Behind the house, there was a hill that I knew led to a frozen lake.

"This is yours?" she said. "All of it?"

"My father's, actually. We came here a few times when I was little. That was before he started acting like if he missed a single day of work, he'd be replaced. After that, I started going skiing with friends during Christmas break."

I stopped, not believing I'd mentioned skiing with friends. Beasts didn't ski. Beasts didn't have friends, and if I had, it opened up questions, lots of them. It was strange, because I felt like I could tell her everything, tell her things I'd never been able to say to anyone, or even to myself. But I couldn't really tell her anything.

But Lindy hadn't seemed to notice. She was already out of the car, streaking across the freshly shoveled path in her pink robe and fuzzy slippers. "Oh, how could anyone not come back to this . . . this wonderland?"

I was laughing, stumbling out of the car ahead of Will and Magda. Pilot looked freaked out, like he wanted to run and bark at all the snowdrifts. "Lindy, you can't go out in your robe. It's too cold."

"It's not cold!"

"You're warm from the car. It's below freezing."

"It is?" She spun around, a pink dot on the white. "So

I guess it'd be a bad idea to roll in all this wonderful, fluffy snow?"

"A very bad idea." I trudged toward her. I wasn't cold, nor likely to get cold. My thick coat kept me warm. "Wonderful and fluffy soon become cold and wet, and if you get sick, we can't play outside." *But I could warm you.* "I've brought appropriate clothing."

"Appropriate?"

"Long underwear." I saw the driver bringing our suitcases, and I pulled my costume around my head. I pointed to the red suitcase. "That's yours. I'll bring it to your room."

"It's so big. How long are we staying?"

"All winter if you want. We have no jobs, no school. This is a summer resort area. Some people come to ski on weekends, but the rest of the time, it's deserted. No one will see me if we go outside. I'm safe."

She glanced at me a second, almost like she'd forgotten who she was with. Could she have? Then she was spinning in circles again. "Oh, Adrian! All winter! Look at the icicles hanging from the trees. They're like jewels." She stopped and picked up a handful of snow, pressed it into a ball and threw it at me.

"Careful. Don't start a snowball fight you can't win," I said.

"Oh, I can win."

"In your robe?"

"Do I hear a challenge?"

"No challenges yet," Will said, walking Pilot toward the

house. "Let's put away the suitcases and get some decent clothing on and have breakfast."

I picked up Lindy's suitcase.

She mouthed, *Decent clothing?*

I mouthed back, *Long underwear*, and we broke up laughing.

My father had prepped everything as I'd demanded. The house was clean—the wood shone, and everything smelled of Pine-Sol. A fire blazed in the fireplace.

"So warm!" Lindy said.

"Oh, were you cold, miss?" I teased. I carried the suitcase to her room, which made her scream some more and jump up and down because it had its own fireplace and a handmade quilt, not to mention a bay window with a view of the pond below.

"It's so beautiful, and no one lives here. I haven't seen anyone for miles."

"Hmm." Had she been looking for someone, a way to run?

As if in answer to my unspoken question, she said, "I could be happy here forever."

"I want you to be happy."

"I am."

After breakfast, we put on our parkas and boots and went outside.

"I told Will we'd mostly study on weekends," I said, "since that's when people are here. Now, are you still up for that snowball fight?"

"Yes. But can we do something else first?"

"Anything. I'm at your service."

"I've never had anyone to make a snowman with me. Can you show me how?"

"It's been a while since I made one too," I said. It was true. I could barely remember a time when I'd had friends, if I had. "First, you have to make a small snowball and—this is the hard part—you don't throw it at me."

"Okay." With her mittens, she packed a snowball. "Oops!" It hit me in the head.

"I told you that was the hard part."

"You were right. I'll try again." She made another—and threw it. "Sorry."

"Oh, this is such war now." I picked up some snow. I didn't need mittens, and my paws were very good for making snowballs. "I am the world champion snowball fighter." I threw one at her.

It ended up deteriorating into an all-out snowball war—which I won, by the way. But finally, she made a snowball and handed it to me for the snowman.

"Perfect," I said. "We'll be experienced ice sculptors by the time winter's over."

But what I wanted to say was *I love you*.

"So now you roll it on the ground to make it bigger," I said. "Then, when it's as big as you can stand, that's the bottom."

She rolled it bigger. Her face was getting pink and her

green eyes shone, set off by the green jacket I'd chosen for her. "Like this?"

"Yeah. You have to keep changing direction, or else it gets like a jelly roll."

She obeyed, pushing it around, barely making a dent in the knee-deep snow. When the snowball got to the size of a beach ball, I joined her, pushing shoulder to shoulder.

"We work well together," she said.

I grinned. "Yes." We changed direction at the same time, until finally the bottom ball was finished.

"The middle ball is the tricky part," I told her. "It needs to be big enough, but you still have to be able to hoist it up onto the first ball."

We made the perfect snowman, then a second one, a snow woman, because no one should have to be alone. We went to Magda for carrots and other stuff, and as Lindy put in the carrot nose, she said, "Adrian?"

"Yes?"

"Thank you for bringing me here."

"It was the least I could do."

But what I really wanted to say was, *Stay. You aren't my prisoner. You can leave at any time, but stay because you love me.*

That night, I went to bed without locking the front door. I didn't tell Lindy I was doing it, but she could see if she had the eyes to. I turned in early. I lay in bed, listening for her footsteps, knowing that if she approached the door, if I heard it open, I wouldn't follow her. If she was to be mine, she would be mine on her own terms and not because I forced her to be. I stayed up, watching the digital clock click the minutes away. It reached midnight, then one. I heard no footsteps. When the clock reached two, I crept as quietly as an animal can creep out into the hallway, then across to her room. I tried the door. I had no excuse to give her if she caught me.

Her door had a lock on it, and I expected to find it locked. In the beginning, back in Brooklyn, she'd made a big show of locking it, in case I entered to do what she called, "some unspeakable thing." Lately, she hadn't made a show, but I assumed this door was locked.

It wasn't. The lock didn't stop my hand, and my heart fell to my stomach because I knew that if it was open, it meant she was gone. She'd snuck out when I'd taken a wink of sleep. If I opened the door, I'd find her gone. My life was over.

I stepped in, and against the quiet of this snow-draped land where no other humans were for miles, I heard breathing, soft as the snow itself. It was her. Her, sleeping. I stood for a moment, afraid to move and wanting to watch her. She was still there. She could have left, but she didn't. I trusted her, and she trusted me. Lindy shifted in her bed, and I froze. Had she heard the door open? Had she heard my heartbeat? In a way, I wanted her to see me, watching her. But she didn't. Her arm reached to pull the covers closer. She was cold. I crept slowly into the hallway and found the linen closet where we kept the extra blankets. I chose one and crept back into the room and fluffed it out, so it fell perfectly over her. She snuggled into it. I watched her for a long time, the moonlight hitting her red hair, making it shine like gold.

I went back to bed and slept as one can sleep only on a cold night in a warm bed. In the morning, she was still there. She came out holding the extra blanket, a questioning look on her face, but she didn't say anything.

From that night on, I never bolted the door. Every night, I lay awake wondering. Every morning, she was still there.

5

We'd been there a week when we found the sled. It was Lindy who found it early one morning, high on a closet shelf, and gave a shriek that brought all of us out of our rooms to see what animal had attacked her. Instead, we found her pointing.

"Look!"

I looked. "It's a sled."

"I know. I've never had a sled! I've only read about them."

Then she jumped up and down until I pulled it off the shelf for her. We both looked at it. It was a big sled, light, polished wood with barely used metal runners and the words FLEXIBLE FLYER painted on it.

"Flexible Flyer. It must really be like flying to race down a hill like that!"

I smiled. We'd made an army of snowmen ("Snow people," Lindy said) in the past days, and just the day before, I'd woken early to clear a section of pond for skating. Lindy had come down, hours later, to find me still at it with my shovel. Pond clearing was hard work. But it was worth it when she exclaimed, "Skating on a pond! I feel like Jo March!" and I'd known exactly what she meant, because she'd forced me to read *Little Women* weeks earlier, even though it was a girl's book.

Now I stared at the sled, remembering. My father had bought it when I was little, five or maybe six. It was a big sled, the kind that could take more than one person on it. I'd stood at the top of a seemingly endless hill, afraid to go down on my own. It was a weekend, so some other boys were there doing it, but they were older than I was. I saw another father and son. The father positioned himself on the sled, then let his son sit in front of him and wrapped his arms around him.

"Can you go with me?" I'd asked.

"Kyle, it's no big deal. Those other boys are doing it."

"They're big boys." I wondered why he'd brought me if he didn't want to sled.

"And you're better, stronger. You can do anything they

can do." He started to put me on the sled, and I began to cry. The other kids were staring. Dad said it was because I was being such a baby, but I knew even then that it was out of pity, and I refused to go alone. Finally, Dad offered one of the older boys five dollars to go with me. After the first time, I was fine. But I hadn't been on a sled in years.

Now I patted it. "Get dressed. We'll go right now."

"Will you show me how?"

"Of course. Nothing could make me happier." *Nothing could make me happier.* Since I'd been with her, I noticed I'd started to talk differently, pretentious and prettified, like the characters in the books she loved, or like Will. Yet it was true! Nothing could make me happier than the idea of standing with Lindy at the top of a snow-covered hill, helping her onto the sled and maybe—if she let me—going with her.

She was wearing her pink chenille robe, and she leaned to polish the sled's runner with the belt.

"Come on," I said.

An hour later, we were at the top of that same hill where I'd gone with my dad. I showed her how to lie, face first on the sled. "This is the most fun way."

"But scary."

"Do you want me to go with you?"

I held my breath for her response. If she said yes, if I went with her, she would have to let me put my arms around her. There was no other way.

"Yes." Her breath hit the air in a puff of smoke. "Please."

I breathed. "Okay." I pushed the sled to the last flat place before the hill began to slope downward, then sat on it. I motioned for her to sit in front of me. I wrapped my arms around her stomach and waited to see if she would scream. But she didn't. Instead, she snuggled more tightly against me, and in that moment, I felt like I could almost kiss her, like she would almost let me.

Instead, I said, "You're in front, so you navigate." With my nose, I felt the softness of her hair, smelled the shampoo she used, and her perfume. Through her jacket, I could feel her heartbeat. It made me happy to know she was alive, was real, was there.

"Ready?" I said.

Her heart beat faster. "Yes."

I gave the ground a kick and held her tight as we coasted down the hill, giggling like crazy.

That night, I built a fire, one of the many things I'd learned to do since becoming a beast. I had chosen soft pinewood for kindling and cut it into small strips. These I placed on some sheets of newspaper, and I put a hard log on top of those. I lit a match to the paper and watched as it all caught fire. I stood a moment, then took a seat beside Lindy on the sofa. A day before, I might have taken a separate chair. But now I'd had my arms around her. Still, I sat about a foot away from her and waited to see if she'd complain.

"It's beautiful," she said. "A winter snow and a blazing fire. I never had a real fire in a fireplace before I met you."

"Especially for you, milady."

She smiled. "Where are Will and Magda?"

"They were tired, so they went to bed."

In truth, I had suggested that they stay in their rooms. I wanted to be alone with Lindy. I thought maybe, just maybe, this could be the night.

"Hmm," she said. "It's so quiet. I've never been any-place so quiet before." She turned around and knelt on the sofa to look out the window. "And it's dark. I bet you can see every star in the world here. Look!"

I turned too and got closer than before. "It's beautiful. I think I could live here forever and never miss the city. Lindy?"

"Hmm?"

"You don't still hate me, do you?"

"What do you think?" She looked at the stars.

"I think no. But would you be happy to stay with me forever?" I held my breath.

"In some ways, I'm happier now than I've ever been. My life before this was a struggle. My father never took care of me. We scrounged for money from the time I was a child, and when I got older, one of my teachers told me that I was smart and that education was a way out of my life. So I worked and struggled at that too."

"You're really smart, Lindy." It was hard to speak and hold my breath too.

"But here, with you, it's the first time I've really been able to play."

I smiled. The hardwood in the fireplace began to catch fire. I'd succeeded.

"So you're happy, then?" I said.

"So happy. Except . . ."

"Except what? If there's anything you want, Lindy, all you have to do is ask, and I'll give it to you."

She looked at some point in the distance. "My father. I worry about him, what might happen if I'm not around to run interference. He's sick, Adrian, and I was the one who took care of him. And I miss him. I know you must think it's stupid to miss someone who's been so mean, who left me without a look back."

"No. I understand. Your parents are your parents, no matter what. Even if they don't love you back, they're all you have."

"Right." She turned away from the window and sat down, looking at the fire. I did the same. "Adrian, I *am* happy here. It's just . . . if I could only know he's okay."

Had the whole thing been a setup? Was she nice to me only because she wanted something from me? I remembered her, on the sled, snuggling into my chest. That couldn't all have been fake. Still, my head felt tight, like it might explode.

"If I could just see him for a moment . . ."

"Then you'd stay here with me?"

"Yes. I want to. If only—"

"You can. Wait here."

I left her there, watching me. The front door was unlocked. She had to have noticed. She could disappear into the night, and I would let her. But she wouldn't. She had said she was happy. She'd be happy to stay with me if only she could check on her father. Once she saw that he was happily partying with his druggie friends, it would all be good. I knew how she felt. I'd watched my dad on TV more times than I would admit. She could see hers too.

She was still there when I returned. I gave her the mirror.

"What's this?" She peered at the silver back, then turned it over to see her face.

"It's magic," I said. "Enchanted. By looking at it, you can see anyone you want, anywhere in the world."

"Yeah, right."

"It's true." I took it from her and held it up. "I want to see Will."

In an instant, the image shifted from my beast face to that of Will, up reading in his room, illuminated only by moonlight. I handed it to Lindy. She stared at it and giggled. "It really works? I can ask it to show me anyone?"

When I nodded, she said, "I want to see . . . Sloane Hagen." At my questioning look, she said, "She was this snobby girl at my school."

The mirror changed immediately, to an image of Sloane, looking in the mirror also, picking a zit. It was a big one, and white gunk oozed out.

"Ew!" I laughed at the image.

Lindy laughed too. "This is fun. Can I look at someone else?"

I started to say yes, then remembered her saying she'd had a crush on me. What would happen if she asked the mirror to show me to her? Would she see this very room?

"You said you wanted to see your father. We can do other stuff later. You can even see the president. I saw him in the Oval Office bathroom once."

"Wow, you're like a threat to national security." She giggled. "Okay. We'll do that next. But first"—she gazed into the mirror—"I want to see my father."

Once again, the image changed, this time to a street corner, dark and dirty. A junkie lay there, virtually indistinguishable from every other homeless person in New York. The mirror panned close. The guy was coughing, shaking. He looked sick.

"Oh, God." Lindy was already crying. "What's happened to him? This is what he comes to without me there!"

She was sobbing. I put my arms around her, but she pushed me away. I knew why. She blamed me. It was my fault, all my fault for making her stay.

"You should go to him," I said.

As soon as I said it, I wanted to push the words back into my mouth. But I couldn't. I would have said anything to make her stop crying, to make her not mad at me. Even that. I still meant it.

"Go to him?" She looked up at me.

"Yes. Tomorrow morning. I'll give you money, and you can take the first bus."

"Go? But . . ." She'd stopped crying.

"You're not my prisoner. I don't want you to stay here because you're my prisoner. I want you to stay because . . ." I stared at the fire. It was burning fast and brightly, but I knew if I left it, it would burn out. "I want you to leave."

"Leave?"

"Go to him. He's your father. Come back when you want, if you want—as my friend, not my prisoner." I was crying too, but speaking very slowly, to keep my voice steady. She couldn't see the tears on my face. "I don't want you as a prisoner. You only had to ask to leave. Now you have."

"But what about you?"

It was a good question, one I couldn't answer. But I had to. "I'll be fine. I'll stay here for the winter. I like being able to go outside and not have people stare. And in the spring, I'll go back to the city and be with my flowers. In April. Will you come to see me then?"

She still looked unsure, but after a moment, she said, "Yes. You're right. I can see you then. But I'll miss you, Adrian. I'll miss our time together. These months . . . You are the truest friend I've ever had."

Friend. The word struck me like the ax I'd used to cut up the kindling. *Friend.* That was all we could be. But then, I was right to let her go. A friendship wasn't good enough to break the spell. Still, I longed for that friendship, at least.

"You have to leave. Tomorrow, I'll call a taxi to take you to the bus station. You'll be home by nighttime. But please . . ." I looked away from her.

"What is it, Adrian?"

"You can't expect me to say good-bye to you tomorrow. If I come down to say good-bye, I might not let you go."

"I shouldn't go." She looked at the comfortable fire, then at me. "If it would make you so sad, I shouldn't."

"No. It was selfish of me to keep you here. You go to your father."

"It wasn't selfish. You've been nicer to me than anyone I've ever known." She grabbed my hand, my disgusting clawed hand. I could see her eyes were tearing up.

"Then be nice to me by leaving quickly. It's what I want." I pulled my hand—gently—from her grasp.

She met my eyes, started to say something, then nodded and ran from the room.

When she did, I walked outside into the snow. I had on only jeans and a T-shirt, and the weather was bitter, so bitter that the cold soaked to my bones in seconds, even with my extra insulation. I didn't care. I wanted to be cold because it would be something to feel, something other than this sudden emptiness and loss. I looked up, waiting for the light to go on in Lindy's room above. I watched her shadow silhouetted against the curtains, moving around the room. Her window was the only light spot in the black, bone-cold night. I looked up higher, searching for the moon. It was hidden by trees, but I found stars—stars with more stars behind them, then more behind those, millions of stars, more than I'd ever seen in my life in New York City, more than all the lights there. I didn't want to see stars. I couldn't bear their beauty and their numbers. I wanted only the lonely, airless moon. Finally, Lindy's light went out. I waited until I knew she slept. I couldn't imagine what it would be like to sleep beside her. I couldn't bear to imagine that anymore. I tore my eyes from the window and found the moon behind a tree. I crouched, threw back my head, and howled at it, howled like the beast I was, the beast I always would be.

6

The next day was a Saturday, the day we usually studied together. But instead, it was the day Lindy left. After I called her a taxi and checked the bus schedule, I retreated to my room to watch her in the mirror. I had thought I'd leave her the mirror to take with her, to see and remember me. But I decided I couldn't part with it. If I couldn't have her, I wanted to be able to watch her. If I gave her the mirror, she might not look at me at all. She might prefer to forget me. I couldn't handle that.

So I watched her pack her things. She took the books

we'd read together and a picture of our first snowman. She had no pictures of me. Finally, I stopped wallowing and went to breakfast. When I got back to my room, Will was there.

He was holding the book we were reading, but he said, "I've just been to Lindy's room, and she said the strangest thing."

"That she was leaving?"

"Yes." Will gave me a questioning look.

"I told her to go. Now can we change the subject to something more cheerful? That *Les Miserables* sure was a funny book."

"But, Adrian, it was going so well. I thought—"

"She wanted to leave. I loved her too much to make her stay. She says she'll come back in the spring."

Will looked like he wanted to say something else, but finally, he held up the book. "So, what did you think of Inspector Javert?"

"I think he'd be great as a character in a Broadway musical," I said, laughing even though I didn't feel like laughing. I checked the clock. Lindy's taxi would be there any minute. Her bus left in about an hour. If this had been a movie, one of those chick-flick romantic comedies, there'd be some dramatic scene where I ran to the bus station and begged her to stay, and Lindy, finally realizing how she felt about me, would kiss me. I'd be transformed. We'd live happily ever after.

In real life, Will asked me what I thought of Victor Hugo's political views in *Les Miserables*, and I answered him,

though I don't remember what I said. But I knew the minute (9:42) the cab pulled into the driveway to pick her up.
I sensed her arrival at the bus station (10:27) and knew the
time (11:05) when her bus left the station. I didn't watch
these things in the mirror. I just knew. There was no movie
ending. There was only an ending.

I didn't go back to the city that winter. Instead, I stayed in the
country, taking long walks every day, where only the other
beasts, the wild ones, could see me. I began to memorize the
flight pattern of each winter bird, the hiding place of each squirrel and rabbit, and I thought I might do this every winter. It was
great to be outside. I wondered if this was how the Abominable
Snowman got his start. I'd never believed in stuff like that
before. Now I was sure it was for real.

I admit I used the mirror to spy on Lindy. Without the
roses there, it became what the roses had been—my life, my
obsession.

In my defense, I only allowed myself to watch her an
hour a day. By doing this, I learned that she had found her
father, that they'd moved to an even shabbier apartment in
an even worse neighborhood in Brownsville, that she was
going to a rough-looking school. I knew this was my fault,
that she was stuck in that school because she'd lost her scholarship to Tuttle because of me yanking her out of school
to be with me. I watched her walk to school, past gutted
buildings covered in graffiti, past wrecked cars and hopeless children. I watched her in the halls at school, narrow,

crowded halls with boarded-up lockers and posters on the walls that said things like YOU CAN SUCCEED! I thought how she must have hated me.

March—I stopped watching her during daylight hours. But watching her in the evening was worse, because there was nothing to say she missed me or thought of me at all. She studied her books, just like she had before I knew her.

Finally, I started watching her just at night, when she slept. Every night at midnight, I looked at her. At that hour, I could fantasize that she was dreaming of me. I dreamed of her all the time. By April, when she hadn't come back, I knew it was over.

The snow lay in patches on the ground, and the lake ice was melting. It floated like icebergs, waking the frogs underneath. The melting mountains became waterfalls, and that meant tubing and rafting and tourist season.

"Have you given any thought to going home?" Will said one day at dinner. It was a Saturday. I'd stopped walking outside and had spent the day staring out the window, ducking as cars—probably full of antiquers—drove by on our rural route.

"What home?" I said. "Home is where your family is. I don't have a home. Or maybe I am home." I looked at Magda, who sat across from me. In the past months, she'd pretty much stopped being a servant. "I'm sorry," I told her. "I know you never see your family. You must think I'm an ungrateful—"

"I do not think that," she interrupted. "I have seen such

a change in you these past two years."

I stiffened at "two years." It hadn't been, not quite, but it was close. My time was nearly over. It might as well be all over because there was no chance anymore.

"Before, you were a cruel boy, a boy who lived to make people sad. Now you are kind and thoughtful."

"Yeah, kind and thoughtful." I shrugged. "Lot of good that does me."

"If there was any justice, this horrible spell would be broken, and you would not have to do this impossible thing."

"It wasn't impossible." I played with my soup spoon. I'd gotten good at eating with claws. "I just wasn't good enough."

I turned to Will. "In answer to your question, I was thinking of staying here. In either place, I'm stuck inside, a prisoner. But going back to the city would only remind me of what I've lost."

"But, Adrian—"

"She's never going to visit me, Will. I know it." I'd never told him about the mirror, so I couldn't explain now that I was watching her, that I saw no sign that she missed me. "I can't go back and wait and wait for her if she isn't going to come."

That night, when I picked up the mirror for my nightly ritual of watching Lindy sleep, I got Kendra instead.

"So when will you be returning to the city?"

"Why is everyone asking that? I like it here. There's nothing for me in the city."

"There's Lindy."

"Like I said, there's nothing for me in the city."

"You still have a month."

"It's impossible. It's over. I failed. I will always be a beast."

"Did you love her, Adrian?"

It was the first time she'd called me Adrian, and I stared into her weird green eyes. "Did you change your hair, sort of a layered thing? It's a good look for you."

She laughed. "The old Kyle Kingsbury would never have noticed my hair."

"The old Kyle Kingsbury would have noticed—he'd have ragged on it. But I'm not the old Kyle Kingsbury. I'm not Kyle Kingsbury at all."

She nodded. "I know. And that's why I'm sad that you're saddled with Kyle Kingsbury's curse." It was almost exactly what Magda had said. "Which brings me back to my question—the one you so cleverly evaded. Did you love her?"

"Why should I tell you?"

"Because you have no one else to tell. Your heart is breaking, and you have no one to confide in."

"So I should pour my heart out to . . . you? You ruined my life. Now you want my soul? Fine. I loved her. I love her. She was the only person in my life who really talked to me, who knew me without the looks, without my famous father, and still cared about me—even though I was a beast. But she didn't love me." I wasn't looking at the mirror.

I couldn't because even though my tone was sarcastic, my words were the truth. "Without her, I have no hope, no life. I will live in misery and die alone."

"Adrian . . ."

"I'm not finished."

"I think you are."

"You're right. I'm finished. If I was at least normal, I might have had a shot with her. I'm not talking about the way I used to look, but it's asking a lot to expect a girl to be interested in someone who isn't even human. It's sick."

"You're human, Adrian. You have a month. Don't you want to go back, just for that one month? Do you have so little faith in her?"

I hesitated. "I'd rather stay here. I'm not a freak here."

"A month. What do you have to lose, Adrian?"

I thought about that. I had already given up, had accepted that I was going to stay a beast forever. To go back to having hope, even for a month, would be so hard. But without hope, I'd have nothing, nothing to look forward to but being a beast, trapped in a house for the rest of my life, to sitting in my Dad-financed brownstone, putting crap on my roses to make them grow better, working my way through every book in the New York Public Library, and waiting to die.

"A month," I agreed.

7

I went back to New York. The guy who'd supposedly been taking care of my roses was a major screwup. Half the plants were dead while the others needed pruning bad and only had single blooms. "A different beast would eat this guy," I told Will.

But I didn't really mind. The roses were mine to tend and no one else's. The disastrous result only showed that they needed me. It was nice to be needed. I wondered how it would be to get a pet, maybe a cat because they didn't need to be walked.

Of course, maybe I'd end up like one of those crazy old people with, like, sixty cats. And one day, the neighbors would complain about the smell, and it would turn out I'd died and the cats had eaten me.

Still, it might be nice to have a cat. As long as it didn't dig in my roses.

For now, I decided to dismantle the greenhouse. I wanted to spend my winters up north, and return each spring to sit in my walled-in garden, in the sunlight.

I was beginning to plan for a lifetime of being a beast.

And yet, every night, I took out my mirror and watched Lindy sleep. I wondered if she dreamed, dreamed of me as I dreamed of her.

I guess Will wondered too because one day he said, "Have you heard from Lindy since you've been back?"

It was May fourth, less than two days from *the* day, a month since my return to the city. I was in the garden with Will. We'd just finished reading *Jane Eyre*. I hadn't told him that I'd read it months before, after that day on the fifth floor with Lindy. I thought of that day all the time, even though the green dress I had hidden under my pillow had long since lost her scent. It had been a perfect day, a day when I'd thought maybe it was possible for her to love me.

"I never would have thought I'd like a book called *Jane Eyre*," I told Will, changing the subject. "Especially since it's about a plucky British governess."

"Sometimes we surprise ourselves. What was it you

liked about the book?"

"Well, I'll tell you what I didn't like about it—Jane was too good. She loved Rochester, and she had nothing in the world, no family, no friends, no money. I think she should have stuck with Rochester."

"But he had an insane wife hidden in the attic."

"No one knew about it. And he was her true love. If you're in love like that, nothing should stand in your way."

"Sometimes you have to take care of things first. I had no idea you were such a romantic, Adrian."

"Not that I have any reason to be."

Will flipped his copy of *Jane Eyre* over in his lap, waiting.

"The answer is no," I said. "No, I haven't heard from Lindy."

"I'm sorry, Adrian."

"But that gets me to what I *did* like about the book," I said, walking to where I'd planted my miniature roses. The "Little Linda" was reviving nicely. "I liked that when Rochester and Jane were separated, he went to the window and called her name: 'Jane! Jane! Jane!' And she heard him, and even answered. That's what true love should be like— the person should be part of your soul and you should know what they're feeling all the time."

I plucked one rose from the bush and held it to my cheek. I wanted to see Lindy in the mirror even if it meant excusing myself from this conversation with Will, even if she didn't love me, didn't miss me at all. But it was no use, wallowing

261

in missing her. I looked at Will. "So what will we read next? Something about war, I hope? Or maybe *Moby-Dick*."

"I am sorry, Adrian."

"Yeah. I am too."

The next night. May fifth. Ten thirty. Less than two hours left. In these two years, I had lost all my friends, a girl I'd thought loved me, and my father. But I'd found true friends in Will and Magda. I'd found a hobby. And I'd found true love, I knew, even if she didn't love me back.

And yet my face, my horrible face, stayed exactly the same. It wasn't fair. It wasn't fair.

There was a full moon out, like the night months ago when I'd told Lindy to leave. But this was the city, and there were no stars over stars. I went to the window and opened it, meaning to howl at the moon as I had that night. But this time what came out was her name.

"Lindy!"

I waited, but there was no answer.

I checked my watch. Almost eleven. And even though I knew there was no hope, I couldn't keep from going to my mirror, early just this once. I held it up. "I want to see Lindy."

Almost before it could show her to me, a shriek pierced the air.

It was her voice. I would have known it even if a hundred years had passed. I'd thought I would never hear it again. So close—I ran to the window to look for her.

Then I realized the voice came from the mirror.

I picked it up again and held it close to my eyes. It was dark, all dark, so I could barely make out anything, the neighborhood or the girl who screamed what I now realized was my name.

"Help me! Oh, please help me, Adrian!"

But as my eyes grew used to the dark mirror, I could make out shapes, buildings. I'd seen the neighborhood by day. Was she walking those streets at night? She was. But as my eyes focused more, I saw she wasn't alone. A shadowy figure walked with her. He held her arm and forced her up a flight of stairs into a boarded-up brick building.

I was running now, not even thinking, into the street. No cabs in sight, and I knew none would pick me up. So I dashed toward the subway station I'd watched so often, but hadn't entered in over a year, still holding the mirror. The street was bright with the full moon and the streetlights, and though it was late, I pushed through a crowd of people heading in the opposite direction on the sidewalk.

"What was that?" someone cried, and all looked after me, but I was just a shadow in the distance by then. I was running, running so fast after that one voice, the one person in the world who called my name so I could hear it.

I hadn't bothered to put on my coat, so I wore only jeans and a T-shirt, nothing to cover myself. I ran down the street, a beast to the world. Maybe they would think it was a costume. There were things just as strange in the city. But I was running, and someone screamed, someone pointed. I kept going, and finally, I disappeared into the ground.

That should have been the end of it. The rush hour was long over, and the subways usually weren't crowded late on summer nights. I jumped the turnstile. I was in luck—the train was there. The train was there. It should have been empty, but there were some Mets fans on the way home from a game.

I crashed through the doors, and there were swarms of people, mobs of them, sitting on every available seating surface, parents with kids on laps, people clinging to metal straps, holding on to seat backs. I thought maybe I could hide in the crowd. I tried to blend with everyone else.

Then I heard a scream.

"A monster!"

It was a little boy, his face paralyzed with fear.

"Try to sleep, honey." His mother patted him on the back.

"But, Mommy, no! It's a monster."

"Oh, don't be silly, dear. There's no such thing as—"

She looked up. Her eyes met mine.

And then a dozen, a hundred eyes were on me.

"It must be a mask," the mother said.

From behind me, someone grabbed my face, my head. They were pulling on me. No choice. I had to let my claws out. I turned on them.

And then the screaming started.

"Beast!"

"It's a monster!"

"Beast in the subway!"

"Call the Transit Authority!"

"Call the police!"

And soon, it all mushed together into screaming, the screaming I'd spent two years hiding to avoid. Bodies were swarming, all around me, swarming to get me, to get away from me. I held them off with my claws and my teeth. Cell phones opening. Would I be arrested? Taken to jail or the zoo?

That couldn't happen. I had to find Lindy.

Lindy.

Lindy needed me. Around me, the screams continued. I felt fists beating on my back. I stared at the mirror, tried to memorize the building, the street where she was, to see the address. I worked toward the door. More screaming, and bodies pushing against me, hot in the May night.

"Don't eat me!"

"Are the police coming?"

"Couldn't get a line. Too many calls from one place."

"Don't let him out!" a man's voice screamed.

"Are you kidding? Someone push him out before he eats someone!"

"Yeah. Push him onto the track."

I stood, paralyzed with fear, amid that roiling crowd. It couldn't end like this. I couldn't die so close to seeing her, to saving her. She'd called me. I'd heard it, crazy as it was. I had to find her. Once that happened, I could live or die. It wouldn't matter.

I knew what I had to do.

When the train shuddered to a stop, I lunged for the exit. A man tried to jump in my way. I searched for a weapon and found the only one I had. The mirror. I raised it high, then sent it smashing down on his head. I heard the glass shatter. Or perhaps it was his skull cracking. Or both.

The glass shattered all over the car, and there were people running in all directions, more screaming, screaming so loud that it was impossible to remember the silence that had been my life for so many months. I let the mirror fall to the floor, knowing that with it, every chance was gone but this one, every chance to see Lindy again.

The crowd was renewed, swarming around me, and I lunged through them, letting out a mighty roar that scattered them. And then I was down on all fours, in the position that made me fastest, fiercest, running for the exit.

"Push him on the track!" someone yelled again.

"Yes! Push the monster onto the track."

Bodies, pressing, pushing against mine, the heat and smell of them. The doors closed, and the train pulled away, and they were pushing me, pushing me. I knew that once the train was gone, they'd succeed in pushing me onto the tracks, maybe hold me at bay until the police came. Or the next train.

That would all be all right if not for Lindy.

All the nights I had spent trying to control my beast-like rages, to sheathe my claws and cover my fangs, were over now. My fangs were bared. My claws were uncovered. I lunged through the crowd. I was not a man, but a lion, a bear, a wolf. I was a beast. My roar shattered the subway station, covering every noise, the trains, the people. My claws met flesh, and crowds scattered. If I was caught, I would surely be killed. I pushed through the crowd and ran—no, bounded. Yes, bounded like an animal on four legs up the suddenly empty steps to the street.

Outside, the air was quiet. It wouldn't last. I took off, still on four legs because it was the fastest, surest way. There were few people on those streets at that hour, at near midnight. But even tough-looking gang members parted at the sight of me.

I had no mirror to guide me, only a memory, memory and animal instinct. I remembered where Lindy had been. I remembered her screams. I heard them again in my ear. I followed them. A block. Another. I still felt like I was being chased. It didn't matter. No one could catch me. I followed Lindy's screams through an alley and down a side street, into a doorway, up a stair, and into a room.

It was there that I stopped.

8

I stared at them. The man held her arm. "No money, huh?" he growled. "Your father said you'd be good for it. But if you don't have money, there's other ways to pay."

"No! Let me go!"

"Lindy?"

Man and victim turned. It was Lindy, all right. My instincts, animal though they were, had been true. The man—the monster—held her hair. He held a gun to her head.

"Lindy!" I started toward her.

"You're here!"

"Don't move, or I'll shoot."

He held the gun to her head. He could not hurt her. I hadn't come this far to have him hurt her. Without knowing it, I let out a low growl, an animal about to spring.

"I mean it," he said. "Don't—"

He stopped. He saw me, and his beast eyes met my beast eyes, and the animal I was smelled his fear.

"What the—?"

"If you harm her," I said in a voice more animal than human, "I will kill you."

"Don't eat me!" he yelled.

And he turned the gun from Lindy to me.

That was all I needed. I lunged. My teeth were in his arm, my claws in his neck. A shot rang out. My teeth were in his neck.

And then he stopped moving.

I threw him off me and crumpled to the ground.

I was bleeding. I wasn't supposed to bleed. I looked away. The bleeding didn't stop. Maybe my skin couldn't heal over the wound if the wound held a bullet. That would make sense. But it hurt.

Lindy was running to me, stumbling over the wounded gunman. "Adrian, you're here."

"I'm here," I agreed. The world was getting fuzzy, so fuzzy, fuzzy and dark, and clean and sweet-smelling as a rose.

"But how did you know?" she said. "How'd you know where I was?"

"I knew." My stomach hurt where the bullet was. "I knew by . . ." *Magic. Love. Animal instinct. As Jane knew of Rochester.* "I just knew." I reached for her.

"I should call the police. Or an ambulance." She started to go.

I thought of the mob in the subway, of a police officer arriving here to find me, taking me away, of dying in a squad car, alone, of losing Lindy when I'd finally found her. I grabbed at her arm. "Please. Please, no. Stay with me. Be with me."

"I wanted to be with you." She was sobbing now. "You told me to come back in the spring. And I wanted to. My father was screwed up like always, and he promised to go into rehab, get a job. He did for about a week. But then he quit. He said he didn't have to work just because I wanted him to. It was the same sort of thing he always said, but now it was different."

"Why?" I tried to keep my voice normal. If she knew how hurt I was, she would leave, go for the police. I hurt so much. So much, like the life was seeping through my skin. I didn't look down because I knew it would be a bloody mess.

"Because I'd been with you. Before, I knew only what it was to be his daughter, to live day to day and wait for it to be over. But now I knew what it was to have someone talk to me, care for me . . . be with me . . . and . . ."

270

"Love you?" The words were a gasp, and from the corner of my eye, I could see my watch hand move. 11:59. I'd set it that morning. It was over. But I was with Lindy. It was enough. "Why didn't you come back?"

"I wanted to come, but I'd lost the address. My father had taken me to your house by force, and now he wouldn't tell me where it was. He lied when I asked him, or said he didn't know. But I remembered your house was near a subway station. I could see it from the window, remember?"

I nodded.

"So I decided to go to every station in Brooklyn, then look for a house nearby with a greenhouse. I went to a different one, every day after school. But it was going too slowly, and tonight I decided I would find you. If I had to walk through every inch of Brooklyn, calling your name, I'd find you."

"Calling my name?"

"Like *Jane Eyre*. I just reread it last week, and I thought of you—how the lovers were separated, and—"

"Lovers?"

It was so hard to keep my eyes open. She was with me. I could just stop now.

"No! I should get an ambulance. If anything happened to you, I—"

With difficulty, I pushed myself up. "I love you, Lindy."

It was midnight. It was over. I would be a beast always. But Lindy was back. She was here.

"I know I'm too ugly for you to love," I said. "But I'll always . . ."

"I love you too, Adrian. But please, let me—"

I grabbed her arm back. "Then kiss me. Let me have the memory of your kiss, even if I die."

It was too late. It was too late, but she leaned forward anyway, and kissed me, my eyes, my cheeks, and finally on my lipless mouth. I was fading away, but I tasted her, felt her. This was all I wanted. Lindy. Now I could die happy.

And in the corner, I saw a shadow, moving.

"Watch out, Lindy!" I said with suddenly renewed strength. The air smelled funny all of a sudden, like roses. But it must have been my imagination. "Behind you!" I yelled.

I saw the man. I tried to make for him, to go after him and bite him as I had before. But my whole body felt numb and tingling, heavy, as if I already had died. I saw Lindy lunge for the gun on the floor. Then, struggling, four hands grabbing for one object. Gunfire, glass shattering. Then the shadow ran for the door.

Lindy turned to me. She held the smoking gun.

"Adrian?" She stared into the darkness like she couldn't see me. The world was black and spinning. The air smelled heavy with roses now. And under my hands, I felt something. Rose petals. They were everywhere, under my hands and on my body, and even in Lindy's hair. Where had they come from?

"I'm here, my love." Did I say *my love? Me?* But my body

felt so nice, like nothing could ever hurt me again. I didn't hurt anymore. Was I already dead?

Still, she stared strangely. Finally, she spoke.

"Kyle Kingsbury? But . . . where's Adrian?"

I'd misheard. "I'm here. But what did you call me?"

"Kyle Kingsbury, right? From Tuttle School. Maybe you don't remember me, but you once gave me a rose." She stopped, looking side to side. "A rose . . . Adrian!"

"Lindy . . ." I put my hand before my eyes, and it was a human hand. A man's hand. So perfect. A man's arm. I touched my face. A man's face! "Lindy, it's me."

"I don't understand. Where is the boy who was here before? His name was Adrian, and he was—"

"Ugly? Hideous."

"No! He was hurt. I have to find him!" She started for the door.

"Lindy!" I struggled to my feet. My strength was returning, and when I looked down, there was no blood, no pain. I was healed in every way. Lindy ran to the door, and I ran after her, for I was better. I was alive and well, and I caught her hand in mine. "Please wait."

"I can't, Kyle. You don't understand. There was a boy here, and he was—"

"Me." I grabbed her other hand. "He was me."

"No!" She struggled to get free, but I held her hands. "No, he wasn't you."

"Please." I pulled her toward me. I was taller than Kyle

had been before, and strong. I pulled her toward me so she couldn't leave. She thrashed against me, hitting and kicking. "Please, Lindy, just close your eyes, and you'll know that what I say is true." I wrapped my arm around her and put the other hand over her eyes.

In a second, she gave up, mostly. I said, "One night, there was a lightning storm. You came downstairs, frightened, and we made popcorn—two bags—and watched *The Princess Bride*." I stopped. She was frozen. "Do you know my voice, Lindy? When the movie was over, you'd fallen asleep. I picked you up and carried you to your room."

She leaned against me now, like she needed me for support.

I continued. "You woke in the darkness and spoke to me. You said my voice sounded familiar. It was familiar. It was me. Kyle. Adrian. We're the same. I will always remember that day because it was the first time I had hope, the first time I spoke to you without you noticing how hideous, how less than human I was. The first time I thought that maybe you could love me."

She turned to me. "Adrian? But how?"

"Magic. A witch put me under a spell—I would say a cruel spell, but it really wasn't because it led me to you."

"How was the spell broken?"

"Magic. It was magic, and the magic is called love. I love you, Lindy." I leaned and kissed her. She kissed me back.

"Adrian!"

"Yes." I was laughing. I couldn't help it.

"Can you take me home now?" she said. "Your home."

I nodded. "We'll take the subway." I looked down at my clothes, my too-large beast clothes. "I know I look a little strange, but probably no one will notice."

Mr. Anderson: Welcome to tonight's chat.

Grizzlyguy: Hey, everyone. There's some people I'd like you to meet.

SnowGirl: Hi, I'm Snow White. But not *that* Snow White.

RoseRed: You always say that. It sounds dumb.

SnowGirl: You're just mad bc I got the guy!

Mr. Anderson: Ladies, ladies . . .

Grizzlyguy: Anyway, this is Snow White. We're engaged.

BeastNYC: Hi, every1. There's someone I wanted every1 2 meet also. This is Lindy. She broke my curse. I'm not a beast anymore!!!

LilLindarose: Hi, everyone. Nice 2 be here.

SnowGirl: Congratz

RoseRed: That's great.

Mr. Anderson: I've been wanting to talk to you, Beast. I heard about a beast loose in the subway system. Was that you?

BeastNYC: Of course not!

LilLindarose: Figment of everyone's imagination ;)

BeastNYC: But we did happen 2 get 2gether on that exact day.

LilLindarose: Draw your own conclusions.

Froggie: I hv sum news 2

BeastNYC: What is it, Froggie?

Froggie: Iv met a princes

Grizzlyguy: Really? Did she kiss you or whatever you needed to break the spell?

Froggie: Nt so far bt she sez she will.

BeastNYC: That's great, Frog. How'd you meet?

Froggie: She ws playin w her GameBoy & she dropd it in my pond. I dryd it of 4 her & she sed shed kiss me.

Mr. Anderson: Wonderful, Froggie!

Froggie: im not getting my hops up. princeses can B unreliable.

Mr. Anderson: So this is interesting. It seems like everyone's finding true love.

BeastNYC: Not everyone.

Grizzlyguy: He means SilentMaid. V sad.

BeastNYC: Yeah. I miss her.

Mr. Anderson: As I was saying . . .

Froggie: OMG princes is heer GG wish me luk

Froggie has left the chat.

Mr. Anderson: Well, maybe we all should call it a night. Congrats to the happy couples. Will there be wedding bells soon?

SnowGirl: Definitely. I mean, if you help a guy kill a dwarf, he should marry you.

RoseRed: She was always like that, out to get something for herself.

BeastNYC: Not for us right now. We're still in hs. But someday . . . . .

LilLindarose: Someday . . . .

BeastNYC: Anyway, night. And thanks for the support.

BeastNYC has left the chat.

PART 6

Happily Ever After

1

A minute later, when we stepped from the building, we saw the police cars surrounding the place. A crowd of people and news reporters from every station including my dad's were there. And there was the guy, the lowlife pusher who'd been holding Lindy. He was talking to them.

"It's him!" he shouted when he saw us. "The beast that attacked me."

A buzz came from the crowd as they saw me, then saw I was no beast.

"That's the beast?" the female reporter from my dad's station exclaimed.

"He was different before. He had fangs and claws

and . . . hair all over him."

The reporter turned to Lindy, obviously hoping to salvage her story. "Miss, did you see a beast?"

"Of course not." Lindy looked up at me. She touched my hair. "I never saw a beast. But that man . . ." She turned to the pusher. "He attacked me. He might have killed me, but this guy burst in and saved me."

"I told you," the pusher yelled. "He's the beast. It's magic that changed him."

"Magic." Lindy's laugh was a little forced, a little fake. The crowd laughed too. "Magic and beasts only exist in fairy tales—or maybe drug-induced hallucinations. But heroes and villains are real."

Now the mic was in my face. "Did you see a beast?"

"No. I didn't see a beast." I took the mic from the reporter, authoritative, like my dad would have been. "But if there's a beast, maybe he's just a regular guy with a skin condition or something. Maybe he just needs some understanding. Maybe we judge people too much by their looks because it's easier than seeing what's really important."

The reporter snatched the microphone back. "Well, that was sappy." She turned away from me and spoke to the camera. "No leads in the mysterious case of a beastlike individual who terrorized subway passengers in Brooklyn tonight."

The crowd began to disperse. An officer grabbed the pusher. "Not so fast, buddy. I ran your ID. It seems you got a warrant outstanding . . . and we found that gun she was talking about." He turned to Lindy and me. "Would you mind coming down to the station to give a statement about what happened?"

"Not at all, officer," I said, thinking how much that would piss off my father, not to mention how freaked he must have been by the whole "Beast in the Subway" story, especially when he saw coverage on his own station. He was probably sitting in my living room already.

"I'll go anywhere," Lindy said, "as long as he goes with me."

The officer rolled his eyes. "Kids in love. Crazy."

He might have muttered something more, but I didn't hear him. We were too busy, kissing.

2

It was hours before we returned home, but when we did, Dad was there, watching *CBS Morning News*. The slide behind the reporter said, BEAST IN THE SUBWAY?, and showed a wolflike creature. Dad's tie was off. He looked rumpled.

"You know anything about this, Kyle?" He gestured toward the television set, not seeming to notice the change in me.

"Why would I?" I shrugged. "Obviously, I'm not a beast."

He looked up then. "No, you're not, are you? When did that happen?"

He meant did it happen before or after the news story. I didn't answer his question. "Dad, this is Lindy."

"Nice to meet you, Lindy." He gave her his best newscaster smile, at once managing to take in her Jane Austen T-shirt, old sneakers, and off-brand jeans while completely missing her face. Typical. Would it have killed him to make eye contact with her? "Well, this calls for a celebration. Shall I take you out for breakfast?"

Also typical. Now that I was normal, he was all about spending time with me. I glanced at Lindy. She wrinkled her nose.

"I don't think so," I said. "I have to go talk to Will and Magda since they've been with me the whole time. And then I'm gonna crash. I've been out all night." I enjoyed the look on his face when I said that. "But hey, we'll have to do it real soon." *Like, in a year or so.*

After he left, I went up to find Will.

It was barely five, so of course Will was asleep when I knocked on the door. I knocked louder.

"Adrian, maybe this should wait until later. He's asleep." Lindy leaned toward me. "And I can think of other ways to kill time. I missed you so much."

"Me too." I kissed her. I thought of the winter. I'd been as dead as one of my roses, but I hadn't wanted to admit it to myself. "But I need to talk to Will right now. It's important. I think you'll see why. I know he will."

I knocked harder. "Open up, sleepyhead."

From inside the door came a muffled voice. "Time's it?"

"Time to see the light. Open up!"

"I'll sic Pilot on you."

"He's a helper dog, not a watchdog. Open the door."

At first, there was no other sound, and I thought he had gone back to sleep. Then, just as I was ready to bang on the door again, I heard footsteps. The door opened.

I watched as the light hit Will's eyes.

"What the—" He looked left, then right, his eyes focusing on me like they never had before. "But how . . . who are you?"

"It's me, Adrian. And this is Lindy. Can you see us, bud?"

"Yes. At least I think I can. But maybe it's all a dream. You led me to believe you were hideous, a monster."

"And you led me to believe you were blind. Things change sometimes."

Now Will was laughing, dancing around the room. "Yes! Things change! I can't believe it. And Lindy? Is this you? Have you come back to Adrian, then?"

"Yes. I still don't understand it, completely, but I'm happy. So happy." She hugged Will, and Pilot, who was usually well behaved, seemed to realize that his services as guide dog weren't needed because he jumped up and down, barking and licking everyone's hands. So Lindy hugged him too.

When we finished jumping around, celebrating, I said, "Where's Magda?"

If Kendra was true to her word, something should have

happened to Magda too. She should have been reunited with her family. But now I didn't want her gone. I needed Magda, wanted her to stay. I ran down the hallway to Magda's room, Lindy following me. I pounded on the door. There was no answer.

When I opened the door, the room was empty.

"No!" I practically crushed Lindy's hand in my grip. She gave me a weird look, and I remembered what a great day it was, what a perfect day. Still, I said, "I didn't get to say good-bye. She left without saying good-bye."

"Magda?" When I nodded, Lindy said, "Oh, Adrian, I'm sorry."

I started to leave the room. But suddenly I caught a glow from something on the bed. I walked toward it.

It was a silver mirror, just like the one I'd smashed the night before on the subway. But this mirror was not smashed, and looking into it, I saw my reflection, perfect as I remembered—straight blond hair, blue eyes, even a tan. When I opened my mouth, perfect lips moved over white teeth. And at my side was the perfect girl, the perfect girl for me.

I said, "I want to see Magda."

At once, Kendra's reflection appeared.

3

"Where is she?" I said to Kendra.

"Meet me on the roof," she said. "The sun's about to rise."

We went to the fifth floor. I hadn't been there much lately. Now, being there with Lindy, I remembered all the lonely days I'd spent there, sitting on the sofa, and the day we'd been there together too. It was wondrous when life gave you a second chance. I opened the window and hoisted myself onto the roof. Then I put out an arm for Lindy.

The roof was flat with a ledge around it, so we could walk. The sun was rising. New York City at sunrise is one of the most beautiful places in the world. People make a big deal about the skyline, but it's nothing like watching the pink sun seep through the buildings, especially when you're holding hands with the girl you love.

I kissed that hand. "Look. Is this the most incredible morning or what?"

But Lindy wasn't looking at the sunrise, or at me. Instead, she was looking off to the side. I followed her gaze and understood.

Kendra was there. It was the first time I'd seen her since the spell. She was beautiful, as she'd been that day, her hair flying purple and green and black around her face, her robes black. And behind her was a flock of crows, stretching across the sides of the roof, black and green and purple in the rising sun.

"Kyle, you look great."

"Adrian. I prefer Adrian."

"Me too, actually. Suits you." She stepped up to Lindy. Or rather, she floated. It almost seemed like she was flying. "And Lindy, we haven't met, but I'm Kendra."

"Kendra, the . . ."

I'd filled Lindy in on all the details of Kendra while we'd waited in the police station that night.

"You can say it," Kendra said. "The witch. I know what I am. There are some who would call me a wicked witch. I'm the one responsible for the spell on Adrian."

"And are you proud of that?"

"A little bit. He's a better person than when he started."

Lindy didn't look so sure, but I nodded, knowing it was true.

"But I'll admit my previous spells weren't as successful. In my youth, I tended to be impulsive—turn someone into a frog first, ask questions later. The other witches got on me, said that by using my powers too frequently, I might draw attention to witchcraft and set off a wave of witch hunts as big as Salem. As punishment, I was sent to New York City to work as a servant. I was told not to use my powers at all."

"But you did," I guessed.

She nodded. "I did because I was placed in the home of a teenage boy so horrible and insensitive that I felt I had to teach him a lesson. I cast a spell."

"Gee, thanks."

Beside me, Lindy squeezed my hand.

"The other witches were appalled. I had cast a spell—a big, obvious one that could end up in an incident like . . . oh, say, a beast on the loose in the New York subway system. They were particularly concerned that I'd chosen the son of a news personality as my victim."

"Yeah, that sucked of you."

Kendra rolled her eyes. "So they said I would stay with him forever, in the form of that same family servant."

"Magda?" I got it. "So Magda isn't real?"

"She's real." With a wave of her hand, Kendra transformed. Now she was Magda. "She is I, I am she."

"Wow," I said. "This is . . . I thought you . . . I mean, Magda was my friend."

"I am, my love," Kendra, now Magda, said. "I cared about you from the first and wanted you to be happy. I could see the sadness in you that made you not see the true beauty of life. That was why I did what I did."

"And what about Will? Is he a witch too?"

Magda shook her head. "No. I knew about Will, that he would be kind to you and teach what you needed to learn. And I, a humble servant, suggested to your father that he find a blind student to tutor you. Will needed a job and now, because of your unselfish wish, he has regained his sight."

"But there was another part to that wish. I wished you . . . that Magda could be reunited with her family."

"And so I was—at midnight, last night."

"I don't get it."

"I wish you luck, Adrian." She placed her hands on my shoulder and on Lindy's, and I felt a bolt of electricity, like when you accidentally put your finger between an electrical plug and the socket. I wondered if she was putting a spell on us. I looked at Lindy to see if she was morphing into a hyena or something, but she seemed okay.

"Luck?" I said.

"Not that you'll need it. You have earned your love far more than most couples your age. Unlike most, you really know each other and are thoughtful of each other. When you allowed Lindy to leave and return to her father,

I knew it would work out."

"Wish you'd clued me in."

She ignored this. "And now, through your wish for Magda, I am reunited with my family."

"What do you mean?"

"Can't talk anymore. They are waiting."

She waved her arm and disappeared. At least, I thought she had. But Lindy pointed down, and that's when I realized that a crow occupied the exact spot where Magda had been standing. It was a beautiful crow, large and sleek, with black wings reflecting purple and green in the rising sun. She hopped over and joined the others and, as one, they rose over our heads and east, toward daylight.

"Wow," Lindy said when they were out of sight. "That sucks."

"What does?"

"I was waiting—politely—for her to stop talking. But if I'd known the nice lady was going to transmogrify into a crow, I'd have been quicker about making a request."

"What kind of request?"

"Well, I'm really happy that we're together, of course. But I loved you the way you were. Before. I thought Kyle Kingsbury was cute and all, but Adrian was the one I fell in love with. I didn't see you as a monster, not after a while anyway. I saw you as unique. Special. I think I loved you almost from the first. I just didn't know."

"So you want me to be a beast?" I said.

She shrugged. "I guess that's not really practical, huh? I mean, it *is* easier to go to the movies and stuff with your boyfriend if it's . . . um, not a news event."

"Easier to apply to colleges too."

"Agreed."

"So what's the problem?" I said. "I'm the same, no matter how I look."

"I guess. But I was sort of thinking that maybe she could change a couple things about you, since she's a witch."

"Like what?"

"Basically, you're tall, blond, and perfect."

"I don't know about perfect."

"Ten out of ten shallow high school girls surveyed would agree you're perfect."

I thought of Sloane. "Okay, let's assume for the sake of argument that I'm perfect. So?"

"That's why I wanted the changes."

"Like what? You said I'm perfect."

"Oh, I don't know. A bump on the nose, or maybe a wart. Twenty pounds in the gut or maybe a big zit on your forehead."

"I see." I took Lindy's hand. "And why would you want that?"

"Because you're *perfect*. And I'm . . . well, not. Guys who look perfect generally don't go out with girls who are, you know, average. Maybe Adrian King loved me, but will Kyle Kingsbury stay around, or can he do better?"

"Better?" I went from holding her hand to hugging her. "Lindy, you loved me when I wasn't even human. You kissed me when I had no lips. You saw what was deep down inside me when I wasn't even sure about it myself. Believe me, there's no way I could do better. I think you're perfect."

"Oh, if you say so." But she was smiling.

"I do. I'll look whatever way you want me to. But do you think this happens to everyone—being turned into a beast, then changed back because of true love? Most people wouldn't even believe it could happen, but it happened to us. Magic. For the rest of our lives, we'll go to school and have jobs and eat breakfast and watch TV, but we'll know that even if we don't see it, there's magic in the world. Face it, this is happily ever after, true love like in fairy tales."

I kissed her again. She kissed me back. We stood there, kissing, until the sun was fully up in the sky and the morning sounds of the city had begun.

Then we went downstairs and made breakfast.

EPILOGUE
Senior Year

"Hey, your name's on this." Lindy's tone is derisive as she passes back copies of the Tuttle homecoming court ballot.

Yeah, Lindy and I went back to Tuttle. It took some string pulling on Dad's part to get us back in, but our classmates welcomed us back into the fold—that is, if whispering behind my back that I'd flunked out of boarding school, been involved in a scandalous affair with the headmaster's daughter, or had a nervous breakdown can be considered welcoming back. At Tuttle, it probably was.

"He *must* have had a nervous breakdown," I heard Sloane Hagen say one day when Lindy and I passed her in the hall. "Or maybe he took a blow to the head. Why else would he go out with a nothing like her?" Apparently, she'd been serious about my calling her if I transformed back. She'd mentioned several times that she was waiting for a call. She was still waiting.

Now I look at the ballot. Sure enough, there's my name. "Must be a typo."

"Right."

"I haven't seen these people in two years. Why would they nominate me for homecoming court?"

"It couldn't possibly be based on looks, right?"

"Maybe so. Whatever." I crumple the ballot into a ball and try to score a basket with it in the trash can. I miss and head to the front of the room.

But the teacher reaches it first. "Mr. Kingsbury, I believe this is yours," he says. "In the future, there will be

296

no three-pointers in my AP English class."

"Yes, sir."

"There's no special treatment around here, Kyle. For anyone."

"Yes, sir." I salute, then shove the ballot into my pocket and head for my desk. "Jerk," I whisper to Lindy.

Lindy looks at the teacher. "What Kyle means is, he's *very* sorry, and it won't happen again."

Around us, people are giggling. I notice that hardly anyone's filling out their homecoming ballots. I count three wastebasket basketballs, waiting to be thrown as soon as the teacher turns his back again, two paper airplanes, and one origami piece, not including the people who are just letting the ballot sit while they text-message. "We don't have to go to the dance, by the way," I tell Lindy. "It's pretty lame."

But Lindy says, "Of course we're going. I want a real corsage from you—any color rose you like—and I have the perfect dress."

The teacher must have decided we'd spent enough time *not* filling out our ballots because he starts class, and we go over an hour of English lit that Lindy and I, at least, already know from our years of homeschooling with Will.

On the way out, I corner the teacher. "Nice guy, ragging on us."

Mr. Fratalli shrugs. "Hey, you wouldn't want people thinking I was showing favoritism just because we happen to live in the same house."

"I wouldn't mind." But I'm joking and put my hand up for a high five. "See you later, Will?"

"Much later," Mr. Fratalli—Will—says. "I have school tonight. Don't want to have to teach little snots like you forever."

Will's going to school too. Grad school, so he can be an English professor. But I made sure my dad wrote him a great recommendation to teach at Tuttle for now.

"Oh, yeah," I say. "Well, we'll keep the pizza warm for you."

"I'd think you'd be studying too hard to have time even to order pizza."

"Then you'd think wrong. This class is easy compared to what we used to do."

After school, Lindy and I usually take the subway to the house in Brooklyn where we still live with Will. My dad offered to move me back into his Manhattan apartment after my transformation, but I think we were both relieved when I said no. I wanted to have someplace for Lindy to stay. So now we all stay together.

"Do you want to walk over to Strawberry Fields?" I say to Lindy as we leave Tuttle. We do that some days, to look at the garden.

But today, Lindy shakes her head. "I want to go see something at home."

I nod. *Home.* It's still such a bizarre and beautiful word for me, to have a home where I can come and go, a place where people actually like me.

When we reach the house, Lindy disappears upstairs. Her room is still on the third floor, and I hear noises from above. I pick up the mirror we always keep in a place of honor in the living room, the repaired mirror that Kendra brought the day the spell was broken. "I want to see Lindy," I tell it.

But as I knew would happen, I see only my own face. The magic is over, but its effects will live forever. There was definitely magic in Lindy and me getting together.

Lindy comes down a few minutes later.

"Where is it?" she says.

"Where's what?" I'm polishing off a box of Cheetos and a glass of milk. I've finally figured out where everything is in the kitchen.

"Ida's dress," Lindy says. "I'm going to wear it to the dance."

"*That's* what you want to wear?"

"Yeah. What's wrong with it?"

"Nothing." I take another handful of Cheetos.

"Is it because it's not new?"

I shake my head, remembering my comment to Kendra. "Around here people buy *new* dresses for a dance." I want to slap that guy except—oh yeah—he was me. "It's just . . . I'm not sure I want other people to see . . . to know about . . . never mind. It's fine."

"Are you sorry you're not going with some homecoming queen girl or something?"

"Yeah, right. No. No. Stop asking me stupid questions. It's fine."

She smiles. "Then where's my dress?"

I look away. "In my room, under my mattress."

She gives me a funny look. "Why would it be there? Were you *wearing* it? Is *that* why you don't want me to wear it?" She's kidding, but even so . . .

"No." I start downstairs to get the dress. I don't expect her to follow me, but she does. I walk through my rooms, past the rose garden, then lift the mattress and take the green satin from the space between it and the box spring. I remember the days when I used to smell her perfume, though I would never tell her about it in a million years. Still, I remember the first day I saw the dress, the first day I saw her in it, being so afraid to touch her, but hoping maybe she'd love me. "Here. Put it on."

She examines it. "Oh, it has a few beads hanging. Maybe you're right about not wearing it."

"You can get it fixed. Take it to the dry cleaner. But first put it on." Suddenly, I very much want to see her in it again.

A moment later, she's wearing it, and it is exactly as I remember, the cool green satin contrasting with the warm pink of her skin. "Wow," I say. "You're beautiful."

She examines herself in the mirror. "You're right. I'm gorgeous."

"And so modest. Now I have to ask you something."

"What's that?"

I hold my hand out to her. "May I have this dance?"

AUTHOR'S NOTE

There are many animal bridegroom tales from different countries and cultures. In them, "the Beast" is presented, variously, as a snake, a lizard, a lion, a monkey, a pig, or a creature with body parts of various animals, such as a winged snake. He has angered a witch or fairy and been cursed in this way until he finds true love, or a wife. In most versions "Beauty" comes to live with, or marries, the Beast because her father has stolen an item (usually a flower). The Beast is kind to Beauty and she realizes she loves him more than she initially believed. Her realization of this causes the curse to be broken. In one version, the courtship of Beauty and the Beast is through letters, and presumably, the Beast is an impressive writer. But typically, he is a simple man/beast. In several versions, including one by the Brothers Grimm, the Beast is human by night but an animal by day, and in this way, the tale is similar to the Greek myth of *Cupid and Psyche,* where Psyche marries handsome Cupid, but since he only comes to her after dark, her sisters persuade her that he is a monster. *Cupid and Psyche* is perhaps the earliest variant on this tale.

In *Cupid and Psyche*, Psyche, when she leaves Cupid, must go on a quest to get him back. This occurs in several other stories, and I have incorporated it into my story.

The version most familiar to American audiences was written in eighteenth-century France by Jeanne-Marie Le Prince de Beaumont (though sometimes credited to Charles Perrault of *Cinderella* fame), adapted from an earlier novel by Gabrielle Susan Barbot de Gallan de Villeneuve. In this version, a traveler stumbles into the garden of a Beast, steals a rose for his youngest daughter, a beautiful but bookish girl, and is going to be killed until he promises to return. The daughter returns in his stead to become the Beast's prisoner. In the Beaumont and Villeneuve versions, unlike most others, the fairy who placed the curse takes a somewhat active role in the courtship of Beauty and Beast, appearing to Beauty in a dream and reassuring her, then returning after the curse is broken, to congratulate them on their prosperous love. It is from this I conceived Kendra's continued involvement in the plot of the book, though in this case, her

302

involvement is with the Beast himself.

As a writer, I write about what disturbs me, and what disturbed me about many versions of *Beauty and the Beast* was that beloved as Beauty is said to be, in each case, her father gives her over willingly to the Beast, in order to save his own life (the Disney movie version is a gentler version of the tale, in which Belle's father has no choice in the matter). Thinking of this led me to think about the Beast himself, how he was alone in the castle, possibly abandoned by his own family, the circumstances of which are unexplained in most versions. So the romance is really the story of two abandoned teens who find each other. As a young adult writer, I hear often of the negative portrayals of parents in my genre, but I am convinced that YA has nothing on fairy tales for evil parents (see, e.g., *Hansel and Gretel, Snow White*). This was how I conceived my story—unsugarcoated, though still with a happily ever after.

Readers interested in other Beauty and the Beast stories may wish to check out *Beauties and Beasts* by Betsy Hearne, which contains stories from different countries, and *The Dragon Prince: A Chinese Beauty & the Beast Tale* by Laurence Yep. Young adult versions include *Beauty: A Retelling of the Story of Beauty & the Beast* by Robin McKinley, *Beast* by Donna Jo Napoli, and *The Rose and the Beast: Fairy Tales Retold* by Francesca Lia Block, which contains various fairy-tale retellings, including a short Beast tale. *The Rumpelstiltskin Problem* is a book by Vivian Vande Velde, conceived because the author was disturbed, as I was, by inconsistencies in a traditional tale.

Readers are probably familiar with the Disney movie version of *Beauty and the Beast*. But they may wish to watch the movie version of the tale, *La Belle et la bête*, directed by Jean Cocteau (in French, with English subtitles). It is, admittedly, this version of the Beast I visualized when creating Adrian.

Want more

BEASTLY?

See the story through Lindy's eyes!
Here is

LINDY'S DIARY

APRIL 30

Having a crush on the hottest, richest, most popular guy in school = not <u>too much</u> of a cliché, right?

Well, um, yes. Yes, it is. Have I, Linda Owens, the same Lindy who reads Gabriel Garcia-Márquez and Ayn Rand (even when they're <u>not</u> required for school) and who skipped lunch every day in third grade in order to donate a flock of chickens to a family in Guatemala, become as shallow as Sloane Hagen and her posse, liking a guy just based on looks?

Well ...

Not <u>just</u> looks ...

The fact is, I like to think there's something more to Kyle Kingsbury. The money is irrelevant. I like him <u>despite</u> his money and his looks. That's my story, and I'm sticking to it.

Maybe I'm fooling myself.

Our school, Tuttle, is the kind of school where you find kids whose parents are Broadway producers, minor rock stars, second-generation Kardashians, people whose grandfather invented Pop-Tarts. But Kyle still gets more than his fair share of attention not only because his father is a network news anchor, but because of Kyle's own gorgeousity. People get used to it after a while—or they pretend to. But at the beginning of the year, when the new middle schoolers start, it must be hard for him.

Once, in September, I saw this in action. He was trying to leave after school when these two girls accosted him.

"Hey," one said, "Is your dad Rob Kingsbury?"

Kyle nodded and said yes, he was.

"We watch him on the news all the time," she said (giggling).

I was thinking what did she want, a medal, but Kyle was super-polite and thanked her for watching.

"What's he like?" the girl asked.

Before Kyle could get out his answer that Rob Kingsbury was just like everyone else, the other girl started asking all these questions. Did his dad help him with his current events homework? Did he get to go on trips with him? Was his dad part of the Liberal News Media her father said was ruining this country? Did they have anyone special to trim their nose hair? And Kyle, who's usually super-confident, like handsome, popular people are, was looking <u>really</u> uncomfortable, so uncomfortable that I violated my personal policy of not speaking to the cool, rich people (which is pretty much everyone at this school) and walked up to him.

"Hey Kyle," I said, "did you forget?"

He gaped at me. "Forget what?"

"You did forget! Chemistry tutoring? My place? 3:00?" I looked at my watch. "It's almost that now. Come <u>on!</u>" I didn't want to touch him. I mean, I <u>did,</u> but I didn't want him to think I was a stalker, so I just gestured to him to follow me.

"Okay, okay." He turned to the two girls. "Sorry, gotta go."

And then, he actually took <u>my</u> arm and walked to the door with me, the two girls still following us with their eyes.

When we reached the street, he turned to me.

"Sorry I forgot our chem tutoring session and, um . . . your name?"

He stared at me, and his eyes were the same color as the Mediterranean Sea in pictures of Greece (eyes are the windows to the soul, you know), and for a second, I didn't quite understand what he'd said, so I stammered, "What?"

"Your name. If you're tutoring me in chemistry, I should know it."

"Oh...wh..." Those eyes! "Linda Lindy."

Of course he didn't know my name. Why would he? I wouldn't be on his radar. He only looked at hot girls.

"Pretty," he said. When I looked at him, surprised, he said, "In Spanish, _linda_ means 'pretty.' My dad wanted me to take Mandarin to make me more marketable, but I took Spanish because it's easier."

He was still holding my arm, still talking too. Good thing, because after the big gesture of rescuing him, I had nothing. I choked out, "Any language is valuable."

I take French, the language of romance. Was he saying I was pretty? Pretty doubtful.

"Funny how I forgot that chem tutoring session," he said. "Especially funny how I forgot to take chemistry. That's a tenth-grade class."

"I know." I take chem, even though I'm only in ninth. But that's because I'm a total drone. People who look like Kyle Kingsbury don't have to study and people with his money don't have to worry about getting a scholarship. I added, "You seemed like you needed rescuing. Sorry if I was wrong."

I raised my hand in what was supposed to be a

friendly good-bye wave. Obviously, my work was done here. But because he was still holding my arm, we ended up sort of moving closer together.

"You weren't wrong," he said. "Does it make me a spoiled brat if I say I hate all the questions about my dad, all the idol worship? I mean, I'd say he puts his pants on one leg at a time, but he usually has some young girlfriend to do it for him . . . joke."

I shook my head, no, it didn't make him a spoiled brat. I was going to say something then, like what's the big deal. His dad read the news—he didn't make it. He probably didn't even write it. But that was insulting, so what I said was, "It must be rough."

When, in fact, I didn't think it was all that rough. What's rough is being a scholarship student at a school like Tuttle Prep. I came here because I thought there'd be more people like me, aka studious nerds, people who would relate to me. In fact, no one does. Being poor seems to be an insurmountable barrier around here. It's not like people totally shun me. It's more subtle than that. They'll sit with me at lunch or study with me, but I have no close friends . . . well, other than teachers.

He nodded. "Rough-ish, I guess. The thing is, I

barely know my father."

He looked at me like he was expecting some big reaction. When I had none, he said, "Does that surprise you?"

I shook my head. "I bet a lot of people could say that about their parents."

"Could you?" he asked.

When I nodded, he said, "So your dad's some captain of industry, leaving you to be raised by the nanny?"

I said, "Not exactly. There are all sorts of reasons people don't really know their parents, or their dad, in my case. My mother died when I was little."

He nodded, like he understood, and started to say something. "So, Lindy—means pretty why do—"

But I never got to hear the end of the sentence because that was when Sloane Hagen, Kyle's Pole-Dancer-Barbie of a girlfriend, showed up and he had to leave.

But he winked at me and said, "See you around," and for months after, when he saw me in the hall, he would smile or at least nod, and I sort of convinced myself that we had some kind of connection. Or, at least, that he knew who I was—even though the reason Kyle doesn't know his dad is because his dad is a

$10-million-a-year news anchor.

And the reason I don't know mine is because he's a drug addict.

Even so, I try to engineer ways to see Kyle, to wave to him, like getting off at the 79th Street station, near where Kyle lives, instead of going all the way to the Lincoln Center station near the school, so I can grab coffee and watch him walk by before I, too, walk on to Tuttle, about fifty feet behind him.

Or maybe I just do it because I need the exercise. Ha!

MAY 5

The main flaw in my whole Kyle-and-Lindy-take-the-Long-Island-Railroad-into-the-sunset scenario is Sloane Hagen.

I'm willing to consider the remote possibility that Kyle Kingsbury is unexpectedly deep. Sloane—not so much. Describing her as a Barbie doll is actually sort of insulting to Barbie. Barbie, however plastic, has had many brilliant careers as veterinarian, Olympic athlete, and even paleontologist. And she's traveled the world. If Sloane travels, it's only to shop.

Still, she's the prettiest girl in school, and Kyle's the hottest guy, so there's some kind of law they have to be together.

And he's taking her to the ninth-grade dance.

I know this because I passed her at school yesterday. She was staying late for cheer practice (surprise, surprise). Me, I tutor after school. I heard her describe her dress on the phone to him ("It's black and has very little material") and demand an orchid corsage in exchange for whatever currency girls like Sloane use

to get guys like Kyle. It's amazing that, for some people, this is their life. Sloane Hagen's biggest problem is
whether her hot boyfriend buys her the right kind of
corsage. I sort of wish he'd screw up and buy the wrong
one. Which is better than a lot of things I could wish.

At least, I'll be at the dance too. I'm taking tickets
as part of my work-study.

Le sigh.

MAY 10

Tonight, when I got home, there was a man on our door-step, lurking. I knew he was looking for my dad. I'd seen him before, hunched over, with knifelike features, the wolf in his eyes. My dad's pusher. If he was wait-ing to make a delivery it was bad. If he wanted to be paid, that was worse.

I used to feel like confronting those guys, asking them how they could do this, how they could sell drugs to a pathetic middle-aged man who'd lost everything and couldn't deal with the world. My sisters told me not to. These guys didn't see Dad as human. They weren't human themselves. Now, my sisters are long gone, but I know they were right.

So I walked around the block.

Four times.

When I came back, the man was gone. I knew that meant Dad was inside.

Someday, something really bad is going to happen. I don't know whether to hope I'm around for it or hope I'm not.

My father had his back to me when I came in. We didn't acknowledge each other. I couldn't look at him. So I started picking stuff up off the counter.

He said, "Do you have to do that? It's really loud."

That was all he could say to me?

No, no, actually, it wasn't. He followed up with, "We got any food?"

I was holding a loaf of day-old bread from the grocery store where I work part-time. For a second, I really wanted to chuck it at his head, but I said, "There's bread."

I set it down on the table on the other side of the room, figured I'd make him walk to get it at least. But he said, "Make me a sandwich. Will you, sweetie?"

And I gave in like I always do. "We only have peanut butter," I told him.

He grumbled a little but finally said, "Sure." I restrained myself from saying that he could go out and work and earn money for something better than peanut butter. It didn't help. I made the sandwich and thrust it into his shaking hand. I didn't even wince at the network of railroad tracks on his arm.

I went to the library to do my homework, wondering why I'd even bothered to come home.

When I got back, the sandwich was untouched. I took it down to the Dumpster before the roaches (or rats) got it.

Sometimes, you wonder when your handsome prince is going to show up and rescue you.

I know that's not a popular sentiment, or a PC one. A modern woman is supposed to take care of herself. But I've been taking care of myself since my mom died, when I was seven. That's when Dad went off the deep end. My sisters helped when they were there, but after a while, they bailed. I don't really blame them. For the past two years, if I wanted to eat, I found food. If I wanted a roof over my head, I made sure the rent was paid. I worked. I tutored. I begged the landlord for more time. If I wanted to go to school, I got myself there. No one does anything for me.

So I know when I meet the right guy, it's not going to be someone like my dad. It's not going to be someone who needs me. It's going to be someone who can, for once in my life, be a hero.

I'm hoping guys like that still exist.

MAY 23

He spoke to me!

I was beginning to wonder if I'd hallucinated our previous conversation (followed, as it was, by eight months of silence on his part, punctuated by the occasional could-be-my-imagination nod in the hall). I realized that, okay, maybe we <u>hadn't</u> made a connection that day back in September. Maybe, I thought, Kyle Kingsbury is exactly the kind of jerk people think he is. Maybe he'd been playing me before, and he really did think I was beneath him.

But tonight, he spoke to me, not only spoke to me, but actually gave me a flower.

Here's how it happened.

I was taking tickets, like a pathetic drone, wearing this white blouse they made all the workers wear, so I looked like a total geek, when Kyle showed up with Sloane. I noticed immediately because people started gathering around the table when they came in, trying to bask in their light. But something was off.

I don't know if Sloane was just not speaking to

Kyle or if she was actually high, but she flounced in ahead of him, not making eye contact, and joined her covey (or is it coven?) of friends.

Kyle, looking like he needed a friend too, leaned against my table and produced two tickets. "That one's for her, when she decides to come in." He jutted his thumb at Sloane.

I ripped his tickets and noticed he was holding a corsage, a white rose with a light blue ribbon. I've always loved roses.

"Pretty flower," I said.

He glanced at it, flipping it in his hand like he'd forgotten he had it. "Oh, yeah."

I wanted to say that a white rose represented purity and innocence, but I recognized that it would be a completely dorkified thing to say. So, in trying to avoid saying the dorky thing I said nothing at all. I looked away, pretending to count the ripped ticket halves.

Yet he still stood there. I felt his presence, magnetic. Stupid Sloane doesn't know how lucky she is. If I could go to a dance with Kyle, have him give me a rose, I'd be completely happy. Or, at least, happy enough not to be a complete . . . never mind!

"Hey, do you want it?" he asked.

"What?" My head snapped back toward him.

He held up the flower. "Here. Take it."

"That's not nice."

"What isn't?"

"Goofing on me, pretending you're going to give it to me, then taking it back." That had to be it, of course. Why would he give me Sloane's corsage? If there's anything I've learned in these years of being my father's daughter, it's how to protect myself.

He protested. "I wasn't pretending. You can have it." He held it up. The ribbon exactly matched his blue eyes. "It's not the right color for my girlfriend's dress or something, so she won't wear it. It's going to die, so you might as well take it."

I glanced at Sloane. Her dress was black, which goes with everything, but probably the corsage wasn't expensive enough for her. Sloane probably needed an orchid fresh-picked today in Brazil and airlifted in for her pleasure. With a ribbon made of thousand-dollar bills.

"Since you put it that way." I started to take it from him but, at the very last minute, he pulled it back. "Let me."

And he pinned it on my ugly blouse. I let him. The

gesture had more intimacy than I'd expected, the back of his hand brushing my neck as he pinned it on.

"Thanks," I said. "It's beautiful."

"Enjoy it . . . Linda." He smiled.

And for that second, it was like he and I were the only two people in the room. I inhaled deeply. Some roses, the ones you buy cheap from guys on the street, don't have much scent, but this one did. I remembered my father, in one of his lucid moments, telling me that smell was the sense most associated with memory and that whenever he smelled a certain lemony-scented perfume, it reminded him of my mother (which made me want to either buy a lifetime supply of it or destroy every bottle). I know that, for as long as I live, I'll associate the scent of roses with him, with Kyle. I was trying to think of something to say, something more than thanks, but he'd already moved away and was talking to, of all people, Kendra Hilferty, this emo girl from my chem class.

I inhaled again. Probably better to dream.

The rest of the night, I took tickets and picked up discarded cups and tried not to pay attention to Kyle laughing, Kyle talking, Kyle being crowned dance royalty. I mean, it's too pathetic to be stalking the popular guy. But I enjoyed watching him. He was so opposite the way I was, so full of life and energy and yet, I knew he and I were alike deep down. Deep down, we were both lonely. He was just better at hiding it.

I took the rose home and pressed it between the pages of <u>Atlas Shrugged</u>, which is the biggest book I own.

Hokey, I know, but I honestly believe that sometimes, there's more to people than meets the eye.

He's gone.

Kyle hasn't been to school in over a week, not since the night of the dance.

The rumors are all over the place. He got mono. From Sloane. He got a modeling contract in France. He went to Florida to live with his mom. No, he's in rehab. And then, he's going to boarding school next year. Sloane is shockingly quiet on the subject. In fact, she's dating someone else.

WHERE IS KYLE??????????

Though I'd rather believe he has mono, rehab is the most persistent rumor. It's probably true. It's typical, after all. There are no heroes in the world, only good-looking villains. People at school relish this gossip. On Kyle, drugs sound glamorous, I guess, like something rock stars do. But I only have to look at my father, emaciated, sick, shaking, willing to do anything for his next fix, to know that ADDICTION IS NOT SEXY!

I wish him in Florida with his mother instead, and at night, I look at his picture in the yearbook, or I open the pages of <u>Atlas Shrugged</u>, inhale the waning scent of the rose he gave me, and dream of what might have been.

Stupid, stupid girl.

JUNE 13—A YEAR LATER

I haven't written in a while, over a year, actually. I guess that's telling. It's sad how often I used to write about Kyle Kingsbury, but what else in my life was, or is, interesting?

Still, I like the idea of a journal. It keeps my head straight. But the sad fact is, I have nothing to write about, nothing except my clichéd crush on a strung out pretty boy.

I suppose I should write about my everyday life—interesting. That's what Samuel Pepys did. His journal (circa 1665) is filled with detailed and ultra-scintillating accounts of the wine he drank, the cloaks he wore. It's considered an important primary source for information regarding life in 17th Century London.

But I doubt anyone will be researching 21st Century Brownsville or consult my diary if they are. Still, I'll try to be better. I need to write. It makes the real world seem far less real.

JULY 13

In case I was worried about not having enough to write about, I shouldn't have been. My father always provides material, sooner or later.

In this case, he's completely insane!

Usually, I'm pretty good at ignoring noises in the night. This is an important skill for people who live in New York City and even more so for people whose fathers are engaged in low-grade criminal activity—particularly if those people need to study. I've slept through banging on the door, even gunshots.

But tonight, my father burst into the apartment. He was messed up, babbling about cops who were going to arrest him, drug dealers, a monster, a freak. His hands were shaking and his eyes were wide. If he wasn't high, he needed a fix.

I asked him to go sleep it off. Repeatedly, I asked him. Tell me in the morning. He wouldn't leave.

Finally I got the story (if any of it was even true) out of him.

He was bad in debt. His pusher, a mean mother

named Hob, wasn't taking no for an answer this time. He'd threatened to hunt me down, to kill me (me!), if Dad didn't pay him.

"How much do you need?" I reached for my wallet, which I kept in my pocket at all times, figuring this was just another scam to get drug money from me and too tired to resist.

But he said, "Too much. You don't have it."

And then, he started to cry. He couldn't pay. He was freaking out, but finally, he'd come up with a solution.

With surprising clarity, he told me about it. He'd called an old friend, a hitherto completely unknown-to-me friend who owed him a favor. I was surprised he had any favors to call in, but he actually had a lot of details. The friend lived in Brooklyn. He traveled a lot, but he had a son my age, a freakish kid who needed a companion. I could stay with him until it blew over and it was safe for me to come home.

A freak? Were there even freaks anymore? I asked my dad what he meant by freak, and that's when the lucid moment ended. He started describing a creature more animal than man, a wolf-boy with fangs and claws, hair all over his body. "But he'll protect you," he promised.

Yeah, right.

I was pretty sure my dad was delusional or, let's face it, stoned out of his mind. There's no such thing as a wolf-boy. Well, not outside of the movies.

"Right. You want me to live with some stranger? What if he...attacks me?"

"There's someone else living there, a housekeeper or something. It's the only way. Please, Lindy. It's the only way to save us, um, you."

At this point, I couldn't process any more of this, especially not on an hour's sleep. I told him to go away. I'd talk to him in the morning.

I've been up ever since.

The obvious fact is, my father is kicking me out of the apartment and coming up with some lame story to hide it. I should probably be happy he even found me someplace else. Do I need my father? To live? Well, no. I've been making my own money since I was thirteen and got kids at Tuttle to pay me for "helping" them with papers. At worst, I'll end up in foster care, which probably won't be any worse than where I am now. I certainly don't need him for emotional support, though I'd miss him. He is my dad.

But there could be real danger. My father's friends

aren't exactly professors at Columbia. That's for sure. We've been on the lam before. Once, when I was nine, we hid in Staten Island for almost a year with a friend of his, and my father never left the house.

My father is never concerned about me or my safety only his own. And yet, he seemed so afraid just now that I wonder if he really could be, for once. When I was little, he used to hold my hand when I crossed the street. He used to kiss my knee when I fell. Maybe it's like that again.

Doubtful. Would I be any safer with some "friend" my father could produce? Possibly. Once, before my mom died, my father was a respectable person. Maybe there's someone from that previous life who still cares about him, who would take pity on him, take pity on me.

The teenage freak son is a strange detail, strange even for my father. Freak. An odd, obsolete, un-PC word, a <u>lonely</u> word that sounds like something from the Victorian era. There were news stories about the man in Indonesia whose skin looked like tree bark, the conjoined twins in Iran, joined at the head. Could he be like that?

It's intriguing. I've always felt like a freak myself.

When I went to school in the neighborhood, the kids would stare at me because I was reading, because I cared about school. Now, at Tuttle, I'm freakish for other reasons.

But what would it be like, to wear my freakishness on the outside, to have it be obvious to the world?

Or is it already?

In Jane Eyre, one of my favorite books, there is a point where Jane realizes that she will never have freedom (liberty, she calls it, since it's a Victorian novel), because of her condition of poverty, plainness, and friendlessness. But at least she may have a different kind of servitude. This is what inspires her to leave her position as a teacher at the horrible Lowood Institution and, instead, become a governess. A new servitude, but one of her own choosing.

I don't know if what my father says is true, or why my father wants me to go live with this wolf-boy, this freak, but suddenly I know I won't run away from it. I know that, like Jane, I will go.

I just have to get something from my father in return.

JULY 19

It's happening. I'm going. Today. Maybe I'm crazy to go along with my father. Yet my life up until now has been so crazy that even craziness seems somehow sane.

I told my father I'd go on one condition. I will go if he goes to rehab.

He was surprisingly agreeable. He said that this experience showed him that he really needed to get help. He'd hit bottom. Still, I called my sister Sarah and got her to agree that she and her (big) boyfriend would pick him up and take him in. They promised not to take no for an answer.

I didn't tell her why, that I was going to live with some stranger. She might try to talk me out of it, and I'm determined to go.

So I'm going.

Which, amazingly, probably isn't the craziest thing I've ever done.

JULY 20

I'm here.

I don't know what I was expecting, a dungeon, maybe, or a torture chamber, my captor in a hood or one of those medieval masks, invisible servants or clocks and candlesticks like in the <u>Beauty and the Beast</u> cartoon.

Maybe.

I got none of it. My new "home" is a normal brownstone in a neighborhood too nice for me to know. No wolf-boy in sight. Instead, when I got here, the door was opened by a man who said his name was Will. He said he was the tutor. He's blind.

I said, "My father has the crazy idea there's a monster here." I glanced over at him, and he looked down.

"No monster, miss," Will said, "My employer is a young man of, I am told, unfortunate appearance. He doesn't go outside because of it. That's all."

Man, he really was a freak.

I asked him if that meant I was free to leave if I changed my mind. Will nodded, but said, "Yes, but my employer struck a deal with your father, I believe—your presence here in exchange for his cooperation in not reporting certain criminal acts which were caught on tape. Which reminds me . . ." He reached into his pocket and took out a bag I knew all too well. "Your drugs, sir?"

WHAT??? I glared at my father. The liar. LIAR! He'd lied about everything. There was no danger, at least, no danger to <u>me</u>. He just wanted me to come here to keep his butt out of jail. LIAR.

Why was I surprised? Everything my father did was a lie.

"He caught me on tape," my father admitted. "Breaking and entering."

<u>Of course.</u>

"The drugs would result in a serious sentence, I believe," Will said.

My father nodded. "Minimum mandatory—fifteen years to life."

Un-freaking-real. "And you agree to this?" I demanded of Will. "My imprisonment?"

He said, "My employer will treat you well—better, probably, than . . ."

I laughed. It was blackmail, that's what it was. And

he was saying the blackmailer would treat me better? And yet, he might be right. I got it. Wolf-boy had seen my father. He knew he was a total scum. He was lonely and thought I'd be safer here than with him. He was probably right—even if he was a blackmailing scumbag. I should have left. But, in some little codependent place in my heart, I didn't want my father to go to jail. I had to do this. I wanted my father to go to rehab.

A new servitude. I have to make the best of this. After all, what's the worst that can happen? You can't be held captive in the middle of New York City. If it got too bad, I could always scream and someone would come.

I hoped.

I gave my father a look that said he owed me, and he was gone. Gone without even saying good-bye. I wanted to cry but I found I couldn't.

Will, seeming to sense how deflated I felt, changed the subject.

"I can tell you've had a hard day, even though it's only ten o'clock. Come. I'll show you to your rooms."

"Rooms? With an s?"

"Yes, miss. They're beautiful rooms. Master

Adrian—the young man I work for—wants you to be happy here."

I laughed. Happy. Sure thing.

I noticed he locked the door with a key. The sound had a terrible finality. What had I done?

Still, I followed him upstairs. I thought I saw a shadow on the staircase, but it might have been my imagination. I didn't want to see Will's "employer," the wolf-boy my captor. Just because I was staying didn't mean we were going to be friends.

He did, indeed, mean rooms.

When we reached my suite, the first thing I noticed were the words Lindy's Room painted in gold on the door. Stalkerish much? The second, once I opened it, was the scent of roses that greeted my nose.

Roses. I thought of Kyle. Poor, stupid Kyle. But, of course, he wasn't there. That night seems so long ago.

I have to admit, I gasped when I entered the room. I found that the scent came from a hundred roses, maybe more, all in vases on every surface.

Will must have sensed my confusion. "My employer grows roses," he said.

"He grew these?"

"He thought you might like them."

I nodded and entered.

I've never been a materialistic person. But then, I've never had much to be materialistic about. Is it wrong that I felt better about the place once I saw that my "rooms" were a whole floor of the house, that they had walls freshly painted a creamy yellow, my favorite color, and wooden floors and crown moldings? A madman wouldn't create such a palace for someone he intended to rape and murder, would he?

But maybe this was his game, like this play I once saw, where this elderly couple kept inviting young girls back to their home using a ruse, when really, they intended to kill them.

But, even if that wasn't it, did he think we were going to have some kind of ROMANCE, like he created this romantic hideaway for me, and I was going to fall in love with him when he'd basically kidnapped me?

What have I gotten myself into? I could always leave, if I don't mind my father being thrown in jail. I shouldn't mind, but sad to say, I do.

Will reassured me that Adrian meant me no harm, that he was just lonely. "Perhaps if you give it a chance, you won't find it so terrible living here."

I checked out the closets, looking for torture

devices, handcuffs, ropes.

Instead, I found clothes, lots of them, what looked like the entire juniors department of Bloomingdale's, all my size, too. How had he known my size? That sounded really stalkerish. And where was I going to wear this stuff? To entertain him? For this romantic fantasy he was having?

But in the next room, I found a surprise I did like. Books! Books from floor to ceiling and not just any musty old books, but books by my favorite authors—by Kurt Vonnegut, Hunter S. Thompson, and Jane Austen. The complete Shakespeare and the complete M. T. Anderson. Even some cool non-fiction titles. There were ladders to reach all the way to the top.

I was a prisoner, but the prison library was excellent.

On one table in the corner, I found an e-reader with a note that said, "In case I forgot anything."

I don't like to think I can be bought, but if I could, this guy definitely knew the currency. Roses and books—I could survive in these rooms forever.

I said, "When I was a kid, I used to like to go to the library because it was safe there. That's how I got to love reading so much."

Will said, "You're safe here."

I laughed. "Safe?"

Will said, "Yes, safe. That story, whatever your father told you, is a lie, but you _will_ be safe here. I wouldn't go along with it if that wasn't the case. Adrian only wants a companion. Live here a year. I'll tutor you, and you can take the state tests, like the home-schooled kids do. At the end of the year, you'll be alive, safe, and a year closer to graduation. Can you say the same if you stay with your father?"

I thought about it and said, "I think I need to be alone now."

Will nodded and left. I walked around a bit more, examining, then I collapsed onto the bed and started to cry—not because I'm trapped here. I came here of my own accord. No, I was crying because I realized Will was probably right. I probably _was_ better off here, here where I am warmer, cleaner, safer than anyplace I've ever been before. Here, there's no risk of being evicted, no risk of evil men pounding my door at night. Some people never have to worry about those things, but I'm not so lucky.

After I finished crying, I spent the next two hours reading a book of Shakespeare's sonnets, comfort food

for my uncomfortable mind. At noon, there was a knock.
I ignored it.

"Excuse me, miss. I have lunch."

It was a woman's voice, a maid, maybe. Not wanting
to be rude, I opened the door.

She had been in the act of leaving a tray. Now, she
held it out. "Hello, you must be Linda. I am Magda."

"You work here?" I asked.

She told me she did, and that if I told her what I
liked for lunch, she'd buy it.

Like Will before her, she assured me I was safe.

I told her thank you, but I wasn't hungry.

An hour later, I found a note under my door. It said:

> Dear Lindy,
> Welcome! Do not be afraid. I hope you
> will be comfortable in your new home.
> Whatever you want, you only have to ask.
> I will see that you get it immediately.
>
> I am looking forward to meeting you
> at dinner tonight. I want you to like me.
> > Sincerely,
> > Adrian King

He did think we were going to have some romance! He thought he could trap me, kidnap me, whatever you called it, buy me, and I'd just go along with it. Well, that was definitely not going to happen. I wrote, "NO!" on the note in big letters and slipped it back under the door.

I went back to sonnets.

An hour later, he was there in person, begging me to come out, talking about the favor (!) he was doing, getting me away from my dad. And again, an hour after that, all apologetic. "I hope we can be friends someday," he said. "I understand if you're . . ."

He didn't finish the sentence. I didn't ask him to.

Still, I wondered what he looked like, what had happened to him. Clearly, Will couldn't tell me, and I hadn't believed my father.

Where were Adrian's parents? Now that I knew Dad's story was a lie, I wondered if any of it was true.

I wondered where my father was too, if he was safe. Much as I hated what he did sometimes, he was still my father.

JULY 22

The past three days, I haven't left my room at all. I'll admit I've been sulking, a luxury I don't get at home. I've talked to no one except Magda, and her only because I don't want to be rude when she brings my meals. Each time, she brings a different rose, a different color, and each time, she points it out to me, saying something like, "If you cut a rose in early morning, it lasts longer," or, "A coral rose symbolizes admiration and friendship." Each time, I thank her and go back to reading. In two days, I've read all of Shakespeare's sonnets and four plays. I'm halfway through a book, <u>The Woman in White</u>, which is over seven hundred pages long. I'm starting to lose touch with reality, but reality sort of sucks.

Since I've always lived in apartments, I'm used to hearing other people's sounds that have nothing to do with me. I've long known that our neighbor, Mr. Estevez, farts every morning at 5:30 and that when the Wolfs (or is it Wolves?) have a fight about money, she threatens to move in with her sister. I know that Angela Lester, who lives downstairs and isn't much older than I am, has two kids, a boy and a girl. When I can hear from her voice that she's had it, I offer to watch them.

This house is a little different, though. I live with these people, but I don't know them. I guess that Will and Magda live in the bedrooms above mine. Sometimes, I hear Spanish-language radio from the left side or NPR from the right. I wouldn't mind discussing NPR with Will. The kitchen and common areas are below me, and I smell cooking smells and hear vacuuming or Magda singing during the day. She has a beautiful voice and loves opera.

Since the first day, Adrian has made no attempt to speak to me. I assume his rooms are either on the top floor of the house or in the basement, not connected with mine. Only late at night do I hear someone pacing the halls below me, someone surfing channels, watching old movies on TV, someone who can't sleep. I'm sure it's him. Adrian.

I suppose I should be happy he's not up here, attacking me in the night, and I AM. Believe me, I am.

But the weird thing is, I'm starting to feel lonely. Yes, I'm getting a lot of reading done, which is great, but I sort of wish Adrian would ask me to come out again. Or Will would offer to tutor me. I might say yes this time. I miss talking to people.

Adrian is downstairs right now. I can hear the television go on and the channels being changed. He settles on a movie, <u>Forrest Gump</u>. I hear Robin Wright yelling "Run, Forrest!"

He obviously has decent taste in movies. I mean, most guys my age, unsupervised, would be watching porn or, at least, something with lots of explosions.

Maybe I'll watch it too. Up here in my room.

Good-night for now.

July 23

I had the strangest dream.

I fell asleep early and woke to hear a clock striking midnight. Funny, I'd heard no clock before. I couldn't get back to sleep, so I went to find my book.

That's when I saw the bird. I'm pretty sure it was a crow, but it sat on the top of my doorframe, like the raven in Edgar Allan Poe's poem "The Raven," and like that raven, it was tap-tap-tapping.

"What?" I said.

Then, the crow transformed into a woman, and she began singing in a strange, almost unearthly way, operatic, yet without words or maybe with strange, garbled words, and in a tune that was equally mangled. She sounded almost like a theremin, this weird instrument they use in old horror movies.

The weird thing was, I recognized her. It was Kendra, from my school, that girl who'd been talking to Kyle the last day I saw him.

She was dressed all in white, a flowing dress that surrounded her like a Greek goddess's robes. She raised her hand, beckoning to me to follow her.

I did. She left the room. I don't remember the door opening but I followed, as if by magic, out of the room and down a staircase to the second floor. This, I knew, was the floor I'd seen when I came in, the living area of the house. I hadn't looked around much. Now I did.

The room was beautiful, with shiny wooden floors and high ceilings, but it barely looked lived in. No mess, for sure, but nothing personal, either—no photographs, no books, magazines, or art, even on the walls, as if it had been put together hastily, more like a decorator's model than a real home.

Kendra beckoned to me from the window, where she had gone seemingly without walking. I obeyed and stood by it, wanting to drink in the full moon. When I was little, I always imagined the moon following me down the street. Now, in someplace so lonely and different, it comforted me to see it still.

When I reached the window, I stepped back.

I had been wrong to believe no one was awake. Someone was, and he was out in the greenhouse. My own room had no window that overlooked it, but now that I saw it, I gasped.

Hundreds of roses—red, yellow, pink, coral, white, even purple—roses climbing on trellises to the ceiling, roses in pots on the ground, lining the walls as hedges, hanging like a bridal veil. This, too, persuaded me that I was in a dream. Who had ever seen so many roses in one place?

In the middle of the greenhouse, a shadow moved.

Was it him? Adrian?

I had been avoiding him all these days. Now, I really wanted to see him, but just <u>see</u> him, not talk to him. Part of the reason I'd been avoiding him, I realized, was not just fear of what he might do to me, but fear of myself. I was afraid he'd be hideous and, more than that, I feared my reaction to him. I've always prided myself on being kind, being understanding. But my father had called Adrian a monster, my father, who'd seen all kinds of ugliness. What if I cringed when I saw him? What if I cried? What if, like Esmeralda in <u>The Hunchback of Notre-Dame</u>, I found I simply couldn't look at him at all? I didn't want to be shallow, cruel. I wanted to be better than the students at Tuttle, who'd looked down on me because I didn't have the right clothes, the right family, the right money. What if I wasn't?

Now, though, maybe I could see him without him seeing me. The living room was dark, the greenhouse well lit. I stepped forward.

He had been partially hidden by the roses, but now, as if he knew I was watching, he came into view. He was pacing, I realized, and when he stepped out from behind the vines, I could see his face.

I gasped. My father hadn't been wrong or crazy or strung out. Adrian was a monster. He looked like no one I'd seen outside a movie. At first, I could only see his body. He was tall, tall and slim, and if I'd seen him from the back, I'd have assumed he was handsome, but as soon as his face became visible from the shadows, I knew he wasn't.

Blond hair—fur—covered every inch of his face and what I could see of him. His hands had claws, but his face was weirder. The nose, long and wolflike, sloped downward to a mouth with white, fanged teeth. The hair on his head had been brushed to shield as much of his face as possible, but it did little good. It was blond and long and from beneath it, I could see the most beautiful wide, blue eyes. They seemed to glow, somehow, from the darkness. They seemed to meet mine.

348

I realized he was looking at me. Could he see me staring? Of course not. Yet those blue eyes—oddly familiar—seemed to plead with me.

Again, I backed away. I stumbled across the dark room, half expecting footsteps to pursue me. None came. I didn't see Kendra again, in human or bird form. Not caring how much noise I made, I stumble-ran upstairs, slammed and locked my door. I staggered to bed. Only then did I realize I was crying. Not for me, not for me, for him. I wanted to hate, not pity Adrian, yet how could I not pity someone who looked like him, someone so pathetic and twisted and ruined? What accident could cause such a thing? No accident, other than an accident of birth. What would it be like to be this way, to have people run from you?

And yet, his roses were so beautiful. He understands beauty.

I had seen him. I could look at him now, I thought, without cringing. Part of me still hated him, wanted to hate him for making me pity him. Before, I could live in the world, not knowing that someone like Adrian existed, and not somewhere far off, not like the cleft-palate babies you see in magazines, the blind beggars in Slumdog Millionaire, but really, in my own neighborhood.

I couldn't ignore him. I pictured the pleading look in those eyes. I had to take pity on him.

Still, I cried, I cried for him until I fell asleep.

Or had I always been asleep? I was dreaming wasn't I? I looked up and saw Kendra, still standing there, still singing weirdly. Then, her mixed-up words became real ones. She sang:

> Now, his name means darkness
> But once, it meant beauty.
> His face is hideous as a thorn
> But within, he is a rose, maybe.
> Go to him.
> Go to him.

That was the last thing I remembered before I fell asleep for real. When I woke next, it was midday. No sign of Kendra, but my room was filled with roses of every color.

The fact is, I'm stuck here, whether it's because my father needs me to be or because I need to run away from my life, I'm here, alone. Adrian is stuck here too, lonely, ugly, so desperate for companionship he was willing to resort to blackmail to get it. But I understand

now. I understand, and it would be cruel for me to
ignore him.

I understand, and I know that, tonight, I will do as
Dream Kendra said.

I will go to him.

JULY 24

All day, I sat on my bed and tried to read, but I was restless, excited, I realized, at the thought of meeting Adrian. I'd sworn to stay in my room forever, but when it came down to it, it was just too difficult. I've never been good at sulking. When I was a kid, if I argued with a friend or one of my sisters, I'd pledge never to speak to her again. I usually lasted an hour, maybe less.

And, of course, I always forgave my dad, too.

It was the same here. If I knew I'd be safe, I'd give the guy a chance, just to have someone to talk to.

So when Magda came to bring me my oatmeal, I stopped her.

"What's he like? Why does he want me here?"

She looked a little surprised, then shrugged and said, "He is lonely. That is all."

I nodded and took the oatmeal. It was as I thought, not a murderer or rapist, just a freakish, friendless boy, a lonely soul. Like me.

"And you . . . like him?" I asked Magda.

She said she did.

It makes sense. After all, isn't it always the handsome, outgoing, "normal" guys who turn out to be dangerous wack jobs? Every time they arrest a guy for killing tons of women, his neighbors always say they never suspected. That he was perfectly normal.

Wouldn't it then follow that deformed, reclusive freaks are actually safer than normal people?

Well, it made sense in my head.

I waited for nightfall. After everyone was asleep, I picked up the dinner dishes and brought them downstairs to the kitchen, just to have an excuse to be there. I made noise so he'd know I was up. I heard him in the living room, watching television. I listened at the door. It was some sporting event that must have happened hours earlier. Still, it comforted me that he was watching sports, not some History Channel special about virgin sacrifice. Finally, after a minute, I went in.

His back was to me. He said, "I'm here. I want you to know so you won't freak."

<u>Freak.</u> Even I cringed at the word, but I stepped toward him.

For one moment, everything froze. Me, standing there, the baseball game on television, Adrian, staring ahead but—I now knew—not really paying attention to it. The room was shadowy-dark, and I could only see the back of his head. It was so normal.

Then, he turned to meet my eyes.

At close range, in the dim light, I found I was more fascinated than repulsed by Adrian's face. I stared at the counterclockwise whorls of fur at the edges of his nose, the eyes human, but wider set than my own. On its own merits, his face wasn't ugly, wasn't repellant at all. On its own merits, Adrian's face had an almost cat-like beauty.

It was just . . . he was supposed to be human.

He saw me staring and looked down. "Please. I won't hurt you. I know I look this way, but I'm not . . . please. I won't hurt you, Lindy."

I started babbling, trying to cover my faux pas of staring at him with the greater faux pas of too much talk, too many stupid things I don't want to remember. He started trying to change the subject, talking about the dinner we'd eaten, what a good cook Magda was, normal stuff, anything to shut me up. He <u>sounded</u> perfectly normal.

Which made me feel sorrier for him.

"When I used to live with my father," Adrian said,

still talking about the food, "he never wanted Magda to make Latin dishes. She just made regular stuff then, meat and potatoes. But when he left us here, I didn't really much care what I ate, so she started making this stuff."

He meant his father. His father had left him. I said, "What do you mean he left you here? Where's your father now?"

He looked away, as if he knew he'd said too much, but he said he lived with Magda and Will, that Will was his tutor. I could tell he was trying to keep it very normal, trying not to upset me. It was all so abnormal, though. But then, what in my life wasn't?

"Tutor?" I asked, just to keep the conversation as normal as he wanted it.

"A teacher, really, I guess. Since I can't go to school because . . . anyway, he homeschools me."

And I wondered. "How old are you?"

"Sixteen. Same as you."

Sixteen. My father had said he was a teenager, but he was all alone. Of course, I was alone too. "Where are your parents?" I asked. He knew I was just as abandoned as he was.

He didn't say it, though. Instead, he said, "My

mother left a long time ago. And my father . . . well, he couldn't handle that I looked like this. He's into normalcy."

My mind flooded with questions. Had he always looked this way? Was his father cruel to him? Did he treat him like a freak, like in <u>The Phantom of the Opera</u>? The house, all of it, was beautiful, but how could he live here, how could he grow up with no nurturing? Of course, my father didn't exactly nurture me either, but at least I could try to live a normal life. Just thinking about him, trapped here, brought tears to my eyes. Now, it was I who looked away.

"Do you miss him?" I asked, still not looking. "Your father?"

He shook his head. "I try not to. I mean, you shouldn't miss people who don't miss you, right?"

I nodded, and said something about my own father, so he'd know I understood, even though I couldn't, not really, not the <u>level</u> of it. We were the same, motherless, fatherless, both freaks in our own way. We were the same. I was here because I was meant to be.

Adrian was the one who changed the subject away from our mutual patheticness. He asked if I wanted Will to tutor me, too. I heard myself saying yes. I felt myself meaning it. I feel like, maybe, I was meant to be here, meant to help this poor guy.

He told me they were reading Shakespeare's sonnets. Then, he invited me to see his rose garden.

"I'd like that." I said I would meet him there tomorrow.

And after a few more stupid statements on my part, a few more awkward ones on his, I started up to bed.

It has begun.

Only when I reached my room did I think to ask what else they were studying, what math, what social studies. Funny how Adrian had homed in on reading, on literature, as if he knew it was what I loved. Does he have Magda spying on me, to know I read all day? Crazy. I went back downstairs but stopped.

As I approached the living room, I heard a voice, quietly whooping. Through the door, I could see someone, a boy my own age, more human than not, doing a wild victory dance around the room.

I smiled. It could wait.

JULY 25

I woke at three, and at four, and then again at five.
Each time, I thought I heard noises downstairs. Each
time, I tried to go back to sleep. Finally, at six, I gave
up and took out Shakespeare's sonnets. I flipped to
my favorite, "Sonnet 54." I chose it in honor of the roses,
and of the day.

> O! how much more doth beauty
> beauteous seem
> By that sweet ornament which truth
> doth give!
> The rose looks fair, but fairer we it deem
> For that sweet odour, which doth in it live.
> The canker blooms have full as deep
> a dye
> As the perfumed tincture of the roses,
> Hang on such thorns, and play as
> wantonly
> When summer's breath their masked
> buds discloses:

But, for their virtue only is their show,
They live unwoo'd, and unrespected
fade;
Die to themselves. Sweet roses do not so;
Of their sweet deaths are sweetest
odours made:

> And so of you, beauteous and lovely
> youth,
> When that shall fade, my verse
> distills your truth.

I know some people would call it a cliché, reading Shakespeare's sonnets. A lot of my Tuttle classmates complained about reading all that old stuff, but I loved feeling the connection to Shakespeare, to someone who lived hundreds of years ago but who was still a real man, a man who sniffed roses and thought about beauty. Sometimes, it's like I know Shakespeare better than I know anyone.

At seven, Magda brought me breakfast, and at eight, I fixed my hair and got dressed, and at nine, exactly, I went downstairs to the greenhouse.

Adrian had obviously prepared for me. Vivaldi's <u>The Four Seasons</u> was playing on the speakers, and he'd pulled a table and three chairs out to the greenhouse. There was even a vase of roses on the table. He seemed nervous. At least, he was talking kind of fast, but he showed me each variety of rose in the greenhouse, describing the different types, floribunda, hybrid tea roses, even one he said was called the "Little Linda."

"Do all your roses have names?" I asked him. Meaning, had he named a rose after me? That was ... weird.

But it turned out to be okay. He explained that when the horticulturalists develop a new rose variety, they name it, and actually, that sounded right. I think I read that somewhere before. The rose called "Little Linda" was tiny—Adrian called it a miniature—and yellow, my favorite color.

Standing there, inhaling the glorious scent of all those roses, my mind went immediately to Kyle and that night at the dance. Poor, stupid, probably drug-addicted Kyle. If I just closed my eyes, I could pretend he was there. Once, when I accidentally brushed up against Adrian's arm, I was imagining he was Kyle, and I felt a shock of electricity all through my body. If only he was Kyle.

But no. Kyle isn't what I want, isn't what I <u>should</u>

want. If I'm honest with myself—and I try to be—the main thing Kyle had going for him was looks. Maybe Adrian will have everything else. Maybe we can be friends.

I could use a friend, actually, and by the looks of it, so could he.

So I admired each rose, which wasn't hard. They were as beautiful as their owner was strange. And it was flattering to have someone try so hard to impress me. No one had ever cared before.

Adrian offered to cut some of the roses for me, but I said, "Maybe I'll come back to see them," and then, I made myself take a long look at his face and was struck, once again, by his beautiful, catlike eyes. Hadn't Kyle's been the same blue? Maybe. But that was where the resemblance ended.

Then, Will showed up. Adrian told him I was there, and he acted all happy and announced we'd be reading Shakespeare's "Sonnet 54."

!!!!!

"No way! I was just reading that this morning," I said.

Will asked Adrian to read it aloud, and it was beautiful. He read beautifully, and when we discussed the sonnet, Adrian seemed to understand it better than most of the kids in my class. Okay, his understanding was a little surface-y, like someone who'd looked the poem up on Wikipedia or something. But that was way more than I was used to. I mean, he actually <u>cared</u>.

I said, "I love these old sonnets."

"Why?" he asked. "I mean, not that I don't. I was just wondering why <u>you</u> love them?"

I laughed. "It's okay if you don't love them. At my school, people kind of thought I was a mutant because I loved every moldy old poem we read."

God, why did I keep saying stuff like "mutant"? But I kept going. "I love Shakespeare, the ancient Greeks like <u>The Iliad</u> and <u>The Odyssey</u>, Chaucer, even Thomas Malory. But the people in my class, they wanted to analyze song lyrics or something."

He didn't reply, but I talk when I get nervous, so I kept going. On and on and on and on, saying pretentious stuff like, "I think that it's not really possible to understand the new things without seeing their origins. I mean, there would have been no <u>Once and Future King</u> if Malory hadn't written <u>Le Morte d'Arthur</u>, and there would be no song lyrics if we hadn't first read Shakespeare's sonnets. You know?"

Clearly, he didn't know. He was staring at me, that weird, fixed stare I often got from classmates, like I might possibly have gone off the deep end, babbling about my favorite subject. Literally, no one got me unless they were a 70-year-old English teacher.

"I'm sorry," I said. "I know I get carried away." I vowed not to tell him about how Shakespeare was like a personal friend of mine.

He shook his head. "No. No, not at all. Man, that is just so . . . I never thought of it that way. Wow. I mean, wow! Hearing you talk about it like that, it makes me want to read all that stuff. What was that last one you said, <u>Le Morte d'Arthur</u>? Is that like King Arthur? I'm really into heroes."

"Me too!" I found I could look at him now, without even thinking about it. "I have Tennyson's <u>Idylls of the King</u> in my room. They're poems about Arthur. Epic poems." I tried not to sigh a little when I said "epic." I glanced at Will. "Maybe we could read them sometime, Will?"

Will said, "Don't look at me. I'm just furniture."

Adrian laughed and said, "Please, Will. It would be . . . epic."

And he wasn't joking.

We moved on to math then, in which Adrian was really smart, and then history. He had some decent thoughts on the French and Indian War, a war teachers usually brush over. Apparently, he and Will had actually <u>discussed it</u> in depth.

By the time we went upstairs to have lunch, I was thinking this might not actually suck as bad as I thought it would.

———

JULY 26

Yesterday's entry was interrupted by Adrian, who knocked on my door, first off, to ask me if I was having dinner with them (I was) and secondly to make, he said, a confession.

"A confession?" I asked, thinking, Okay, this is the part where he tells me he actually _does_ intend to sell me on the black market after all.

But he said, "I don't know squat about poetry."

I laughed and said, "Sure you do. You had a lot to say about sonnet fifty-four."

He said, "I cheated. I looked it up. Will told me ahead of time what we were going to do, and I studied. I didn't want to look stupid in front of you."

Wikipedia. Just as I thought. Playing with a girl's feelings about poetry.

He said, "Stupid and ugly is a deadly combination."

Aaaaannnnd . . . I forgave him. I said, "You're not stupid. You're great at math—can't fake that. And you had a lot to say about the French and Indian War." I cringed, realizing I hadn't contradicted his assertion that he was ugly. I couldn't. He would know I was lying.

He said, "Ah, well... Will and I read <u>The Last of the Mohicans</u>."

I smiled. "See, I haven't read that."

"The important thing is," he said, "I lied about Shakespeare. Yes, I lied because you have to try harder when you look like a supervillain, but I don't want to lie to you. I want to be friends, which requires total and complete honesty. Usually, I'm one of those people you talked about, the people who don't understand why we read the moldy old stuff."

So did he come to insult my taste? But then he added, "Until now. Hearing you talking about Shakespeare and all those other writers really made me want to read them."

I still didn't know if he was making fun of me or what, but then he said, "Will you teach me about poetry?"

That was all I needed, all I needed to start babbling on about every poem I'd ever read in my entire life. If you think I didn't recite parts of "The Love Song of J. Alfred Prufrock," you don't know me very well. And then, I started on "Dover Beach," and he listened like he was actually you know, <u>listening</u>.

I got to the last stanza, the part that goes,

> Ah, love, let us be true
> To one another! for the world, which seems
> To lie before us like a land of dreams,
> So various, so beautiful, so new,
> Hath really neither joy, nor love, nor light,
> Nor certitude, nor peace, nor help for pain;
> And we are here as on a darkling plain
> Swept with confused alarms of struggle and flight,
> Where ignorant armies clash by night.

He got really excited. "Hey, I know that poem," he said. "Wasn't that in <u>Fahrenheit 451</u>?"

I remembered that yes, it had been. The part where the fireman, Guy Montag, reads poetry to his wife and her friends, to show them why books shouldn't be burned.

"That book was awesome," he said. "It was the first book I ever really loved, and it started me reading all this other science fiction, like Asimov and Toffler."

Now, science fiction is the one genre that totally makes my eyes glaze over, but it was cool that he read, and I actually liked Fahrenheit 451. I told him so.

Which led to another fifteen minutes of talking about that.

And, at the end of it, I realized I'd been standing there with him for almost an hour and I hadn't once thought about how weird looking he was, hadn't once thought about how I was a prisoner here. Hadn't thought about my father or school.

And then, Magda called us for dinner and Adrian said he would read Shakespeare and he would read Tennyson's Idylls of the King and anything else I wanted him to read, if I would just forgive him for his lie, and loan him the books, which he was pretty sure I had.

I gave him Idylls of the King and by this morning he'd already read "The Coming of Arthur," "Gareth and Lynette," and all the way to "Merlin and Vivien." He confessed he'd stayed up most of the night to read them. Before Will came, we sat and read "Lancelot and Elaine" together, and I swear I thought I saw him wipe a tear from his eye when Elaine's body was borne down the Thames past Camelot, but I pretended not to notice.

But Will, who showed up just then, did notice. He

was all, "Was that sniffling I just heard? Are you <u>cry-ing</u> Adrian?"

Adrian laughed at that and said Will's supersonic blind-person hearing was obviously failing him and that he was <u>not</u> crying. I assured Will that it had been me and told him what we'd been reading.

So then, Will calls Adrian a heartless beast for not crying over one of the most touching passages in English lit.

I sort of froze at the word <u>beast</u>, but Adrian laughed and said, "Poetry's for sissies!"

Adrian was an unusual guy in more ways than just his appearance.

I want to ask him more about himself, about what it's like to be like he is, but I guess it would be too embarrassing. There are plenty of things I don't want him to ask me about either. So it was fine just to talk about poetry.

September 1

It's been a few weeks since I've written, mostly because I've been so busy <u>reading</u> to keep up with Adrian. Also, watching baseball, because it turns out he's a major Yankees fan and so am I.

Between watching the games and discussing the Yanks' chances at the pennant, we have sort of a running game of Can You Top This? where our childhoods are concerned.

It went like this:

Me: Did you ever <u>play</u> baseball?

Him: Nah, my dad wasn't much for throwing a ball. He offered to have the maid practice with me, but it didn't seem like real baseball that way.

Me: Understood.

Him: We did watch a game on TV . . . once. But we never went to a game because, you know, the shrieking mobs with pitchforks would have made things uncomfortable.

Me: (nervous laugh, but tucking away the information that he'd always looked like this) Aren't you going to ask me if my dad took me to any ball games?

Him: Sorry. I thought it might be a sensitive subject. He didn't exactly seem like the type of guy who'd put buying peanuts and Cracker Jacks high on his priority list.

Me: It's true. Most of our Cracker Jack budget has been going for <u>actual</u> crack lately. But when I was little, we used to go.

And then, I stopped joking and told him about how it was, back when my mom was alive. We were a normal family, my two sisters and I. Mom was a paralegal. Dad was an English teacher at Tuttle, which is how I got so interested in poetry and stuff like that. But then, when my mom died, he sort of freaked out, started doing drugs. Prescription stuff first, to help him sleep, but then, it was easier to get the other stuff. He got fired from Tuttle. My sister Sarah, who'd been going there, had to drop out and go to public school. She never forgave him. But when I got old enough to go to middle school myself, she told me we should call them, give them a guilt trip about firing my dad (even though, really we knew they'd had no choice), get them to give me a scholarship. After all, I had the grades for it. That's how I started going to Tuttle.

"Did you like it?" Adrian asked, and that set off a whole other train of thought because, no, I hadn't liked it. I'd hated it. I mean, yes, I'd been physically safe at Tuttle, unlike at my old school or even at home, but I hated going someplace where everyone was rich and beautiful and treated me like I was vaguely—if I'm honest here, not even vaguely—dirty compared to them just because I was poor. The fact is, here, in this apartment, where I'm being held <u>prisoner</u>, I'm actually happier than I've been in a long time, and these people— this freakish boy, blind man, and their maid—are the closest I've had to a real family since my mother died. We have dinner together. And yesterday, Magda taught Adrian and me to make flan for dessert. Will and I do yoga every morning, and we have a baseball pool going. For the first time in my life, I feel like I'm part of some- thing. Maybe it's Stockholm syndrome, but if so, I'm moving to Stockholm.

Finally I said, "No, I didn't really like it. I mean, it was a good education, but the people there were snobs."

"I'm sorry," he said.

"What are you sorry about? They'd have been just as snobby to you."

<u>More</u> snobby I was thinking. He looked thoughtful,

and for a second, I was worried I'd hurt his feelings.

But then he said, "Well, that's obvious. Good thing neither of us have to go there, right?"

And I agreed that it was a good thing, then changed the subject back to baseball. Fortunately, we had a lot to talk about.

OCTOBER 23

Last year, when Kyle Kingsbury gave me that rose at the dance, I thought that whenever I smelled roses, I would think of him.

I was wrong.

It's fall now. It has been three months since I came to live with Adrian, three months, studying every day in his rose garden. Now, the scent of roses has become hopelessly, irrevocably associated with Adrian. Sometimes I think I've become used to it, and I ask him if we can study someplace else for a day so the next day, I can experience it anew.

It's hard for me to believe I missed the beginning of school. I wonder if people have even noticed I'm gone. If they have, they probably just think I went back to my old school. I don't miss Tuttle, where I was so invisible.

Other Things I Don't Miss
—Guys lurking on our doorstep
—Weird noises outside at night
—My dad not coming home for days or nights on end

—Being alone and frightened

Sometimes I do worry about my father. I don't know if he actually went to rehab. Chances are, he didn't. But I push that fear back. After all, he ditched me here. I've at least earned the right not to obsess over him.

Now, my life has routine. Here's my schedule.

6:30 a.m. Wake up

6:45 a.m. Yoga with Will

7:45 a.m. Shower and dress

8:30 a.m. Breakfast

9–2:00 School with Adrian and Will

2–5:00 Reading/quiet time (usually with Adrian)

5:00 p.m. Adrian and I help Magda with dinner

6:00 p.m. Dinner

7:00 p.m. More time with Adrian

Through the windows, I can see the leaves hanging red and orange on the trees, then falling. (This neighborhood, what I can see of it, is beautiful, with tree-lined streets, unlike what I was used to.) I wished we could go out and play in them.

I mentioned this to Adrian.

"I'm sorry," he said. "I know I wrecked your life."

This wasn't what I meant. I said, "No, no you didn't. Not really. I understand."

"Understand what?"

"What it's like to be lonely, to be alone. I've been alone all my life, even if there were other people around."

"You ever see an animal in a cage?" he asked. "Once, I saw a tiger at the zoo. He had this tiny area, and all day long, he'd walk from left to right, sit down, stand up, walk back, then front, and repeat. It was really sad, because he was supposed to be a TIGER, and he didn't even have the freedom of a housecat."

"That's weird."

"That's how I feel sometimes, like that tiger."

I nodded, watching him. Adrian has the grace of a tiger, and the power. I get the feeling he could really hurt someone if he wanted, but with me, he's like a kitten. I said, "Me too. All my life, I felt exactly the same way. I like being here with you. I only wish we could go someplace, not be inside this house all the time."

"I'd like that too. I know it's not fair of me . . ." He stared out at the flowers in the greenhouse. "I keep you here, like one of my roses. You should be able to go out places."

"Not just that. I wish you could go out too, go to the park, enjoy the fall leaves."

"I wish. It's just . . ."

"I know. You're worried someone will see you."

He shook his head. "Not that. Mostly, I'm afraid you'll leave."

"I won't."

"How can you say that? I'd leave if I were you."

"You're not me. I could leave if I wanted to, Adrian. You think I couldn't find a way out if I wanted?"

He looked doubtful, but then he glanced around. He must have realized I was right. There were no bars on the windows. When I'd first come, I'd assumed I was locked inside, but now, I realized the only things standing between me and the door at night were a blind man, an old woman, and Adrian himself. I knew none of them would ever hurt me. I knew I could leave. It was my own decision to stay.

"So why do you stay?" he asked.

"I don't know. I guess . . . I've never had a friend like you. Maybe I've never had a friend, a good friend. I'm happy here, happier than I've ever been. I feel safe for the first time in my life."

I knew my words—the word _friend_—were crushing him. He didn't think of me as a friend. I knew from the many times I'd seen him gazing at me. I knew it from the times our arms brushed over our books and I felt electricity in the air. I knew he thought of me as much more than a friend. Adrian loves me, and I know it.

And I know it because I feel the same way about him.

I love him.

It's crazy, right? I love him. I love that he cares about poetry. I love how funny he is. I love that I feel safe with him. Yet, I can't be _in_ love with him.

Anyone might think it's his looks that are standing in the way. But I got past his looks long ago, in a few days. I can see into his soul, and it is <u>beautiful</u>. The real problem is, Adrian needs me too much. And I can't be with someone who needs me, not anymore. I mean, I know he doesn't want me to be a nursemaid or anything, but if I was with him, I'd be trapped in this house, unable to have a normal life . . . just like I'm trapped with my father.

If this were a fairy tale, there would be a curse on him, and I'd have to kiss him or marry him or say I love you to break the curse. But this is reality, and there's no such thing as magic, and no matter what happens, he will be him, and I will be me. And the world will be the world. Am I using his neediness as an excuse not to love him, because I really am icked out by his looks, really don't want to love a freak? No, that's not it. I _do_ love him, despite or maybe <u>because of</u> his looks, but I can't do this. I can't. I can't spend my whole childhood saddled with my father, then spend my whole adult life saddled with someone else needy. I know it's not his fault. He just wants someone to be with. It just can't be me.

So I love him, but I'll never tell him.

I said, "Maybe, one day, we'll be able to go, to play in the leaves."

OCTOBER 25

This morning, when I went out to the greenhouse to study, I found a surprise.

Leaves. Hundreds, thousands, maybe millions of them, brown and yellow and red and orange, in bright piles on the concrete floor. Some were so high they almost covered the rosebushes.

I stood, openmouthed, until I heard footsteps, then turned to see Adrian standing there.

"How did you do this?" I asked him.

"It wasn't easy. I was up half the night, in the street, with a flashlight and a rake, gathering them. I couldn't even see which ones were pretty. I just took them all. Then, I brought them in here and sorted out the best ones for you."

I looked back at them. They were even more vivid than the leaves on the trees.

"They're perfect," I said.

"You were right before. I don't want to go outside. I don't . . . I can't let people see me. It would be too embarrassing."

I said, "You're not that bad."

He shook his head. "I can't take the chance. What if someone took pictures, posted them online ... made fun of me? What if everyone came to stare at the freak?"

I nodded, understanding. I wanted to say the world wasn't like that, but I knew the world. I lived here too.

"But I would do anything for you, Lindy, anything else, at least. If you want leaves or flowers or . . . diamonds, I'll get them for you."

He seemed so earnest, and it made me sad because I knew I couldn't make him happy the way he wanted, so I changed the subject. I ran through the leaves, then stooped to pick some up and threw them at him. Then, I collapsed in one of the piles.

He followed and lay down next to me, but gently so as not to hurt me. Adrian is always a gentleman.

"I think we should take the day off from school," he said, "to play in the leaves."

"Like a snow day," I agreed.

So we did. We ran and jumped in the piles and threw the leaves at each other (and at Will when he came down, suggesting we start with geometry), then raked them all back up and started over again.

It may have been the most fun I've ever had.

NOVEMBER 29

It's November, after Thanksgiving. Christmas season.

When I was a little girl, when my mother was still alive, Christmas was a lot of fun. We did all the usual corny stuff, baking cookies and skating at Rockefeller Center, got pictures on Santa's lap.

Then, she died, suddenly the day after Thanksgiving. Christmas died with her.

Since then, what I do for Christmas is read.

When I was little, my sisters used to read me <u>The Night Before Christmas</u> and <u>How the Grinch Stole Christmas!</u> Then, <u>The Best Christmas Pageant Ever</u>, followed by all Laura Ingalls Wilder's books. I loved reading what the Ingalls girls got for Christmas, even if it was only a stick of candy. My favorite was <u>On the Banks of Plum Creek</u>, when Laura and her sisters got the presents off the tree at church.

When I was ten, my teacher gave me <u>Little Women</u>, and two years later, I found Dickens's <u>A Christmas Carol</u>. Laura and the March girls and Ebeneezer Scrooge, that's who I spent Christmas with.

I asked Adrian if he could get me these books. "We could read them aloud together," I said, "get in the holiday spirit."

"That's all you want to do for Christmas? READ?"

"I like reading and we're stuck in the house anyway." I was sorry I'd said that. "And I LIKE READING. Don't you have any holiday traditions?"

"Sure," he said. "I like watching It's a Wonderful Life as much as the next person."

"I do that, too," I said. "Let's definitely watch that."

He nodded. "Definitely. But isn't there ANYTHING else you want to do? I have sort of an unlimited budget, thanks to my dad's guilty conscience. And I really want to make Christmas nice for you, for us."

I thought about it, all the things other people had done that I wished I could do. Riding in a one-horse open sleigh sounded like a bit much to ask, so I said, "We could make cookies, maybe even a gingerbread house. I bet Magda could help us with that. And ... we could get a tree."

It probably would sound stupid to most people, but I really wanted a tree. We hadn't had one since I was little, but I always saw them in people's windows, especially near school, all decorated and with lights and stars on top. Every year, I went to Rockefeller Center and the department stores and just gazed at the beautiful decorated trees. I knew exactly the kind I wanted, with lots of different little ornaments, each with special meaning. I hoped to have a tree like that someday, with my family.

Adrian smiled then. "We have a winner. I'm way ahead of you."

He gestured me out toward the greenhouse. When I got there, I saw a tree, a live pine tree in a pot. It was so tall it almost scraped the ceiling.

"I wanted a real one," he said, "a live one that wouldn't have to die ever. If you want it up in the living room, we could probably move it out. I thought the light was better here."

"It's beautiful." I inhaled the scent of pine, now mixing with the roses. "Did you get decorations too?" I hoped he hadn't. I wanted to choose them myself.

He shook his head. "I wanted you to pick. White lights or colored? Glass balls or little toys and stuff? A star at the top or an angel?"

"Oh, an angel," I said, "with blond hair, like my mother." Then, I realized I should ask what he liked too. "What did you used to have, with your father?"

He said, "We haven't had a tree since my mother left."

Of course he hadn't. It was like we were two halves of an oyster shell, and when you put us together, it hid the gray gunk inside.

So we decided to choose together. We spent the afternoon on Macy's website, choosing each ornament, garland, and string of lights, including a yellow-haired angel for the top.

And then, today, Magda went and got it all. The four of us decorated the tree together (Will helped with the lights), like a real family, maybe better than most real families, singing Christmas carols and having hot chocolate. Magda made a special soup she said they ate at Christmas in her country.

We chose white lights because we both agreed we wanted them to look like the stars. Adrian got them to blink and twinkle. When we finished everything, we all stared up at the tree, silhouetted against the sky.

Well, all except Will. He said, "It's beautiful. The beauty, it brings tears to my eyes," and he gave a big fake sniff.

We all laughed, and that's when I noticed the snow was falling outside. The first snow of the year settled on top of the greenhouse windows while we stayed in, warm and dry, watching it.

It _was_ beautiful. In fact, I'm looking at the tree now, as I write this.

It still is.

December 15

Adrian suggested that, since it was winter break for New York schools, we too should take a break from studying and do holiday stuff. Here are some of the things we did.

<u>Made a gingerbread house</u>: I found instructions on the internet. Adrian wanted to make a gingerbread brownstone, but I thought that might be too hard. I told him we should make a regular house this year. Then, next year, we could do something more advanced.

He looked at me, surprised. "Will you still be here next year?"

I remembered then what Will had said when I first came. "Live here a year." It had implied I could, or would, leave after that. But I hadn't thought of it since then. Still, maybe they hadn't planned on my staying any longer.

"Do you want me to be here next year?" I asked.

He met my eyes with an intensity I'd never seen before, then looked down. "I want you to stay forever, Lindy, but I want you to be happy."

"I am happy," I told him, and I meant it. But would I always be happy? Can I be happy here alone with Adrian, no school, no college, no life? Was it enough for me forever? No. Of course not. But he was smiling and it's Christmas, so I didn't say it. I was happy, am happy now, and I want Adrian to be happy too. There would be enough time for sadness and separation later.

I changed the subject. "So, a regular gingerbread house, but we need to get a <u>lot</u> of candy."

Adrian agreed. "In fact," he said, "I was thinking you could do most of the baking and I could actually be <u>in charge</u> of candy."

"You think so?" I asked.

"I do," he said. "You're sweet enough."

<u>Watched a bunch of hokey Christmas movies:</u> Specifically, we've watched <u>Elf</u>, <u>A Christmas Story</u>, <u>Home Alone</u>, <u>A Christmas Carol</u>, <u>Scrooged</u>, and of course, <u>It's a Wonderful Life</u>.

"Wow," he said when <u>It's a Wonderful Life</u> was over. "That was great."

"You act like you've never seen it before," I said.

"Well, I might have exaggerated how many times I've seen it. I saw it once, when I was twelve, but I get it more now. It makes me wonder how the world would be different if I'd never been born."

I thought about that. I knew my father would be dead many times over without me, which gave me more than a twinge of guilt over the fun I was having without him right now. I wondered where he was, if he was okay. Stupid, right?

"Makes me want to do something nice for someone," Adrian said.

"Me too," I said.

I told him how, last year, I bought some toys and things for these kids in my building, the Lesters, because I knew their mom couldn't afford presents.

He was impressed. "Could _you_ afford presents?" he asked.

"Not really. But I saved up and bought them some cars and teddy bears and left them on the doorstep."

"That was really nice of you," Adrian said. "Maybe we should do it again."

Truth be told, I'd mentioned it hoping he'd suggest it. Last year, I'd only been able to get small toys with money squirreled away from my paycheck. Maybe together, we could do more this year.

So I told him about them, the boy, Kenneth, and the girl, Kiana, funny and creative, how their mom was sort of a friend of mine when we had time for it. Adrian and I spent the rest of the afternoon talking about what type of gifts to buy. Adrian thought we should get them things to play with together, but I pointed out that, when you're poor, sometimes it's really important to have something all your own. Finally, we decided to do both: art supplies and LEGOs they could share, and then a baby doll for Kiana and Tonka trucks for Kenneth.

"Should we sneak in and deliver them?" Adrian asked.

"Um, that's a good way to get shot in my old neighborhood," I said.

So we ordered the toys and arranged for them to be delivered to their apartment. I wish I could see their faces when the presents come, but I can imagine.

I told Adrian I loved that we were doing this, and he said, "And I love..."

But then he stopped. I knew what he was going to say. He loves me. I think I love him too. But I can't tell him that. I can't. This has been a wonderful, sweet fantasy but it can't be anything more than that, I know.

"Do you want to send anything to your father?" he

asked. "Christmas dinner, maybe?"

I frowned. "He probably doesn't even live in the same place anymore." Eviction loomed large in our lives, and it would be even more likely now that I wasn't there to manage things.

"I'll find out where he is, and we'll send something," Adrian said. "I'll make sure he's safe. Lindy, I would do <u>anything</u> for you."

The thing is, he's said that to me before. And no one else <u>ever</u> has.

December 16

I've decided I'm just going to have fun. It's Christmas. I'm young. I'm not going to worry about the future, about hurting Adrian's feelings, about leaving him. I'm not going to think about my father, either. I'm just going to enjoy this time. I deserve it. If it can't last forever, at least I'll have it now.

December 24

Tonight is Christmas Eve. I wish I could say it was weird, not spending it with my father, but that's happened before. More than once. Some years, he showed up stoned or late. Other years, he didn't show up.

But this year, I'm not alone. Adrian asked me if I usually went to church Christmas Eve. I haven't, not since my mother died, but suddenly, I really wanted to, so I said I did. "Will you go with me?" I asked.

And then I regretted it, because he frowned and shook his head. "I wouldn't feel comfortable in a crowd like that, but maybe Magda could . . . you wouldn't leave, would you? Not on Christmas Eve?"

His eyes, wide and bright blue, seemed so concerned and his strange face so sweet. Of course, I said, "Leave? No, I won't leave. I'll never leave. In fact, I don't want to go at all without you. We'll just stay home and watch a service on TV."

Of course, leaving was the last thing I'd do. I was where I wanted to be.

That was when he mentioned that there was a

church down the street holding a live nativity, where they acted out the Christmas story. "I could take you to that," he said. "It's outside. I could stand in the shadows."

Much as I wanted to tell him he didn't have to stay in the darkness, I knew he wouldn't believe me. And I knew he was right, too. I agreed to go.

So tonight was the first time I've been outside, out anywhere with Adrian. He wore a coat with a big hood, and gloves. He held my hand as we walked down the street. It was sweet. I knew his hands were ugly underneath the gloves, but it didn't matter. I squeezed his hand.

He squeezed mine back.

As planned, we stood in back, in the shadows, and even so, whenever anyone turned around, Adrian cringed and hid. This is how it would be, I knew, if we were together. Always hiding, always concealed.

He started to say something, but that was when the music started, and the performance began. It was just kids our own age, dressed as angels and wise men. They had a real donkey and some sheep. At one point, I noticed a shepherd's Nike sneakers, but still, it was beautiful. After all, it was the story of two outsiders with nowhere to go. I <u>so</u> related, and for a while, we were just silent, in the cold night air and under the stars together.

And then we came back and drank hot chocolate, and Will insisted we hang up stockings even though we told him we weren't kids anymore. "You never know what will happen in the dark," he said, and somehow, I just know those stockings will be filled by morning.

And now, I'm awake in my room, thinking, remembering.

I got Adrian a present. I had Magda go out to buy it, a bound volume of Hans Christian Andersen's stories. I know he's too old for fairy tales, of course, but I thought he might appreciate them anyway. Several of the stories involve transformation, like "The Ugly Duckling." But I think the one he'll like best is "The Nightingale." That's always been my favorite. It's about an emperor who prefers the singing of a gaudy mechanical bird over a real nightingale. But then, when the emperor is dying, the song of the plain-looking real bird restores his life.

Of course, Adrian isn't plain-looking. Still, I think the message of goodness over beauty is a valuable one. I wish the world knew it.

I've never been so excited about Christmas before!

December 25

Christmas Day! I woke early and ran downstairs to see the beautiful tree before anyone else. But Adrian was awake and beat me to it.

Even though it was morning, snow had fallen on top of the greenhouse, so the light was dim. Adrian had lit the tree, and it shone in the darkness. We stood and watched the lights twinkle for a few minutes. Then we thought to check our stockings.

As we suspected, some secret Santa had filled them with candy and little books of poetry.

Then Will and Magda came downstairs, and we went up and had breakfast before opening our other presents. We wanted to make it last longer.

But after breakfast, we did open them. Will loved the gift Adrian and I chose for him, new speakers so NPR would be even clearer. For Magda, we'd chosen sweaters and earrings, and Adrian asked his father for an extra bonus check to send home to her family far away. Will bought us a chess set and promised to teach us how to play.

Then Adrian picked up my gift. "Oh, boy," he said, feeling it. "It's a book."

"The best kind of gift?" I said.

He smiled, and I noticed again how lovely his eyes were, how unexpected the color against his strange face. If only everyone could see him as I did, see how beautiful he was.

"The best gift is having you here," he said. "I was so afraid you'd leave last night. I would have let you go."

I shivered at the thought of it. "I'm not going anywhere."

I held my breath as he fumbled with the paper. His hands aren't like other people's, and sometimes, little tasks are difficult for him. Still, I didn't offer to help. I didn't want to embarrass him.

Finally, he opened it and read my inscription. I had written:

<u>Adrian King and Hans Christian Andersen—two men who taught me about magic!</u>

He looked away, saying, "That's so sweet."

I wanted to read "The Nightingale" right away or "The Little Match Girl," because it was a Christmas story, but Adrian laughed and said there was time for reading, plenty of time, and told me to open his gift for me.

It was then I realized Will and Magda had disappeared. I could hear Magda upstairs, singing Christmas carols while she cooked, and Will had said something about trying out his new speakers. We were alone.

Adrian reached up to a high branch of the tree and found a small box I hadn't noticed, and suddenly I was terrified. Was it a ring? Did he mean to ask me to marry him? I couldn't say yes. I'm only sixteen, and I can't commit to this, to anything right now.

And yet, I don't want our time together to be over, either. If he asked me and I said no, it would be all awkward with him. I didn't want that. I wanted everything to stay the same, perfect.

Throat clenching, I fumbled with the paper almost as much as Adrian had.

I opened the box, and I could breathe again.

It wasn't a ring.

Inside the box was a tiny pendant in the shape of a rose, silver or maybe platinum petals, with one tiny diamond like a dewdrop. It hung on a silvery chain.

I sighed. "It's so beautiful," I told him, immediately removing it from its box so I could see it more clearly.

He said he'd offer to put it on me, but probably I'd do better myself. He looked sad when he said that.

"I love it," I said as I fastened it on my neck. "Thank you."

"I wanted you to have something to remember me by even after you leave."

And suddenly, I was hugging him, assuring him I never intended to leave.

"You will," he said.

"I won't." I felt his heart beating, my chest against his. It was warm in his arms, and I wanted it to be true, wanted this moment, this day, this lifetime-in-a-year to last forever. I wished nothing would change and I'd always be happy just to be here. I wanted to tell him I loved him, but I didn't. I couldn't. He'd take it the wrong way, or maybe the <u>right</u> way, and I couldn't hurt him. And then, Will and Magda came back downstairs, and the moment was over. Still, I squeezed him harder, saying, "This is the best Christmas I've ever had."

Adrian pressed his face against my hair and said, "me too. God, me too."

DECEMBER 26

I just had another weird dream. Again, there was the fairy girl, who looked just like that Kendra Hilferty. Now she was dressed for winter fun in a green velvet dress with white fur collar and cuffs, like the Ghost of Christmas Present. Again, she sang. This time, it was to the tune of "Hark, the Herald Angels Sing."

Things aren't always as they seem.
So—voilà—you have this dream.
Adrian is a great guy
If you'll just give him a try

See him through much different eyes
You will have a big surprise.
If you trust yourself to love
You will be in heaven above!

And then, she started to dance.
Like a Rockette.

And then, she turned into a whole LINE of Kendra Rockettes, kicking and singing:

> Please give Adrian a chance!
> So we can finish up this dance!

And they disappeared—poof—as I awakened.

Was my subconscious telling me to stay with Adrian? Of course, that's what I want. But what I want hasn't always been right. I mean, what I've wanted all these years was to fret and worry and try to care for a father who will never get better, to sacrifice what I want in the process. And maybe Adrian is just another substitute for my father, another someone who needs me.

So my subconscious might not have the best judgment.

And, um, why is my subconscious showing me dancing Kendra Hilfertys?

Answer: My subconscious is nuts!

Still, I know I love Adrian. He's kind to me and good and decent. I love his roses, and I love that he really will do anything for me, even read poetry. I love his courage and his sweetness, too. And, of course, unlike my father, Adrian is nice to me and tries to make me happy.

I'm wearing the necklace he gave me. I know I'll never take it off, no matter what.

December 26, later

I had barely slept when Magda shook me awake. "Come," she said, "we are going on a trip."

A trip? My thoughts were all muddled, and for a minute, I wondered if it was a big lie. I've lived with these people for five months, but maybe they were just gaining my trust and now they're going to ship me to South America and sell me. I thought about running, but I was too tired.

Magda led me downstairs, where Adrian and Will were waiting.

"Where are we going?" I asked.

"Trust me?" he asked.

And yes, I did. I trusted him. I wasn't used to trusting people, but I did.

"We're going someplace great," he said, "someplace you'll really like. At least, I hope you will."

He held out my coat and gloves. I put them on. He, too, had on a heavy coat and a scarf, hiding his face. As we walked around to the back door of the house, he held my arm lightly, and I trusted him.

There was a limo out back. A freakin' stretch limo!

"Are we going to the airport?" I asked, thinking of South America again.

Adrian shook his head. "I'm taking you to see snow. Like you wanted. Why don't you go back to sleep?"

Adrian gestured at my seat belt. "I wouldn't want you to get hurt."

Obediently I fastened it, then just as obediently, I slumped over and pretended to sleep.

I felt so warm beside him.

I remembered that, a few days earlier, I'd complained that I wanted to go out in the snow. Was he taking me someplace where we could play outside? Would he really do anything I asked, just because he loved me so much?

I knew he wasn't asleep, but he thought I was. We crossed a bridge, then another. He took off his scarf and gloves. (The limo had this screen between us and a driver, so he couldn't see us.) I could feel him stroking my hair.

I snuck a peek out. The sky was starting to get light, and soon, I stopped seeing gray buildings and instead saw tall, snow-covered trees like on a Christmas card. Adrian had fallen asleep, finally, and I was tired, so tired, and so comfortable that I did too.

I woke, maybe hours later, and everything had changed. Now, there were not only trees but hills covered in snow. I shook Adrian awake.

"Where are we?" I asked. "Are we still in the United States?"

He laughed. "Still in New York." Then he told me he was taking me to see real snow, not just gray, city slush. "Where we're going we can go outside and roll in it."

No more sleep. I'd never been outside New York City before, but now I saw farmhouses, decorated with bows for the holidays, even silos and cows and horses. People really lived here—on farms like in the Little House books! I saw that the hills were mountains now, looming high above everything. I wanted to go out and run in all that glorious snow.

Finally we pulled off the main road and onto a side street, then in front of a huge, beautiful house surrounded by snow-whitened pines. Adrian told me that this was where we were staying, that it was his father's house, where he used to come when he was a kid.

The trees here all looked like Christmas trees.

I couldn't believe it. I jumped from the car, even

though I was still in my nightgown and the coat, and ran around and spun and danced and threatened to make snow angels before Adrian and Magda urged me to put on warmer clothes.

And they had brought warmer clothes—a whole big suitcase full. Adrian said we can stay <u>all winter</u>! No one else is here, and we'll be able to make snowmen and skate on the lake and curl up by the fireplace and read!

I have never been so happy!

December 26, even later

We've been outside, making a snowman(!) and having a snowball fight. We made snow angels and fed bread crusts to the birds. I saw a cardinal and lots of crows. This place is a wonderland.

But one thing is bothering me.

When we first got here, Adrian told me he used to come here with his father, when he was a kid.

"That was before he started acting like if he missed a single day of work, he'd be replaced," he said.

And then, he said IT:

"After that, I started going skiing with my friends during spring break."

Friends? Spring break? Adrian had had friends? He'd gone to school? How?

That must have meant he'd been normal once, that he hadn't always looked this way. Yet I know he said he'd been this way as a child. He said his father couldn't take him to a baseball game.

What had happened to him? And why didn't he want

me to know the truth?

He changed the subject, and we've had a wonderful day together. Still, I wonder what it is he doesn't want me to know.

December 30

Four amazing days! I feel like I've crammed my entire lost childhood into four <u>amazing</u> days! We've snow-shoed! We made a fort! We rode a snowmobile and made s'mores in front of the fire. And today, when we came back from all of it, the UPS guy had left a package on our doorstep.

Adrian lit up when he saw it. "I was waiting for this."

He let me open the box. Skates! Two pairs—one for each of us. Mine were pure white leather with shiny silver blades. They are maybe the most beautiful things I've ever owned!

"I tried to talk the others into it," Adrian said, "but they were wusses about it."

"It's, like, three degrees out there!" Will said.

"It's <u>nine</u> degrees," Adrian corrected.

"Yeah. Big difference," Will said.

So it was just the two of us, alone at the frozen lake at the bottom of the hill. When we walked down, Adrian had already cleared the snow from one big section. It shone in the late afternoon sun, and I felt like

Jo March in <u>Little Women</u>.

"Is it safe?" I asked, remembering that Amy March had fallen through the ice.

"I'd never take you anyplace that wasn't safe."

I looked at him—at his beautiful blue eyes—and I knew he meant every word. My heart stuttered a little, but then I turned away.

I confessed I hadn't skated in years, and then only at ice-skating rinks with railings and smooth surfaces (and horrible, rented blue plastic skates). The pond had bumps and ruts where snow had frozen to the ice. There was, for sure, no Zamboni here.

"I'll show you how," Adrian said. "The railings are just a crutch anyway."

"Some people need crutches," I said.

"Not you, Lindy. Come on. Take my hand."

He had no gloves on. I'd never held his hand without gloves. I was a little scared, more of the skating than that, but I smelled the pine trees and felt the cold stinging my face. I wanted to go and use my pretty skates. Finally I took Adrian's hand. Together, we stepped out onto the ice.

"Just walk," he said. "Hold out your arms, and if you feel like you're going to fall, it helps to bend your knees a little."

I did as he said, and to my amazement, it all came back to me, and I was a six-year-old girl, skating at Prospect Park. When Adrian realized I didn't need him to hold my hand anymore, he skated backward in front of me, watching.

"Isn't this better than some fake ice at a rink?" he said.

There it was again. Had he skated at a rink before? Something else to indicate he'd been normal once.

But I said, "Much better." A flock of Canada geese flew over in a V. "You don't see that at a rink."

"Race you!" he yelled, and he turned and started skating faster, so fast I couldn't keep up. When he came around behind me, I said, "Let's hold hands again."

Obediently, he took mine. "I like holding hands."

"Me too. But can I ask you something, something personal?"

"Maybe."

I took a deep breath, uncertain. I didn't want to insult him. But I wanted to know him, the real him. "You haven't . . . always looked like this, have you?"

He didn't answer, and so I started to list the things.

He'd mentioned skiing, having friends, going to school, skating rinks.

Finally, he said, "No, I haven't always been this way. Does it matter?"

"I just wondered . . ." I wanted to ask him how it happened, what it was like for him. "It must have been hard."

"It was hard. That's why I don't like to talk about it. It was like everything I thought was true suddenly wasn't. My father, people I thought were . . . they weren't there anymore. They couldn't deal."

I nodded. "Like when my mother died. Everything changed."

"Exactly." He looked down. "I'm sorry. I didn't want to talk about it because it . . ."

"Hurts?"

He nodded. "I should have known you'd understand."

And then, he dropped my hand and skated, lightning fast, around the ice. This time, he didn't call to me to join him. Had I offended him, insulted him with my question? I couldn't tell. He went around, faster and faster, and I remembered what he'd said about the tiger in the cage. Maybe sometimes he just needed

412

to run. I watched him, his power and grace, and even though he might be freakish in some ways, in others, he was so, so beautiful, so full of life and energy.

He went around three times, not looking back, just flying, but after the third time, he fell back in step. He didn't even seem out of breath.

"I'm sorry," I said.

"For what?"

"For . . . asking you about something you didn't want to talk about, for making you feel all weird."

He shook his head. "I _am_ all weird, but it's not because of you. I just like to go fast. I don't get that many opportunities."

I told him I liked to watch him, and then, I begged him to do it again. And again. He happily obliged, and I yelled and clapped each time he passed. He really was like a wild cat, graceful even in his heavy clothes, and finally free. I could tell he knew it, knew it and liked impressing me. After a while, he even shed his jacket, knowing he was safe, knowing no one was watching but me.

"It's so great to get out and just go."

"It is. We should do it every day while we're here."

"We will."

After another hour, we went upstairs and had soup by the fire, even though we'd exercised way too much to be cold, and for the first time, I wondered if it wouldn't be bad to be like this forever, me and Adrian, holed up in our private house in the middle of nowhere, like characters in a Brontë novel—like Jane and her blinded Rochester at the end of <u>Jane Eyre</u>. Would it be that bad?

What have I seen of the rest of the world that would make me think I'd miss it so much?

And his looks? His appearance has become irrelevant to me. It would be even less relevant here, where we can walk outside freely, away from the harsh gaze of the world. After all, aren't we both equally strange, equally damaged?

The only difference is, my damage is inside.

Perhaps I love him, not merely despite but because of his appearance.

Maybe that's what makes him perfect for me.

But do I love him enough to give up everything else?

December 31

The answer is yes.

Yes. I love him enough. I love him so much that nothing else matters, not what everyone thinks, not normalcy, not conforming to some picture of what people should look like or be, not even the fact that, yes, I'll be trapped here, maybe forever. It doesn't matter. After all, unlike with my father, it's not Adrian's fault he's like this. He's not weak like my father. Rather, being like this has made him stronger.

When I first moved into his house, I made a big deal, every night, of locking my door so he wouldn't be able to come in, wouldn't attack me. Now, I know he would never do something like that. I don't lock my door anymore. I feel safe. I never thought he'd come in.

But last night, it was colder than usual when I went to bed. Bitter, really. And, later, when I woke up, the night air nipped at my skin.

Then I felt an extra blanket settling onto me.

I saw his shape. I knew it was him, but I pretended to be asleep. The scene was too intimate. Still, I felt warmed by more than wool.

I snuggled into that blanket and knew I could stay here forever. Someday, I'll not only let him into my room. I'll invite him.

Someday soon . . .

December 31 (Later)

We've had the most wonderful day! This morning, I was up early, rummaging through the closets (what? me, snoop?), and I found a sled! A SLED! I've never been on one before.

But now I have. It was the most incredible experience, flying down a snowy hill, the wind in my face. I was a little scared, but Adrian and I went together. He held me. It felt so warm and safe in his arms. I wanted to stay there forever.

I will stay forever. I plan to tell him tonight. I love him.

The only thing is, I want to check on my father. Just one last time. It's stupid, I know. Maybe it seems like a step backward after so many months without this crazy, codependent relationship. Still, I worry.

But tonight, I'll tell Adrian, and we'll start the new year together!

JANUARY 1

Last night, New Year's Eve, was the night I was going to tell Adrian I loved him. I think Adrian suspected it too. At least, he made the scene very romantic. There was a fire in the fireplace, and I noticed Will and Magda were nowhere to be seen. When I asked Adrian, he said they were watching Times Square on television. Outside was bitter cold, but the fire was warm, and Adrian sat beside me on the sofa—not too close, but we'd be closer soon enough.

It was quiet, so quiet. The only sounds that penetrated the silence were the crackling wood and the wind from outside. I turned to gaze out the window. It is so dark here, which makes the stars more prominent. There were a multitude of them, and just when you think you've seen all of them, there are more. What looks like a cloud is really the Milky Way. I pictured it as a white hill for sledding angels.

Adrian was watching, then he said, "Lindy, you don't still hate me, do you?"

I smiled. He was so sweet. I said, "What do you think?"

"I think no. But would you be happy to stay with me forever?"

It was like he'd read my mind. I looked at him, remembering how I'd once tried to avoid doing so. Now his face wasn't disturbing. It was just his face, the face of my beloved. His eyes were so beautiful and hopeful. He drew in his breath, and I could tell he was holding it, awaiting my answer. I thought about leaning toward him, thought about kissing him. Maybe I should have. If I'd kissed him, everything might have been different.

Instead, I spoke. I told him that in some ways, I was happier than I'd ever been. I liked being with him.

The fire was hot, hotter than before. He said, "So you're happy then?"

Yes, I told him. "Except..."

"Except what?" I saw the concern on his face.

So I said it. "My father. I worry about him, what might happen if I'm not around to run interference. He's sick, Adrian, and I was the one who took care of him. And I miss him. I know you must think it's stupid to miss someone who left me without a look back."

"No. I understand. Your parents are your parents, no matter what. Even if they don't love you back, they're all you have."

I knew he did understand. He loved his own father too.

I turned to look at the fire and said, "Adrian, I am happy here. It's just . . . if I could only know he's okay. If I could only see him for a moment."

He looked sad, then panicked. But then he said, "Wait here."

And then, he left. I heard him running up the stairs to his room. He returned several minutes later with an object. He handed it to me.

It was a mirror, a silver mirror, ornate, like something from another time. I stared into it, and I saw my face. I looked worried.

He told me it was a special mirror. "By looking at it, you can see anyone you want, anywhere in the world."

I laughed. Of course I didn't believe him. But then he took it from me. He held it up, saying, "I want to see Will."

And then, it was the most bizarre thing the mirror or spy cam or whatever it was changed to a picture of Will. Or not a picture, but the actual moving Will, up in his room, wearing the same clothes he'd had on before.

How was this possible? Magic? Of course not. It must be some incredible technology. He had everything money could buy, after all.

"Can I try it?" I asked.

He nodded and handed me the mirror, telling me that, by asking, I could see anyone. I said, "I want to see . . . Sloane Hagen." I wanted to choose someone Adrian didn't know, in case it was a trick, and Sloane's was the first name that popped into my head.

But sure enough, there was Little Miss Perfect . . . and she was popping a zit!

"Ew!" I said. Adrian laughed too.

And then I wanted to see more people. In particular, I wanted to see Kyle. I'd always wondered what had happened to him.

But Adrian reminded me about Dad, so I asked to see him.

The image changed from Sloane's brightly colored bathroom to a gloomy New York street, far from the lights of Times Square. At first, I couldn't make out anything but gray snowdrifts and garbage.

Then, the garbage moved. It was a man! He coughed.

My father! He was homeless, on the street. He was sick!

My throat clenched, and, despite my resolve not to care, my resolve to live my own life, I started to cry. I started crying and I couldn't stop. I had been wrong to think he could survive without me, wronger still to think I didn't care. This was all my fault. No, not <u>all</u> my fault. My father's fault too, and Adrian's fault for making me stay, making me care about him, making me think I could be anything but some junkie's daughter. Making me think things could be different when they can't.

He tried to put his arms around me, but I pushed him away. It wouldn't work. Maybe he could live in this fantasy world, but I couldn't. I had to have cold, bleak reality.

So I was surprised when he said, "You should go to him."

And then, in minutes, it was settled. I would leave. Tomorrow. Today, now. On the first bus. He would give me money, and I would go to the very street where my father now was. I would rescue him once again, as usual. Then, later on, I'd come back to Adrian, maybe once he got to the city. I wasn't really mad at him. I love him. But it doesn't matter. I can never be the same. Clearly, I can't leave my father. I can never have my own life.

I know it's the right thing to do, the humane thing. Still, I didn't want Adrian to know how close I'd come to chucking it all, to staying with him forever.

So I said, "I'll miss you. You are the truest friend I've ever had."

I could see that my words were a knife in his gut. Yet, it seemed kinder than the alternative, for him to know I love him, but that I'm leaving anyway.

It hurts me, too. But what else is there to be than my father's daughter?

JANUARY 1 (STILL)

Now, in my room, I envision some "deleted scenes" version of our story playing out. In it, I tell Adrian I love him. Our eyes meet. Then, our lips. I take his hand and lead him upstairs. I tell him I'll never leave him. I mean it.

If this was a DVD, I'd love that alternate ending.

January 1, Later

I'm gone. I left on the first bus. I'm on it now. I didn't even see Adrian before I left. He said that if he came down to say good-bye, he might not let me go. He couldn't handle it.

I guess I understood that at the time. But now, by daylight, as I speed back to a city I'd never left before but which I was willing, for a moment, to leave forever, it makes me sad and lonely. I always have to handle stuff alone.

I've been staring out the window for about an hour. I get to see the mountains by daylight, and the Hudson River, sparkling in the morning sun. But the mountains look cold and mournful, and the sun off the river hurts my eyes and makes them tear up. I wonder if I'll ever see Adrian again. The past week, the past five months, seem like a kind of dream, one from which I'm being painfully wrenched awake.

I pass some boys, one pulling another on a sled, and I remember how, just yesterday, that was me. Now it's over. In a way, I hate Adrian for taking me out of

my life, for making me think anything could be different . . . and I hate him for sending me back too.
Maybe if he'd said, "Don't go," it would have given me
the excuse I needed to stay. But I know that's wrong. I
have to go. He was good to let me. He was always good
to me.

JANUARY 1, EVEN LATER

I'm back in NYC, and I'm in a limo!

When I reached my station, I saw a man holding a sign that said, "Linda Owens." I asked him what he wanted.

"I've been instructed to pick you up and also to give you this." He handed me an envelope.

When I opened it, I found an ATM card and a note that said, <u>Stay safe and come back.</u>

Maybe I'm not actually angry.

JANUARY 1, MUCH LATER

I found my father. At first, when he saw me, he started yelling—yelling!—at me to leave. And I was ready to! I knew it was because he thought Adrian would turn him in. But once he let me talk, and I explained that Adrian had released me, that he'd never forced me to stay, that he wasn't going to the police, my father stopped screaming and let me take him to a clinic.

Then I went to the bank and checked the balance on Adrian's ATM card, and it's enough for rehab, rent, whatever I need. I didn't want to take the money, not when I'd left him, but I had to, for my father.

Money sure does fix things, doesn't it? Except for things that can't be fixed.

Like broken hearts.

JANUARY 8

It's been a week since I came back to the city. My
father is in rehab, so I don't have to deal with that, and
I'm staying with our old neighbors, the Lesters, while
I look for a place that will have us once my father
comes home. Every time I see the kids playing with their
Christmas toys, I remember Adrian.

I haven't heard from him. I guess I didn't expect to.
I know he was upset that I called him a friend and
nothing else. I understand, but it still hurts.

I enrolled in a school near here. The magnitude of
its suckishness goes without saying. I called Tuttle,
but since I basically just didn't show up for school, I
lost my scholarship, and they're not really sympathetic.

So everything's pretty much horrible, as expected.

JANUARY 10

I miss him.

JANUARY 11

I miss him. I wonder what he's doing right now, if he's off in the woods, walking in the snow, or skating without me. If I close my eyes, I can picture him, gliding around and around the lake, faster and faster, maybe fast enough to forget all about me.

JANUARY 12

I found an apartment. It wasn't easy as a teen, and my dad's not exactly a safe bet. But it got easier when I offered to pay cash.

Adrian hasn't tried to contact me. Is that because he doesn't care? Or because he thinks I don't?

JANUARY 13

I wonder if he watches me in the mirror ever.

School is an epic fail. Someone made fun of me yesterday for answering a question about <u>The Great Gatsby</u>, and it's supposed to be Honors English.

I miss Will too, and Magda.

JANUARY 14

It's strange how quickly my life with Adrian became my life, how wherever he was became home. I miss home. This isn't it.

JANUARY 15

Dad's back, full of promises to stay straight, get a job, do better, be a father. I wish I could believe it. I'm going to try to.

Still nothing from Adrian.

JANUARY 22

Dad's been clean a whole week, which is nothing, but it's a lot for him. Maybe losing me and being on the streets was a wake-up call. Maybe it inspired him to do better.

But what that tells me is, I need to be here for him now, taking care of him, not off somewhere with Adrian.

It's hard because I know Adrian needs me too.

And because I love him.

JANUARY 25

It's probably not helpful to sit around wallowing in what might have been. I need to worry about what is. I'm not going to write for a while. I have no time.

MARCH 1

My father didn't come home last night. His bed hasn't been slept in. There have been other things, including some scary-looking guys on our doorstep. Funny how those guys can find you, even when you move.

Or, probably, my father found them.

But maybe I'm wrong.

MARCH 10

I'm not wrong. He's using again.

439

MARCH 30

He's using again. I can't deny it anymore. He says he doesn't have to work just because I want him to, that he liked it better when I was gone. It's like my old life all over again, only worse, because now I've tasted something different. It's like spending years watching nothing but reality TV, then someone gives you a ticket to a Broadway show.

The night before I left the house upstate, I talked to Will. He was upset that I was leaving. "To paraphrase Mr. Bennet in _Pride and Prejudice_," he said, "without you, the conversation will lose much of its animation and all of its sense." Will's so like that.

I had laughed, though I didn't feel it. "Flattering," I said, "but Adrian and Magda are perfectly sensible."

"I know," he said, "but we'll still be lonely without you, all of us, but especially Adrian. You can come back, if not here, then in the city. We'll be there in spring, no matter what. Will you come to us then? In the spring?"

I assured him I would.

Spring. It is bitterly cold now, colder still in our

apartment. Yet, the vernal equinox—the first day of spring—was last week, and the forsythia is beginning to bud, if not bloom. He should be here soon.

I will go to him. I realize I should never have left.

APRIL 7

I don't remember where the house is, which sounds crazy, but every time I saw it, it was dark and someone was leading me. I never thought about having to find it.

Now I do. I want Adrian. I asked my father where the brownstone is, but he won't tell me.

I've decided I'm going to go to every subway station in Brooklyn and look for a house with a greenhouse. I know he was near a station. I could see it through the window. I just have to find the right one.

It's April now, spring by anyone's definition. He must be back.

I will find him.

APRIL 8

I started looking today, after school. No luck. I'll keep looking, though. I'll find him.

APRIL 9

Nothing today. And we got a notice on the door for unpaid rent. Adrian's money ran out, and even though I'm working without my tutoring jobs, it's hard to make ends meet. Have to beg the landlord to wait.

APRIL 12

I found a house today I thought was it. But when I knocked on the door, an older woman answered. Wrong house.

Some good news. I applied back to Tuttle, and they approved my scholarship. I can go there in September.

If I last until September.

APRIL 20

Today, I saw a house I was sure was it. It was in Park Slope, near a train station, and also near a church that looked like the one where we saw the live nativity. It had a greenhouse in back.

I knocked on the door. No answer. Yet I was sure it was his house. I knocked and knocked and called and called. Finally, I climbed up a tree across the street. The branches were shaky, creaky, but I had to check.

When I did, I saw that all the plants in the greenhouse were dead. I knew then it wasn't the right house. Adrian would never let anything happen to his roses.

Have to keep looking.

Maybe he doesn't care. Maybe he's dead. Maybe it's time to give up.

MAY 22

My life is falling apart.

My father is gone. He said something about laying low, and I haven't seen him in a week. And yesterday there was an final notice of eviction on the door. So, soon, I'll be on the street.

And through it all, the thing that worries me most is . . . does he still remember me? He meaning Adrian. Does he still even care? Does he love me? Does he know I love him?

MAY 23

I never sleep in school. I just don't. But today, I'm just so tired, so WEARY, that I actually fell asleep at my desk in English class.

That's when I had the strangest dream, the type of dream I used to have when I lived with Adrian.

The setting of my dream was like <u>The Persistence of Memory</u>, that painting by Salvador Dalí, the one with the melting clocks. There were clocks everywhere. More than that, everything in the room was melting, the desks, the classroom door, even the blackboard. The room was empty, like my smarter classmates had already evacuated. I started to leave too, careful not to touch the lavalike desks.

That's when I saw her. Kendra. She was dressed in a red jacket and gray pants, like the White Rabbit in Disney's <u>Alice in Wonderland</u>. She held a giant pocket watch. She sang:

> You're late! You're late
> And if there's anything I hate

It's girls who say they are in love
But won't substantiate!

"What?" I said to Kendra/Rabbit. "Won't substantiate? I looked all over the city for him!"

"You didn't look hard enough. Or long enough. And,
besides, he was still up in the country most of the
time you were looking in the city. And now . . ." She sang
again. "You're late, you're late, you're late, you're late,
you're late, you're—"

"I get it! Can you possibly give me any useful
information in these dreams?"

"Time's a-wastin'."

"I know. My life is falling apart."

She shook her head. I noticed her long ears made a
shaky sound when she did, like a real rabbit. "No, not
for you, silly girl. Time's a-wastin' for <u>him</u>."

"What do you mean, for him?"

She sighed and waved her arm. Suddenly, she
was transformed into the creepier-looking white
rabbit from Tim Burton's <u>Alice</u>. I became aware
of the clocks again. They seemed to be melting
faster, running, sliding off the furniture and onto
the floor.

She started singing again, a strange tune I didn't recognize.

> I placed you in this scene by Dalí,
> To let you know it would be folly,
> To wait too long, so don't delay.
> To find him, you must go today.

"I've gone <u>every</u> day." A clock slid off the desk in front of me and toward my feet.

"But not the right place. Or rather, you were in the right place, but at the wrong <u>time</u>." She tapped her pocket watch. "And time is of the essence."

I jumped to avoid the sliding clock on the floor. "So you're saying go back somewhere I've looked before?"

"Duh."

"But where?"

She checked her watch. "I've already said too much."

"You've said nothing."

"I'm late!" Her voice seemed small and far away. "I'm late!" Smaller still.

"Wait!" I screamed.

That's when I noticed all my classmates staring at me like I was crazy. Maybe I was.

Still, I know what I have to do. Look for him. As soon as I get out of school, I'll go. I'll go everywhere I've been before, and I'll find him.

Today.

MAY 24

It was a suspenseful day yesterday, and a more suspenseful night.

When I woke in class, the melting clocks were gone. I was in school, and it was almost three o'clock. I knew what I had to do, as soon as school was over. I had to find Adrian.

I started with the subway. In the dream, Kendra said to look where I'd already looked. I know it was just a dream, but it had seemed so real that I decided to follow her advice.

But by evening, I was frustrated. I decided to go with the long shot, go back to the apartment, see if my father was there, if he could tell me where Adrian was. Maybe he would if he thought Adrian would give him money.

I got off the subway and was almost to my apartment. It was dark, almost 10. I ran faster.

That's when somebody grabbed me.

"Where is he?" a voice demanded. I couldn't see his face, but the voice was a low growl in my ear, and I felt something hard—a gun—against my back.

"Where's my father?" It amazed me how calm I was.

The man cursed. "He owes me."

"I don't know." I thought of Kipling. If you can keep your head . . . I told the guy, "I haven't seen him in a week, but I'll tell him—"

"Save it. Scumbags like him can disappear without a trace."

Didn't I know it?

He shoved the gun against me. "I want the money from you. Now."

I didn't have it. But I couldn't tell him that, so I said, "Okay. I have to go back to my apartment to get it. If you'll just . . ."

And, suddenly, I knew exactly where Adrian was. The house. The one in Park Slope with the dead green-house. It all made sense. If he'd stayed upstate too long, he wouldn't have answered the door. Even though he'd gotten someone to tend the plants, that person might have let them die. I knew he was there.

"I have to get on the subway," I said.

The guy started calling me things I can't bear to write here. "Don't play games with me. I know where you live." With the gun, he forced me toward my own apartment, the last place I wanted to be trapped.

Still, I went inside and pretended to rummage in the drawers, in the closets, looking for it, saying stuff like, "He used to keep it under the mattress." All the while, I wanted to scream out for Adrian. The guy was getting impatient, and I said, "If you'd just let me call my boyfriend . . ."

"And have him tell the police? I don't think so."

"He wouldn't. He'd give you the money. He'd do anything for me."

I should never have let myself get sucked back into this world.

"You're not going anywhere," the guy said.

Despite the gun, I tried to break for it. He was between me and the door, so I lunged for the open window and screamed into the dark street, screamed Adrian's name. Even though I knew he couldn't hear me, my fear and love and desperation combined to tear the sound from my throat. I thought of <u>Jane Eyre</u>, when Jane hears Rochester's anguished cry across the moors. I was looking for magic.

It didn't come. The guy pulled me from the window and, again, demanded his money.

I had to admit I didn't have it. I begged for more

time. What good would it do to kill me, after all?

But the guy wasn't buying. He grabbed me. I screamed, and he slapped me hard. I fell on the floor. He jerked me up by the arm. I screamed again.

"Shut up!" he yelled, and I did. My head was spinning, spinning from the slap. The room was starting to blacken, and I thought it was my vision blurring. But then, I looked up, and I saw black-winged angels, circling like crows. The angels, all of them, had Kendra's face. The thunder of their wings drowned out everything else. I was hallucinating. The guy was saying something, something I couldn't understand.

"Let me go!" I shrieked.

A giant Kendra-Angel swooped at the guy's head.

"Lindy!"

Kendra? No, it wasn't Kendra's voice. It was another voice, a man's voice, so familiar. I turned toward it, as did the gunman.

Through my blurred vision and the flying Kendras' wings, I saw him. Adrian! It was Adrian. A dream. It had to be a dream, just like the angels. Adrian was clear across town. He didn't know where I lived. He never left the house.

And yet, he was rescuing me.

It had to be my imagination. And yet, my imagination was so clear. It said, "Lindy!"

"You're here!" I said.

The man said, "Don't move, or I'll shoot." I felt the gun against my head, and yet all I thought, all I cared about thinking, was that Adrian was there, for real there. Adrian was rescuing me like a hero, _the_ hero I always wanted.

I heard a low growl, as if somehow, seeing me like this brought out his animal, his beast tendencies. He crouched low, like a tiger about to spring. I felt the guy shaking.

Adrian spoke, and somehow, his voice was huge, thundering, terrible.

"If you harm her," he said, "I'll kill you."

I felt the gun leave my head and turn toward Adrian.

And then, so many things happened at once. Adrian sprang, snarling at the gunman. A shot rang out. I screamed and screamed. Then the guy was on the floor. Adrian was on top of him, his claws in the guy's neck.

Black Kendra-Angels circled the room, singing, and the guy lay unmoving on the floor. Adrian threw the guy off of him and crumpled to the ground.

I lay frozen. A Kendra-Angel offered me her hand, helped me up. I ran toward Adrian.

"You're here!"

"I'm here," he agreed, softly, weakly. Above our heads, the Kendra-Angels were singing and sprinkling something. Rose petals?

I leaned over him and felt wetness. Blood? No! He couldn't be shot, couldn't die. I loved him more than I'd imagined, not like a friend, not like some weak thing I had to care for, but as what he was: A hero. <u>My</u> hero.

"I should call the police. Or an ambulance."

"No!" He grabbed my arm. "Please. Please, no. Stay with me. Be with me."

I had to get help. I couldn't let him die. Yet he held my hand, and I was talking, babbling, explaining all the reasons I hadn't come back to him, hadn't found him until now, until it was maybe too late. I started telling him how everything had been different, living with my father after him.

"Why?" His voice was so weak.

"Because I'd been with you. Before, I knew only what it was to be his daughter, to live day to day and wait for it to be over. But now, I knew what it was to

have someone talk to me, care for me... be with me...
and..."

"Love you?" His words were a gasp. Oh, God, I had
to get help. I couldn't let him die. Yet he kept holding my arm, keeping me there, as if my being there
was enough. I stood. Around me, the Kendra-Angels were
circling. They were singing something I couldn't understand. One of them cuffed me with her wing, pushing
me back toward Adrian. But it was crazy. I had to get
help.

I said, "I should get an ambulance. If anything
happened to you, I—"

Adrian pushed himself up. "I love you, Lindy. I know
I'm too ugly for you to love, but I'll always..."

Around me, the Kendra-Angels were singing and I
was crying. "I love you too, Adrian. But please, let me—"
Again, I stood. Again, they pushed me back. Adrian
grabbed my arm. "Then kiss me," he said. "Let me have
the memory of your kiss, even if I die."

Die? But then, I understood what the Kendra-Angels
were singing. "KISS HIM! KISS HIM!" Over and over, they
sang it. "KISS HIM!" Their voices reached a crescendo,
and the wind off their wings literally blew me back
onto the floor beside him. "KISS HIM!" they sang

460

I kissed him. His forehead. His cheeks, wet from my tears. His mouth. The air smelled of rose petals, and the Kendra-Angels were singing like, well, angels. Was he dying?

And then he yelled, "Watch out, Lindy!" and I felt the guy grab me. Somehow, I got his gun in my hand. Somehow, I fired it. There was smoke, glass shattering.

Rose petals, falling everywhere.

I turned to Adrian.

He was gone. Gone!

"Adrian!"

In his place, on a bed of roses, lay someone else.

KYLE KINGSBURY?!?!?!?!?!

"I'm here, my love," he said.

It was a hallucination, just like the rose petals and the Kendra-Angels. Maybe it was all a dream. Maybe Adrian had never been here at all. Maybe I'd been attacked. Maybe I was dead.

I wouldn't mind, if I could only be with Adrian.

In my vision, I spoke to Kyle.

"Kyle Kingsbury? Where's Adrian?"

"I'm here," he said. "But what did you call me?"

Stupid, snobby Kyle. Still thinking it was all about him.

"Lindy, it's me," he said.

"Where is the boy who was here before? His name was Adrian, and he was—"

"Ugly? Hideous."

The nerve! "No! He was hurt. I have to find him!" I started for the door.

He chased me. "Please wait."

"I can't, Kyle. You don't understand. There was a boy here, and he was—"

"Me." He grabbed my other hand. "He was me."

Crazy. But then, he asked me to close my eyes, and after a while, I did, just to make him let me go. He was holding me so hard.

"Do you know my voice, Lindy?" he said, and he reminded me of one night when we'd watched a movie together. He said, "When the movie was over, you'd fallen asleep. I picked you up and carried you to your room."

That <u>had</u> happened. And his voice. His voice was so familiar. He continued. "You woke in the darkness and spoke to me. You said my voice sounded familiar. It was familiar. It was me. Kyle. Adrian. We're the same. I will always remember that day because it was the first time I had hope, the first time I spoke to you without you noticing how hideous, how less than human I was.

The first time I thought that maybe you could love me."

I finally started to understand. Kyle was Adrian? Adrian was Kyle? "But how . . . ?"

"Magic. A witch put me under a spell—I would say a cruel spell, but it really wasn't, because it led me to you."

Magic. Magic like melting clocks and Kendra-Angels. The mirror. Somehow, it wasn't that hard to believe.

"How was the spell broken?" I said.

"Magic. It was magic, and the magic is called love. I love you, Lindy." He leaned and kissed me.

I kissed him back because, finally, I understood. Kyle was Adrian, and Adrian was Kyle. It was like one of my books, like a fairy tale, and I was the princess, the one that transformed him with my love, my kiss. And, in turn, he transformed me from a lonely, unloved girl to a romantic heroine.

OCTOBER 23

It's been a while since I've had time to write, so let me catch you up.

Adrian and I are still together. For a while, I wasn't sure what to call him, particularly after he explained to me that he'd changed his name from Kyle to Adrian after finding out that "Kyle" meant "handsome" while "Adrian" meant "dark one." Now, he _is_ handsome and isn't dark, so it seems like Kyle would be right. Yet it's Adrian I came to love.

"How about Stud Muffin?" he suggested when I told him this.

"Adrian it is," I said, and it has been. People at school call him Kyle, but that's because they don't know him like I do.

School? We're both back at Tuttle for senior year. I got my scholarship back, and Adrian's dad (surprise, surprise) managed to pull some strings for him, too. It's kind of weird, seeing Sloane Hagen in the halls. She glares at me as if I stole her boyfriend—and maybe I did. But the guy I'm dating isn't the same guy who dated Sloane. He's changed completely. Yesterday, for example, I saw him talking to this new guy, a ninth grader. The guy has a stutter and really bad acne. Kyle was talking to him about tennis team tryouts.

The old Kyle would never have bothered with someone like that. He wouldn't even have bothered with me.

"The old Kyle would have made his life miserable," Adrian said when I mentioned it to him. "Don't remind me about that guy."

"There was always some good, deep inside him."

"Yeah, real deep. So deep you'd need an archeologist to find it."

"I saw the good in you," I said.

"You see the good in everyone. That's what I love about you."

I said, "I love you, too." And I did.

The person I don't see at Tuttle anymore is Kendra. No surprise, really. What I found out about her was, she was the witch who turned Kyle into a beast. Because he was apparently such a jerk to her at the dance (and in general), she placed a curse on him, and someone had to kiss him to end it. I did. Oh, and after it was all over, she transformed into a crow and flew away.

Yes, you read that right.

But the weird thing is, once I knew Kendra was a witch, I started thinking about all those dreams I'd had about her.

Like, were they really dreams?

Or was she there, in person, trying to help Adrian and me get together?

Another thing she did with her magic was, she gave Will his sight back.

Will is a teacher at Tuttle. Adrian and I still live with him in the brownstone in Brooklyn (which was, btw, the one I saw that day). Adrian told his father it was because it wasn't worth the effort of moving back in with him, just for one year of school, but we all knew that wasn't the whole story.

And my dad? I haven't seen him, not since he left that last time. Adrian doesn't have the mirror anymore, so I can't even spy on him that way. It's probably better. I've realized that, sometimes, you have to let people go.

But I'm really glad I have someone to hold on to.

eXTRAs

BEASTLY

DELUXE EDITION

Lindy's Diary wasn't enough?
Get more info on the characters from *Beastly*,
hear about Alex Flinn's visit to the movie set,
and discover Sloane's MO.

Plus, a sneak peek of Alex Flinn's next book,
Bewitching, starring Kendra!

All About Lindy

What's on her playlist?
"Call Me When You're Sober" by Evanescence
"Beautiful" by Christina Aguilera
"The Ballad of Mona Lisa" by Panic! At the Disco
"Bleeding Love" by Leona Lewis
"Christmas Lights" by Coldplay

Favorite book
Jane Eyre. I love the part where Jane says, "I am not talking to you now through the medium of custom, conventionalities, nor even of mortal flesh; it is my spirit that addresses your spirit; just as if both had passed through the grave, and we stood at God's feet, equal—as we are!" (Yes, I've memorized that, but I had to look up the punctuation—there are a lot of semicolons there.)

Oh, I've also spent quite a bit of time with *The 7 Habits of Highly Effective Teens.*

Favorite place to hang out in New York City/Brooklyn
I live at the library—usually the Riverside branch by school. Sometimes, I don't want to go home.

Favorite word (hello, crossword puzzles!)
Bildungsroman. It means "coming-of-age novel." I read a lot of those. I read a lot of everything. When I typed this into

Word, it told me I'd misspelled it when I hadn't. I love when I know a word and Word doesn't.

Biggest dream

I want to be a speech therapist and work with kids with problems, maybe even travel the world and help people.

Biggest fear

That I won't make it out of here.

All about Kyle

What's on his playlist?
"Tik Tok" by Ke$ha
"Ego" by Beyoncé
"Panic" by Sublime With Rome
"Give Me Everything" by Pitbull
"The Time (Dirty Bit)" by Black Eyed Peas

Favorite movie
Inglourious Basterds. The French chick is kind of hot, and the German one is REALLY hot.

Favorite place to hang out in New York City
Union Square. I like crowds, mostly because they all turn to look at me. I really should get into modeling.

Life goal
To have a life goal by the time I'm twenty-five. Until then, I can just get by on my looks.

Best perk of having a rich dad
Money can buy love. It can buy lots of things.

The thing I'd never admit
Sometimes, I go to school early or just hang around Union Square or the park, waiting for people I know to show up, because I can't stand being alone at home with only the maid.

All About Adrian

What's on his playlist?
   "Brick by Boring Brick" by Paramore
   "Transatlanticism" by Death Cab for Cutie
   "You Wouldn't Know" by Hellyeah
   "Every Teardrop Is a Waterfall" by Coldplay
   "Angel" by Sarah McLachlan

Favorite book
   The Hunchback of Notre-Dame by Victor Hugo. I don't think I need to elaborate on why.

Favorite place to hang out
   Considering I'm confined to the house, I don't have a lot of choices.

Biggest dream
   To find a FURminator strong enough to make me look normal. j/k. To find true love, of course.

Biggest fear
   That no one will ever love me and that I'll die a beast and be eaten by the multiple cats who will be my only friends.

Biggest regret
   What do you think my biggest regret is? I regret messing

with that Kendra girl and getting turned into a beast. Other people do worse things and get away with it. I mean, not that it hasn't been a learning experience and all, but next time, maybe I could read some books or take an online course or something.

All About Kendra

What's on her playlist?

Symphonie Fantastique by Hector Berlioz (particularly the final movement, "Dreams of a Witches' Sabbath")

"Stride la vampa" from *Il Trovatore* by Giuseppe Verdi

"Lorelei" by Ella Fitzgerald

"Rhiannon" by Stevie Nicks/Fleetwood Mac

"Born This Way" by Lady Gaga

Favorite book

The Harry Potter series. Not because it bears any resemblance to my life, but I'd like to have gone to witch school and played Quidditch. Also, I love going to midnight movie premieres.

Favorite place to hang out

The Catacombs in Paris are quite charming in springtime.

If you could have lunch with anyone, living or dead, who would you choose?

First off, I try to avoid having lunch with the dead. They smell bad and they're messy eaters because food falls out of the holes in their faces. Oh! You mean if I could have had lunch with them back when they were still *living*? Because, if so, I'd probably invite Marie Antoinette or maybe Mussolini. Maybe a stern talking-to would have helped. If not, I could have straightened them out with a spell.

Favorite use of your powers
Shape-shifting, definitely. I never have a bad hair day!

Biggest regret
Immortality can be lonely. Most of the people I cared for are long dead.

Stars in your eyes—
questions for Alex about the movie:

Q: *Beastly* was made into a movie and you got to go to visit the set. Tell us what it was like. Did you get starstruck?

A: Visiting the set was fun. The movie was filmed in Montreal, both on a soundstage and in a real house that served as Kyle's home. We got to visit both, but they were only filming on the soundstage when I was there. We saw two scenes in two days. The first was the scene where Kyle is thinking about letting Lindy go. The second scene was where Kyle and Lindy were reading poetry together and the seasons change behind them. It was filmed in front of a green screen.

The producer told me they get about two minutes of usable footage in a day. That struck my family as very little, but when you think of it, I think I probably average about two pages a day writing. Some days it's more, some days less, and that doesn't count revision. So that sounded about right.

We met Alex Pettyfer and Vanessa Hudgens on the set. My kids were thrilled. They both seemed nice and polite. Neil Patrick Harris was also there, but we didn't get to meet him because he was "blinded" by these special contacts that made him actually unable to see. However, we did meet him at the premiere, and he was just as awesome as you'd want him to be.

I also taped an interview, parts of which they used on the special features on the DVD.

Q: There are differences between the book and the movie. What did you think when you saw the movie in its entirety?

A: The movie was cute—definitely the type of movie I would like, even if I hadn't had anything to do with it. The most important thing to me, with romances, is that the romance itself seems genuine, which it did here. I thought Kyle and Lindy had good chemistry.

I wasn't expecting the movie to be the same as my book. I've been going to movies based upon books I like my whole life, and I can name maybe one where I thought the movie was a true adaptation of the book. Usually, you go to a movie because you want a visual or you want a two-hour version of a 350-page book. This is what I tell teens who write to me. It's not my book, and they can still read my book as many times as they like! In fact, I encourage that!

That said, I wondered about some of the smaller changes, such as changing Kyle's last name from Kingsbury to Kingson. Also, in my book, Kyle and Lindy read Shakespeare's "Sonnet 54" together. In the movie, Kyle tells Will that sonnets are "obvious" and they read a modern poem instead. While I thought the poem was cute, I did laugh when one of the reviewers of the movie said that the characters "denounce Shakespeare's sonnets . . . as clichéd and prefer to recite . . . "Having a Coke with You."

But I also liked some of the additions, like the scene at the zoo, when Kyle and Lindy are talking about the mother elephant. Overall, it was a great experience, and I thought the movie was, as I said, adorable.

Q: Alex Pettyfer is SO cute! Who was your celebrity crush when you were a teen?

A: I really loved John Travolta. He was in the movie *Grease*, which I know my kids and a lot of their friends have seen, even now. He's still a great dancer and still has beautiful eyes.

Q: You are the author of other modern fairy tale retellings, including *A Kiss in Time*, which is an edgy take on *Sleeping Beauty*, and *Cloaked*, an adventurous mash-up of lesser known fairy tales. Who would you cast as Princess Talia and Princess Victoriana in movie versions of those books?

A: Talia: There are actually a lot of reader-made trailers for *A Kiss in Time* on YouTube, and the usual casting for Talia is Ashley Tisdale. I really like Ashley Tisdale, but I'm sure she'll move on to more adult roles. At this point, my dream Talia is Jennette McCurdy from *iCarly*. She is funny with the right amount of sass. AnnaSophia Robb would be another strong possibility—she's so beautiful that you could believe she was gifted by fairies, and she was funny in *Charlie and the Chocolate Factory*.

For Victoriana, even though she isn't blond, I could picture Leighton Meester in the role. When I wrote the character, I was picturing Paris Hilton, but I doubt she can act.

Oh, and Abigail Breslin as Meg, the real heroine of *Cloaked.* I just loved her in *Zombieland,* among other things.

Q: What is it about fairy tales that draws you and, of course, readers after hundreds of years? What never gets "old" about them?

A: I think fairy tales work for us because they exemplify our greatest hopes (for heroism, redemption, love) and worst fears (that we aren't, in fact, paranoid, but that there are actually people out there who wish us ill) and, for the most part, allow us to conquer the latter and gain the former.

Sloane: Up Close and Personal

Here's something no one knows about me: When I was younger, my ears stuck out so bad I looked like a loving cup.

You might think people at school were kind and understanding about this minor defect. I mean, it wasn't my fault. And they'd heard years of lecturing about no bullying, zero tolerance, "It isn't big to make others feel small." I've heard those lectures myself. But, if you thought that, you'd be severely wrong. Little kids can be complete jerks. I got called Dumbo, Minnie Mouse, Dogface, and the ever-imaginative Big Ears.

When someone beat me up, my parents enrolled me in karate classes. It was supposed to be self-defense, but I'll admit I was pretty into it—so into it that when this one girl, Ramsey Taylor, asked me if I could hear the sun come up, I kicked her in the mouth.

Of course, *I* got in trouble. Because, you know, when people are asking you if your mother had an affair with Bugs Bunny, you're just supposed to ignore it. Ignoring it is the go-to solution for grown-ups. They love to blame the victim.

Anyway, I got thrown out of school. I was homeschooled for the rest of the year, and that's when I got plastic surgery.

I sense your disapproval. Some people will say that children getting cosmetic surgery symbolizes everything that's wrong with our society. Well, those people should have to walk around with ears so big they knock stuff over.

I started a new school that fall, a school where no one

knew me *or* my ears. Oh, and I changed my name from Sylvia (after my grandmother) to Sloane (after cool, rich British people).

I devoted myself to fitting in. From that day on, I had no clothes, no possessions, no *opinions* that weren't shared by ten other people. I talked my mom into letting me get highlights, and when it came time for braces, I made sure my dad knew he had to spring for Invisalign. I was never going to give anyone reason to make fun of me again. People might hate me, but if they do, it's because they fear me. Which is a lot better than being some pathetic loser.

But, sometimes, I wonder if anyone actually *likes* me.

I especially wondered that with Kyle.

Kyle was my boyfriend, back in ninth grade. He was the most popular guy in our class. It was always fun to be with Kyle, not only because he got invited to all the cool parties, but also because he had this wicked sense of humor. He could imitate people so well you thought they were in the room, and he always made funny comments.

But, sometimes, I worried he was making funny comments about *me*. When you've been one of the weird, unpopular people, you feel like you're always one of them. I laughed at Kyle's jokes, but part of me always knew I could have been the butt of them.

I knew Kyle wouldn't have given me a second look if he'd seen me with my old stick-out ears, my crooked teeth. Yet, what was I supposed to do—*not* go out with the cool, handsome, popular guy because he wouldn't have liked my rabbit-esque former self? I'd worked hard to look the way I looked. I deserved to reap the benefits.

Still, I always looked for proof that he loved me. Like, at the ninth grade dance. I asked him for one thing: an orchid corsage. It was meaningful because I remembered when I was little, my older sister, Elizabeth, went to a dance, and her date brought her an orchid. I always wanted one. To me, an orchid corsage equaled love.

Kyle showed up with a rose. Not only that, but when I called him on it, he said the maid screwed up. The. Freaking. Maid. Like, he didn't even care enough to buy it himself.

Okay, so maybe I was a little hard on him. Maybe I was a complete bitch. But really. And then, he gives the corsage to some defective, working the ticket table, obviously to get revenge on me. And *then*, he wanted to *leave early*. What a jerk. I mean, getting crowned dance royalty might have been NBD to Kyle, but it was pretty much the pinnacle of my entire existence. It meant not only that I was pretty, but that I was loved.

I was assertive with him. I told him no way was he going to ruin the biggest night of my life. But later, I was a complete puddle. I should have broken up with him right after the dance. Instead, we went back to my apartment because I'm just *that* desperate for approval.

But the next day, he went all weird on me. I mean, I knew he had a cruel streak. I saw what he did to Kendra. I just thought he at least sort of cared about me.

He didn't. He actually pretended he had some kind of curse placed on him, to make him ugly. I guess he assumed I'd break up with him if he wasn't hot, but I knew he was trying to get rid of me.

When he pulled that crap, I kicked him to the curb. But then, he disappeared for two years, and I wondered if maybe it hadn't been a trick after all. Maybe it had all been true, and I'd become as mean as those kids in my grade school class. What he'd said about witches and spells—was that possible?

Now, Kyle's back and completely normal looking, so it must have been a trick.

The weird thing is, though, he's dating this really nothing-looking girl named Lindy. What's up with that?

**Read an excerpt from
Alex Flinn's next novel,**

BEWITCHING

If you read fairy tales, and who doesn't, you might believe there are witches all over the place—witches baking children into gingerbread, making princesses sleep hundreds of years, even turning normal teenage boys into hideous beasts to teach them a lesson. But, actually, there are only a few of us. The reason it doesn't seem like that is because we're pretty long-lived. We live hundreds of years, as long as we don't find ourselves fueling a bonfire.

Which leads us to another quality of witches: We move around a lot. It's easy for us to get into trouble, and sometimes, we need to beat a hasty retreat (in the dead of night or on the business end of a pitchfork) to another town or another country.

So that explains the existence of many tales from different times and places, many of which involve the same witch.

In quite a few cases, that witch was me. My name is Kendra, and I'm a witch.

Here's my story—well, some of it. It involves romance, drama, even death.

It started in England, many years ago; 1666 to be exact. When I was a teenager, the first time.

Girl to Woman to Witch: England, 1666

When Mr. Howe called from the street to ask if I had any dead for him to bury, I told him I did. The chore did not tax me, not physically, though I was but four and ten and small for my age. Little Lizzie, my youngest sister, weighed barely more than a sack of flour even before the plague ravaged her body and our village. After months of hardship, she weighed even less. I hated to give her over to the gravedigger, but what choice did I have? I had no parents left. I had next to no one.

"Are ye alone now, Kendra?" Mr. Howe asked me.

I shook my head. "No. There is still Charlie. And Charlie will be well."

He seemed doubtful but only said, "I am sorry."

3

I nodded and did not wait for him to take her. I could not. I was accustomed to death now, accustomed enough to know not to dwell upon it. It was the only way to survive.

The first to leave had been Sadie, my older sister. How we had wept and regretted, not merely because Sadie was kind and good, but also because she was only a month from marriage to Henry, the dairyman's son, who would have kept our large family supplied with sorely needed milk. Young Henry had not even come to Sadie's funeral. Too scared was he of catching the dread disease himself. He caught it anyway, though, and was gone in two months' time, too long to blame Sadie. People in our town were all looking for someone to blame for what happened.

The reverend had told us to have the funerals out of doors, that we should not spread the disease, but it had not helped. The reverend also told us to stay in the village, so as not to spread the plague abroad, but those with means had left nonetheless. Those with means did as they wished. The reverend lived still, but his wife was gone.

Next was my youngest brother, John, a mere babe and barely known to us. Still, we said a few words over him. Babies dying was sad business, but not unusual.

By the time Mother died, there was no funeral, no time for prayers for the dead, only prayers for the living—that they might stay that way.

They did not. The month past had been a whirl of vomiting, fever, complaints of painful limbs and swelling blisters on arms and legs, cracked lips begging for water and death, so much death. One by one, all who I loved were ripped from this earth as I stopped being a child and became a woman, a sad one. By the end of it, Father and another brother and sister were lost to me, their bodies dragged out between checking to see if the hen had laid and tending the cow.

Two days ago should have been a particular blow, for it was James whose body Mr. Howe took from me, James, my twin, whose shadow I had been even before we were born. But I had no thought for James or any of them. Had I thought of anything besides how to get food, had I thought of why I, alone, was given the dubious gift of health, I would have lain down beside those once-loved bodies and succumbed myself. Yet the good Lord, if good he was, did not see fit to have me die. He saw fit to have me find scant milk from the cow and no eggs from the chicken and to care for my sick brother—my now only brother—Charlie, age eight, in the luxury of a house that had once held nine but now needed room for only two.

Human beings, I had learned, could become used to anything.

This morning, when I went out to collect our one egg, I found, instead, that the hen had died. Then, all the losses I had suffered came down to this one loss. I sat in the sparse hay, buried my head in my hands, and sobbed.

And then, I plucked that stupid chicken and cut and boiled it for, at least, if Charlie was going to die too, he could die with a good, hot chicken soup in his belly.

But Charlie was too sick to eat, and as I turned away from

him, I knew I must try Lucinda.

Lucinda Baker was our town's healer, a woman who knew how to use herbs to cure illness. Once, she had been my friend, but when the plague struck us, Mother had warned me away from her. There were those, Mother told me, who said Lucinda was a witch and that witches were the ones who had started this plague. She worried that, were I too much in Lucinda's company, suspicion might fall on me by association, particularly because I had always been thought strange due to the odd bright green color of my eyes and a moody nature that differed from the other village girls. Perhaps Mother knew that Lucinda had begun to instruct me in the use of herbs. Lucinda told me that she saw the gift in me and believed I could someday be a healer like her.

Were healer and witch one and the same? Perhaps. It mattered not now. If a witch was what my brother Charlie required, then a witch was what I needed. There was no mother to caution me otherwise. There was no one but me now, and I would risk all to save Charlie, even being seen in the company of a known witch.

Thus, I made my sad way through the town, a town which had once been a bustling village of over three hundred, now so empty and silent that I could hear the wind in the trees, even at midday. I passed one, maybe two others, trudging as wearily as I did, but there was no talk, no laughter, no wagon wheels, nothing to drown out the wind.

My step quickened as I came to Lucinda's house, and for

the first time in weeks, something other than despair gripped my heart. Hope held my hand and tugged me closer. Lucinda could help Charlie. I was sure of it. I only wished I had come sooner.

The cottage, made of brown bricks, neatly laid, was strangely silent. Only one black crow perched on the eaves, staring down at me. I approached the doorstep with a fawn's cautious steps and gave an almost silent knock.

Nothing.

I knocked again. Still nothing but the crow's caw.

"Who is that?" A voice from the street shook me in my shoes. I turned and thought for a moment I saw a ghost.

But no, it was Mrs. Jameson, mother to Anne and Alice, two uppity girls who had teased me about the ugliness of my flaxen hair. Still, I felt close to weeping at the sight of a familiar face.

"Mrs. Jameson! It is Kendra Hilferty!"

"Kendra!"

I ran down the stone pathway to embrace her. But when I reached the street, Mrs. Jameson's arms were closed. "Kendra, what are you doing here?"

I faltered. "I was . . . visiting . . . Lucinda."

"Visiting?" The expression on Mrs. Jameson's face was strange.

I thought it best to change the subject. "How are dear Anne and Alice?"

Her face crumpled like papers in flame, and I knew.

"Gone," she said, "all gone."

"All?" I was sorry now to have thought them snobbish girls. "Mr. Jameson too?"

She nodded. "Of my family, only I have been fated, nay cursed, to survive."

"I am the same," I said. "My brother Charlie, he is the only one who lives yet, and I may find him gone when I return." It was the first I had thought it, and I glanced back toward the house. Had death become so routine for me? Was I turned to a monster?

Then, she did take me in her arms, and we held each other and wept and wept as if weeping were the cure for our troubles.

Finally, I said, "I beg your leave, Mrs. Jameson. I was searching for Lucinda, that she might have some herbs for Charlie."

She looked at the house, and her eyes seemed to burn. "Lucinda Baker was a witch who brought the plague upon all of us!" she spat.

Was that what was being said? "'Twas George Viccars who brought the plague from London on a bolt of fabric. Besides, Lucinda is my friend."

"If she is your friend, you may be a witch as well, and should be hanged as one."

"How can you say such a thing to me? My family is as dead as yours. I only want—"

"Oh, Kendra." Her face broke, and she began to sob again. "I know what you want. Would that you could have it, but it is too late. Lucinda is gone."

The crow on the eaves cawed and turned its black head away.

"Some say she left in the night to avoid those who threatened to try her by water. Others say she came to a different end."

I glanced in the window, which was black and empty. Lucinda was gone and, with her, every last impossible hope. I wanted to fall to the ground and weep, but I had not time for that. Instead, I said, "Perhaps there is something left in her garden for Charlie."

Mrs. Jameson nodded. "I am sorry for your losses, Kendra."

"And I for yours. Perhaps . . ." I stopped. I had been about to say that perhaps she could come and live with us, that we might not each be alone. Yet I knew I would not be staying in the village. I must leave the site of all this tragedy and go far away. "Perhaps I will see you again."

She nodded again and moved on.

I ran to Lucinda's garden and gathered what I could of the different herbs. I tried to remember the uses for each. Yarrow, to heal wounds and reduce fever, dandelion for boils, horsetail for strength. I piled all into my apron. In the back of the garden was an herb I did not recognize, yellow and pointy as a cat's claw. The crow swooped down upon it, as if pointing it out. I did not know its use, but something told me it was the most valuable of all. I took a bunch.

The crow cawed as I shuffled away home.

Charlie lived still, and slept. I watched as a shiver wracked his frail body. Without stopping to check for fever, I went to the well, then the stove. I spent my morning brewing teas and making salves, the afternoon forcing them on him.

By nightfall, he had improved not at all. Lucinda's herbs had failed me, and Charlie's chills had worsened. The boils on his neck seemed redder. Abandoning medicine, I took his hands and began to pray, pray as hard as I could, even knowing that it would not be enough. God, it seemed, had not time for us, certainly not time for me. Who would blame him, for there were so many sick, not only here but in all England, maybe all the world? As I prayed, the telltale odor of rotten meat met my nostrils, and I knew it would not be long before Charlie too was dead, before I was alone, all alone in the world.

And then, along with my tears, my prayers became more fervent, more desperate, only the words changed to something beyond my comprehension. I leaned forward, holding Charlie's hand, and felt my own fingers vibrate with a strange energy that combined with the words and flowed from me to Charlie, from Charlie back to me, until the room spun and filled with a strange, sparkling light. I was light-headed from hunger and despair, arms throbbing with the effort of saving him, bizarre ancient words coursing from my lips. I did not know what was happening. I only knew that something was, something stronger than prayer, something stronger than grief had hold over me.

Finally, I collapsed from exhaustion.

I woke to the morning sun's first rays and to Charlie's voice.

"Kendra? Kendra? I am tired of always lying around."

I started. "What?"

"I am tired of lying in bed. I want to go outside and play with Tommy and James."

He was alive! Alive, and wanting to run and play. I rushed to put my hand to his forehead. His fever was gone and the boils on his neck were gone, gone as if they had never existed. I lifted the covers and examined the rest of him. All gone. He was well!

"Stop it, Kendra. What are you doing?" He squirmed away from my touch. "Where is Mother? She will let me go out."

"Shh. Mother is very sick, in her bed over there." I gestured at the pile of empty blankets and hoped he would not look too closely. Charlie was alive!

Now, what should I do? I decided there would be time enough for the grim task of telling Charlie of our parents' demise. I said, "If you can be quiet all day today, I will bring you some chicken soup and tell you a story and tomorrow, yes, tomorrow, we will go outside."

He nodded and said, "I am hungry."

Warm the soup. I must warm the soup. But I stood too quickly. I stumbled, and the room spun purple around me. I thought of Mrs. Jameson's words: *You may be a witch as well.*

Three thoughts whirled past me, over and over:

Charlie was cured. I had cured him.

It had been a spell I had cast.

I was a witch.